FEARLESS LIKE US

BOOK 9 IN THE **LIKE US SERIES**

KRISTA & BECCA
RITCHIE

CHARACTER LIST

Not all characters in this list will make an appearance in the book, but most will be mentioned. Ages represent the age of the character at the beginning of the book. Some characters will be older when they're introduced, depending on their birthday.

The Security Team

These are the bodyguards that protect the Hales, Cobalts, and Meadows.

KITSUWON SECURITIES INC.

SECURITY FORCE OMEGA

Akara Kitsuwon (boss) – 27

Thatcher Moretti (lead) – 29

Banks Moretti – 29

Farrow Hale – 29

Oscar Highland-Oliveira – 32

Quinn Oliveira – 22

Paul Donnelly – 28

Gabe Montgomery – 22

PRICE KEPLER'S TRIPLE SHIELD SERVICES

SECURITY FORCE EPSILON

Jon Sinclair (lead) – 40s

Greer Bell – 30s

…and more

SECURITY FORCE ALPHA

Price Kepler (lead) – 40s

Wylie Jones – 40s

Tony Ramella – 29

…and more

The Meadows

Ryke Meadows & Daisy Calloway

Sullivan — 21

Winona — 15

The Cobalts

Richard Connor Cobalt & Rose Calloway

Jane — 24

Charlie — 22

Beckett — 22

Eliot — 20

Tom — 19

Ben — 17

Audrey — 14

The Hales

Loren Hale & Lily Calloway

Maximoff — 24

Luna — 19

Xander — 16

Kinney — 15

The Abbeys

Garrison Abbey & Willow Hale

Vada — 15

A NOTE FROM THE AUTHORS

The Italian used in this book is an Italian-American language developed by Italian immigrants. It is an incomplete language and uses Italian, English, or both. Different Italians speak different dialects in certain areas, and what is used in the Like Us series is prominent on the East Coast. Words may vary in pronunciation and spelling in different communities. A glossary with pronunciations for Fearless Like Us is included at the end of the book.

Fearless Like Us is the ninth book in the Like Us Series. Even though the series changes POVs throughout, to understand events that took place in the previous novels, the series should be read in its order of publication.

Fearless Like Us should be read after *Wild Like Us.*

LIKE US SERIES READING ORDER
1. Damaged Like Us
2. Lovers Like Us
3. Alphas Like Us
4. Tangled Like Us
5. Sinful Like Us
6. Headstrong Like Us
7. Charming Like Us
8. Wild Like Us
9. Fearless Like Us
10. Infamous Like Us
11. Misfits Like Us
12. Unlucky Like Us
13. Nobody Like Us

1

Sullivan Meadows

SO, DAD, I'D LIKE YOU to meet my boyfriends. Akara Kitsuwon and Banks Moretti.

Those words hang in the air like the smoke cloud after a bomb drop. I can't close my eyes. Can't look away from my dad whose brows furrow in utter fucking confusion. Before I have a chance to explain—like really fucking explain—he speaks.

"I didn't hear you fucking right, Sul," he says. "Say it again."

Oh fuck.

Fuck, fuck, *fuck.*

How am I supposed to say this *twice?!*

My mouth dries, and I instinctively look behind me at Akara, who usually comes in with the save. When words fail me in social settings, he takes over…but usually not with my dad.

Usually, I can manage to form some kind of coherent sentence in front of him. My dad is the last person to really care when I struggle to say what I mean, so typically, I try to reach the point. Fucks and all. But his intensity right now, in this moment, is setting my feet on fire.

I want to run away, but I stay still and let the heat scorch my soles.

Akara picks up my distress signal, then looks to my dad. "Ryke—"

"Wait, let her fucking talk." He zeroes in on me. "Sul?"

God, my dad is so fucking *intense.*

Feel the moment.

Yeah, feel the *fucking* moment—what was I thinking?! There is no back-peddling, no laughing this off with poorly placed dick jokes.

Swimming forward is all that makes sense, and I hope the man who taught me to float as a baby isn't about to see me drown as an adult.

And if Akara and Banks wished I didn't explode this news to my dad first, I can't tell. All of us are stopped at the base of the rock face, and they remain completely guarded, like they're on-duty about to protect me from an enraged horde of so-called fans.

Only that horde is one person, and I'm hoping with *everything* in my soul and body that he's not soon-to-be enraged.

"Um..." I have two fingers to my lips, lost in contemplation, and I drop my arm fast. "Fuck...so what I said was, I'd like you to meet my boyfriends." I wave my hand from Akara to Banks, like this needs actual *physical* indication of what I mean.

His death-stare burns into Akara, then Banks, with more confusion than anger, I think. And I'm also hoping. *Please, fucking please.*

"Boyfriends?" He shakes his head, brows knotting. "I don't... fucking understand."

"The three of us are together," I say quickly, my pulse speeding out of fucking control.

His confusion is setting me on the cliff's edge—the one that we just climbed in the quarry. Like I'm no longer grounded. Like I'm falling forward without a harness. I wonder if my dad feels the exact same.

Like he's being pushed off the same cliff.

By me.

He holds up a hand. "Wait, so you're with Akara?" He shifts his weight, an angry fucking shift. He runs his hand aggressively across his scruffy jaw. His eyes nail into Akara. Both men are unblinking.

"Dad, *Dad*," I call out until he looks at *me*. Once he does, I tell him clearly, "I'm also with Banks."

He tries to shake his head, but the movement is cemented. His neck is tight. "What?" His face hardens to stone. "What the fuck, you can't...you're..." He exhales roughly, painfully. "You're fucking with me. The three of you are playing some fucking practical joke on me."

He's waiting for one of us to jump out with the punchline.

Banks hangs his head slightly so he's not towering over my dad. But his eyes lift up with his brows as he tells him, "We're not joking, sir."

Without falter, Akara adds, "Sulli is telling you the truth."

My dad is barely breathing. His carriage is barely rising. He's just *rock* burning from within, and he turns to me. "This better be a joke, Sulli."

Hurt builds pressure on my chest. "You know me better than that," I say. "I would never make this into a fucking joke." Winona, *maybe*. She likes trying to get a rise out of him. But me?

No.

"The daughter *I* know would also never date her fucking *bodyguard*." His voice rises in the quarry.

"Two bodyguards," I correct. Un-fucking-helpful. But I need this to be crystal clear.

Akara and Banks stay stoic, skilled in deescalating situations, and this situation does not need any kind of fucking *escalation*.

My dad's nose flares. "*Two* bodyguards." He zones in on *them*. "Get the fuck away from her." We're not even touching, but I know he sees me as his little girl, and he's wishing for a whole mountain range of separation between us.

"Ryke—" Akara holds up a hand to cool the air, but the air is already laced with my dad's fury.

"I said get *the* fuck away from my daughter," he growls.

Oh God. Oh fuck. Oh Jesus.

This is not good.

Akara and Banks don't move a muscle, and Kits is the one who says, "No."

My dad drops his rappelling gear. Spooled rope falls to the dirt. His harness thuds, and rage is piling up in his eyes. Before he moves forward, I shout, "Dad!"

He looks to me. "Get over here, Sulli." He points to the spot beside him.

"No," I say, pain lancing everywhere. "They're not hurting me—"

"They were supposed to protect you—*that's fucking all*. That was the fucking end of it!" he shouts, more at them than at me. "You're her fucking bodyguards." His glower intensifies on my boyfriends. "You two—you had *one* fucking job. One!" At the base of the mountain, everything feels louder, even his wrath. I feel more like a small creature in the vast greatness of nature, not the girl raised by wolves.

Banks somehow is able to hold eye contact. "We have kept her safe, sir."

"Fuck you," my dad sneers. "If you think keeping her safe was making a move on my daughter—"

"Dad!" I yell even louder and take a step forward. "I kissed them! I made the fucking move!"

His face contorts in a series of horrified emotions. "They reciprocated, Sul. They abused their fucking power and trust—"

"What about Jane?!" I shout in hurt. "What about Moffy?! They both *married* their bodyguards!"

"They're not my kid!" he screams. "You're *my* daughter!" We're hot and sweaty from the rock climb, our shirts soaked, and the sun beats down on us through the canopy of trees. Yet, the real fire is the tears that build in his eyes, in my eyes. "The day you were born, I cried in fucking pain, in fucking *agony* because I thought I'd lose you and your mom, and I knew, while I held you in my arms, that I'd be there for you your whole life, no matter what—I'd fucking be there. *You're my kid.*" He points to his chest, eyes reddening with so much emotion that pummels me. "As a father, as *your* father, I'd never let anyone harm you or fucking manipulate you or come into your life and abuse the power that I'd granted to protect you when you were a *kid.*"

"I'm an adult now," I cut in, eyes wet and raw. "And I've made an *adult* decision to be with them." *Please, fucking please accept this.*

"They're your bodyguards, Sulli!" he shouts like I don't get that.

"I'm twenty-one!" I yell back. Pain chokes me. What's happening. What am I destroying right now?

He keeps shaking his head like this is all going wrong. My feelings are the same, but the origin is different. He runs a rough hand over his face.

I rub my wet cheeks.

Fuck.

Fuck.

My dad exhales roughly but he catches my gaze and says, "Please come here, Sullivan. *Please.*"

We're both begging each other for different things. Only half my pleas are in my mind. I start to shake my head.

He holds out a hand, pleading. "Protecting you is what they're *paid* to do. What they've done isn't fucking right, Sulli."

His words are like a swift punch to Akara. He jumps in, "You don't understand, Ryke—"

"I don't even want to fucking look at you," my dad snaps, but he spits out, "You...*you* are her brother!" The disgust in his voice almost bowls me back.

My brother?

"What...?" I cringe.

Akara puts a hand to his chest. "Hey, I get that's what you wanted me to be towards her but—"

"That's what you have been," my dad growls.

"No, it's not!" Akara yells into a frustrated noise. "I'm *not* her brother, Ryke! I've never been her fucking brother!"

My dad takes angered steps forward.

"Dad," I warn. "*Dad.*"

He stops at my side. "You've always treated her like a *sister.* There wasn't one fucking day you didn't!"

Oh my fucking God.

"*You* put that into the universe!" Akara shouts so loud that veins protrude in his neck. "Not me. Not her! The closest thing she has to a brother is Maximoff—and I promise you, I'm not that!"

Banks plants a calming hand on Akara's shoulder.

I cover my face, feeling sick thinking my dad believed we were like siblings.

My dad looks murderous. "How can you not see the fucking issue here?" He outstretches his arms, then points at Akara. "She trusted you to *protect* her. And fuck you for taking advantage of—"

"I didn't!" Kits screams.

"You fucking did!"

"I LOVE SULLI!" The power in his voice rings the air. "That's what this is about—not money, not a damn job! I fell in love with your daughter, *that's it!*"

"So she doesn't pay you a fucking dime to protect her?!" my dad shouts back, barely digesting Akara's proclamation. "Tell me she doesn't?!"

He's fallen in love with me.

I nearly sway back from the conviction in Akara's voice, from his face that looks torn in agony. Like he's about to lose me.

I wish my heart wasn't being torn apart right now because I'd love to just hang onto the words he screamed into the world.

Let them guide me where I need to go.

I exhale a big breath and look to the man beside Akara. I hold onto Banks' gaze, which stays on me with a kind of comfort I could walk right into. Even several feet away, his eyes whisper against my anxieties and fears, *I'm right here, mermaid. I'm right here.*

Akara breathes through his nose, so pent up with anger that he has to turn his back to my dad. He tries his best to cool off, even as Banks squeezes his shoulder.

I think my dad can't conceptualize that I'm dating both men because he's solely focused on Akara and his role as a *bodyguard* in my life.

My dad keeps going. "It's not about money, but you're getting money from her to do a job! Instead, you did what?!"

No one says anything as the rhetorical question lingers. Quiet seeps into the taut air. The longer we just stand and breathe and *feel,* pain and guilt continue to twist my dad's face—guilt, I think, for agreeing to put Akara on my detail for all those years.

I don't want to hurt my dad. That was never my intent in all of this.

As more pain snakes around us, I want to yell about how Moffy and Jane pay their husbands to protect them, but my throat is swollen closed. My dad is fueled by something I can't understand. I'm not a parent.

And the trauma surrounding my birth has left scars that are ripping back to open wounds.

Wind picks up, and birds caw in the distance. My dad turns his glare to the ground. "Sulli," he says to the earth and dirt, then up to me. "You're coming home with me. Right fucking now."

Tears threaten to spill from my eyes. He's just protecting me. *He's just protecting me. He's just protecting me!* Then why does it hurt so fucking much? I don't want to choose between my dad and them.

It was wishful thinking, wasn't it?

To think I could *have it all* with no horrible consequences.

I don't want to lose my dad.

I can't.

I can't.

Silence eats between us.

My dad glares up at the sky, then down, then back to Akara and Banks. Fists are clenched at his sides. "Sulli, get in the fucking car."

The car isn't even in sight. We have to hike the trail back to the parking lot first.

Akara has a hand on his head, breath shortened and face practically shattered. Banks is unblinking, staring into me as I look from Kits to him, back to Kits, back to him.

Banks nods once to me like, *it's okay,* but his eyes are bloodshot. Has he blinked at all? Is he barely breathing too?

I want to run towards them.

Into their arms.

Not away.

I've finally found that *can't-eat-can't-sleep, reach-for-the-stars, over-the-fence, World Series kind of stuff.* A movie quote my mom always recited from *It Takes Two.* Love that she always talks about, and I think back to those days in Yellowstone under an October sky. Where pain and fear after the animal attack were washed away to utter peace and solace. How fucking *scared* I was—how I couldn't let go of a gun, but they were there; *they were there.* And through glassy eyes and staggered breath, I let go of my fear and embraced both men, and then I couldn't let go of them. Because nothing else felt better.

Nothing else felt more right.

My heart called me in their direction—it's been calling me towards them—and running away will destroy so many pieces of me.

"Let's go," my dad says, picking up his fallen rappelling gear.

"No," I breathe out my decision in a wave of pain. "I'm going back with Akara and Banks." *I have to.* And I start to walk to them.

Banks rests a comforting hand on my shoulder, and my dad turns his gaze back on me, narrowed in on his hand and my shoulder.

Something snaps in my dad, and he lunges. Dropping the rope again, he frees his hand and shoves Banks hard.

"DAD!" I scream.

Banks staggers back several feet away from me. My dad stalks forward like he's going to rip Banks to shreds. Akara is pulling Banks even further *away* from my dad, trying to protect him.

"DAD!" I scream again, rushing after him. I trip over the rope.

My knees hit the dirt.

"You fucking touch her, and you're *dead*," he growls. "You fucking hear me?"

No, fuck. No, no, no.

"We already have, sir," Banks says.

I look up just as my dad swings. He punches Banks in the jaw, and Akara wrenches Banks back so forcefully that *Akara* takes the second blow to the stomach.

"NO!" I'm crying and clawing at the dirt to stand. "STOP!" I scream bloody murder, barely able to see the scene through my tears. "I LOVE THEM! STOP! PLEASE FUCKING STOP!" My voice is horrific and hoarse, and my dad instantly backs away like I rattled him awake.

He blinks hard and breathes heavily. Two hands fly to his head. I've never seen his anger directed anywhere near the people I love.

"Dad," I say, softer this time. I pick myself up, dirt coating my hands, and I stumble towards him.

2

Sullivan Meadows

MY DAD CAN'T MEET MY eyes. Something raw floods them, something that wells a pit in my ribs, and I want to excavate the *hurt* but I don't know how. I've never felt this before, not from him.

"I'm leaving," he says, almost in a whisper. "Before I do something…" He grimaces, his scowl darkening, and he pinches his eyes. Because he did already do something.

Banks spits a wad of blood on the dirt.

Akara is coughing from getting the wind knocked out of him.

My lungs burn from breathing so hard. "I don't want to leave this conversation like this. Can't we talk it out?"

He drops his hand from his face. "I'm not good at talking," he says roughly, staring at the ground, then the sky, then the distance to the parking lot, then wincing at me. "Call your fucking mother, Sul." His eyes well up the longer he stares at me, so he just turns around.

He walks away slowly, like each step is a thousand pounds in agony. I know it must be excruciating for him to leave me here. When he thinks I'm in harm's way, all he wants is to keep me safe forever.

But he punched the two men I'm in love with, and is there any coming back from that?

As he disappears through the woods, leaving behind his gear, the pain surges inside me. I've never really been at odds with my dad or my mom. It feels worse than disappointing them.

It feels like I've lost my dad.

I rub the dirt off my palms in a trance.

"Sulli," Akara breathes.

I blink back more tears and turn to my boyfriends. They've come closer, and their concern envelops me.

"I'm so fucking sorry," I say, throat scratchy and tight. "I didn't think he'd react like this. I mean, I knew he might be hostile at first, but not to the point where he'd hit you guys." I glance up at Akara, then Banks. Not thinking, just doing—I reach up and cup Banks' unshaven jaw, inspecting the cut on his lip. Time slows, but the hurt stays in our silence. "I'm *so* fucking sorry."

Banks tries to smile, but it's faint and weak. "Not the first time someone's tried to hit me, mermaid."

"Won't be the last," Akara says, but he can't force a smile either. He exhales a tensed breath. "Shit. I wish that went *a lot* better."

"I shouldn't have told my dad," I realize and drop my hand.

"No, hey, you did the right thing," Akara assures.

Banks nods. "We all agreed to do what you feel—you did that."

I try not to burst into tears. But I really fucking love them right now, for making me not feel like shit about the consequences of my decision today. Not only did I implode my relationship with my dad, but I put them in the crossfire of his anger. And I didn't prepare them to deal with that heat.

I hug Banks' side, then I hug Akara's, and they squeeze back before I pick up the abandoned rappelling gear. I want to hug them longer. I want to roll around in the earth with them and pretend what happened was just a fucking nightmare and not real.

I want to kiss them, but turning back around feels like swimming through tar. If I just gather all the safety equipment, then maybe my mind won't descend into *replay* mode.

Locking carabiners.

Non-locking carabiners.

A pull cord.

Rope.

Rappel device.

Two harnesses.

Check, check, check, and more checks.

Banks scans the wilderness around us. "Nothing good ever happens in quarries."

The comment chills my bones.

I glance over at him. "This isn't the same quarry where..." *Where his brother Skylar died.*

"No," Banks shakes his head once, then lightly kicks a pebble. "Haven't been to that quarry in forever."

"Something good did happen here," Akara contends.

"Yeah, you got the wind knocked out of you," Banks teases.

Akara manages a half-hearted laugh. "Uh, *no.*" He playfully shoves Banks' shoulder. I almost smile as Akara winks at me, then says, "Someone climbed a sweet rockface today."

Banks bounces his head, his mouth nearly curving up as his gaze meets mine. "I remember that. She looked pretty happy on the descent."

I was.

I am.

"Yeah, that was a good climb...one of the fucking best," I mutter, throat still swollen, and I try to hang onto the happiness before I unleashed the bomb. I remember the closeness I felt with my dad at the peak. We just bonded in an intangible, spiritual way over a route he loves, and then...

Boom.

I blew it all up.

Was it worth it? I don't fucking know. But I can't imagine *hiding* this part of my life from him, so I'd have to share eventually.

As these thoughts toss and turn in the quiet, we all hike along the trail. Akara holds my hand while Banks rubs my back, then rests a strong arm around my shoulders.

Until we reach the parking lot, in public, and they let go. After piling the climbing equipment into the green Jeep, I slide in the back of Booger.

Banks is driving, and Akara fusses with the faulty air conditioning in the passenger seat. Behind them, I lift a knee to my chest and stare out the window. Headed back to Philly.

I replay my dad's words over and over. His actions.

His hurt.

Their hurt.

My hurt.

How there was no painless way this could go, and I don't want to be afraid to lose my dad. But I'm fucking *terrified*. He's my rock. He's been there to turn to my whole life, and now what? Should I even forgive him for his anger? Does he even want forgiveness?

Will we never speak again?

The thought obliterates me. I bawl into my hands, sobbing as pieces of me that have never torn are being shredded apart.

3

Akara Kitsuwon

JUST AS I GIVE UP FIDDLING with the A/C, I hear the sound of Sulli's sobs. I turn. Banks tries to turn but keeps half his gaze plastered to the road.

Sulli shields her face in her hands. Practically buckled forward. She's not someone who easily hides her emotions, and being her bodyguard—being her *friend* for years—I've seen her upset before. Only, these aren't hot, angry tears or frustrated ones of defeat.

These are rare, guttural, and *broken*. And they're a right hook to my heart. Not a second waiting, I'm gone. Crawling over the middle console, I slide into the backseat and wrap my arms around her.

"Sulli," I whisper.

She cries against my chest, unable to unglue her hands from her face.

I hug her closer. "Your dad loves you. This isn't the end." Ryke has to come around. There's no way I'd let her relationship with him just perish because of me.

Fathers.

I don't have one anymore, but she does. And he's always been good to her. Up until today, he's been good to me too.

Her staggered breathing starts to ease up a little.

Behind the wheel, Banks rotates for half-a-second to check on her. He frowns, looking as concerned as I feel. "If your dad just needs to get another punch in to let off some steam," Banks says as he switches lanes, "I'll let him have at it."

"No," she mumbles in her palms. "No…more…" The next word comes out garbled.

Banks glances in the rearview. "What'd she say?"

"No more fighting," I tell him.

I catch the faint rise of his mouth. And the smile on my face surprises me. Looks like we both find Sullivan damn cute in this moment, and I'm not jealous.

Actually, I'm loving that Banks sees what I see. And I love that seeing him love Sulli doesn't freak me the hell out anymore.

But I'm not naïve. I know being in a relationship with the same girl will be *complicated*. Probably in ways that none of us are prepared for— because how the hell do you prepare for this?

It feels like just yesterday I learned poly romances happen in real life and not just fantasies.

Banks drives past a minivan. "Is it fighting if I let Ryke hit me?"

"Still fighting," I tell him.

And he's still my responsibility. One of my guys on Kitsuwon Securities. Only now we're…attached? Metamours? Something that has grown strong and will hopefully grow stronger. The inverse would ruin everything.

Sulli breathes better, but her next words sound fractured. "It… hurts."

I touch her hands that still shield her face. "One day, it won't, and we'll all laugh about this."

"He's a good dad," Banks tells her.

Sulli sniffs loudly, uncovering her face. "Fuck." She intakes a sharp breath. Her face is splotchy, and I brush my thumb over her cheeks. With a raspy voice, she asks, "How can you both be so fucking cool about him? Especially after it got physical?"

Banks lifts a shoulder. "It's not every day a father hears the shit that he heard. Can't expect him to take it easy. Not sure I would've either in his position." He speeds up to pass some oncoming traffic. "I am pissed he walked away though."

"He had to walk away," I tell Banks. "He would've decapitated you."

"But she wanted him to stay to talk it out. And he should've just sucked it up, pulled up his fuckin' undies and *talked*."

I shoot him a look. "You think *that* was a 'clusterfuck'"—I use his word that he muttered to me on our hike back to the parking lot—"it would've been a hundred times worse if he stuck around."

Honestly, I didn't really expect Sulli to tell her dad—of all people—about our relationship first. I doubt Banks expected that bomb-drop either, but we know these families. I'd be terrible at my job if I was shocked that Ryke ended up swinging.

He's known for talking with his fists.

"Yeah, I think Kits is right," Sulli says sadly. "It's good that he left before anything else exploded."

"Like Akara's confidence," Banks says.

I look to Sulli. "Please kick the back of his seat for me."

She almost smiles and she barely nudges his seat with her foot. To me, she says, "I reserve aggressive seat-kicks for the real fucking assholes."

Banks laughs hard.

Yeah, she's referring to *me*.

I playfully fling her hair in her face. Light touches her eyes, and I help her peel off a strand of hair that stuck to her wet cheek.

She rubs her runny nose with her palm. "Cum...fuck...snot is... everywhere. I'm a fucking—"

"Bombshell," Banks interjects.

She blushes.

Banks has that effect on Sulli, but she's also eyeing one of my arms that stays wrapped around her waist. With my other hand, I search the backseat pockets for tissues.

Suddenly, a blue T-shirt catapults at Sulli.

She catches.

I stop my hunt. Noticing a bare-chested Banks driving the Jeep. He stripped for her. Classic Moretti move, giving the shirt off his back.

"Banks the Barbarian," I quip.

"You're letting this barbarian drive," Banks says with a crooked smile.

"You know it."

Sulli nearly smiles too, and she lifts the tee to her nose, smelling Banks' scent. After a few inhales, she wipes the snotty mess on his tee, and her attention returns to me. "I've never seen you that angry, Kits." Her green eyes look like the wild we just left. "Not like that, anyway."

Hands back on the wheel, Banks chimes in, "You popped off."

"I didn't," I refute.

"You did," they say together, and out loud, Sulli wonders, "Was it because my dad was the one who went at you?"

"No, but," I start to explain when I catch a glimpse of the traffic up ahead. "Take the next right, Banks."

He takes a sharp right, the Jeep whipping fast. *Shit.* Just as Sulli starts to careen towards the door, I clutch her waist and pull her halfway on my lap.

Her breath hitches. And she grips onto my sculpted shoulder.

Is she okay?

I skim her with concern that we both recognize as something ancient and then I look into her with desire that feels raw and freshly discovered. My pulse upticks. This is still so new between me and her. A fledgling romance that we've let fly free around us.

I brush a few pieces of hair out of her face. Letting my fingers trace the carve of her squared jaw and along the softness of her pink lips.

"Thanks for the save," she breathes, and I wait for her to slug me, but she drinks me in for a second before glancing to the driver's seat.

Banks is catching glimpses of us through the rearview mirror. And she seems to be in her head about him.

We *really* need to go over the ground rules together. At least have some sort of consistent plan so she's not paranoid about time and attention given to us and so jealousy isn't a habitual monster.

What I know: I like watching them kiss. And Banks likes watching us kiss. More than anything, he probably hates chauffeuring us around, and the only reason he hasn't called me back to the front seat is because A.) Sulli likes me back here and B.) I'm his boss. I order him around.

Keeping her partially on my lap, I try to take Sulli's mind off our relationship. "So Ryke has laid into me before. If it were up to your dad, he'd be the one protecting you twenty-four-seven." I think back to how I yelled at her father.

That was *not* how I wanted that to go.

At all.

I sigh. "I just lost my shit back there because of what he said."

"That you're her brother?" Banks lets out.

Sulli cringes.

I glare. "Don't even, man." I bow forward a little towards him. "And I might've popped off at her dad, but at least I don't have a death wish. Remember when Ryke threatened to kill us if we touched her? Remember what *you* said?" I mimic Banks. "*We already did, sir.*"

Banks is unbothered. "I wasn't going to lie. It's not like I said I fucked his daughter."

Sulli goes pale. "God, he really would've fucking killed you."

I adjust the radio on my waistband to pull Sulli a little closer. To Banks, I say, "When would you like me to hold your hair back while your head is on a guillotine?"

"Your head is gonna be beside mine, so that honor is hers."

"Oh no," she says strongly, "I'm not watching either of you die. Count me the fuck out."

Banks and I exchange a brief smile, then I notice how Sulli grimaces, staring out the window. My face sobers. "What's wrong, Sulli?"

"A part of me just really wants Runaway Sulli gone." She balls up Banks' tee. "I want to ensure you two aren't headed for anything fucking bad, not without me."

She is here. She didn't leave us.

Before either of us can make a comment, she asks me, "Why did my dad lay into you back then?"

I can't even remember if she heard anything. It's years back, and if she was there, maybe she forgot too. "It was mostly about security logistics when you turned eighteen," I explain. "Like I said, he wanted to be in control of protecting you. But I had to stop listening to his orders, and I took yours. It was a rough transition for him."

"You're his baby," Banks says plainly.

Sulli lets out a long groan, cheeks flaming. "It's not fucking fair." Is she embarrassed? She's avoiding our eyes.

"Sul?"

"He should be treating me like a woman, Kits. It's what I am. *I'm a fucking woman.*" She sounds as defensive as she does passionate.

I smile, "We know, string bean. No need to convince us."

The nickname usually grants me a punch to the arm, but her lips seem to ache to rise instead.

Banks checks the mirror before switching lanes again. "If you were underage, we wouldn't have made a move on you."

She shifts a little on my lap.

Fuck.

Her ass grinds down against my cock, whether unconsciously or consciously—it ripples a shockwave through my entire body. I flex my muscles, and I kiss her cheek lightly.

"You've both only done it to me once," Sulli mentions. "And by *it*, I obviously mean putting your dicks inside me."

I heat up at her crudeness and the fact that only clothing separates Sulli from sitting on my cock. "Due to time and opportunity constraints," I tell her. "Not because I don't want to be inside you."

Her dad just yelled that I'm a *brother* to her, and I want to make clear I'd love to fuck her. Slowly, deeply, with my hand pinning her wrists to the bed. In ways we definitely haven't yet, because she was a virgin.

Slow.

Go very, very slow with Sulli.

Banks glances briefly at her, then the road. "You worried it won't happen again?"

"I guess I just need some reassurance that my dad didn't scare you guys away. He can be intense."

"I'm not going anywhere," Banks says.

I nod, "We knew who your dad was before we slept with you."

Her lips fall in thought, like she just realized something disastrous. "I know who my dad is, too. But right now, I can't tell you if he'll be blurting this all over the family gossip networks or keeping it to himself." She lets out an exasperated breath. "*Fuck*."

That thought lingers in the car, even as I hold her tighter.

I *really* don't like the idea of Ryke Meadows being the one to tell everyone about our relationship. It should come from Sulli, Banks, and me.

Only way to fix this is to start telling more people. It's what we discuss on our way back home. By the time we enter the Philly apartment complex and rise up the elevator, we agree that we won't change our first decision. No mega announcements. We'll tell everyone casually when we see them.

Only issue is that Thatcher and Jane are still on their honeymoon. I'm at least glad my friend didn't insist on being Jane's bodyguard during the trip. Gabe Montgomery was the better option. The bodyguard has been part-time temping and part-time protecting Jack Highland-Oliveira, who needed more security after being with Oscar. With Gabe on Jane's detail during the honeymoon, Thatcher can relax, *and* he can personally see if Gabe has what it takes to make it on the full-time roster.

Banks fiddles with the keys to our apartment door. We still live three floors below Sulli's penthouse. Before we go to Sulli's place, we're making a pitstop to change out our battery packs and get Banks a new shirt.

Sulli nibbles on a vegan granola, crinkling her nose in slight distaste.

I keep my eyes alert on the hallway. Comms crackle in my ears, and I listen for a second. No one speaks. But someone is pressing on the mic and breathing weirdly.

Great.

Just great.

I pull out my phone to text in a group thread. Take your sticky finger off the mic.

Since Thatcher is taking time off work and he's the lead, I'm picking up his tasks. Like being aware of SFO's whereabouts.

Oscar: Copenhagen with Charlie, *I think*. (Last update was 48 hrs ago.)

Quinn: New York with Luna, *I think*. (Last update was 15 hrs ago.)

Farrow: Philly penthouse with Moffy and their son Ripley, *I think*. (Last update was maybe 4 hrs ago.)

Donnelly: the Hale house with Xander, *I'm positive*.

Thatcher: Switzerland

Banks: right in front of me

Pinning down SFO is becoming a game of "pin the tail on the jackass" that I suck at, and the only way I feel like a winner is to have Thatcher back.

Banks opens the door, and we push into the apartment. Immediately, the wind is stolen from my lungs at who I see.

4

Akara Kitsuwon

QUINN: PHILLY SECURITY APARTMENT, *I know because I'm looking at him.*

Balancing a plate of avocado toast on his knees, Quinn watches college football on TV, but music is blaring over the game. He bobs his head to the beat of a pop song I've never heard. When he sees us, he upnods.

"*Volume down*," I call out to the stereo. The music automatically lowers.

"That one was actually pretty good, wasn't it?" Quinn licks avocado off his finger and checks the song on his phone. "It was RuPaul's 'Condragulations'. Oscar sent me a playlist after we went to the drag show together last night."

Last night?

I try to not let out a sigh. Well, it looks like Oscar wasn't in Copenhagen yesterday like I thought. Don't know where he is now.

I'm a *rusty* lead (but a pristine boss). Back when I worked for Triple Shield, I used to be better-than-decent at locating the guys.

"Things are going better with your brother?" I ask Quinn since him and Oscar are actively spending time together off-duty. And I'm still paying for their therapy. Money well spent, especially if they can bury any kind of hatchet.

Even a Polly Pocket sized one.

"Yeah. We're cool." Quinn leans back, his floral shirt opened and bare-chested underneath. It's November on the *East* Coast, but Quinn is the poster boy for trending LA fashion. He's been a total babe magnet since the FanCon tour, and I really don't want to be the killjoy of his early twenties as an asshole boss.

I do believe achieving a balance between work and play is possible in this job.

I found that with Sulli early on. Friendships with your client make every day more worthwhile.

You fell in love with your friend, Nine.

Okay, I do *not* want Quinn to befriend Luna and then fall in love with her. Ryke Meadows is one thing, but Loren Hale is a different breed of dad. He has the power to destroy Kitsuwon Securities out of spite.

Anyway, I'm positive that Quinn doesn't have a buddy-guard relationship with Luna. He's said he's more like her big brother.

Nothing to worry about.

Quinn notices Sulli slipping into the kitchen, then us lingering. "What's going on, guys?"

"I can tell you what's not going on," I say with not much heat. "You radioing me your location."

"Do you need to know what I'm eating for lunch too?" He holds up his plate. "5 out of 5 *best* avocado toast I've made all month. Want a bite?" His teeth rip into the bread.

I have not missed this part of the job. Don't want it. Need Thatcher ASAP.

Banks pats my shoulder. Like it's all over my face, he says, "My brother will be back soon."

"Not soon enough," I breathe.

He smiles, then studies Quinn and his food like he's flown in from outer space. "We look like the mimosa-sipping, avocado-eating type?"

Sulli calls out, "Don't knock it till you try it."

Banks glances over at her, and a soft smile plays at his lips. Like her words were more than just words, but also a memory they shared.

Time. I want more time with her, but I've also had *years* with Sulli that Banks will never have. It's not a contest, and we're all in this together.

It'll be easier once people like Quinn know the truth. So we can stop hiding.

Quinn's eyes scrunch at Banks. "You get hit, bro?"

Fuck.

His bottom lip is puffy, skin more reddened too.

Banks shrugs. "On-the-job horseshit." It's not a complete lie. We were on-duty when Ryke decked him.

While I head to the kitchen to grab an icepack for Banks, Sulli is already halfway in the freezer. She pulls out a bag of frozen broccoli. I take it, and she tries to whisper, "He's not more hurt than he's letting on, right?"

Banks promised he'd tell us when he has another migraine. But we both know he'd rather hide his physical pain.

"I think he's okay." *He better be.*

She eases.

I want to steal a kiss—the moment is there, but thinking *rationally*, I touch my knuckles to her knuckles instead of lips to lips. She makes a strange face, red creeping up her neck.

Yeah, that was awkward.

Ice.

Banks.

I wave to Sulli, losing all sense of *smoothness*. What the hell is going on with me? Leaving, I cast a single glance back at Sulli in the kitchen.

She raids the pantry and hunts for something better than a vegan granola bar. Her dark hair is tumbling out of a messy bun, splayed long over broad shoulders. She's beautiful.

She's always been beautiful.

And I realize I've never really loved anyone like I love her. Dating a friend is one thing—dating a friend that I considered *life-long* feels like racing down the best black diamond slope. Exhilarating, nerve-wracking—or what a Meadows would say: the greatest adventure.

I center myself and hand Banks the frozen broccoli in the living room. He's rifling through a storage bin on the bookshelf, searching for the battery packs.

"Is it that bad?" Banks asks about his face, pressing the broccoli to his mouth. We speak quietly since Quinn is still on the leather couch.

I scrutinize his swollen lip. "Ryke definitely wasn't holding back."

"Fuck-a-duck," he grumbles.

"Hey, at least he didn't break your face."

Banks lets out a short sound, an almost-laugh, and I pick up the remote, lowering the volume of the TV.

Quinn peers up from his phone. "You guys want to hang at Saturn Bridges tonight? A girl DM'd me on Instagram—she's bringing a bunch of her friends."

Banks stiffens, then locks eyes with me.

Quinn adds, "I told her I'd ask my roommates since you're all single."

We're *not* single.

A plate clatters in the kitchen. "Cumbuckets," Sulli curses. She dropped a dish?

"You okay?" Banks calls.

"Uh, *fuck*...yeah."

Banks abandons the batteries to go help her.

Unclipping my radio, I pick up his task. "We can't go out, Quinn."

"Damn. Alright. Maybe Donnelly will be free then."

I head to the kitchen, batteries in hand.

Sulli is whispering up at a six-foot-seven Banks. "You want to fucking tell him first?" Her voice is pretty loud. "He's like two seconds from setting you both up on blind dates—or with the chicks he brings home. Which is great—I'm sure they're so fucking rad and *cool*." She groans into her hands.

Quinn is looking over here.

"You have nothing to worry about, mermaid," Banks whispers better. "You're the coolest chick I know."

"The raddest," I chime in, joining their huddle.

Hands falling, she smiles from him to me, then I extend an arm over her shoulders. "Kits," she says, "what's the plan?"

"He's our roommate. We'll tell him."

Quinn calls out, "There should be some bread you can eat in the pantry, Sulli." He thinks she's distressed about food right now. He knows she's on a vegan pact with her little sister, and Sulli has been down in the dumps over *no eggs, no dairy.*

So he's not far off.

"Have you ever gone vegan?" Sulli asks Quinn, a vegetarian.

"Once, and it was way too hard for me. I felt like I was slowly wasting away."

Sulli's eyes bug. "Fuck."

I twist a strand of her hair around my finger. "You're not wasting away, Sul. I won't let you." My knuckles brush the edge of her jaw.

Her cheeks flush, gaze dipping down to my lips. Tension draws between us, one that we've been refusing to lean into these past few days. I remember the knuckle-bump from earlier and the awkward beat afterwards.

For real, I just want to kiss Sulli like she's my girlfriend. Because she *is* my girlfriend. And a kiss shouldn't cause an earthquake of chaos.

Everything *romantic* has been a secret. But today, the three of us are choosing to set that secret free.

I drop her hair and then I hand Banks one battery pack.

He subtly gestures to Quinn. "I've got this one."

"You sure?"

Banks nods, and the three of us move out of the kitchen. We stand around the living room, and Banks says, "We have something to tell you, Quinn."

"Okay...?" Quinn actually mutes the TV, confusion on his face. I can't even imagine what the hell he's thinking. His puzzled eyes ping between us. "What's up?"

"Akara, Sulli, and me..." Banks makes a motion with his finger, circling us. "We're in a relationship together."

I pipe in fast, "We're telling everyone ourselves, so keep this to yourself, okay?" *That's an order*, I wish I could add.

Quinn jerks back like someone slapped him. "Wait, you two are fucking?"

He's looking between *me* and *Banks*.

That's what he got out of that?

Sulli has her hands on her head and mutters, "Fucking fuck."

Banks mumbles something, tossing the frozen broccoli behind us, in the sink.

And before I can cut in, Quinn's hands shoot in the air. "Not that I'd care! Seriously, you do you—"

"We're not fucking," I say curtly.

Quinn nods slowly. "…right, so it's like…a relationship without sex. Like a platonic thing. A bromance." His eyes light up with the snap of his fingers. "It's what the four of us have. Four single roommates forming bromances. Yale boys are going to be jealous."

Banks gives him a look. "Donnelly is a Yale boy."

"So the three of us then." Quinn holds out his knuckles.

Sulli is hiding her face in her hands.

I'd like to never see another knuckle-bump again. That'd be great.

This is going way less hostile than the conversation with Ryke but about a million times more awkward. I need to get behind the wheel of this train wreck. "We're not talking about roommates. This is about *Sulli*."

She uncovers her face. "I'm dating them—Akara *and* Banks."

Quinn listens, unblinking.

I'm righting this further on the damn tracks. "We're in a polyamorous relationship. Look it up, Quinn." I grab Sulli's hand and look to Banks like *follow me*.

"What they said," Banks adds to Quinn before taking the directive. We leave and then enter the bedroom that I share with him.

As soon as I shut the door, Sulli's hands fly to her head. "We fucked that up."

"*I* fucked that up," Banks rephrases. "Lesson learned, hand signals don't do shit."

"It's a practice round," I say to them. "We'll get better at it." I unspool the wire of my mic and fit a new battery pack into the radio. I have to at least believe that. We're going to be telling way too many people for us to keep bombing this hard.

Sulli studies our small bedroom for a brief second. It's minimal. No personality or artwork or photos of family. Just two full-sized beds that belong to me and Banks, pushed against either wall, and two end tables, one dresser.

Our lives are so far outside this room. It's a pitstop. Not a home.

She sniffs her sweaty shirt, wandering closer to the half-window— which is the *only* window in the room. This apartment was cheaper because of the shitty views. Terrific for me, since I pay for everyone's housing, and Oscar's studio apartment in New York is costing me a tiny fortune.

"Want a shower?" Banks asks her while he pulls a clean blue T-shirt over his head.

"Yeah…but maybe later…" Her mind is somewhere else, especially as she checks her phone. Little wrinkles of distress line her forehead.

Banks and I share a look.

Ever since we left the quarry, she's been worrying about her parents. I want to help Sulli solve this crisis, but the only solution seems to be *calling* them. But that just might make everything ten times worse.

Banks and I finish getting rid of the dead batteries, and Sulli stretches her muscular arms over her chest. She shakes out her limbs and lets out a humongous sigh.

"You want to talk about it, Sul?" I ask.

She finally uncorks her bottled thoughts. "I just don't understand *what* I need to do for my dad to see me as Adult Sulli and not Teenage Sulli. I've already moved out. Do I need a job? Is that what makes an adult, *an adult?* Earning your own money?"

"It's not about money," Banks says, clipping his radio back on his waistband.

She sinks down on my bed, her green eyes lifting up to us. "I've never really had a job besides being an Olympian—but I was still a teenager back then." Her professional athlete days are over, but those were important her whole life and to who she is.

I was there.

I know what winning gold meant. The tears in her eyes. The pride on the podium. All her hard work had an ending, and the new beginning has been constantly shifting with her desires.

Sulli collapses backwards and stares hard at the ceiling.

I wonder if she's thinking about how she hasn't given a lot of thought to a paying career. At least, she hasn't brought it up to me lately. I grew up rich, but not the kind of rich that owns mega-yachts and boards private planes.

She's lived a privileged life. Able to travel, to climb and swim without setting monetary goals. I've always seen Sulli as a free spirit, chasing the essence of the earth and water, and I never saw myself as the man *paid* to follow her.

I'm *sworn* to protect her. I'd give my life for Sulli's life, but Ryke wasn't wrong. She does pay me. Kitsuwon Securities is a business that Sulli and her cousins choose to use, and we have expenses. But why does it feel weird now?

She shouldn't have to pay me to protect her.

I'm her boyfriend.

It comes free.

Sulli's face twists in a thought. "Maybe my dad doesn't respect me as an adult because I'm living off my trust fund."

I doubt that. "Hasn't Ryke lived off familial wealth too?" I ask. "Your grandfather owned Hale Co."

"Which my dad walked away from."

Loren Hale is the CEO of the billion-dollar baby product company. Hale Co. is best known for diapers, strollers, baby oil, shit like that, but their logo is actually on popular air fresheners, skin care lines, facial washes, and even the first-aid kits Farrow packs in his trauma bags.

So Hale Co. is massive. Something I'll never achieve in my lifetime, just being realistic.

Sulli reminds us, "Most of my dad's income comes from doing sports drink sponsorships for Fizzle."

Her mom is the heiress to Fizzle, along with her aunts, but I'm almost positive most of Sulli's family wealth is tied to the billon-dollar soda empire.

But she's told me that before her grandfather died, he set funds in trusts for her and Winona, and he made sure they were shareholders in Hale Co.

She's a double heiress.

Or what she's said to me, *a double fucking heiress.*

She has enough money to live luxuriously for the rest of her life. I've been working since I turned eighteen. All college aspirations burned out fast. I wanted to run a gym, and college felt unnecessary. More like a roadblock to success than a building block.

Her frown deepens. "If not age or money, then what makes an adult? Responsibility?"

Banks pops in the new battery. "No, then my brother would've been a four-year-old adult."

We laugh, but I end up saying, "For me, it was *death.*" The bedroom quiets as they listen. "Losing a parent at seventeen just woke me up to a reality I wasn't really ready for." I take a beat. "One day I was excited about playing drums on a college field, then the next, I wanted to burn the application and never pick up sticks again."

Death changed the course of my entire life.

The legacy of my family felt more important to immortalize than some adolescent love of playing drums.

Banks clips the mic to his collar. "By your logic, you're saying her mom or dad need to die for her to be an adult."

I shove his arm. "Not what I meant, man. And maybe it's just different for everyone."

He bobs his head.

Sulli rises onto her elbows. I can tell she's still distraught at defining adulthood.

Banks catches her gaze as he slips a toothpick between his lips.

"What do you think?" she asks him.

He lifts a shoulder. "Hell if I know the right meaning of anything, but I do know that no one should be telling you who *you* are but you."

She breathes in stronger. "I want so fucking badly to just listen to my own voice and feelings about who I am. I know I'm a woman, but I want my dad to see me as more than just his little girl too."

She cares about what he thinks.

So do I.

I want Ryke Meadows' respect. I wish I could be like Banks and say, *whatever the fuck.* Screw it. But I can't shrug this off.

Probably because I don't like to lose, and there has to be a solution. A way out.

I'm lost in thought when Sulli tosses a small pillow at my chest. "Kits?"

I focus on her. "Maybe you shouldn't pay us anymore, Sulli."

"What?" she winces.

"This is a bad idea," Banks mutters, gnawing on the toothpick.

"I have to pay you, Kits, for your *protection* services. You're my private security. I'm not letting you work for fucking free."

"I can manage it."

Can you, Nine?

I hear my dad's voice in my head.

"How will you afford rent?" Sulli asks. "How will you pay Banks' salary?"

By crunching a shit ton of numbers.

I push back my black hair. "Just let me handle the business end, okay?"

"My dad got in your head," she realizes. "You know who knows nothing about dating a bodyguard? Ryke fucking Meadows. My dad has *no clue* how this all works. You know who does? Moffy and Jane. They've made it work."

I'm rigid. "Farrow and Thatcher aren't running the company, Sulli. *I am.*"

Moffy and Jane are paying *me.*

I pay their husbands.

Her shoulders slowly drop, realizing that this makes a difference to me.

Banks keeps shaking his head like it's still a *bad idea*.

But one thing I know about my friend, he'll follow me into any bad idea I have.

5

Banks Moretti

WE EXIT THE BEDROOM and start cooking. Quinn can't stop staring at the three of us like we've all grown horns and tails in the past three minutes. But I'm not hiding out in the bedroom. The mermaid is starving, and we're doing our best to whip up something edible for Sulli.

The kitchen is in direct line of sight to the living room, and Quinn still stares.

Hell, maybe he's just watching Sulli try to sauté this pound of broccoli. She pushes around the vegetable on the frying pan like it's diseased.

I angle towards her. "Stroke it any gentler and it might jump out at you."

She snorts. "And what, try to kiss me?"

I crack a smile. "No broccoli is kissing my girlfriend." I reach over her head and flip on the fan as smoke mushrooms up.

She elbows me softly with a blushing smile. "Broccoli is the moldy armpit of vegetables. I wouldn't let it near my lips unless it was the only thing in your freezer."

Which, it was.

I grab a spatula and help her scrape up burnt pieces. "You hate most of what you *can* eat and love everything you can't."

"You think I should quit being vegan?" Sulli asks.

"Unless you really are withering away, I think you should do whatever you want. If that means challenging yourself, then go for it." We look over at each other at the same time, and I add, "But like Akara, if I see you withering, you better believe I'm going to pick you up and fling you across my shoulder."

She laughs into this overwhelmed smile that takes my breath away. "And then what?"

I almost feel choked. "And then I'll carry you to the nearest McDonalds. Get you the *biggest* McFlurry."

"Extra Oreos."

"All the Oreos."

Good grief, I'm in fucking love. And by some grace of God, I have Sulli for longer than a day or week or month. I can only hope this'll go on for years, but I'm trying not to look too far ahead and miss out on what's right in front of me.

She's stopped cooking. Letting me take over, but I'm just as terrible of a chef. The best cook among us is leaning against the fridge, texting.

Sulli watches Akara, then looks to me, "What happens to the three of us if not everyone takes our relationship as well as Quinn?"

Is Quinn taking it well?

On the couch, he pretends to be reading Akara's *Fortune* magazine. But he's peering coyly at us like we're strange beasts in a stranger zoo.

"We stick together. Come what may," I whisper to Sulli. "Nothing's gonna pull us apart."

"Not even your brother?" Sulli wonders, concern flooding the prettiest green eyes.

She's worried he'll take it badly.

Truth: he probably will. But Sulli chose me and Akara over her father. And I'm picking her over everyone else.

"Whatever happens," I whisper, "we'll always choose you like you chose us. No matter which direction I'm pulled in, I'm headed in yours."

She breathes in, and I take her free hand, twirling her in a circle until her back ends up against my chest. I tuck her closer while we burn some vegetables together.

And then my phone buzzes on the counter.

I stretch an arm and grab my phone. My mouth curves up seeing the Caller ID. What timing.

How are the cats? – Cinderella

Alas, the six-foot-seven Cinderella is texting. It'd be better if Thatcher were actually here right now. That way he could see my eyes roll around the fuckin' room. He goes to Switzerland for his honeymoon, and the guy forgets how good of a cat sitter I am. Typical. I shift back from Sulli to text my brother: Alive. Well fed. You and Jane will see them tomorrow. Don't panic before then.

One second later, he replies.

I'm not panicking. – Cinderella

I'm about to put my phone down when he texts again.

I'm coming home tonight. – Cinderella

"What?" I say out loud, too shocked to cage this thought.

Sulli rotates more to me. "What's wrong?"

Boiling water starts bubbling over a pot on the stove—the pot Akara was supposed to be watching. I drop my phone this time to grab the pot and lift it off the heat.

"Shit, sorry," Akara says, glancing up from his phone.

Akara usually ranges from mediocre to subpar in the kitchen. I'm still smack dab in the terrible range, but I guess I found something I'm good at. Keeping a pot of boiling fuckin' water from overflowing isn't an achievement I'm going to be gloating about any time soon.

When the water simmers, I set the pot on the stovetop. "My brother is coming home *tonight*," I announce.

Akara nods like he already knows. He pockets his cell. "He just told me, too. Thatcher and Jane are cutting their honeymoon a day short because of the cats."

I let out an annoyed breath. "What a fucking *stunad*. I'm doing a good job cat sitting."

Akara smiles. "It's not you. Jane misses them. Thatcher won't admit it, but I think he does too."

He definitely has a gooey soft spot for those pussies.

Not so sure I'm going to be a soft spot in my brother's heart after he learns about my current relationship status. Thatcher would be on guard in any scenario that involves me dating Sullivan Minnie Meadows. Even when he knows I had a Jupiter-sized crush on her, he was throwing down crash pad after crash pad in front of me. Like he knew I was about to plummet out of the side of a plane without a parachute on.

I know my brother like I know myself.

Maybe even better.

He's my twin.

And I know, for a certain fuckin' fact, nothing will have changed in his eyes. I'm head-over-heels in love with Sulli, but Akara is paddling in the same lovesick boat as me. Thatcher won't jump for joy over this "triad." He's going to think I'm gripping the short end of the stick, and one day I might not be gripping it at all.

But I've been through that insecurity in Yellowstone, and I'm over it. A choice has been made, and we all chose each other. That's enough for me.

Right now, I'm not worried about being the odd one out, but I'm buckling up for Thatcher's worry to assault me tonight.

I grab the box of rotini from the cupboard. After a quick check on the ingredients, I confirm there's no egg and I toss the contents in the water.

More smoke plumes from the frying pan. "Cumbuckets," Sulli curses.

"I have it." Akara quickly takes the pan off the heat, but he doesn't see me pass to throw out the pasta box. Heat lances my wrist, the pan bumping into me.

"Shit." Akara loses his grip on the pan and drops it.

Broccoli scatters across the ground.

Sulli stares at the vegetable for a second. "That's where broccoli belongs, and you know, I'm not too sad it's there." Her eyes hit mine. "Are you okay?"

"All good." Just a small burn. Nothing I can't handle.

Akara cringes. "I'm sorry, man."

"Maybe the three of us shouldn't be allowed in a kitchen," I say.

Akara laughs. "Hey, I'm all for takeout."

Cheering escalates on the TV, and we glance towards the living room. Quinn's still eagle-eyeing the fuck out of us, even behind the *Fortune* magazine. And I don't even think he realizes he's doing it.

Akara looks back. "How about we *take out* the remnants of this pasta to the penthouse? Maybe we won't have an audience there."

"Right on," I nod.

Sulli says, "Sounds like a fucking plan."

We're able to finish cooking the pasta. Strain it. Divide it into three different paper bowls. No vegetables. No spices. I stare at my bowl of overcooked, *musciad* rotini that literally has only a splash of olive oil.

My mom would be wearing a thousand different expressions of disappointment if she saw this mess. Christ, even Thatcher would be giving me shit.

We ride the elevator up to the penthouse. Hand-to-heart, it feels like there's no storm ahead on the ascent. No worries. No cares in the world. Just three knucklefucks in an elevator carrying bowls of disgustingly bland pasta.

Akara keeps glancing at the red welt on my wrist. "You should ice it."

I wear a slight smile. "You should stick to being the boss and not the doctor." I stab my fork into the pasta. "You're not supposed to ice burns."

He sends me a look. "And suddenly Banks has an MD."

"No, I have an MG. I make guesses. But *our* MD told me not to ice burns."

"Farrow?" Sulli asks.

"Yeah. The night of the townhouse fire, my dumbass was icing a burn with cold vending machine drinks." That night I only really had minor burns. Nothing that doctors needed to treat. Nothing that left permanent scars. Not like my brother who still has lasting reminders of that horrible fucking night.

Akara bows his head with a pained expression. "Top five worst nights of my life." He physically pinned me down when my brother ran into the fire. When I thought I'd lost Thatcher, Akara made sure he didn't lose me too.

I clear a tight knot in my throat. "Yeah, let's not talk about it then." Both of their gazes soften on me.

Akara pats my back. "I see burying painful shit is still the Moretti standard."

"Not that easy to break," I say lightly, but I know if I could, I'd break the silence with them. I already told them I had an older brother. *Skylar.* They know about his existence and his exit from this world, but I haven't been able to really describe *that* night to either of them.

It's not just fourth or fifth in my Worst Nights ranking.

It's number one.

The absolute motherfuckin' worst. And seeing as how my dad is working for Akara now, I'm not too peachy keen on shading my dad into some kind of villain. What he said to me at twelve-years-old was just about as villainous as they come. Akara can't know.

I can't tell him.

Maybe one day I can tell her.

"And here I am," Sulli says, stabbing her pasta, "the *over-sharer.*"

I can't help but smile. "You can always overshare with me, mermaid." She leans closer to me, and I wrap an arm around her shoulders.

"Funny, I was going to say the same thing," Akara says with a teasing smile on Sulli, "Minus the *mermaid* part."

Sulli elbows him. "That's the best part."

Fuck it, I'm gloating.

Akara looks unafflicted. Confidence at 110%. I'm at 100%, and I'm A-okay with losing a battle of arrogance if the winner has a surplus.

Akara says, "You melted when he said you can overshare."

"Banks is good with words," she professes.

Nobody has ever said that about me before. I stare down at her with a swelling feeling rising in my chest. I'm already six-seven, but fuck, I feel a thousand-feet taller.

Akara leans down and whispers in her ear. Loud enough that I can hear. "I'm better with my hands, Sul." His fingers trail down her spine towards her ass.

Hot fucking damn.

I watch her squirm a little. Hell, I *feel* her squirm since my arm is around her shoulders. Her breath shortens, and he whispers, "There is still so much I want to do with you." The depth in his voice makes his words sound greater. Like he's lamenting about more than just sex. Like he's yearning for time.

"Kits," she nearly whimpers, then lightly pushes his arm before grabbing onto him, bringing him closer to her other side. "So the mighty leader is becoming the follower now since you're following Banks' lead?"

Because he copied me?

I cock my head to him.

"*Never*," Akara scoffs. "If Banks led us, we'd all end up in a dark, dank jungle in a ditch."

I laugh hard. Because it's true.

Ding.

The elevator stops and slides open to the penthouse foyer.

Sulli uses her keys and unlocks the door to 9000 square feet of *home*. Her home.

My job has always had me standing outside rich, *lavish* settings, peering into a world that couldn't be more unfamiliar to me. Then Thatcher went off and married a Cobalt. Attaching the Morettis to the Cobalt Empire is still a fucking weird combo.

But inside, my brother fits well in both worlds.

Me?

I don't see myself acclimating as well as he did, but strangely enough, the penthouse doesn't feel so unfamiliar. The walls aren't dripping in one-of-a-kind oil paintings. Diamond chandeliers aren't hoisted overhead.

The penthouse might be big, but it's dressed with familiarity: brick walls, earthy brown woods, and photographs hung of Sulli's family, Jane's family, Maximoff and Luna's family.

As soon as we step inside, a skateboard whizzes across the floorboards. Not a soul on the thing.

Luna races after. "Sorry!"

The skateboard curves towards us, and Akara grabs the board before it collides into Sulli's ankles. Luna rolls to a stop, panting, and Orion, a black-furred Newfoundland puppy, leaps after her. Luna lovingly pats his head.

Why the fuck the dog catches my attention first—I have no clue. Because Luna's face is *covered* in googly eyes.

Now I have trouble looking into her *real* eyes.

"Hey, Luna," Sulli raises her bowl of pasta in greeting.

"Howdy." Luna smiles, pulling her long, light-brown hair off her shoulders.

I nod to her. Not as close to Luna as I am to Xander. But I worked so long for the Hale family that I saw Luna grow up more than I ever saw Sulli.

She flashes the Vulcan salute.

"This is yours." Akara waves the skateboard before handing it to Luna.

"Thanks." She tucks it under her armpit. "I'm trying to teach Orion how to skateboard. It's going…" She glances at Orion who circles her feet excitedly. "Not so great." She sniffs the air, then makes a face. "What's that?"

"Fucking pasta," Sulli says.

"It's barely pasta," I add.

Luna rubs Orion behind his ears. "Is it supposed to smell burnt?"

"Okay, that's it," Akara decrees, "we're not eating this shit." He takes my bowl, then Sulli's, stacking them onto his bowl. "I'm ordering us actual takeout."

"Thank fucking God," Sulli exhales.

I smack Akara's chest with the back of my hand. "My savior."

"Jesus is your savior," he says into a short laugh.

"But you can call Him up on speed dial. Tell Him I'd like a pizza. Heaven-sent."

Sulli and Luna laugh, and Akara mimes a phone to his ear. "Hello, God, I'd like to report a sin—"

"Alright, alright." I wear a slow-rising smile. "We all know my ass is headed for hell anyway."

Akara gives me a strong look like I'm wrong, and before Luna turns to leave, Sulli quickly steps forward and says, "Oh hey, do you have a sec, Luna? I have to tell you something important."

Let's do this.

I unpocket a canister of toothpicks and slip one between my lips. Though I'm ready for any hellfire, I feel like I need to strap into the walls. Just in case this all goes fucking sideways.

"Sure," Luna says with a frown. "Is everything okay?" She sets her skateboard down, and Orion hops on, then off, then darts in another direction. Luna watches her energetic dog go but doesn't bother calling him back or chasing him down.

"Yeah." Sulli crosses her arms. "Um, it's just kind of fucking hard to explain—I mean, it's not that hard. But…" She blows out a breath.

Akara and I are staring at our girlfriend. Waiting to see if she needs one of us to pull the grenade.

Luna says, "It can't be anything worse than I've done." She pauses. "Do you want to talk in private?" She means away from us.

"No, it's about Akara and Banks too."

With his free hand, Akara gently shuts the door behind us, and I lean a shoulder on the wood.

Luna pries only one googly eye off her cheek. "Are you all going on another road trip?"

"Not anytime soon," Akara answers.

Sulli shakes out her limbs again. "Alright, so here it is." She rests her hands on her hips. "Luna, I'm dating Banks *and* Akara."

"Both?" Her eyes are saucers with a growing smile. Add in those googly eyes, and it's almost comical.

I feel my lips try to lift.

"Yeah, *both*," Sulli nods. "It's pretty new to us. We started dating in Yellowstone, but I always thought I'd have to pick one of them in the end. Until I talked to Beckett about polyamory. And it's something the three of us want to be in—a polyamorous relationship."

Knew Sulli could do it.

Luna starts nodding. "Yeah, yeah, I've read about poly relationships in some fics online." Her lips rise more, reddening her cheeks. "That's really cool, Sulli." She bursts into a bigger smile, then says, "You're dating two dudes at once. It's like the ultimate fantasy."

"But it's *real*," Sulli emphasizes.

"Yepyep, I know," Luna says fast. "I won't judge. Everyone likes all sorts of different things." Luna shrugs. "It's something I like reading about in sci-fi fics, but I don't know if I could ever do it."

Sulli nods a hell of a lot.

Akara and I exchange a look. *She's nervous.* Maybe because Luna is someone who seems game for most daring things. But Sulli is the one swimming towards those rapids.

We're with you, mermaid.

Luna continues, "Dating one guy is already a lot of work, especially with our parents..." She trails off. "Are you keeping it secret from them?"

"Not really," Sulli says. "My dad already knows. It's a long story."

Luna looks horrified. "Uh-oh."

Akara whispers to me, "That's putting it mildly."

"Rah." I drop the *ooh* to the *rah.*

"Maybe you, uh, shouldn't tell Moffy," Luna says. "If your dad had a bad reaction, then my dad would be out for blood. And you know Moffy goes three-fourths Loren Hale."

Three-fourths out for blood.

Pack me up and ship me out, I'm prepared for war.

Surprisingly, Sulli is too. "I have to tell him, Luna. I can't keep anymore fucking secrets. It's hard enough dating, but dating *in secret* sucks."

Luna's gaze goes gentle. "I get it. *Not* that I'm dating anyone in secret." She looks right at Akara.

Akara stiffens. "Is there something I should know?"

"No," Luna says quickly. "Forget I was here." She hops on the skateboard and rolls away. What the fuck…?

"She's dating one of the guys?" I ask Akara.

"Quinn," Akara guesses with heat. "*Shit*."

"No," Sulli snaps. "She just said she's *not* in a secret relationship. Believe her."

He touches his chest. "I'm not *not* believing her. But she is definitely hiding something, Sul. And if it's not being with Quinn, then what else?"

Sulli buries her face in her hands and groans. "Don't make me break a secret."

I bite on the toothpick. "I'll be fucking damned, she knows."

"Our little secret-keeper," Akara muses with a sigh.

Sulli reappears. "I'm not little!"

We smile, and Akara tells her, "Banks and I will figure out the mystery without you, so you don't have to break a thing."

I cock my head to her. "Looks like you're dating the Hardy Boys."

She laughs into a smile, but just as she opens her mouth to speak, we hear a voice echoing from the kitchen. A voice that deadens the air around us. That drops Sulli's face. That tenses my muscles.

I turn to Sulli. "What in the hell is your grandmother doing here?"

6

Sullivan Meadows

GRANDMOTHER CALLOWAY.

All my life my mom and dad made sure to limit my exposure to my grandparents. Every single one.

Like Grandma Sara, my dad's mom, who I see even more sparingly. She lives a modest life in New Jersey, but I know it wasn't always that way. At one time, my dad said she lived for money and revenge.

At one point, she was even married to Jonathan Hale. I barely knew my alcoholic grandfather before he died. The one who ensured Nona and I had money set-up from Hale Co. When I was younger, I even tried to contact him at summer camp. I partook in a stupid séance. After our cabin rattled, I raced outside with a baseball bat. I was *sure* it was him.

Recently, Luna told me it'd been Eliot and Tom playing a prank.

Sometimes I wish I could ask Jonathan why he cared about me and my sister. He cut my dad out of everything financially in the end. But he gave us something.

But Mom and Dad always told us that our grandparents had made some irreparable mistakes raising them. Mistakes that they didn't want to slide down the generational ladder and affect us.

So most my life I've had stadium seats watching the close relationships Grandmother and Grandfather Calloway had with my cousins. There were times I did envy the sleepovers the Cobalts had at the big mansion in Villanova, the Hales usually included too (with the exception of Moffy). He never spent much time around our grandmother.

I remember my jealousy from Jane having our grandfather's number (in case of emergencies). He's not even in my cellphone contacts. Growing up, I loved the small moments when Grandfather Calloway would bring me chocolates, because he knows Mom and I could live off chocolatey things. Un-fucking-fortunately, he's so often quiet and hidden behind his wife.

But even more recently, all that envy has evaporated into dust. Grandmother Calloway's true colors have all but farted out into the air, and they're not pretty.

Being frank, I always knew she had a royal stick up her ass. She thinks my mom could've landed someone better than my dad. Someone proper. Someone with less *fucks*. And if I weren't an Olympian, I sometimes wonder how much I'd be worth to her.

So I'm not too shocked to find her *literally* clutching the pearls at her neck. Her Birkin is hooked on the crook of her arm, and at first, I think she's aghast at the interior decorating: butcher block counters, forest-green cupboards, and four velvety yellow stools hugging the long island, complete with a deep sink.

No glitz or real glamour.

But she's not critiquing the cupboards.

Or even my pile of dirty dishes in the sink.

She's standing at the refrigerator while Maximoff and Farrow square off with her in front of the sink, and I realize we've walked into a very bad showdown.

"You need to call them *now*," Maximoff says coldly. "Tell them not to come."

What the fuck is going on?

Farrow glances our way, noticing Akara, Banks, and me sliding into the kitchen. Akara immediately heads for the trash to toss the pasta and paper bowls.

Grandmother Calloway briefly glances to me. "Sullivan, dear…" She eyes my sweaty shirt, then forces a tight smile. "Tell your mother I said hi and that we should grab lunch soon."

"Maybe you should tell her yourself," I try to say without being too rude. But for one, I'm more apprehensive than eager to call my mom, and for another, if my mom is avoiding my grandmother's calls, it's because she doesn't want to talk to her.

Fucking duh.

A noise catches in her throat like I was offensive.

Moffy cuts back in and repeats with force, "*Tell them not to come.*"

She makes a show of blowing out a dramatic breath. "That's a little overboard, Max. They're on their way right now."

"Who?" Akara asks. He's in full-on security mode, hand already slinking to the cell in his pocket.

Grandmother Calloway ignores him, but Farrow answers easily, "Delivery men. She bought Jane a wedding present that's being delivered today."

"I didn't *buy* my granddaughter anything." She bristles. "I've been waiting for someone to wed in this family, so I can *give* them this family heirloom."

Fucking ouch.

Maximoff and Farrow got married *before* Thatcher and Jane. Moffy goes rigid next to his husband, jaw setting down like he's grinding his teeth.

Farrow is usually cool, calm, collected, but he's staking knives into my grandmother. His hand slips into Moffy's hand.

I swear she prickles more.

And I grow hot with anger. "You can leave now," I snap.

"Excuse me," Grandmother balks at me. "Sullivan, you can't speak to me that way."

Fucking leave! I almost yell, but I temper my building rage. Winona has a hard time controlling her anger, and I don't want these hotheaded fragments to take over. "I don't think you should be here," I say less concisely, less angrily.

"Well, I am." She humphs.

"Sulli is right," Moffy says. "If you wanted to come here, you should've called."

"My grandchildren live here. I don't need to call."

Farrow rolls his eyes, then says, "See, we need to establish *boundaries*. If your grandchildren are saying they want you to call, then you need to call before you arrive. It's that simple."

She purses her lips. "Well, I don't see Jane anywhere. She lives here too, and this gift is for her."

Moffy cracks a few knuckles.

Akara tenses more, then leans over and speaks hurriedly to Farrow. "Delivery men are coming up here?"

I wonder if this is a security breach.

Farrow shakes his head. "Man, no one is coming up here. It's not happening."

Grandmother Calloway makes a noise. "It's not for you to decide. Jane appreciates sentimental gifts."

"What is it?" Banks asks.

Grandmother Calloway waves a hand at him like he's a fly. "It's a wonderful surprise for my eldest granddaughter." *And a surprise for all of us.* Her eyes are on Moffy. "Don't deprive your cousin of that just because of your issues with me."

Moffy hesitates, brows knitting in doubt.

Farrow glares harsher at her.

"I'd ask Jane right now," Moffy says. "But she's on a plane—"

"Then it's settled," Grandmother Calloway interrupts quickly. "We'll have the delivery men set it up in the living room." She checks her diamond encrusted watch. "Look at the time. I have tea with some friends." She struts towards the door. "Take care, Max—oh my Lord!"

Luna pops into the kitchen. Googly eyes still on her face. "Hey, Grannie," she says casually as she grabs a Fizz Life out of the fridge.

Grandmother Calloway's face goes red. "Luna, dear. You have something on your face."

"You were leaving," Maximoff says firmly before their interaction can last any longer.

I could fucking applaud. Maybe even do a cartwheel. Because she actually nods curtly and heads out the fucking door.

Good riddance.

Farrow is quick to follow her out, untrusting. I don't really blame him on that front. She's the reason Jane had to deal with the Cinderella ad, and now she's personally delivering her a "surprise" wedding present. I don't envy how obsessed our grandmother is with Jane's life.

Akara clicks his mic. "Akara to Quinn, go to the lobby. Don't let any delivery men into the private elevator."

Just as he says the words, my phone buzzes.

Maximoff's chimes.

Luna's lets out a galactic *ping-ping-ping*.

Farrow's phone vibrates on the countertop.

Along with them, I check my phone and see the group chat labeled *Roommates*.

Thatcher and I will be home in an hour. Let's do charades!
I can't wait to see all your faces again. — Jane

Charades.

Oh fuck. Stress builds on my chest. I didn't imagine telling my roommates about my relationship during a game of fucking charades. Alright, it's only a *slight* screwball in the grand scheme of things. Maybe a game will ease the tensions and be the perfect time.

Maybe this will all go superbly well.

Maybe I'm just fucking fooling myself.

7

Akara Kitsuwon

"A LION!" DONNELLY shouts.

Luna prances around on all fours, taking her turn at charades. "Nope," she says from the ground. Others on her team throw out incorrect guesses from the blue, mod sofa.

Jane, Sulli, and Luna decorated most of the communal areas, and of what Sulli told me, the living room is 50s *Mad Men* inspired. With the brick walls and family photographs, some part of the penthouse still reminds me of their townhouse that burned down.

Flames flicker in the gas fireplace and warms everyone on this cold November night, but Team O-Squad (Sulli, Luna, Donnelly, Farrow, and Jack), headed by Oscar, is snuggled under heaps of blankets and cradling bowls of popcorn, pretzels, and some kind of Filipino chips Jack brought over.

Team A-Squad (Banks, Thatcher, Jane, Maximoff, and Quinn), headed by me, has been showered with a couple stale bags of Fritos. Normally, I'd butter up my team like Oscar. *Normally*, as a team captain, I'd even be all-in on winning. But my concentration, attention, complete brain capacity is zeroed in on Sulli and Banks.

Romance.

My love life.

Something that I've never fretted over. Something that I've never placed before career success or Security Force Omega. I never met anyone important enough.

But that's a lie. Because Sulli has always been there, and she's *always* been my greatest importance. *You were in so much damn denial.*

I push back my thick hair, only for the strands to fall forward.

"Panther," Jack guesses.

Luna shakes her head. "Uh-uh." She crawls even slower across the floor.

"Sloth?" Farrow throws out.

"Nope."

Luna isn't on my team, so I stay quiet.

Banks and I are sitting on round, pincushion ottomans, and I've reached a point where I just want this *out*. The anticipation feels like a splinter underneath the bed of my fingernails. My muscles are pulled taut, and the only thing loose is the beer bottle hanging limply in my hand.

"Anteater!" Donnelly shouts.

She can't tell him if he's close to the answer. But she continues on crawling.

I take a tense sip of beer.

Comms chatter is dead tonight since all of SFO is here. Their radios are unhooked. Earpieces out. Except I have mine in, my radio switched to a frequency for temp bodyguards. Oscar took tonight off to spend with his husband and younger brother. I'm listening in case the temp on Charlie's detail has problems.

So far, no issues on the security front.

And I'm vaguely interested in charades because I already know this game is going to be cut short.

Hopefully by *me*.

Banks and Sulli could be the ones to unleash the final blow, but I want to. It makes the most sense for it to be me. Not just because I have experience in hosting "team meetings" fit with messy news—but because no one is so personally connected to me here like they are to them.

I have no blood relatives in the audience. No one who cares too deeply.

My closest friend is Banks' twin brother, and I'm sure Thatcher will have more to say to Banks than to me. So I need to be the one to rock the boat.

Luna makes a hissing sound.

"The stray locked in the bathroom," Oscar guesses.

Jane gasps from my side of the room. "I take offense; LJ has never *hissed* like that."

Banks says into a swig of his beer, "Little Jane hissed at me earlier while I was taking a piss."

"Same," Donnelly pipes in.

Sulli jumps up. "Stop the clock, Jack. Foul play from A-Squad, they're interrupting our team's time." She looks to me like I'm going to contest her rules. Normally, I'd smile and say, *your call is just interfering with the pseudo-interference, and you want extra time, Sul.*

But I'm not invested in charades right now. I'm just invested in her.

Jack pauses the timer on his phone.

"LJ is still unsure of the dogs, is all," Jane professes. Six of seven cats are all over her and Thatcher, purring against their ankles, nudging their hands, and curled on their laps. Happy their parents are back from their honeymoon.

Thatcher is officially home, and my friend's homecoming is going to be derailed by me. Could I have planned this news-drop a lot better? Yeah.

Definitely.

I could've bought him some whiskey or a pack of Guinness. I should have gifted him something before his head is going to roll.

But hey, at least *Grandmother Calloway* got her surprise present delivered here on time. And I hate that I had to let delivery men through the door.

But Jane hated her present even more.

A humongous white grand piano is sitting among us like an elephant in the room. Untouched and given the side-eye every other minute.

Jane can't even play piano.

No one here can.

Anyway, maybe it's for the best that none of this tonight is planned. Nothing the three of us have done so far has been.

Love isn't planned.

No way would I have planned something this complicated. A triad? A V-triad? It happened, and I don't want to go in any other direction but forward with them.

"LJ wouldn't normally hiss," Jane concludes.

Thatcher glances over at the hall bathroom, where they're keeping the tiniest cat tonight. They're trying to introduce Little Jane to different areas of the penthouse, away from the dogs. "I'll check on her, honey," Thatcher says before leaving Jane's side.

Once he disappears, Jane sips a beer, "We can proceed."

Jack restarts the timer.

Shit. Thatcher better hurry back. I can't announce this without him here.

Luna hisses again.

"A feral cat!" Sulli yells out.

"Yep!" Luna hops to her feet.

Oscar tosses a potato chip in his mouth. "Exactly what I said."

He gets a stink-eye from Jane.

"Team Cobalt," Oscar reinforces, pointing to his chest.

"More like shit-stirrer," Farrow says with a smile as he claps for Luna with Donnelly, Sulli, and Jack. Oscar joins in the applause.

O-Squad is beating the shit out of us right now.

Five to nothing.

Thatcher, Jane, Maximoff, Banks, and Quinn are on the losing end with me.

Banks nudges me. "How'd they get so good at this game?"

"Sulli's on their team."

She's too competitive to just give up that easily. I would've picked her on our team after being nominated team captain, but Oscar chose her first.

"Wait, wait," Maximoff says to everyone as Luna ventures back to the sofa. Even his ten-month-old son on his lap looks up at him. Ripley is squeezing his stuffed animal, a yellow parrot with an eyepatch.

Baby needs a bodyguard.

Soon.

I have to create a mess before I clean that one.

"You can't hiss. I swear that's against the rules," Maximoff declares.

"Hissing isn't talking," Luna says into a shrug. "Jane's rules were just *no talking.*"

Jane cringes. "Technically, that is what I said, old chap."

Maximoff replies to her in French.

She nods sympathetically, and Maximoff hands Jane the bowl of papers, full of charades topics.

Sulli swigs harder from a beer, staring at the ground.

You just won a round, Sul.

But she knows my turn isn't next.

I set down my beer and massage my palms. Unable to peel my eyes off Sulli. Before the game even started, we agreed that we'd announce our relationship during one of our turns.

Our team chose Banks to go first. But he wasn't about to open charades with a bomb drop. Sulli has yet to be called on, and my turn should be soon.

The actual anticipation isn't grinding down on only me.

Banks leans into my arm. "What's Quinn doing?"

I find him fast.

Quinn.

Come on.

He's staring so hard at Sulli, he looks like he's trying to penetrate her damn mind.

My muscles tighten. "He has zero chill." Once his eyes ping to me, I send him a disapproving glare.

He scratches his unshaven jaw. "Arkham! Orion!" Calling the two dogs just draws more attention to him, including the attention of *Oscar.*

One of the most perceptive guys I've ever known.

Wonderful.

So very wonderful.

"Mother of Christ," Banks mumbles. "We're fucked."

"Not yet."

Luna is keeping her cool. She laughs at something Farrow and Donnelly say, but even that sends me on edge. I don't know what Sulli knows about Luna, but I'll find out with Banks. Some way or another.

Thatcher comes back before the next round.

Perfect. We're not *that* out of luck.

"Alright, this one is a bit…strange." Jane stands, crinkling the paper. "But I'll try." She takes position in the center of the room and kisses the air in one direction. Then she turns around and kisses the air in the other direction.

My stomach knots.

"Whistling," Maximoff guesses with way too much confidence. Ripley giggles up at his dad.

Farrow's brows rise. "That's what you think whistling looks like, wolf scout?"

Maximoff makes a face. "No talking from the enemy team."

Ripley babbles to Farrow, trying to mimic Maximoff.

Farrow's smile stretches into a laugh. "Okay, Last Pick."

I did pick Maximoff last. I've been around these families long enough to know that Maximoff Hale sucks at charades.

Maximoff groans out, but he's smiling.

There are so many couples here, and it's making me want to reveal my relationship even more.

"You alright, boss?" Donnelly asks across the room.

I lift my gaze and nod once. "Yeah." *I'm fine.*

Just fine.

Cut in and hold an emergency meeting.

Cut in and tell them.

Wait, Nine.

Something tugs at me and stops me from interrupting.

Jane continues. She pushes at the air like she's pushing someone away, and then she turns back and kisses the air on the opposite side.

I can't help but think about Sulli.

About *us*.

Did someone put polyamory as a charade option? I glance to Quinn. He hasn't taken his gaze off Sulli this whole time. Not even as he grabs a handful of popcorn from a bowl.

"Kissing! Love!" Thatcher guesses.

Jane lets out an exasperated breath and shakes her head. She goes back to the other side and mimes kissing someone again.

Thatcher looks between Banks and me. "You two going to guess here?"

He doesn't want to leave his wife high and dry on her round, but the only guess I have is *polyamory* and I'm not about to blurt that out.

"Peacocking!" Banks shouts unhelpfully.

Jane looks like she's imitating her little brother with Beckett's classic *what the fuck* face. I laugh a little into my beer. Three more air kisses, and the timer goes off.

Thatcher gives Jane an encouraging nod. "That one was hard."

Banks whispers to me, "That's what she said."

"To you or to me," I joke, hanging onto that levity with Banks.

He slaps my chest, then steals my beer, downing the rest.

Thatcher overhears our whisper-fest and gives us a strange look. Like something has changed. He's not on the outs.

But I'm closer to his brother. Closer than I've ever been.

Dirty thoughts infiltrate. I picture Sulli's hand...but Banks' cock. That image heats my blood.

"Cheating," Jane says.

That word ices me over in an instant. Hair stands up on my arms.

"What?" I ask.

"The answer was cheating," Jane clarifies. "I was kissing two guys."

Great.

Great.

That's what cheating is considered these days? I run a hand through my hair.

Sulli slumps further on the sofa next to Luna, who whispers to her, then throws a blanket over their heads.

Banks whispers, "I wish Sulli were on our team."

"She is metaphorically."

We're all on the same team.

Jack rifles around the papers in the glass bowl.

Oscar shakes Quinn's arm. "You alright over there, little bro?"

"Huh?" Quinn turns to his brother.

"Look at you," Oscar grins, "you're crushing on Sulli."

"*Oscar.*" Quinn looks horrified. "I don't have a *crush.*"

Don't look over here, Quinn.

Don't look over here.

He looks over here.

Shit.

I glare.

Oscar eats popcorn slower, studying me way too closely.

Now we're fucked.

I stand up. "Who needs refills?" The quick distraction causes hands to shoot in the air and drink orders to be listed off quickly.

"I'll help," Sulli throws off the blanket, uncovering her and Luna. She follows me fast into the kitchen.

Sulli opens the fridge and practically steps inside.

"You cooling off?"

"Yeah, I'm so hot from this whole night. Like could it get anymore fucking tense?" She pulls out a few beers and hands them over. "And we haven't even told them yet." She takes one more from the fridge and kicks the door closed.

"It's going to get worse before it gets better."

She twists off the cap to her beer and takes a giant swig. More used to the taste of beer than her first taste a couple years back. Honestly, I support the fact that she wanted to drink tonight. Alcoholism runs in her family, but she's never abused alcohol. What concerned me was when she'd pass out after drinking nearly nothing, but that hasn't happened in a long time.

Beer is relaxing her nerves tonight, and I'd be a hypocrite if I said I haven't had a drink while stressed. I'm keeping an eye on her—like I've done for years.

She wipes her mouth with the side of her wrist. "Next person up for charades has to do it."

"Me," I tell her. "It has to be me." I want to kiss her. We're out of sight from the game. From onlookers.

But I play it too safe and kiss her cheek. A peck. An awkward beat tries to pass, but I tell her assuredly, "More is coming later."

Sulli begins to smile. "Promise?"

"Promise." I hook my pinky with hers, then I kiss her knuckles.

Sulli now starts to melt, her smile more uncontrollable. And how stupid I was—to never kiss her earlier. Kissing her didn't ruin what we had. The feelings grow inside me. Infinitely stronger. "Jeez, Kits."

"Jeez, what?"

"You're fucking hot."

I laugh.

"And jeez, I can't believe this is real. We're not just friends anymore."

"It's about to be more real."

"Yeah." She glances back. "I think I'm ready."

Me too.

No more waiting, I release her hand, just to hug her side, and then we return, hearing Jack's round end with more cheers.

"Your team is already taking the L," she whispers to me.

"The team that I want to win hasn't played yet."

Her smile softens.

"Who's up?" Jane asks.

"Me," I say and quickly hand out the beers. As I grab a random slip of paper from the bowl, I meet Banks' eyes. I do my best to silently tell him *it's happening now.*

He must read me because he gives me a nod.

My stomach knots as I unfurl the slip of paper. Slowly, I read the word and make my way to the middle of the room.

Nightmare.

I blink.

That doesn't mean anything. It can't mean anything.

I try not to think too hard about *why* I picked this word in this moment. I don't want to pull at a meaning that isn't there.

Silence blankets the room as everyone waits for me. Time feels slow right now. Like if I tried to take a step, my foot would feel weighted down with bricks.

I lick my dried lips.

You can do this, Nine.

I take a deep breath and face the room. And then I point to Banks and then to Sulli and then to my chest. Without reservation, I make the same motion over and over and over again. Air tenses. The only sound is Oscar's crunch on a popcorn kernel.

Strangely, I breathe easier the longer I motion to Banks, to Sulli, to me.

Over and over and over.

"Two guys...and a girl?" Maximoff guesses.

I motion again and again.

Oscar drops a handful of popcorn back in the bowl. "You finally do it, Kitsuwon?"

Maximoff goes rigid. "What does that mean?"

And clearly, without stopping, I say, "Banks has been dating Sulli since Yellowstone. They're together."

"What?" the Yale boys almost say in unison. *They thought it'd be me and her.*

Jane is beaming. "Oh my God!" She crosses the room excitedly to Sulli and squishes her in a hug.

SFO is confused, except for Quinn, but soon that veers into happiness once they see that I'm not upset. Donnelly, Farrow, and Oscar slow-clap for Banks, and Thatcher wraps an arm around his brother, bringing him closer.

Thatcher…Thatcher is smiling. In the hierarchy here, I'm so often first, and for once, I just wanted Banks to feel what that's like.

Selfless Banks—he's not reveling in *merriment*.

He's looking at me like I'm the biggest fool of all. But I'm not hurt seeing how they love Banks and Sulli together because I really love them together too.

"That's not all," Banks says loudly, causing the room to go still.

"*Kits*," Sulli says, tearing out of Jane's hug. "Tell them."

Everyone is quiet.

And after a beat, I announce, "I've been dating Sulli since Yellowstone too. When we came back, the three of us decided to be in a poly relationship." I barely get the definition out before the mutterings of *what?* and *holy shit*.

Oscar says, wide-eyed, "Didn't see that coming."

The mood shifts. Everyone slowly turns silent. Tension mounts.

Thatcher is stoic and still. He narrows his gaze on me, then on his brother. He cocks his head to the left, signaling a need to talk to Banks.

Banks nods.

"Maximoff," Farrow calls out in concern.

Maximoff isn't letting anything pass through his features. All sharp cheekbones. He's already standing. "Can you hold Rip for a sec." He hands Ripley off to Farrow. "I need to talk to my cousin."

Sulli rises, her other cousins following her out.

I watch as Sulli and Banks are pulled away by family. The three of us are separated in different directions. And I'm left alone with Jack and SFO and what'll probably be a round of probing questions. So I sit on the ottoman, and I pick up a bag of stale Fritos in the awkward silence.

Just wishing I could be in two places at once.

With her and with him.

8

Sullivan Meadows

LIBRARIES HAVE NEVER comforted me like the woods or the water. Like stories my mom grew up telling me.

Standing among bookcases of hardcovers and paperbacks just reminds me of all the pages I've never read, all the stories I've never completed.

My dad loves reading, but he never really advertised that part of himself. Most of his books are kept in trunks. Worn covers and dog-eared pages. Sometimes he just went ahead and donated them after he finished the last page.

While I'm in the penthouse's library, I look everywhere but at my cousins. Jane has said the library brings back memories of Princeton. Floor-to-ceiling bookshelves cover the walls. Green-stained glass lamps on a reading table are turned on, casting warm lighting tonight.

College.

I never gave too much thought to going. Academics took so much time away from swimming growing up that I just wanted to punt every school subject to another dimension. Far, far away from me.

I'd be a big fucking liar if I said I suddenly acquired the drive to study. Cracking open a *textbook* sounds like the devil's armpits.

And thinking about my contempt for schoolwork is not helping ease my nerves. I glance up, like if I stare hard enough, I can see the rooftop pool. It feels miles away.

Grow some courage, Sullivan Minnie Meadows. They're your family, not your foes. I would've said the same about my dad—and look at us now.

Exhaling, I face my cousins.

Luna hops onto the long table, and Jane is rocking a sleepy LJ in her arms. She must've scooped the tabby from the bathroom. I've never seen a cat that loves to be cradled like a baby more than Little Jane.

Moffy crosses his arms, stiff as a board, but through his tough exterior, his eyes—green like mine—seem to hold more questions than anger.

While it might be easier to look at Luna and Jane, I find more comfort with Moffy. He's the one I spent hours upon hours with at swim meets. The one who constantly had my back when assholes teased me about the hair on my arms.

"Sulli the Sasquatch!"

"Look at that gorilla!"

The snickers, the laughter was met with *fuck yous* by Moffy. Even when I stuck up for myself, I always hoped to avoid confrontation. And I attribute the fact that I can control the burning rage inside me to Moffy. Hecklers, haters, fucksticks, and fartholes—he dealt with them so I didn't have to.

I let him fight a lot of my battles, and in doing so, he preserved something peaceful in me. Just like my dad did.

I love Moffy so fucking much. But I'm older now.

"I don't fucking get why you needed to pull me away to talk to me," I say as I climb up on the table beside Luna. I bring my foot up to the surface, knee bent. "We could've had this conversation in front of them. They're our *friends*. Your husbands…"

Moffy uncrosses his arms. "I just thought this might be easier. For all of us. Farrow, Thatcher—all of them—they didn't go through what we all went through, Sul." His eyes toughen on me. "The four of us. Growing up famous."

I touch my frayed ankle bracelet. "I guess that's fucking true."

Luna sways into me with a consoling shoulder-nudge.

I try to smile back.

When it comes to my relationship, I only know where Quinn and Luna stand. If Jane and Moffy were strangers, I might not give a second thought about what they think. But having my cousins' approval means something to me. At the very least, it'd make this easier.

Especially since I don't have my dad's.

Moffy adds, "Plus, I don't really want to hear what Akara and Banks have to say. I'm more interested in your thoughts on all this."

"Me as well," Jane says, her inquisitive, blue eyes on me, even as she curls LJ closer to her zebra-print sweater.

I rest my chin on my knee. "My thoughts are that I'm with Banks and Akara. And I hope you guys can be happy for me."

Moffy is more tense. "How did this happen?" He gestures to his head. "I just can't picture how it went down."

Fuck.

How do I even rehash Yellowstone? "I'll try to explain, but if you're asking me to defend my relationship—"

"You're not on trial," Moffy cuts in quickly. "I promise, Sul." The look in his eyes reminds me of childhood. Where Moffy has always just wanted to protect me.

If I needed him for anything, he was there, and I'm so fucking terrified of losing him like I might've lost my dad.

But maybe I shouldn't be afraid of anything. Maybe I should stop relying on family to save me and believe more in myself.

So I take a breath and go through my first kiss with Banks in the motel, then the next morning my kiss with Akara. The "Bachelorette" style dating, the cougar attack, the night we spent together in a tent, and how we just grew closer. The three of us.

And I couldn't choose.

I didn't want to choose, and then what Beckett told me. And by the time I finish, the tabby cat is on the floor, and Jane has her fingers steepled to her lips, eyes wide. "Did you...?" She stops herself with the shake of her head. "Never mind. I can't ask you that." Her cheeks redden, but the curiosity is killing her.

I stop picking at my anklet. "Did I what?"

Jane asks slowly, "Lose...your virginity?"

Oh fuck. *Cum,* shit. I watch Moffy crack his knuckles, more tensed— if that's even fucking possible! He's like the Tin Man right now.

"You don't have to answer," Jane says quickly.

"No, I can." I drop my foot, legs hanging off the table, and I look Moffy right in the eye. "I had sex for the first time. Once with Akara, once with Banks. And it was *epic*, eye-rolling sex—stuff of legends, and I plan to do it again."

Luna is grinning.

Moffy shifts his gaze, too many emotions rolling over his face. Like bewilderment. Confusion. Maybe wondering why I sound defensive.

I realize this is everything I wish I could say to my dad. I know it's so fucking wrong to use *sex* as a measure of my womanhood. But some part of me believes that others might view my virginity as being too immature, too naïve. I was none of those things while I was a virgin.

I'm none of those things now, but if this is what it takes for my dad to see me as a woman. Then I wish I could yell off the rooftops, *THEY FUCKED ME GOOD! AND I LOVED IT!*

"What's going on with you, Sul?" Moffy asks with more concern.

"You waited so long to have sex, and then just all of a sudden—"

"It wasn't all of a sudden," I say strongly. "It felt right."

"Were they safe?" Moffy asks. "They wore condoms?"

"Yeah, they did." I actually welcome these overprotective questions. They're better than any judgment.

He motions to his head again. "I'm just processing."

Jane touches her cheeks. "It's a shock—you, dating *two* men at once."

"Neither are my first boyfriend," I remind them. "I dated Will Rochester, remember that? And even if they were my firsts—who fucking cares? Thatcher was your first non-friends-with-benefits, Jane. Farrow was your first boyfriend, Moffy. Everyone fucking starts somewhere!" I throw my hands up and jump off the desk.

"We're on your side, Sulli," Luna tells me softly.

"Then why does it feel like Jane and Moffy aren't?"

"It's a shock," Jane repeats like that's an answer enough.

Fucking sue me, because I just want *more*. What if they don't approve, but they're just acting like they do? What if that's just my insecurities biting my butt?

"We don't care that you're dating a bodyguard," Moffy tells me.

I huff. "Fucking cool because my dad *really* cared."

Jane gasps.

"Wait, what?" Moffy narrows his eyes. "Uncle Ryke knows?"

My face heats, and I stare at a fallen library book. "Yeah. It went really fucking badly...we're not talking right now."

"Fuck," Moffy breathes.

Yep.

"What about your mom?" Jane wonders.

"I haven't called her yet." I explain how the blow-up happened earlier today.

They seem to relax. It's not like we kept this secret for that long.

I tug at my T-shirt, sweat-stains dried. "I just want you all to be happy for me like you were happy for each other. Is that too much to ask?"

"We are happy that you're happy," Jane professes, but she's not smiling or jovial or hugging me like she did when she thought I was only with Banks.

"There has to be a *but*," I realize.

Moffy rakes a hand across the back of his neck. "It's different, Sulli. This is a colossal thing you're undertaking that Jane and I have *never* taken."

They're worried about me. No one has blazed this trail before, and so often, Moffy is the one out in front first.

He adds, "It'd be different if it were *just* Akara or *just* Banks."

"Why?" I frown. "Because you think I'm too inexperienced to handle it?"

"Because we're not normal," Maximoff says with so much power that his eyes nearly redden. "We're *not* like everyone else, Sulli. The second the world knows you're dating *two* men at once, you will lose complete and total privacy of your life."

I want to believe I can handle the change. I want to believe I'm someone who can walk into the dark unknown without Moffy leading and Jane carrying the torch so I can see.

I listen to my heart, and I tell him, "None of that matters."

"None of that matters?" Moffy says in utter disbelief like I'm not the same person standing before him. "Sulli, you *hate* the paparazzi and the probing questions. You grew up without even being on *We Are Calloway*. You lived most of your early life with more privacy than any of us here did—and now it doesn't matter?" He runs both his hands through his hair. To the ceiling, he asks, "What the fuck is going on? Have I teleported to another goddamn universe?"

"I know what I signed up for, Moffy." I step closer. "You don't think I'm nervous? Alright, I am." I breathe hard. "Seeing paparazzi hound you and Farrow made me never want to date in public. But my relationship with Will never made a single headline, and maybe I can do this all under the radar again."

Jane drums her lips. "What happens if you break-up? What happens if one of you splinters off? A lot of variables are here." She seems worried, maybe for Banks, her brother-in-law.

"I don't know," I breathe. "Hopefully we don't break-up."

Moffy listens, his empathy calming me.

"And I know that means eventually, we'd need to go public—but one thing at a time, right? We just started dating."

Moffy winces, stares at the ground, then up at me. Something rests behind his eyes that I try to understand, something that looks like years gone by. "I didn't think about marriage or kids or what a future could look like when I first started dating Farrow. I just wanted to be in the moment, so I get it, Sul. I get it."

I breathe in.

"But I'm worried if you don't think about it, you'll get in too deep."

I go cold.

"You can't legally marry both of them," Moffy tells me.

"And what about babies?" Jane asks.

I blanch. "I'm twenty-one."

Jane tips her head. "You may be in your early twenties, but Akara and Banks aren't. What if they want children?"

My throat dries. We've only been dating for about a month. Not all relationships discuss heavy topics that early. And I think about what

Beckett has told me. There shouldn't be a roadmap for relationships. Everyone has their own path. Everyone is different.

They just always believed they'd take the hard paths before any of us.

Now I'm leap-frogging over them.

I find my voice and answer, "I'll cross that road with Akara and Banks when it comes."

Moffy nods repeatedly. "You should think about kids, Sul. You should be thinking about *all* this shit before it's too late. The media—"

"I don't care about the fucking media," I groan.

"They'll eat you alive," Moffy professes, his eyes pleading with me to understand. "They will take everything you love and destroy it, Sulli. They might even pit Banks and Akara against each other—and then what? That leaves you with a bucket load of heartbreak. Shattered. The worst experience of your goddamn *life*. Headlines you can never run away from. Pain you can never take back."

Hot tears threaten to rise. "I love them…and I guess right now, that has to be enough." I exhale a giant breath. "And do I even need your approval?"

"No, but—" Moffy starts.

I cut him off at the *but*. "I'm an adult." My chest tightens with each word. Does every person in my life still see me as this little girl? "I know you both probably look at me like your little cousin, but I'm more than that."

He nods. "Sulli, I want to be happy for you, goddamn, I do."

"But," I say, waiting for that word to drop again.

"But I made a promise to your dad since you were little," he says, "I promised to always protect you, and if I don't warn you how this is going to go, then I'm failing at that." He licks his cracked lips. "We're American royalty. It doesn't matter how much you love them, the world is going to tear you apart. Once you become media fodder, it's too late. I can't protect you anymore. Your dad can't protect you. And you shouldn't have to go through it in the first place."

I'm a Meadows.

I'm supposed to stand on the edge of bridges. On the edge of cliffs. I'm supposed to take the leap of faith into the great, terrifying unknown. And I'm not supposed to do it alone.

But I have Banks.

I have Akara.

Stop running away.

"I want to be fearless with my life," I say in a single breath, "like my parents were with theirs."

Moffy and Jane nearly smile, but I can see they're afraid for me.

Whatever waits at the end, even if it's anguish and torment, I'll have to survive. I inhale strongly, "And if this all goes fucking terribly wrong, I won't need you or my dad to save me this time, Moffy." I hold his gaze, our childhood racing through us. "This time, I'll save myself."

I walk out of the library with those parting words.

9

Banks Moretti

AS SOON AS SULLI GETS swept away by her cousins, Cinderella himself sweeps me off to the game room. Lights to the pinball machine glow, and two calico cats circle around Thatcher's feet.

People talk about love, but what most don't understand is loving someone for all your life. From the moment I breathed air to the moment I die, I'll love my brother.

Hell, before I even knew what love was, I loved him.

I followed him to war. I followed him to security. But for the first time in my life, I'm taking a different path than him. I'm voyaging into an unconventional relationship, and I can see on his face that he's worried for me.

"I expected as much," I tell him.

He frowns harder. "I haven't said anything yet."

I wave at his face. "It's all over your mug, Thatcher *Alessio* Moretti."

He lets out a gruff noise. "Are you just taking my facial expressions as gospel now or are we going to talk about this?"

I lean up against the pool table. "We can talk about it, but I'm thinking you're going to be saying the same shit you said a month ago when you knew I kissed her."

He shakes his head.

Shock jolts me, and I grip the edge of the pool table. "Really? You have a different opinion then?"

"Yeah," he says. "I think you're out of your damn mind."

I roll my eyes and release the tension in my hands. "Same opinion."

"No, this one is *stronger*," he growls. "I get you want to ride this wave into a hurricane, but I'm telling you that you're not the only one in line to get hurt now. Think about Sulli. Think about Akara."

I raise my brows. "You seriously want me to believe that you care more about *their* potential broken feelings than mine?" My brother would take a thousand swords for me. Christ, he'd become the sword. And sure, he's the kind of guy that runs into a burning building for a guy like Tony. But when it comes down to it, I'm not sure he'd *truly* hurt for anyone else but me and Jane.

He stares me cold in the eyes. "I'd tell you anything for you to pull your head out of your ass." His South Philly lilt comes out.

I smile. "Too bad. Head's already firmly wedged up there."

He breathes hard and runs two hands through his hair. "You've had a couple serious relationships in your life, and you think you can handle a *polyamorous* one?"

"Whoa," I hold up a hand. "You think I've had a couple serious relationships? When? Who?"

He frowns and his hands fall to his sides. "High school? Clara?"

I rock back. "Not serious, Thatcher. Not at all." I raise my shoulders. "I think she was dating Bobby Donati the day after we slept together."

"What about Denise? Eleventh grade?"

"That wasn't even close to being a relationship. I didn't let it get that far."

"Why not?"

I shake my head a few times, thinking. "I don't know. No spark? Wasn't feeling it. I was a fucking kid, man." I rub my unshaven jaw, then loosely thread my arms. "Nothing went anywhere but downhill, and I was fine with that. Less attachments."

He blinks hard. "Why'd I think those lasted longer?"

I'm not surprised he read those situations wrong. "Probably because I didn't care to talk about them. And probably because you wanted to think better of me than some playboy fucking around all the time."

Thatcher grimaces. "You weren't a playboy, Banks."

I nod once. Looking back, I just needed an emotional connection to enjoy the sexual one. Wish I could tell Young Banks that before he went and had some miserable fuckin' lays.

My brother wipes his lips. "So to confirm, you've had *zero* serious relationships."

I bob my head. "Affirmative."

"Christ, Banks," he says heavily. "And you think this is a good idea?"

"It's the only idea that makes any sense, Thatcher. Otherwise, I lose her and him. This way I get both. I want both."

His frown lines deepen. "Are you sleeping with Akara too?"

"No," I say casually, not hostile about it. "I'm not attracted to him like that. We're just both sleeping with her."

A question bores through his intense eyes.

"Ask it, man. You're my brother." I would never get offended at anything he said or did.

"Are you both fucking her at the same time?" he asks.

"Not yet."

His eyes grow dark. "You're not exactly *small*."

I nod. "I'm being careful. I would never hurt her."

"I know you wouldn't mean to, but accidents can happen."

I roll my eyes. "Anything else?"

"I don't understand why you're putting yourself through this. There are other girls—"

That one is a knife into the gut. "No," I cut him off. "There's only her." What I have with Sulli can't be replicated or reproduced with just any living soul. If these feelings were that easy to come by, I would've felt them before now.

"Her family won't approve," he says. "It's not going to be easy for you or Akara."

He doesn't mention *our* family. Maybe because he knows their opinions don't matter much to me. I'm like the wind—I go where I want. They know that. I know that.

Her family won't approve.

That's an understatement.

I run my hand over the eight ball. "Yeah, I figured." I toss the eight-ball in the palm of my hand. "Ryke already hit me when Sulli told him about us."

Thatcher solidifies. "Say again?"

"Ryke punched me." I mime a fist to my lip.

Thatcher takes a better look at the reddened skin. Fear for me flickers in his stern gaze, but before he interrogates further, I tell him, "I'm not getting into the details right now." I look him over in a quick sweep. "Do you approve?"

"No," he says, not even hesitating. Not for one second. "Your happiness is my happiness, Banks. And I don't see how this can end happily."

"I'm happy now," I reply. "Doesn't that count for something?"

He opens his mouth. Closes it. Then opens it again. "Sometimes I think about him. Sometimes I wonder how *unhappy* he must have been to keep riding out to that quarry every night."

Him.

Skylar.

Our brother.

Thatcher doesn't break eye contact. "And then I think, all it takes is being unhappy *enough*. To get pushed down to a point where you can't come back up. Your being happy now doesn't change the fact that I believe you'll be unhappy *enough* later."

"Don't do that," I breathe. "Don't throw down crash pads for me."

He swallows hard. "I can't help it. It's what I do."

I'm met with a brick wall. One that wants to protect me, but in doing so, is hurting me. How do I even deal with that? How can I hate him for it? It just causes a wave of pain that I don't know where to pocket or shove down. All I want to do is retreat to what makes sense.

10

Akara Kitsuwon

BANKS IS GONE. Sulli is gone. Normally, I'd feel comfortable with SFO, my men. But Farrow, Oscar, Donnelly, and Quinn have said *nothing* since the room partially vacated. Add in the fact that Jack is here, and I'm more on edge. Jack Highland-Oliveira is my friend, but my relationship being exposed to production (off-duty, sure) is not my ideal scenario.

As I shake the bag of Fritos to cut into the silence, I keep glancing at Jack with slight warning.

Jack is a big smiler, but the awkward tension in the air has slaughtered his California charm. He's almost cringing. "I'm not recording, Akara. I promise."

"Can we get that in writing?"

Oscar wraps an arm around Jack. "My husband has no camera here. I can vouch for that. Frisked him earlier."

Jack laughs. His mega-watt smile is back. "That's what you call frisking?"

Oscar turns Jack's baseball hat backwards. "I'll demonstrate again later, meu raio de sol." He leans in and kisses his husband.

I crumple the Fritos. Glad there's so many *happy* couples here. I really am…*not*. Yeah, I'm not. Right now, I just want to be with the two people who make me happiest.

I interrupt the lovey-dovey shit. "Guys, I don't need anyone vouching for anyone. I just want to make sure you're all good. My relationship shouldn't affect your work. Tomorrow you'll all go to your clients and be clear-headed, okay?"

Donnelly raises his hand.

I feel exhausted. "What?"

He drops his hand. "If you're dead, then who pays our bills? Assuming Ryke Meadows is going to murder you."

"No one is getting murdered." I push my hair back. "If he wanted to kill me and Banks, we'd already be dead."

"He knows?" Oscar almost chokes on a shovel of popcorn.

I nod, and since they might hear the fallout through the rumor mill, I rehash the event in a few sentences and finish with, "That's all I'm talking about Ryke. You want to gossip; do it on your own time."

I hear Donnelly whisper to Farrow, "When did Akara become a crabby patty?" *Patty* sounds like *paddy* with his South Philly accent.

Farrow rolls his eyes, then pops bubblegum he's chewing. "Most likely while listening to you fuckers."

Donnelly blows him a middle-finger kiss.

Farrow smiles, but his lips falter as he catches me staring at his son who's on his lap. Ripley Hale is babbling to his stuffed animal, hugging the parrot against his soft cheek.

Baby needs a bodyguard.

I lift my gaze to Farrow, and he shakes his head, "No. You don't want to talk about Ryke, and see, I don't want to talk about the extremely unnecessary security detail you want on my son. He already has me."

"And if something happens to Ripley—"

"You can say, *I told you so, Farrow.* And it'll be on me as his father." Farrow chews his gum slower. "Finished?"

No. I haven't been ready to shut this door closed. Maximoff and Farrow are way too obstinate together, and they're not budging—but I need to kick inside. Because if Ripley is *ever* in peril, it'll be on *me* and my conscience. And I don't want to see a baby caught in the crossfire of hecklers or paparazzi any more than Farrow does.

But Ripley is the son of two unthinkably famous men. Who were trending a couple days ago just for walking out of a Cinnabon.

Let's make a deal.

"Here's the thing, we can talk about what happened with Ryke more, if you'll just consider putting someone from SFO on Ripley's detail." I already figure he won't trust anyone else but SFO to protect his son.

Farrow lets out a laugh into a smile, "Man, your relationship and what happened with Ryke is none of my business. I don't need to know."

"Redford," Oscar groans, throwing popcorn at him. "I need to know."

"Stamp," Donnelly says in agreement.

Farrow tilts his head back and forth, then says, "Not happening."

I toss the Fritos bag, more frustrated than I like letting them see. But I was just grasping for a silver lining, a win, something good while I'm in a mess.

Farrow looks me over. "I'm not trying to make your job harder, Akara."

"But you kind of are, Farrow."

"Fair enough," he says easily.

He's always been hard to work with, but he's the best on SFO.

I've known him for *years*. Like early high school days. But Farrow doesn't remember me from high school like I remember him. To Farrow, I was just a guy on the drumline.

But *everyone* knew Farrow Redford Keene. The inked, pierced teenager who changed his hair color with the months, who walked the halls like he had no care in the world. Yet, he was the top of his class.

Yet, he hailed from an incredible pedigree of doctors.

Yet, the more everyone tried to get to know him, the more you never could. He was popular but didn't want to be popular.

I never sought him out. Farrow was older and never struck me as someone who wanted more friends.

And then Farrow was one of the first to walk into the gym I opened. I was eighteen, and I was enamored with the guy.

Farrow Keene wants to join *my* MMA gym?

He said he liked how quiet it was. No one to bug him. And *yet,* he told other people about Studio 9. Like a family of boxers who knew more boxers and MMA fighters.

The Oliveira family.

They single-handedly saved Studio 9 from going under. Oscar and Farrow didn't know how in the red the gym was at the time. I never told them.

Maybe Farrow could tell.

Or maybe he just wanted to spend time with his friend at the gym.

He was a pivotal piece in changing my life, and then I changed his by telling him he should join security work. And so like all circular paths, we're here.

Staring at each other and I'm wondering how we're going to affect one another again.

"I only want to be a supportive source in your life, like you've been in mine," I tell Farrow. "Check your ankle."

I was with him during that ankle tattoo. He was back in town at twenty-one. Spent the day at the gym, and we went to the tattoo shop together.

He got the words inked, *live by your actions.*

Farrow nods a few hearty times while touching his earring. "I'll talk to Maximoff about an SFO guard on Ripley."

Oscar and Donnelly do a doubletake.

Shock actually hits me. "Really?"

"Yeah." Farrow runs his tongue over his lip piercing. "I respect you, and I need to show that more. So, I'll talk to my husband. I can't promise it'll go anywhere."

I ease a little. "I appreciate it."

Progress.

That's something.

Farrow nods back, then says, "And don't let these two fuckers pressure you to talk about Ryke if you don't want to."

"Hey," Oscar boos.

"Ryke who?" Donnelly plays dumb.

Oscar says, "Donnelly only knows the word *Cobalt.*"

Donnelly smirks. "My babies."

I almost smile like Jack and Quinn, but after a beat, Oscar grows more serious, then lifts a finger. "I have one concern, Kitsuwon."

"Let's hear it."

"Triple Shield. What happens if Price's men start complaining about our boss dating a Meadows girl? Most are going to be pissed."

I clasp my knees. "That's for me to deal with, guys. If they give you shit, tell me or Thatcher and I'll talk to Price, but so far, we don't know if Ryke has even told anyone, let alone the other security team." Pressure weighs again, and I want to assuage their worries more. "Kitsuwon Securities isn't in any jeopardy." My voice holds as much conviction as I can muster. "It's here for the long haul."

They all nod, their belief in me apparent.

Failure can't be an option. If my security firm flops into a death sentence, they're all out of a job or they'll have to go crawling back to Triple Shield.

As long as I can keep the current full-time client roster—Maximoff, Jane, Charlie, Sullivan, Luna, and Xander—I'm in no danger of bleeding money. There's even a pathway for me to lose Sulli's money and still stay afloat.

I can sell one of our security vehicles. Maybe even reduce my salary again.

Everything will be okay.

"We're here for the long haul too, boss," Donnelly says. None of us are here for the money. Security work isn't a cash cow, but for them to stay afloat, I need the company to make money.

Costs are everywhere. And talk about someone who *needs* cash, Donnelly has been tattooing on the side to earn more. Even though I'm clueless as to where he's spending it all, I know Donnelly can't afford a pay cut.

My insides twist considerably because I don't want to let SFO down. I never have before. Their faith in me is the ground beneath my feet.

11

Sullivan Meadows

BEER BOTTLES LINE my dresser. Bottle caps scatter the ground.

After the announcement and the raw conversations we went through, I retreat to my bedroom and soak in a bath first. Akara and Banks shower in their apartment, and while I climb out, dry off, squeeze my hair—a bolt of panic courses through me. *What if they never come back?*

Staying in their apartment, away from me, would be easier. Just forgetting Yellowstone. Forgetting us. All the confidence I'd built in us seems to wash away with the water in the drain.

By the time I pull on a sea-foam green tank top and step into matching boxer-shorts, my door opens with a soft knock.

Banks and Akara are back with damp hair and a twelve-pack of beer.

Seeing them breathes oxygen into my lungs, and a smile grips hold of me. Once upon a fucking time, my mom told me, "Swimming isn't everything, Sulli."

I was crying after I added four-seconds to my 200m freestyle. I won the heat, but I swam my slowest.

"It's everything to me," I blubbered.

I was seven.

Mom seemed worried. She hugged me close, kissed my cheek, and whispered, "I love that you love the water, but that's not all there is to life. I know it seems like that now, but I promise, there's more to look forward to, more adventures with me and your dad and your baby sister. And when you grow older, you'll find that can't-eat-can't-sleep, reach-for-the-stars, over-the-fence, World Series kind of stuff."

I sniffled, "What kind of stuff is that?"

She brushed my nose with hers. "When you're sad one day, you'll discover that stuff coming around that makes you feel less lonely, and you'll share the quiet and the restless and the loud with them, and life will feel so much bigger."

I finally understand what she meant.

Life feels bigger with them here.

Resting on my velvet, turquoise quilt, we're already halfway through the twelve-pack. The guys tossed most of my sea-creature-shaped pillows on the ground but kept a decent amount of the donut and cupcake ones. They use them for comfort against the hard iron rungs of my headboard.

It feels safe in my bedroom with Banks and Akara.

Away from common areas of the penthouse.

Free from accidentally running into my cousins or SFO and turning up a notch on the *awkward* meter.

But that hasn't stopped me from thinking about all the whispering and fucking gossip happening outside my door.

Well, not *right* outside it. I doubt any of my roommates would be that fucking rude to put their ear against the door, but they are probably huddled in the dining room or kitchen discussing my love life.

Fuck, I hate that sort of attention that looms and shadows. Moffy was right about that, but I need to get used to these *cons* because the *pros* of being with them mean too much to me.

"Luna felt the most supportive, I think," I tell them, sitting cross-legged. "I just wish they'd give *us* a chance before they think it'll all fucking fail."

"I'll drink to that," Banks lifts his beer.

We swig at the same time. Alcohol tastes bitter on my lips, and a warm, fuzziness washes over me from the beer. I'm not really drunk at all. Tonight's events have the best sobering effect, and replaying my talk with Moffy and Jane just about obliterates my buzz.

"Hey, whatever happens *out there*," Akara says to us, holding his beer on his knee while he leans against the headboard—right next to Banks, "that's not as important as what happens here." He motions with his beer between the three of us.

"Fuck 'em," Banks says, "including my brother. But with love."

I smile more, feeding off their confidence. "Yeah, fuck them." I sip beer. "They put us on an island alone together, and they should know what happens next. It's not a break-up like they all fear. It's literally *Blue Lagoon.*"

Akara smiles, twinkling his brown eyes. "You Meadows and *Blue Lagoon.*"

"It's a classic."

Banks wears one of those shadows of a smile. "What, are we all gonna turn into mermaids?"

Akara laughs with the shake of his head, "No, zero mermaids are to be found in this movie. Two kids are stranded, then they grow up on the island together, presumably *alone* and fall in love and fuck."

"It's a porno?" Banks asks.

"*No,*" I cut in. "Ugh, Kits. You're ruining one of the best, most pure movies of all time."

His smile only grows. "They have sex, Sul. I've seen the movie about ten times with you."

I talk to Banks as I say, "Okay, *yes,* they fuck—but it's more like making love. Because when they're on this island together, they're discovering things on their own without anyone's advice or guidebook. No one even taught her what a period was. No one told them about sex, but they listened to what they *felt* while they were out there."

Banks slowly nods, then tips his beer in my direction. "So we're *Blue Lagoon,* stranded on an island together and listening to what we feel?"

"Exactly." Butterflies swarm my stomach, feeling how much Banks just understood me.

Banks swings his head to Akara. "You really did ass-fuck that movie synopsis."

"Hey, it's not a complicated movie." He counts on his fingers. "Stranded. Love. Sex. Babies—"

"Babies?" Banks makes a point of eyeballing me. "She never said anything about babies."

Akara smiles at me, swallowing more beer. "No, she didn't."

Their teasing is setting me on fire. "Where were they going to buy condoms on the island? The fucking Walgreens next to palm tree 1 and 2?"

They laugh, and Banks says, "There's a fucking Walgreens on our island. Unless our asses literally get stranded."

"We'd survive," Akara says with certainty, and I think he's right. The hardest thing for us is going to be integrating with *people*. Our families and the world.

Here on our island, hiding out in my bedroom, hiding out in Yellowstone—it's easy. It's freeing. But like *Blue Lagoon*, sooner or later someone will come find us.

As Akara stretches down for the beer box on the floor, bands of muscle in his traps and bicep stretch, his core contracts. Only wearing red drawstring pants, I can count his abs and the yellow flowers inked around the snake on his upper-chest and shoulder. Black hair touches his eyelashes as his fingers curve around the beer bottle.

Holy fuck.

The rim of my beer rests against my lips. Forgetting to drink. Until Banks catches my eye. His mouth is curved like he caught *me* watching a porno.

My gaze tracks down Banks' scruffy jaw to his dog tags against his white tee and the dark-blue drawstring pants that mold his big bulge way too perfectly.

He takes a hefty swig, then eyes my tits.

I glance down.

Fuck.

My nipples are pushing against my tank top. Totally visible, and I'm not sure anyone has ever aroused me as much as Akara and Banks can.

Once Akara sits back up, screws off the cap, his attention falls on my perked nipples. "Sullivan." The deep, smooth register he uses to say my full name while he takes a strong sip of beer does a fucking number on my body.

His smile appears.

While cross-legged, I dig the heel of my foot between my legs, adding friction against my clit. *Fuck, that feels good.*

I can't even lie about the room just being cold. For one, I want them to know I'm aroused. For another, I'm still way too uncomfortably hot from the mention of *babies.*

Moffy thinks it's best to discuss that future now, but no part of me wants to resurface the topic. And I'm glad they don't either. Maybe they, too, feel like it's too early to bring those complications into the newness of a relationship.

Really, I need something to take my mind off that part of tonight. After a sip of beer, I ask, "How about we play a game?"

"I'm down," Banks says.

"What kind?" Akara asks me.

I finish off the last drop of beer, then I place the bottle horizontally between us. "Spin the bottle."

Banks breaks into more than just a shadowy smile, and Akara shares a grin with him before he asks me, "How long have you been waiting to play this one, Sul?"

It's true that I always opted out. Not that there were many opportunities. Mostly just summer camp shenanigans. My first kiss, I hoped would be with more than just a stranger during a party game.

"Too long," I smile, "but the time feels like now. My first fucking foray into *spin the bottle* with the two guys I trust most." I shift a little closer. "Have you both ever played?"

Banks bobs his head. "Middle school."

"Middle school," Akara answers too. The way they soak me in, I know I've picked the best game right now. Having their lips on my lips sounds too good to be true.

"I figure we can stick with the original kissing version," I tell them, voice a bit raspier. "But we need high stakes. I don't like playing games without losers."

"First to end the game loses," Akara suggests. "Otherwise, we keep playing until someone forfeits."

"I like it," I say. "Quitters never win."

Akara laughs. "A Sullivan Minnie Meadows motto to live by." He drinks to that.

Banks looks between us. "So what happens to the loser?"

The first idea that pops into my head is risky. Really, it'd hurt me the worst if I lost, and maybe that's why I offer it. "Loser has to stop cursing for a year."

Banks whistles. "When you said high stakes, you weren't joking."

"Go big or go home." I wag my brows, but the motion almost instantly reminds me of my mom. I try to maintain a smile, even though a sad pang thumps inside me.

Akara can tell, but thankfully he doesn't mention the momentary sadness. "Lucky for you, Sulli, I only know how to go big."

My smile returns.

"Akara 'Going Big' Kitsuwon," Banks teases.

Akara taps Banks' shoulder with the beer bottle. "Banks 'Going Home' Moretti."

Banks slaps his friend's chest. "Home is where the heart is."

I snort into a laugh.

We're all smiling, and Akara takes extra interest in the game. "We need one more rule," he says. "What happens if the loser accidentally curses throughout the year? There has to be a consequence if they break the punishment."

I shrug. "We'd have to slug the loser."

"No," Banks shakes his head to me. "If you lose, I'm not punching you."

"In the arm?"

Banks scrapes his hand across his jaw, thinking, but more tensed. Akara has lightly slugged me back before, no problem, but my relationship with Banks isn't playful wrestling and competition.

"I'm not losing anyway," I assure him. "You or Akara are."

"You hope," Akara says into a sip of beer. Can he be any fucking sexier right now?

I pulse my heel a little between my legs, digging for more friction. Their gazes roam my body, mostly landing on my nipples and shallow breathing pattern.

Banks nods to me, "I'm rooting for you then, mermaid."

"Just don't lose on purpose. I need some competition."

He has this gentle, affectionate expression that I fall into. "Alright. I'll try to win for you."

I breathe in his sweetness. I've fucking fallen so in love with him. My heart practically soars out of my body into Banks' hands. We share a smile, and I say, "Let's play."

Akara nudges my knee with his foot. "Scoot closer, Sulli."

Moving forward and keeping my legs crossed, the beer bottle and our sexual tension is the only thing separating us on the bed. After everything that happened today, I'm done talking.

I just want to turn off my brain and feel.

"Ladies first, *Lady* Meadows," Akara says, not the first time he's called me *Lady Meadows* either.

"I'm not a proper lady," I remind him, grabbing the bottle.

"Yeah, you're 100% improper." Akara smiles into a swig. "And I love my improper lady."

My heart expands. *I'm so in love with Kits, too.* I touch my fingers to my smile.

Concentrate, Sulli.

This could just be their winning tactic. Distract me and take the fucking prize.

Not today.

The prize is fucking mine. I want the bragging rights. Always.

"Wait before you spin," Akara says, then snags a hardback off my nightstand.

The only book I've actually read more than once. *Tobias Kingly: Gold under Water.*

He fits the biography under the beer bottle. "It'll be easier to spin on this." He flips the cover to the backside, hiding Kingly mid-swim with goggles and swim cap. "So I won't punch his face."

I make a noise. "His face isn't punchable—he's fucking *legendary*, Kits."

"He's an ass."

"You're an ass."

"I'm a *likable* ass," Akara refutes. "There's a difference."

Yeah, yeah.

Banks looks lost. "Am I supposed to know who the fuck this guy is?"

I readily explain, "Kingly is only the *best* swimmer of our generation—"

"Sulli has a crush on him," Akara tells Banks before I can list off all of Kingly's swim records and Olympic golds. "She practically drooled all over Kingly when he signed her book."

"I didn't *drool*," I refute, face flaming at the way Banks is smiling at me. "I just said, *thanks*. He's a swim god, Kits."

"You're a swim god, Sul. He should've been drooling all over *you*." To Banks, he explains, "He's too cocky."

"Another cock," Banks says like Kingly is on his hit list.

"No," I shake my head profusely, "*no,* he's not a cock. He's fucking cool. Kits is cockier than Kingly."

"No, I'm *moderately* cocky. Kingly is a chump. You can do better." He puts a hand to his mouth, feigning shock. "Wait, you already *did*." His smile is making me smile.

We're all grinning, and that's the best place to leave the talk of one of my idols.

Bottle on the book, I give it a good spin. We watch the bottle rotate quickly before slowing down. The neck of the bottle is pointing to...

Banks laughs. "Right down the middle."

I grip my knees, then bite the corner of my lip. "Should I...spin again? Or should I just kiss both of you?"

They look at each other.

"Both," I say, before they can decide between each other. I like when they both win anyway. I crawl closer to Akara, my knee knocking the bottle off Kingly's biography. I'm too fast for Akara to savor my prowl towards him. Just as quick, I place a peck on his cheek. In another second, I place a soft kiss on Banks' right cheek.

I fall back onto my bottom.

"That's not the kind of spin the bottle I was imagining," Banks says with a soft smile.

"Me neither," Akara says to him. "Should we tell her?"

"No, let's see how long this plays out." Banks smiles wider.

I flush. "Hardy har-har. I know spin the bottle is a lot hotter than that. But I'm working up to it."

"We need to help her out of the Kindergarten league," Akara says to Banks, then gives me a sexy smile as he tips beer back. They drink me in like I'm unequivocally attractive, like they're imagining more than their lips on me. Every time Banks' gaze roams over my nipples, I squirm.

Dirty games like spin the bottle aren't in my repertoire, but their confidence is wrapping around my inexperience in the most sensual way possible.

These are the men who took your virginity, Sulli.

I want them to show me more. What feels good. To go on greater, deeper explorations of bodies and heart.

On the nightstand near Akara, the clock glows a meaningless number. It's late-late. Like the kind of late where we're definitely well into the next day but it's still pitch-black outside. Time and sleep are two mega-assholes I don't love. So I'm ignoring both.

"Akara, you next," I say.

He places the bottle back on the book, then spins.

It lands…

On me.

Anticipation and excitement swarm my stomach. He leans forward on his knees, and his hand effortlessly goes to the back of my head. Fingers threading my long hair. Lips an inch from mine as my pulse ascends.

And then he detours to the left, his lips brushing my ear. He whispers, "You want to be worked up to it, Sul." He kisses my earlobe in a featherlight touch. Shivers trickle down my neck.

Just like that, he returns to his spot against the headboard.

I'm utterly fucking breathless. And his mouth never even touched mine.

"That was hot," I say, smokiness to my voice that I can't extinguish.

Banks rests his forearm on his knee, lips rising. "Ear kisses turn the mermaid on. Noted."

"Ear kisses from me," Akara clarifies.

Banks wears a crooked smile. "Is that a challenge?"

"Oh hey, it's not a contest," I remind them, holding out my hands to referee. But they're not even close to tackling. *They're friends. They won't fight.*

"A bet within a bet, though, string bean," Akara tells me. "Aren't those your favorite?"

"Yeah, as long as there aren't any hurt feelings between you two." I look from Akara to Banks with a mild case of concern. If they suddenly despised each other, our triad would crumble apart. There are so many elements to the three of us being together, and their friendship is essential.

"No hurt feelings," Banks assures me, and then looks to Akara. "And I'll take your challenge." He spins the bottle slow enough that there's no chance it *doesn't* land on me. It goes through one full revolution before stopping.

Banks' eyes lock on mine, and the air seems to still. My breathing shallows, then almost stops completely. Being so tall, he uses little effort to close the distance between us. He doesn't pretend to go for my lips—instead, he beelines for my neck. His soft lips brush the flesh just below my earlobe. And his hand dips down to the small of my back. I uncross my legs, and Banks nearly scoops me up into his chest.

Fuck, fuuuck. I'm melting.

Gently, he begins to suck on my neck. My breath shortens, and my gaze is in direct line of sight to Akara.

He watches, and it's impossible to miss the lust in his brown eyes. My pulse descends to between my legs. Banks' lips rise to my earlobe, and the tenderness mixed with the warm, wet pressure drives me fucking wild. This feeling, I could bask in, but I want *more*.

My fists grip the quilt.

Banks. Banks. My eyes flutter, and I force them open onto Akara. His head is tilted, attention completely wrapped around me and my arousal. Unable to break away.

He drinks beer like he's cooling off under the hottest sun. Sitting there watching me, Akara might as well be auditioning for the cover of a fashion magazine. But there is a primal look in his eyes. Like I'm the *need* to his greater thirst and hunger.

Kits. Kits.

Why are they both so hot? I try to gather my bearings. One dreamboat and one beefcake—they're combusting me.

And Banks…

He sucks on my neck again, hitting a sensitive spot that quickens the heartbeat between my legs.

Akara palms the crotch of his red drawstring pants. I'd love to touch him, just to see how hard he's become. To see how much I turn him on.

But I already feel sexy. *Beautiful.* To be desired is totally, completely intoxicating. And I'd rather drown in this feeling than surface for more breath.

Before I can process what's happening, Banks leaves my side. His lips are replaced with cold, uninviting air. He glances to Akara. "You were fuckin' saying?"

"Not bad," Akara says, tipping the beer bottle back to his lips.

My turn again.

Gathering my hair on one shoulder, I try to cool down. *Focus. Concentrate.*

The heat of their gazes penetrates every cell of my body. *Penetrates.* Now I'm imagining their cocks penetrating other parts of my body— which is definitely *not* helping.

I re-cross my legs. Dig my heel into the throbbing place, then I glance up at them. Their hungered, ravenous expressions are consuming me whole.

I want to be devoured like we're animals back in the woods. Like they can't withstand the pheromones I project, and they just need to touch me and caress me and make fucking love to me.

But I foolishly made this a *kissing* game.

The bottle spins out of my hand and lands on...*me*.

"Cumbuckets, ugh."

"Lose a turn," Akara says, then he spins the bottle.

It stops on...

Banks lets out a laugh. "Knew that one was coming." He nods to Akara. "Kiss me, Kitsuwon."

"I'm the one that gives the orders," Akara says into a smile.

"I don't mind it."

"I know you don't."

While they sit shoulder-to-shoulder, Akara barely rotates to place a light, friendly kiss on Banks' cheek. Waiting for the next turn draws eagerness and longing in my body. I shift my heel between my legs back and forth. I feel soaked.

Their touch is the only touch I crave, and I could dream a thousand ways of their hands caressing my body. But no dream has to be wasted with the reality this close.

Banks is quick to take his turn. The bottle whirls, then comes to a stop on me.

He doesn't make a move right away. Instead, he looks to Akara first. "What do you think?"

Akara appraises me with headiness in his eyes.

I cross my legs tighter together to try to stop the pounding between them.

"She's definitely not worked up yet," Akara says teasingly.

"No, I am—I really am," I breathe like I'm running an ultramarathon.

Banks smiles, but to Akara, he says, "Maybe another round?"

"Definitely another round."

What does that mean?

One more round before what?

I want to ask, but part of me craves the mystery more. Banks leans towards me, and his large, callused hand encases my cheek with sultry affection. And his lips brush my chin before descending to my collarbones. He leaves a trail with his tongue.

A whimper catches in my throat. I feel like I'm falling into something overwhelming.

"You're alright, Sul," Akara says as our gazes meet.

I'm going to combust. My fingers curl back around the turquoise quilt. *Deeper. Deeper.* Fill me completely. I remember what that felt like.

Having Banks inside me.

Having Akara inside me.

I'm seconds away from begging for a repeat when Banks pulls away and collapses back against the headboard again. He gives me a long once-over, satisfaction brimming in his own eyes.

"That was...mean," I say.

They both laugh, but in a way that makes me feel really cute. Attractive. Feminine, even. Like I'm the most adorable thing in this room.

I light up in ways I didn't know I could. "My turn," I breathe.

And I spin.

The bottle lands on Akara.

At least the universe, fate, *something* out there is trying to make this somewhat even. I let out a relaxed breath and when I look up, I realize Akara and Banks are whispering something. Banks finishes with a nod.

I don't ask.

Part of me knows I'm about to discover what they're discussing.

Akara moves closer in one fluid motion, then takes my waist in two confident hands and pulls me between his spread legs. Our bodies collide, my hair whips at my face like I've been sling-shotted into him.

All the rounds before were uncontrollably slow. This one is deliriously fast. Unable to think, his lips are on mine. Skin tingling, pulse thumping, Akara guides my lips open with expert force. His tongue, his experience, his hands and knowledge and the fact that he's *Kits* is driving all the desire straight into my heart.

I reach up to touch his head.

He clasps my wrist mid-air. The pressure in his grip sends shockwaves through my body. Our eyes touch with pulsating need. *Holy fuck.*

Akara keeps me bound as he guides my back to the mattress. He breaks my legs apart. Knowing I could just lie here and he would pleasure and devour me is making me a mess of feelings and yearnings. *Kits.*

His thumb circles my hardened nipple that presses against my tank top. *Oh my fuck.* His tongue sweeps my tongue, and I arch my hips into him. He forces them back down with his own build.

I break from his lips to catch my breath.

But he doesn't stop the barrage of kisses against my jaw, then my neck. His mouth brushes lightly over my nipple. I squirm and writhe under him.

And then I tilt my head to the side and see Banks. He watches with heady arousal, his hand lost beneath the waistband of his drawstring pants. Massaging himself as he watches Kits thrust harder against me.

"Fuck," I rasp, shaking. Turned on beyond belief. I remember losing my virginity. How Banks stretched my legs open. How my body was in his care while Akara went deep, and I almost wish he'd grab my ankle.

I'm sure they can tell I ache for more. But right when I'm about to ask, Akara kisses me lightly on my lips.

An endnote.

He leaves me breathless on the mattress. I stare up at the ceiling.

"Sulli?" Kits asks in concern.

"I'm good," I muster before sitting up to face them, winded. "The game is still on." I am *not* a fucking quitter. Not even if my body is screaming at me to forget *spin the bottle* and go straight to harder, deeper pleasure. "Who's turn is it?" I ask. Fuck, I've forgotten.

"Mine," Akara says the same time his phone chimes.

Oh no.

Banks and I give each other a look.

Akara rolls his eyes at us. "I'm not stopping the game for a phone call…" He stares harder at his cell that lies across the room on my dresser. The next chime turns into a ring, ring, *ring*. Until the ringing stops.

And then starts up again.

Akara curses under his breath as he climbs off the bed. "I'm coming back," he says before crossing the bedroom.

Banks is tall enough sitting that he extends an arm over the top of the iron headboard. Both of us watching Akara click into his phone.

"Everything okay?" I ask.

"Yeah, but I have to take this." Akara expels a stressed breath.

"Who is it?" Banks asks.

"Your dad," Akara replies.

Michael Moretti is calling him? He works for Akara now and trains the temp bodyguards.

Banks' face screws up. "You can hang up on him, man."

"I can't, Banks. I need him to know this company is everything to me. If he leaves for any reason, I'm *fucked*."

I cringe, feeling badly for setting the stakes so high. Akara's responsibilities outpace ours by a hundred miles. "We can just say we *paused* the game. You don't have to take the L," I tell him.

He pushes back his hair. "I don't know when I'll be coming back, Sul. It's fine. I lost fairly." He doesn't give me a chance to argue. Akara leaves the bedroom completely, shutting the door quickly behind him.

Banks and I lock eyes across the bed.

I pick at the quilt. "Game over, I guess?" I say, uncertain.

His soft smile peeks. "I don't need a game to kiss you, if you want to be kissed."

"You know I do." I smile more, then glance hesitantly at the door. We haven't really talked about rules, but I just want to be fair. "Whatever we do here, I'll do with Akara when he gets back."

Banks nods, understanding.

I scoot closer until I take Akara's seat shoulder-to-shoulder with Banks. Right up against the headboard, a cupcake pillow snug behind me.

His arm falls around my shoulder, holding me to his side. Our eyes graze each other in the quiet, and my skin still tingles from their teasing. His fingers drift along my cheek, lifting my chin, and our lips touch with sultriness that feeds greater cravings.

I grip his thigh, and he holds my face like I might disappear. The kiss is desperation and life and love, and I never want to leave.

Banks slides my leg over his leg, and he pulls me onto his lap. I barely have time to clutch his shoulders as he draws us further down the bed and rests my back on the mattress.

Oh fuck yes.

He's on top, cocooning me. The beat of my pulse matches my shortened breath. He breaks my legs open around his waist, and I accidentally kick the book and the bottle off the bed. I hear the shatter of glass, and our heads turn slightly but neither of us pull away.

Our eyes trace our lips, and I whisper, "I really love being this close to you."

"Me too." He stares down at me like I'm the most attractive thing in the sea. I'm drowning in a pool of attraction and yearning and overwhelming feelings.

His hand slides up my thigh, his lips nuzzled against the nape of my neck. He touches the sensitive skin, and I shut my eyes in absolute heaven with him.

"Banks," I rasp, in need of more. I reach for his length, his hardness tenting his drawstring pants. I stroke him. A groan rumbles through him.

And there is no thinking next, just total feelings as his lips meld against mine, as he breathes into the kiss like he's breathing life into my lungs. As he sheds my top and bottom, as I tug at his clothing until it's all gone.

Naked, our flesh welds and heats me, and I ache and whimper for more. I'm floating into his muscular build, into his arms, into his embrace, into his care and experience and affection.

I breathe against his mouth, "I need you…in me, *please.*" He's right *there.* His erection is nudging against my heat. My legs are open around him. He even clutches my thigh, spreading me further, and I watch how he soaks in our bodies. I feel utterly fucking vulnerable, but also so safe. Like he's one of two people on this earth meant to connect with me.

"You sure you want to?" Banks asks, studying me.

I clutch his hair. "*Yes, fuck, please,*" I nearly cry out.

He kisses me quickly, then climbs off.

"Banks?"

"I have to get a condom."

Right. *Fuck.*

I check him out while he stands. He's tall, sculpted and masculine, but Banks has a gentleness and light in his eyes that I hold on to even more. He's back in a blink after rummaging in my dresser. We put those condoms there "just in case" for a time like this, but we've always been a little too cautious. Afraid my roommates would find out about *us.*

But now, they already know.

"You want under the covers?" Banks asks, climbing back on.

I realize I'm shivering.

"Yeah."

He whips the quilt. I slip under. He climbs back on top of me, his hands traveling over the length of my legs as he stretches them wider. And then he pulls the quilt over us.

Heat gathers, and his hand roots to a spot above my head. His other hand sheaths his length with the condom.

My eyes widen. *He's so fucking hard.* And big.

Really, really fucking big, and I almost can't believe he's been inside of me before.

While hovered over me, his dog tags hang off his neck, the metal brushing against my collarbone. This'll be my first time having sex on a bed, and I still find myself forgetting to move my hands. They mostly stay planted to his biceps.

Banks kisses me, then touches my pussy. *Fuck ahh.*

I writhe as he massages my clit. "I…" I cry out already, toes starting to curl. "I have to already be…wet enough. *Please.*" I just want Banks *in.* I throb for him.

"You're very wet, mermaid." His husky voice melts me. "But I'm gonna go down on you first."

Yes.

Fuck yes…he's buried further under the covers as he moves back, and I can't see him as he lifts my legs over his shoulders. As he kisses the bundle of nerves. *Holy…*

His tongue sucks and laps, and my hips buck up. Breath hitching, I see stars as I come with a cry.

"*Banks, Banks.*" I reach under the quilt, gripping his shoulder for support. My legs quake, and somehow, someway, I hit another peak.

He pops back up with a sexy noise in his throat, then we're kissing vigorously. I hold on to him for dear fucking life while he curves my leg towards my chest, pulling it higher.

"If it hurts, say *stop*," he breathes.

"I will," I rasp.

Our eyes stay attached the whole time he edges closer. He reaches down, guiding himself gently into me.

I let out a gasp, the pressure overwhelming at first. "*Fuck.*"

"Alright?"

"How far…are you in?"

"Not far."

I nod to him. "Go, *go.*"

He inches more, and I contract around him. Banks grunts a little, his gaze consuming me as much as I just want to devour him in one fucking gulp. But I can't take him that fast.

He inches more and more, then rocks a little. The friction is mind-numbing. I'm so swollen from all the teasing beforehand, and my eyes nearly roll. My fingers dig into his shoulders.

And then he stops moving.

"Banks?" I instinctively arch up my hips, but he grabs my waist, keeping me still.

"You're so fucking tight, Sulli," he says huskily. "If I go any further, I might hurt you, and if I move back and forth, I'm gonna come."

"Come then."

He shakes his head. "Not yet. I want this to last…" The look in his eyes starts to well something up in mine.

"Can we stay…just like this?" I ask. *With him inside of me.*

He nods. "Just like this."

We must be dreaming because the longer we're *just like this*, the more I feel his cock twitch inside of me. The more I pulse around him. For a moment, I pretend we're together on an island.

In nature.

Where it's safest.

Unable to take it anymore, he thrusts in and out. In and out, and I cry so loud, he plants a hand over my mouth. His muscles flex against me as he hits a climax.

As our breaths come down, he kisses me, then gently pulls out. After tossing the condom and wrapping me up in his chest, I glance over at the door. Half expecting Akara to be back.

Should we have waited?

Was this wrong?

But it felt right.

"Sulli?" Banks asks in concern. "What's wrong?"

I'm about to speak, but I yawn, totally wiped. Probability that I'll fall asleep before Akara comes back is astronomically high, but I'll defeat sleep for him. I'll rise into his arms. "Nothing…just, when Akara comes back, can you tell him to wake me up? He can have a turn too…" I might not have phrased that right, but whatever the fuck.

I don't care.

I'm spent.

I love being in Banks arms, and I'd love just as much to be in Akara's if he were here.

"I'll wait up for him," Banks breathes. "Get some sleep."

I nod as I shut my eyes. "I really love you, you know that, Banks?"

The last thing I hear is, "I really love you too, mermaid." And then everything fades into a peaceful slumber.

12
Banks Moretti

THE DOOR OPENS SLOWLY, a sliver of light illuminating the dark room. Sulli remains passed out in my arms, but I carefully sit up in bed as Akara slips inside.

My eyes adjust to the dark as soon as he shuts the door, but I can't figure out how to adjust the metaphorical weight crushing my chest. Guilt. Don't know that fucker that well. But it's currently riding me like a coked-out cowboy. I'm just the dumb horse that can't buck it off.

I swept the glass up earlier, so I don't warn him about the broken bottle as he moves closer. Floor is clean.

Akara gently climbs into bed on the other side of Sulli. He doesn't acknowledge me until he checks underneath the turquoise quilt and white sheets, confirming that she's naked. I'm naked.

Then his eyes lift to mine.

"Akara—" I whisper.

He interrupts in a soft tone, "Stop looking at me like that. It's fine, Banks."

"I should've asked or waited—"

"No," he refutes quickly. "Because when I get the chance, I'm definitely not asking you or waiting. And if we're being honest with each other, I'd probably feel less guilty if I were in your position. So who's the real jerk?"

I shake my head, "Not you."

Akara lets out a soft sound, an almost-laugh. "You're wholesome, a *good son*. Looking back, I made your brother be the bad cop so I could pretend to be nice—"

"You didn't make Thatcher do shit," I whisper. "He's stringent and prickly. He knows he's prickly. You're good at being friendly with your men because you aren't a fucking cactus like my lovably cactus-y brother."

Akara tries to smile, but he looks to Sulli, then back at the phone in his fist. "I'm just hanging on, Banks." He sighs heavily. "The only certainty I have right now is you and her."

I squeeze his shoulder. Everything is starting to slip around Akara, and the financial tolls he's taking, I won't understand. I can't. But I'm the guy ready to move out whenever he calls. Whenever he needs me, I'm there.

As we share the quiet, he asks me, "Did it hurt her the second time with you inside her?"

I shake my head. "I didn't go that far in."

Akara nods a couple times, then says, "I don't expect the two of us to always be together when she's turned on." He exhales an annoyed breath. "Can't really lie, I hate that I missed this."

I whisper back, "She told me to wake her up when you got here. So you could have a turn. Her words."

"So I could have a turn," he repeats with a shocked laugh. "My improper lady." He smiles a little but shakes his head. "No, we'll have our time together later. Let her sleep." He exhales another deep breath like he's shedding today's stresses.

I don't know how that phone call with my dad went, but I don't ask. Avoiding the topic of Michael Moretti has been the name of the game, and I'm not fumbling that ball tonight.

More seems to be weighing on him, though. "You alright?"

Sulli doesn't even stir between us, out cold. Don't blame her. Strange to think today started with a rock climb and her dad's anger.

Akara glances to Sulli, then stares at the ceiling. "I missed out on sex with Sulli because of a phone call with your dad, and I can't even fudging curse about it."

Can't help it. I laugh.

He gives me a look with a fraction of a smile. "It's not fudging funny."

"A year of that and you're gonna give me a permanent side-cramp from all the laughing."

His smile remains as he says, "Can we make a deal?"

"Anything."

"You're not even going to wait for the terms?"

"For you, I'd do just about anything." I tilt my head, letting it sag to the side to meet his eyes. "Alright, *probably* anything."

Akara takes that in for a long moment. Silence ebbs and flows between us, an acknowledgement of what we mean to each other. What we're growing to mean.

"If one of us has sex with her when the other isn't around," Akara says. "We tell each other about it. Let's not keep it a secret. Jealousy isn't here right now, but I think it'd bother me if you two were hooking up on the regular and I didn't know."

"Deal," I say without hesitation. "And just so you know, I feel the same."

He pats my shoulder. "Good talk. Now get some rest. You have work tomorrow."

I scoot back down until my head hits the pillow. My mouth curves up, even as I say, "Yes, sir."

13

Banks Moretti

NOVEMBER SUN BEATS down on the rooftop pool, making an otherwise chilly afternoon more enjoyable in Philly. I have the perfect view of Sulli as she swims laps back and forth with skill and ease. Like a majestic goddess of the sea.

Truth: Akara should be the one up here. Instead, my ass is holding a net gun and watching out for a drone.

He put me on Sulli's detail when the Studio 9 manager called this morning. To quit.

Now he's working through a dumpster fire that I can't help him extinguish. If this had been a security crisis, I'd have his six. No question. But his gym—that business might as well be written in hieroglyphics. I don't understand how it operates, and I have no desire to figure it out.

It just blows because I want to give Akara equal time with Sulli, especially after her and I had sex last night, but I'm unsure how to do that when he keeps sidelining himself. *I* don't control my schedule. He does.

Sulli pops out of the water as I patrol the roof and squint through the bright sun. Thank Mary and fucking Joseph, I don't have a migraine today. The light would be a knife to my temple.

She pulls off her goggles and leans her arms on the poolside edge. "Any flying fuckers out there?"

"Negative," I say. "A shame too. I kind of wanted to use this." I twirl the net gun in my hand.

She smiles, beads of water rolling down her smooth skin. "I'm sure if I stay up here long enough some type of drone will fly in."

I crouch down to her spot. "Is that your way of saying you never want to come out of the water?" I think her next smile is at the sound of my South Philly accent on *water*. Sounded more like *wooder*.

She makes no effort to climb out. "Depends. Would you live in the water with me?"

"Day and night." I stand up. "But I'm no mer-man. I'd probably sink to the bottom."

"I'd save you. No beefcake is dying on my watch."

I laugh into a smile. *Beefcake*. Looking her over, I notice her reddened cheeks and nose. "And no mermaid is getting burned on mine." I grab the sunscreen, then come back and sit down near the edge of the pool. Right beside Sulli, who stays submerged.

She watches me stretch my legs out on the stone patio. "You think Akara is okay?"

I click my mic on my collar. "Banks to Akara, what's your status?"

He rogers up fast. "Akara to Banks, I just closed the gym until I can get a new manager. I'm on my way back to the penthouse."

"Copy that," I say to him, and then to her, I say, "He's on his way."

She breathes out in relief. "He works too much."

I nod. "He puts a lot of pressure on himself."

Her eyes soften. "I fucking get that. When I was training for the Olympics, I had a one-track mind. No time for anything else…or *anyone* else. Sometimes I think if Akara weren't paid to follow me around, I would've been really lonely."

"He was a good friend to you back then," I assume.

"The best," she says into an exhale. "And I want to be a good girlfriend, but it's not exactly easy taking work off his shoulders when I *am* his work. Now he's not even letting me pay for security anymore."

Yep, Akara decreed that this morning. And I thought I was the dumbass. He's on Sulli's detail *for free*. He's still paying my salary, though. Where he's pinching pennies, I don't know, and I'm trying not to stress over money. He'd just tell me, *I'm handling it*. As long as I can afford to take Sulli out on a *nice* date, I'm good to go.

I scan the sky, then look to Sulli. "You might be his work, but I doubt you've been like work to Akara."

She watches me uncap the sunscreen. "What do you mean?"

I lift a shoulder. "You've made him happy. For years, he's stayed on your detail because he never wanted to leave—I saw that. Most of SFO saw that." I block the sun with my hand. "For what it's worth, I think Akara taking time away from you is a fucking dumb move."

She contemplates this and wades more in the water. "So what's the solution?"

"I don't know. I feel the exact same as you. I want to be a good… *metamour*." I cock my head, not sure if the term used to describe my relationship with Akara is catching on or not. Anyway, I continue, "But it feels like the only person who can unsink himself from the hole he climbed in is Akara himself." I grimace, partly from the sun, partly from the quicksand Akara is in. "It's eating at me because I'd love to just jump down and shovel him out."

"Fucking *same*." She sighs. "We can't do anything, can we?"

"Right now, I think we just gotta be there." I hate feeling helpless, but Akara is involved in shit that outranks me *and* Sulli. "Your nose is burning."

"Oh fuck…can you…?" Her voice trails off since I'm already rubbing a layer of sunscreen on her nose. With my fingers, I swipe sunscreen over her cheeks that pull in a smile.

I smile back. "Who fucking knew, mermaids burn?" The rest of her is tan.

We enjoy this quiet moment together, and after I finish rubbing sunscreen along her nose, I try my best to pay attention to the drones. But Sulli is a much better sight than the sun and the sky. Her wet hair glistens in the light, and her green eyes are orbed like world globes.

"You coming in?" Sulli asks with hope.

What I'd give to drop into the water with her. I can't take off my boots. The net gun rests next to me. *Still on-duty.* Maybe if I were Akara, the boss—the one with more leeway to cut corners—I'd cut this one to shreds.

But half-assing my job will only add more stress onto him, my friend, my *metamour.*

"Can't," I say with the raise of my net gun. "I have to keep my boots on."

Instead of sulking, Sulli immediately pulls herself mostly out of the water. She sits right beside me on the stone, keeping her calves submerged.

My chest rises in something close to *longing.* She wasn't kidding when she said *living in the water* was dependent on if I'd be there. I smile down at her.

Sulli swishes the water with her legs, then asks, "Do you think you'll tell your mom about us?"

"Yeah, eventually I hope everyone in my family will know too."

She shields the sun with her palm. "That doesn't freak you out?"

"Not really." I tuck my hair behind my left ear, then right. "No one's gonna give a shit what I do with my life, as long as I'm not in jail or doing hard drugs."

"Do they not care or…?"

"They care about me," I say into a laugh, thinking about the big Italian-American brood I grew up around. "They probably care *too* much. They'll be gossiping at every Sunday meal—hell, centuries from now, my aunts will be clanking skeleton teeth in their graves, not able to shut up about my relationship."

Sulli laughs.

Christ, I love the sound of her laugh. Bright but smoky.

I tell her, "My family is like yours in a lot of ways. They'd drop *everything* if I needed them." We both stare out at the glittering pool while we talk. "But I didn't come from much. They don't expect a lot out of me, other than to be a good person and to be happy. Add in the

fact that my *ma* sees me as the 'free-spirited' one"—I use air-quotes—
"and I doubt she ever really saw me settling down. I'm the son who'll
go fuck off wherever my soul takes me." I raise a shoulder. "Just so
happens it's taken me to you."

Sulli catches my eyes on those last words and breathes in. Her hand
rests on my thigh, and I place my hand atop hers.

Our fingers thread, and she says, "I think I've put more pressure on
myself than my parents have ever put on me."

I nod a few times. "You know, I've been around your families long
enough to know the world expects different things from you. Some
want you to be like your parents—to have the same love story as them."

She snorts. "That's fucking impossible."

I tilt my head gently. "You knew Akara when you were sixteen like
your dad knew your mom."

"Akara is *barely* like my dad," Sulli says adamantly. "Not that I
don't love my dad or my parents' love story—it's epic, unable to be
replicated—but I just know now, today, as I sit here with you, that I
want to go my own way. Ever since Yellowstone, it's been the most
freeing I've ever felt."

I skate a hand across her soft, bare back, and she leans more of her
weight into me. "Other people out there are gonna want you to be *their*
ideal version of Sulli or the Sulli they think they know. But the only
person who knows if they're capable to handle this kind of romance is
you. Not Big Sal down Passyunk or Joey Junior in the row house next
door."

Sulli looks up, squinting. "Are those real fucking people?"

"Yeah," I say, using my hand to block the light from her eyes.
"Though, you're never meeting Joey Junior. He's a fucking prick and
stole my boots in third grade."

She makes an angry face. "If I was better at writing, I'd write him
a fucking letter."

"Yeah? What would it say?"

"Fuck off, Joey Junior. Sincerely, Banks' mermaid."

I laugh, one that rumbles deep in my chest, and as our eyes meet again, I tell Sulli, "I wish your family gave you more credit. I know you can do this without their safety nets."

Sulli rocks into me, "I wish your brother gave *you* more credit too."

I bob my head, both of us exchanging a deeper look, deeper breath together, because we're going through similar issues with similar families who love us too fucking much. No one wants to see us hurt.

I can't look at her for long.

Pulling my gaze to the sky, I scan for drones.

Sulli wrings out her wet hair, wearing a sporty bikini that shows off her abs and tanned skin. Beads of water dry on her collarbones, the longer she's two-thirds out of the pool. "Have you talked to your dad since Akara hired him?"

"No, and I'm hoping it stays that way."

No drones.

Sulli lifts one foot out and holds onto her ankle. "What'd he do, Banks?"

It's always been too easy to talk to Sulli. Shutting her out sounds like hell, and I'm not my brother.

Thatcher loves descending into that kind of self-torment like it's Saturday tee time on a fucking golf course.

I swallow a pit in my throat. "You can't tell Akara if I tell you. He'd fire my dad out of loyalty to me, and he can't do that. Kitsuwon Securities needs him." I take a beat. "I know it might not be fair to put that on you, but *he can't know.*"

And I want you to know, Sulli. I force myself not to add that and put more pressure on her, but maybe she can read those words all over me.

She touches her lips, focused. "It should be alright if I keep some things private between you and me, and vice versa, between Akara and me." She drops her hand. "And even if I can't lie all that fucking well, I'm not that terrible at keeping secrets. I haven't spilled Luna's yet to either of you."

She's not wrong about that.

In the next second, Sulli rotates more to face me. "I want to know about you and your dad, if that's not crystal."

My lip lifts. "You're coming in clear, mermaid."

Our hands are still together. She stares longer at the scars along my fingers. "Did he physically hurt you?"

"No," I say with the shake of my head. "My hands are beat-up from working with them most of my life. I worked on cars growing up."

She nods, knowing I've been a mechanic.

"On the way to Montana, I told you the last thing my dad said to me before he left."

"*You're the dispensable one*," Sulli says with hurt. "That was fucking cruel."

I let out a laugh that sounds bitter and pained. "That was only half of it."

Her face falls. "It gets worse?"

I hang my head, feeling the weight of that night bear on my neck. "I was twelve. It was the night my brother died, and my dad—in all his *anguish* of losing his firstborn son—he decided to turn to his youngest one and tell me, *You're the dispensable one. It should've been you.*"

Sulli's grip tightens around my hand. For me. *She's holding on for me.* Not letting go. "Banks…"

I can't look up. I stare at the water. "It's not even the worst thing he said that night. I can't forget how soulless he looked towards my ma when he told her, *It's your fault. You should've never let him ride out there. He'd still be alive if it weren't for you.* I tried to punch him for coming at her like that, and he put me on my ass in a second flat."

"Fuck," Sulli breathes. "He sounds…"

"Like a monster?"

"Yeah."

I raise my eyes to the sky. *Scanning.* Then I look down at her. "He's been distant ever since that night, ever since the divorce, and Thatcher forgave him without an apology or acknowledgement of what he said. They buried it, and if I can help it, I want nothing to do with him."

"But you also want Kitsuwon Securities to succeed and not fail."

I nod strongly. "Exactly it." I glance over at her. "You gonna tell me that I should tell Akara?" He might be my best friend, but Sulli knows him a bit differently than I do.

"No." She rests her chin on her knee. "He'd probably fire your dad if he knew. Deep down, Akara is as big of a lover as he is a fighter, and he'd hurt himself if it meant protecting you."

He'd do the same for Sulli in a heartbeat.

I nod a few times. "He can't know." And another thought makes me crack a smile. *Jesus.*

"What's so funny?" Sulli asks with an elbow-nudge.

"The boots Joey Junior stole—I was thinking about how my brother gave me his to wear after that, and they were too small."

"Aren't you the same shoe size as Thatcher...wait..." Realization suddenly washes over her face.

"They were Skylar's boots," I say what she's thinking. "We all only had one pair of shoes, and Sky eventually saved up enough money from working at Cinema World to buy another pair for me. We didn't tell our ma, or else she would've scraped up the money. But things were already tough."

"Your dad was a Navy SEAL, right? Didn't he have some money saved?"

"You'd be surprised how fast someone can blow money on shit they shouldn't. Bad investments. Gambling. Not sure about his finances now, but my dad was in deep debt when I was a kid. And he dragged my ma down with him."

She loosely holds her knees. "It makes sense why you said I have a good dad." She takes a sharp breath. "He is *really* fucking good, and I don't want you to think I take that for granted."

"I never thought it," I say. "You might've been given a lot, but you're not ungrateful or some sort of brat. You also have good parents to thank for that."

"Even if my dad is solely Team Akara?" she wonders.

"I'm ready for the *whole world* to be Team Akara."

Hell, some already are. A false rumor picked up steam. One about how Security Force Omega is a group of fake bodyguards and every bodyguard is secretly dating their client.

Akara has been Sulli's bodyguard.

So somewhere out there, fans are already carrying *Team Akara* signs and wearing *Kitsulli* stickers. What they don't know is that *I'm* the number one Kitsulli fan.

Always will be.

Till the day I die.

"Saying that you're okay with Team Akara and feeling it might *feel* fucking different," she warns me.

I squint in the sun. "We'll see."

Just as I say the words, her phone pings across the patio. Sulli drops back into the water and swims to the other side. Once she grabs her cell off the ground, her face twists at the screen. Mostly looking sullen.

"You alright?" I ask.

"Not really," she lets out a heavy breath. "It was a notification that my voice mailbox is full. I haven't listened to any of the ones my mom left, and I can't bring myself to fucking delete them." Her lips descend further. "I'm just not ready…and I haven't even talked to my sister."

"You want to call her now?"

She thinks. "Yeah, maybe I can…" She shakes off her wet hand and touches the phone screen. "I figure she hasn't heard anything yet or else she'd be blowing up my inbox too."

Winona Meadows is more of a mystery to me than some of her cousins. Can't predict whether or not she'd love the idea of Sulli dating Akara *and* me. Like everyone else, I expect her to be firmly on Team Akara, and I understand that loyalty. He's the one with long-lasting memories protecting the Meadows family.

I'm just a guy that showed up in Sulli's life. Late to the party.

Sulli dials a number, phone pressed to her ear. "Nona?"

I watch Sulli's face drop again.

"Oh no, I can call back later—no, you go ahead. You're busy... *fuck*." She adjusts her grip, and I can't hear anything her fifteen-year-old sister replies.

I stand back up, giving Sulli some privacy. I twirl the net gun again, eyeing the sky.

"No, no, no, it's totally fine—go finish your defensive driving class. We can talk another time. Alright...okay. Kick ass, squirt." And then the phone slips from her palm like butter.

She tries to course-correct, hot-potato-ing the cell, but the phone plops into the water. "Fuck, fuck, fuck!" Sulli dives down as I rush over.

She comes back up, swims over, and I toss her a towel while she climbs out of the pool in a panic. "I can't believe I fucking did that." She tries to dry off the cell, then smacks it against her palm. "Turn on, turn fucking on."

"Were you done talking to her?"

"Sort of—the last thing she said was, *I love you a waffle lot*, and now I feel like shit for not saying it back." Sulli shifts her weight from side to side, in distress. "Fuck, *ugh,* I'm already a shit sister for not telling her about you and Akara."

"Hey, hey, hey, look at me."

She looks pained.

I hold her shoulders. "We're gonna figure this out."

"How?"

What would Kitsuwon do? As she squints, I block the sun from her eyes with my hand. Alright, that's what *I* would do. He'd fix shit.

"I have a working phone. We can call her back."

Sulli hesitates. "I don't want to bother her anymore than I did. She gets her license in March, and she's taking some driving classes before then...what if I text her off your phone?"

I pass her my cell. "Go ahead."

Sulli composes a text really fast and hits *send*. "I just told her that it's me, and I dropped my phone in the pool." She adds fast, "And that I love her, I put that in there too." She tries to relax. "I know you don't care who takes sides, but I fucking care. I think I'm stalling on telling Nona because I know she's going to want me to be with *only* Akara." She wipes nonexistent sweat off her brow. "Fuck."

I wouldn't know how to win her sister over.

And that's where Sulli and Akara are more alike. Winning isn't really my forte.

That's their strength.

A faint buzzing sound cuts into the short quiet, and I eye the sky. "There it is." I shoot the net gun at the drone. Capturing the device as it thuds down to the patio. After I shut off the thing, the terrace doors open.

Akara saunters outside, coming towards us in gym pants and a red muscle shirt. He spots Sulli's tension. "What are you two doing?"

I toss the net gun on a lounge chair. "Missing you."

Sulli tells him the full story about her wet phone and short call with her sister. He takes the cell from her, and somehow, he dries the thing off with the towel like he's the Cell Phone Whisperer.

Jesus fucking Christ.

It couldn't have been *that* easy.

Akara shakes his head at me and her. "I leave you two for three seconds."

"Three *hours*," Sulli refutes.

"She almost drowned from lovesickness." I smack his chest. "I had to give her CPR. It was a fuckin' ordeal."

"The biggest," Sulli adds. "Like the size of Banks' dick kind of big."

I start to smile.

Akara gives her a teasing look. "The kind of size you can't take."

"I can take him," she refutes, shoving his arm.

"Like you can take me." He holds both of her arms and walks her backwards towards the edge of the pool. Until he walks right into the water with her. They go down, and I'm laughing when they pop back up. Sulli splashes him.

Akara wipes off the water, then reaches back towards me, capturing my ankle.

I shake him off and just jump in, fully-clothed.

When I come up, we're all closer together. Treading water in a huddle. Akara pushes his wet hair back, his eyes drifting from me to her, and our smiles slowly fade.

He tells us, "I'm shutting down Studio 9 indefinitely."

"Kits—"

"It's okay, Sulli. It's just until I find someone to take Alexis' place." *Alexis*—his manager, or rather, *ex*-manager.

He can't lose Studio 9. He's been trying to preserve the gym like someone preserving a ghost and a legacy, and it's too priceless to let go.

The bad news kicks my ass back onto dry land. I climb out of the pool, leaving those two to tread in the deep end. While I pry off my boots and pour water out of them, Akara calls after me, "Your dad told me he wants to talk to you."

I go still. "Does he really?"

"Wolf Scouts' honor."

Sulli splashes him. "Kits, you were never a Wolf Scout."

"But I *could've* been," he smiles, one that vanishes too fast.

I pour water out of my other boot. "You need me to talk to him?"

"You don't have to," Akara says strongly, knowing me and my dad didn't even speak at my brother's wedding. "I'm not telling you to."

But it'd help him.

If I decline, then he has to go back and tell my dad, *sorry, sir, your son isn't available.* And then he'll have to field the *why* questions and *how come.*

Akara is going through enough. Here's my chance to do something for him, but *goddamn*, I can't believe it's going to be *this.*

"I'll reach out to him," I suddenly say.

By text? By carrier pigeon? By a *fuck you* pizza, I wish. But I'm not that big of a Bitter Betty.

"Thanks, Banks." Akara looks relieved.

Sulli looks a little shocked, but after our talk, I think she understands why I'd do the thing I said I wouldn't. We both want to help Akara, and this is my shot.

14

Akara Kitsuwon

WOLFGANG AMADEUS MOZART blares in my eardrums. Sweat drips down my temples. Pulse pounding, I slam my fists hard into a red bag.

Jab, cross, hook. Jab, cross, hook.

Over and over, I repeat the simple combo. Pent up energy expels from me in short, quick bursts. Out of the corner of my eye, I watch Sulli run laps around Studio 9.

The Studio 9 that I sunk my dad's life insurance money in.

The Studio 9 that embodies my mom's Muay Thai career

The Studio 9 that is supposed to honor their legacy, their lives.

The Studio 9 that has no manager.

I slam another fist, the crescendo of the classical song building more emotion out of me. *Perhaps* I should feel good that Alexis is moving to Chicago to be with her new girlfriend. Selfishly, I can't help but wish singledom on her.

Then I wouldn't have lost my manager—the *best* manager I've ever had over the years, by the way. Without Alexis, no one is running the gym while I'm busy with security.

I don't have time to hire someone else.

Don't have time to second guess any of my decisions. It's been three days since I closed the gym, and I'm no closer to finding a new manager than the day Alexis left.

Uppercut.

Right hook, right hook, *right hook*. I hit harder, gritting my teeth as I slam my gloved fist into the red bag. I expel a single breath and catch movement as Sulli rounds the boxing ring. Her narrowed focus draws me in, and my next uppercut is lighter.

I find myself catching my breath as I apply less force and study my girlfriend.

Girlfriend.

My lips begin to upturn.

Sullivan Meadows jogs with purpose. Like she's training for a championship race. Like this isn't just an afternoon workout at my closed gym. Her drive and concentration never shift, not even as she runs past the wooden lockers, about to circle the area of hanging bags where I am.

Tension unwinds across my shoulders, and my next easy combo is done with an actual smile. I needed this today.

Time with her, even if we're just sharing the same air.

As Sulli jogs through the neighboring row of boxing bags, I slip through them and swiftly step out in front of her.

She collides into my chest in hard impact. I grab the small of her waist, stabilizing Sulli so she doesn't go down. "Easy there, string bean."

She rips out one of her earbuds and speaks. I can't hear her over Mozart blasting on high-volume through my AirPods. I'm about to pry one out, but she beats me to the punch and tears an AirPod from my ear.

"What the fuck, Kits?" *Spice Girls* blares from her speakers, the cord hanging loosely at her gym shorts. "I could've plowed you over."

Plowed me over. She's way too cute. "Impossible, Sul." I lead her backwards towards the nearest boxing bag. "I'm the one who caught you."

With each breath, she smiles more and more. Her ass bumps into the boxing bag. Sulli's green eyes travel down my six-two build. "You hear that?"

I hear my pulse and her pulse hiking up another notch.

I also hear music.

"Hear what?" I ask.

"Our songs. They're fighting each other." She uncurls her fist, one of my AirPods blaring the rage-y classical tune.

"Mozart vs. Spice Girls." I give her a long once-over, moving slowly over her gorgeous legs. "What a match."

"Spice Girls would take the W." Her voice is more breathless, raspy.

Our chests rise and fall against one another. My hands slide to her wrists at her side. There are a thousand things I want to do with Sulli, and a thousand chances I let slip by.

It's not too late, Nine.

My lips practically dance over hers. "You remember that time we switched workout playlists?"

"And I had to swim to Bach?" She drinks me in. "While you worked out to *All Saints* and *S Club 7* for a whole month."

I smile into a laugh. "And I played 'Bring It All Back' on repeat. Security gave me such shit—"

Sulli slugs my shoulder with actual force. For swearing.

Fudge-nugget.

I rub my arm and mock wince. "Not holding back; are you, Lady Meadows?" I used to call her *Lady Meadows* at times when we were just friends. I stopped while we were on rocky grounds after her breakup with Will. But recently, I've been able to see she *really* likes when I say it.

Her cheeks flush. "Just waiting for you to call me *strong* bean."

"I never said you weren't strong," I tell her deeply, because I *love* how physically powerful Sulli is. I kiss the cut of her bicep.

She drops my AirPod, flustered. "Cumbuckets."

We leave Mozart playing on the ground and her girl band playing from the dangling cord on her shorts. Why she hasn't gone wireless—that's just Sulli hating to charge cordless earbuds. She says it's a pain in the ass.

A couple inches taller, I rest a forearm over her head and hold her wrist at her side with my other hand. Staring down at Sulli, I can't help but smile.

I love her strength, but I love the crinkles in her brows and the peeking smile when I say, "But you're also the stringiest string bean that ever did—"

Her hand flies to my mouth. "Take it fucking back."

I press my body closer against Sulli, driving her shoulders further against the boxing bag. We're melded together, and even with the collapse of her collarbones and the breathy "fuck" from her lips—she keeps her hand over my mouth.

So I lick her palm.

"Kits!"

She slugs me again.

I laugh.

Shit—I mean, *shoot* (I need to practice this punishment in my head, unless I want a bruised arm all year).

And I needed that laugh.

I needed this.

You need her, Nine.

She wipes her wet palm down my shirt, tracking the lines of my abs. Tension pools between us, but we stay still.

Quietly, I ask, "Do you care that I switched Banks to Maximoff's detail today?"

"He had to go, right?" Sulli asks.

"Yeah," I breathe. "He's still the floater, and Farrow got a med call."

"It's not like you did it out of spite, then *I'd* care."

I expel a strained breath. "I couldn't do that to him—even if I wanted to spend a millennium beside you. Banks is..." I grimace. "*Good.*"

"That doesn't make you bad, Kits," Sulli says strongly. "Your heart is one of the biggest I've ever fucking known."

I tilt my head, smiling. "That's because my heart has always been the biggest around you."

Sulli inhales that declaration and wears an expression like she's falling backwards.

I still clasp her wrist, and I'm not letting her descend without me.

She glances back towards the gym's entrance, which is locked. "I don't know if you heard yet, but Winona texted me that Ben is okay."

Ben Cobalt was hit hard during hockey practice, pitfalls of the sport. And hence, the medical emergency that whisked Farrow away from his job in security. But I haven't heard any updates yet. Partially because the med team—aka Farrow, his father, and his uncle—keep medical reports confidential.

"Any broken bones?" I ask Sulli.

"None. Just slightly concussed." She explains, "Apparently, Farrow said it's not a bad concussion, but since it's Ben's second one, he's going to monitor him all day."

Which means Banks is on Maximoff's detail all day. Giving me more alone-time with Sulli than I've had in a while.

Sulli uses her free hand to push hair off her shoulder. "I'm fucking hot."

"You definitely are," I whisper, cutting more distance between us with my lips. They brush along hers, then travel lightly over her jaw, down the nape of her neck. Her familiar chlorine and sweet scent dizzy me in a heady rush. Our eyes meet, and I imagine stripping Sulli naked.

Right here.

Bare.

Filling her until she whimpers that pleasured *whimper*. Shi—*hoot*, I'll never get enough of those noises Sulli makes. As though every new and overwhelming touch is welcomed with a cry of *I can't take it but I want more.*

"Kits…" Sulli breathes hard.

I close my lips around her soft skin.

She shudders. "*Fuck.*" And her breathy curse turns into a gasp as I stretch her arms above her head and pin her wrists to the boxing bag.

"Wait," Sulli cuts in, and I immediately drop her wrists.

"You okay?" I skim her fast. *What'd I fudging do? Is she okay?* I'm having flashbacks of our first kiss outside the motel. When she backed up from me, but I doubt she's harboring another short-term secret like the one about kissing Banks.

The three of us are so far beyond that.

I didn't go slow enough with her.

Crap.

Crap.

Sulli needs slower. She's had sex a whopping *three* times, and I'm over here pinning her arms up again like she's used to this shit—*stuff.*

This stuff.

"Yeah—oh hey, Kits, I'm *really* okay. I don't want you to think I don't like that."

"I do think it."

"It's *hot,*" she emphasizes. "It was bad timing on my part…I just want to…" Face flushed, Sulli fumbles with the music in her shorts. She turns off *Spice Girls.* "That's all."

I relax in one breath.

And I end up smiling. "You're letting Mozart beat Sporty Spice?" I name her favorite Spice Girl.

"This one time, yeah. I just know what Mozart and Bach and all the classicals mean to you."

That washes over me. We stare at each other with deeper memories, and I blink back some burgeoning feeling that pricks my eyes. Sulli has been one of the closest friends to me over the years, and I let her into my life, even when other guys cautioned me "don't get close to your client" and "don't be a buddy-guard"—I never thought twice about being friends with her.

It just came naturally.

Like the day Sulli asked why I listen to classical jams during workouts and not rap or throwback hip hop (my go-to genres).

The answer: my mom.

Growing up, I'd spend hours in a Muay Thai gym. One that closed in Philly a little bit after she retired. And I'd watch her train with Bach, Beethoven, and everything in between playing in the background. She loves this music, and so these songs became synonymous to martial arts and her.

Sometimes, I come back to them for nostalgia. To remember those idyllic childhood days gone by.

Other times, I come back to them to feel close to her. Even though she's only a state away, it's always felt like she's wanted to add greater distance between us. To emotionally detach for *my* sake ever since her health took a toll.

Mozart grows louder in the gym and in our quiet. I move back up against Sulli.

Being physical with her is just as overwhelming for me. Like plunging head-first in ice-cold water. I spent so long denying and resisting my feelings that giving in now is a head-rush.

Sulli whispers, "Kits…if you could do anything to me now, what would you do?"

I thumb the hem of her shirt. "I'd strip you. Layer by layer…" I clasp her squared jaw, her lips parting in an aching breath that ripples through me. "Until you're bare against me." Our intimacy is laced with years of friendship, of teasing and pulling, and as we skate towards bearing our bodies, a vulnerability hangs between us that I can feel Sulli gripping on.

"The only security cameras are outside, right?" Sulli asks.

"Right."

"So what are you waiting for then?" Sulli says in challenge.

"The *okay* from you," I whisper, not about to push her in a direction she's not ready for.

Sulli breathes the word like its erupting inside her, "Okay." And I immediately pull her tee over her head. Tossing it aside. As I slowly, *slowly* slide the shorts down her thighs and long, long legs, Sulli touches the back of her sports bra.

"Should I…?" She hesitates. "Or…should you?"

"Me," I kiss her lips, then whisper, "Just watch me. Don't think, string bean."

Sulli lets out a tiny, aroused noise. "Fuck." She places a hand on her forehead, watching as I squat down to slip her shorts off each ankle. I kiss her calf, then up to her thigh, and I graze my fingertips up towards her panties.

Standing fully upright again, my muscles burn, already dying to be against her body. I slide her sports bra over her head. She reaches for my hands, and I hold them and bring her to my chest. "You okay?" I ask in a deep whisper.

"I'm cold," she admits with a laugh.

I smile into a laugh too, and I rub her arms, adding friction. Her tits are driving me wild, but I want to warm Sulli up. She hugs onto me like a koala bear, and I'd rather not detach her.

Gently, I bring us to the mats with a slow kiss. Her shoulders rest against the mat, and I break apart her legs with my knees. While she's only in cotton panties, I shed my shirt, and I return to her mouth. Heat brews between us, as we kiss and I grind.

Her goosebumps vanish.

Breath is hot and heavy, and life feels wrapped around us.

"Sulli," I almost groan.

I clasp her wrists and pull them above her head again. Only now, she's on the floor, and I look into her eyes that swirl with pleasure. I see how she intakes our bodies. How I'm fit between her legs, how her thin panties barely hide her pussy.

And so I ask, "Have you ever pictured this?"

"Yeah." Her breasts push up higher with her lungs. "A lot more recently." She squirms under me.

Blood pumps into my dick. Hardening, I breathe through my nose, and Sulli continues, "I've thought about being naked in your gym…and you doing what you want to me. Taking me…"

"Like *Blue Lagoon*," I tease.

She makes a face like I've dissed the pinnacle of cinema. "Kits—" Her own gasp cuts her off because I've reached down and pushed aside her panties. Two of my fingers circle her clit, and she writhes again at the new friction and sensitivity. "*Holy fuck.*"

Her breathing is all over the place.

I stop touching to pin her arms up again, and as my lips meld against hers, she tries to buck into me. I grind down, thrusting forward. My shorts and her panties separate us, but the illusion is magma in my veins. And Sulli's eyes nearly roll.

"Fuck, fuck," she cries. "Kits, can you…I need…" She tries to reach down and move her panties, but I keep her arms braced.

"Not yet," I breathe, our eyes meeting with headiness. "I'm going to make you feel good, Sulli. Just like you've imagined." I lean down more and whisper against her ear, "You feel me? I'm going to slip my cock inside you and drag each inch in and out so slowly, until you forget what day it is. How does that sound?"

"*Fuck me,*" she cries. "Please."

I smile. "Lady Meadows, *language.*"

"*Kits.*" She digs up into me.

I cup her breast. "You have beautiful tits, Sul."

She smiles into a breathy sound. "Sir Kitsuwon, *language.*"

Our smiles weld in a kiss, and I slip off my shorts and underwear. I taste her excitement, her lust and love, and I crave to be closer. To be deep. To forget all worries and stresses and torments. To just be *one* with her.

While I root her arms above her, I stretch her legs further open, and I whisper against her lips, "Don't forget to breathe." I pull the fabric of her panties aside, not taking them completely off her, and I tease a finger into her heat.

She doesn't just feel soaked. She feels swollen. Aching.

Her legs vibrate. "Kits."

I arch my waist forward into Sulli, driving my erection between her legs. *Her wetness.* The warmth and tightness wrap around me, and I flex my muscles as she contracts.

Pulsing.

Pulsing.

"*Kits,*" she cries, wriggling in my hold.

I thrust, dragging my cock in and out like I promised. She gasps into a softer moan, "*Fuck.*" The hypnotic tempo lights up my core.

Sullivan Minnie Meadows.

The girl I dedicated my life to protect.

I have her bare under me, and I'm fucking her with deep, long strokes. And I almost can't believe we're here. Together.

I'm hanging on to her. *Don't go anywhere, Sulli.* And I wonder what it'd take for this to implode. Because I would lose *every* company, every business—even my gym—if it meant that I still have her this close, this intimate, this soul-bearing and deep.

This'll last.

Us.

Together.

It has to.

I go slow but lift her leg higher. I enter further.

"*Holy fuck,*" she cries. "*Oh fuck.* Oh fuck." Tears crest her eyes. "Akara—*Kits,* it's…I can't…" She jerks in my hands.

I let go of her wrists just to see what she'll do.

She covers her face.

"Sulli," I whisper, still rocking in and out. "Give me."

I grasp her wrists again, prying her hands off her face. Her hips buck up into me. The sensation strikes my brain. *Fudge-it. Ah.*

I blink back stars, and I grind further inside Sulli. With two more pumps, she comes in a high-pitched cry, and I hold her against me while her breath comes down.

"Was that good for you?" she asks.

"Understatement," I smile and gently pull out.

"You didn't come, though?"

"Because I wasn't wearing a condom. And I'm not ready for a literal *mini*-Meadows to be running around here."

"Me either." She eyes my dick. "You want me to blow you?"

I smile at her reddened cheeks, but her words are a fist jerking me off. "Another time." I reach for my shorts. "I just really wanted to get you off, Sul."

"What if I want to get you off?"

My smile grows.

Before I can answer, she says, "You can come on me."

The heat in the room kicks up at her words. My dick still throbs, wanting a release, and she must clearly see that.

"*Please*," she begs.

That does me in. I start fisting myself, and she watches with a heady gaze, lips parted. She tries to reach down, and with my free hand, I clasp her wrist in mine. A whimper catches at the back of her throat and tips me over. Everything that has mounted meets a combustible peak and I come on her chest.

She's grinning like I just gave her a bouquet of roses. *I love her.*

Breathing heavier, I pick up a nearby gym towel and wipe her up. "I'm going to have to tell Banks about this," I mention. "We agreed to be honest with each other."

"I fucking like that actually." She watches as I pull on my shorts. "Do you think you'll go into detail about coming on me?"

I look her up and down, but her body language isn't letting anything through. "Do you want me to?"

Her eyes flit to the ceiling in thought. "I guess it'd be kind of hot knowing you told him about coming on my tits. And vice-versa."

My brows shoot up. "He came on your tits?"

"Oh, fuck. No. I meant *hypothetically*."

I smile. "Hypothetically, yeah, that'd be hot." I do get off imagining Banks and her together. I get off even more seeing it. I'm aware of my turn-ons more than I was. And I know Banks feels the same.

I'm about to mention this, but the worst *fudging* sound cuts into Mozart and our hot and sweet moment.

A phone chime.

My phone, to be exact.

Sulli cranes her neck, eyeing my cellphone on the mats.

I glare at it.

"You should see who it is," Sulli encourages. "It's probably important, seeing as how you're a very important person."

"You're the VIP of my life." I lean back down over Sulli to kiss her lightly. "Can't keep trying to turn that one back around on me, Sul."

"Sure I can." Her tenacity swells my lungs.

The chime sounds again, alerting me of the same missed message.

I give her a soft, apologetic smile. "Hold on." Sitting up off Sulli, I reach for my phone and grab the cell.

She props herself on her forearms.

For a second, I panic thinking Price heard about my relationship with my client. Today is not the day that I want to go to war with Daisy Calloway's bodyguard, who also owns Triple Shield.

As soon as I skim the text, I relax knowing it's not about security. Our news hasn't reached the Cobalt brothers (besides Beckett) or Triple Shield yet.

"Who is it?" Sulli asks.

"My mom." I read the text out loud, *"Everything good here. Don't worry."*

Worry crests her eyes. "Has she been doing alright?"

"As far as I know." I spot goosebumps on Sulli, and I grab the nearest article of clothing. *My shirt.* She rises, our legs interlocking like we plan to do sit-ups together, and I pull my shirt over her head. Baggy on her frame, she fits her arms through the holes while I add, "But that can change at any moment."

"Do you want to visit her?"

I run a hand through my black hair. "I don't have the time." I immediately feel the guilt in those words. "She's in New York. I'm in Philly." I glance at my gym office, where I should be shuffling through the P&L for last month.

I don't move an inch, though.

Am I not worthy of my mom or this gym if I just want to shirk everything aside to extend my time with Sulli?

I say tightly, "I can't close that distance with how much crap I have going on here." I grimace and let out a groan. "Fu—*frick*, I sound like a horrible son."

She shakes her head, a small smile cresting her lips from my *almost* curse slip-up. "You're not. You're really fucking busy. I'm sure she understands that."

Mozart switches to Beethoven on my playlist, and I can't kick the guilt that's kicking me. I stare longer at Sulli.

"You've got that look," Sulli says.

"What look?"

"The 'you want to tell me something' look." She touches her ankle bracelet absentmindedly. "You get these little wrinkles right between your eyebrows." She touches the spot on my face.

I scrunch my brows more. "How long has that been going on?"

She laughs. "It's not an affliction, Kits. It's fucking cute. Sexy, even." She wags her brows.

"*Sexy* is you wearing only panties on the mats underneath me." I lift up my palms. "In my hands."

"In your hands," she repeats with a growing smile. "Yeah, fuck, that's definitely the hottest thing. You win, *this time*." Seriousness reappears as our eyes lock in a solid beat. "Am I right though? You need to tell me something?"

I rub my palm. "Maybe it's not *just* time that's keeping me from visiting her," I confess. I pause, gauging how Sulli is taking this. Her rapt attention wields no judgment. It pushes me forward, and I continue, "She left me, Sul. She made that choice to leave Philly when she was having health problems. She knew I couldn't follow her, but she left anyway." My muscles tighten. "I don't have an urge to go visit someone who chose to be around her siblings over her own son. Especially after my dad died."

Sulli holds my ankle consolingly. "I understand being hurt by the people you love. Icing them out. I think I might be really fucking good at that."

I think about her recently repaired friendship with Beckett. "You fixed that, though. I'm not sure I want to fix this, Sul."

She frowns. "What if your mom gets *really* sick? You won't even visit her then?"

I hold my breath. "If I tell you I won't, will you think worse of me?"

Her fingers slide against my calf. "No, of course not, Kits. But I will try fucking hard to change your mind. Because I do think that's something you'd regret."

Maybe.

I don't know.

I place a hand atop her head in affection. "My little *fucking* conscience."

She smiles. "I'm not that fucking little." She slugs my arm pretty hard. "And that's for the curse." Yeah, yeah, yeah. I fudged it up.

On purpose.

"I was thinking," Sulli says, "you need a manager, and I could use a job."

"You want a job?"

"It'd be nice to have a new goal where my family starts treating me like I'm a capable, responsible adult." She's still pissed her dad is treating her like a little girl. "But maybe it'd be a bad idea. You hiring me might not look like I earned it."

"Good because you're overqualified."

She crinkles her nose. "What? How?"

"You're an Olympian," I remind her with a smile. "You're more suited to run some fitness classes than to manage this place."

Her green eyes bore into me. "I just want to fucking help. You and Banks watch out for me all the time—"

"Literally our job," I twirl a piece of her hair around my finger.

She smiles. "But I'd like to be a positive fucking force in your life, too."

"You're already a positive force, Sul. You're…" I take a deeper breath. "You're what keeps me moving. Besides SFO, you're all I've got here."

She scoots closer and wraps her arms around me. I fit mine around her. My chin rests on the top of her head. It feels good to hold her. It feels like home.

And then a phone starts ringing.

I glare, about to disable every single phone on this planet. We're going back to the stone ages. For my sanity.

"It's mine," Sulli realizes, reaching for her phone.

We break apart a little while she checks Caller ID. Now I'm asking, "Who is it?"

"*Unknown*, but it says they're calling from Philly." She goes ahead and answers. "Hello?" Phone pressed to her ear, I can't hear anything.

Her brows jump. "Yeah…yeah, I'm definitely interested…wow." She starts smiling.

I'm more cautious.

It's the bodyguard in me.

"Thanks, yeah. Sure…I'll look out for the email. Bye." She hangs up, grinning. "That was the swim coach from Warwick University."

Shock arches my brows. "Warwick?"

"It's a private school in Philly."

"Yeah, I know that one. It was one of the few colleges I applied to way back before I bailed on the idea of college." I pause to consider something. "They have a really good music program."

"Is it the college that gave you a music scholarship for drums?"

I smile, realizing she remembers an offhanded comment I must've made years ago. "Yep, same one."

She refocuses back on her phone with the kind of Sullivan Meadows *focus* that has been documented extensively online. Her grin returns in full.

I ask, "Did the coach want you to swim for Warwick's team?"

"No." She checks her email. "Apparently, they have a couple of Olympic hopefuls on the team." She glances up to me. "He's looking for an assistant coach, and he wants me to help train them."

The Sulli I know would have a hard time training someone else for a competition that she's still fit to compete in. But a lot has changed since she retired from swimming, and I'm not sure she's in the same headspace.

"You've been looking for a job. Sounds like it's coming at the perfect time."

She nods. "It feels a little like fate farted in my face, and I'd be an idiot not to take notice."

I smile. "Do I need to have a talk with fate? It can't just be farting around you like that."

She laughs, then says, "I told him to send me the info. I think I'm gonna do it, Kits."

Looks like we're headed to college.

A path I thought I left in the dust. But I'm prepared to protect my girlfriend wherever life takes her next.

I stand and hold out my hand for Sulli. As she grabs tight, I tell her, "I'll lead the way."

15

Banks Moretti

FALL ON A COLLEGE CAMPUS. Yellow, orange, burnt red leaves landscape old brick buildings and the grassy quad. Straight out of a university pamphlet.

Pamphlets that I'd more likely use to blow my nose in than actually read. Nuns at Saint Joseph's didn't bother even talking to me or my brother about college.

We couldn't even afford tuition to the private Catholic school without clocking in hours of volunteer work at bingo halls and canned food drives.

College was for the rich.

For some bougie fuck down the street.

Not me.

What a fuckin' life—look at me now. I flip a college ID over in my hand, my gorgeous mug staring back at me. Not in all my twenty-nine years did I think I'd be given one of these.

After Sulli accepted the assistant coach position at Warwick University, the three of us needed to be logged into the university system. The IDs act as keycards for all the buildings. Including the gym, fit with a competition-sized pool.

I'm here as security. Here to protect Sulli. And this is almost better than being enrolled. No college tuition fees, no mid-terms to pull my hair out over, and I have A+ perks rather than D- grades.

I'm talking *free* collegiate paraphernalia.

The administration has been overly kind to me and Akara, considering we're just bodyguards to their new swim coach. And they loaded us up with an overflowing tote bag.

I carry that tote now.

Black and red water bottles, T-shirts with the "war horse" mascot and the Latin motto *vincit qui se vincit*; notebooks, pens, plastic cups, *tin* cups, sunglasses, koozies, and more. Stuff I don't need.

Stuff that I can't believe fits into one fucking bag.

But Lord knows I like some free shit.

I fit on the black baseball cap.

Welcome to college, Banks Roscoe Moretti.

Our destination: the gym.

"Is this what orientation is like?" I ask Akara while we saunter across campus like we're seasoned students. Settled in, milking this shit for all its worth.

Students chitchat with friends, carrying books and bags of their own, entering and exiting stately brick buildings with either purpose or unhurriedness. Thought I'd stick out like a pimple, but the age range is vast, considering undergrad and grad students mix in with the professors.

And I've already walked past a couple athletes who came close to my height.

Akara wears a red *Warwick U* ballcap and types on his phone, not taking in the atmosphere like me. "How would I know?" he asks. "I never went to college either."

"I thought you toured one?"

"As a bodyguard, not a future student." He glances up from his cell, just as most students disperse quickly into buildings like classes are about to start.

Don't envy that.

Reminds me that I never regretted missing out on college. Like my dad and grandpa before me, the military was always gonna be my path.

Wedged between a dining hall and the Eastcrest "athlete" dorms, the glass-domed gym stands like a proud monument on campus. Alumni must throw their money at *brawn* over *brains* here.

Good thing my girl is legendary when it comes to brawn.

Only sad thing, Sulli isn't here with us. She's back at the penthouse while we're doing some recon of the area before her job officially begins.

I hawk-eye the gym entrance where a couple students are gathered. Like they're waiting for something or someone, these two guys loiter outside the glass doors. Backpacks strapped to their broad swimmer's shoulders, the curly-haired, lean-cut one grips a pair of goggles and the buffer one sports a *Warwick Swim* T-shirt.

They both turn to us as we approach.

"Keypad isn't working," Curly Top tells us. "Someone should be here in a second to open the doors." He studies our ballcaps, then my Warwick tote bag. "Are you a new student? God, please tell me you're not a swimmer."

"Not a swimmer," I reply, avoiding the first question. Getting a better look at Curly Top, I spot a mole on his chin and recognize him from the roster that the head coach sent us yesterday. I've memorized the faces of every swim team member.

Garrett Winthrope.

His last name sounds like a cough drop.

He blows out a relieved breath. "Seriously, man, you scared me for a second. You're what six-six?"

"Six-seven."

"Yeah, I can't compete with that."

Garrett is a hair shorter than Akara, who's six-two.

Gotta say, we're *blending* all too well at college. Our mic cords are tucked behind our ears, threaded beneath the collars of our shirts. Neither Garrett nor his buff friend have questioned the sharp-eyed, observant pieces of us that make us bodyguards and not just easygoing students.

Sulli will be around these guys—hell, she's about to be *coaching* them. So I take mental notes of which one looks dickish.

There's always one.

The buff guy lightly elbows Garrett's ribs. "You know who you *definitely* can't compete with, Gar?" He smiles. "Our new assistant coach."

Akara stifles a smile beside me. Sullivan's reputation as a badass has reached Warwick University. Can't say I hate hearing people talk her up. The whole world should know how incredible she is.

Garrett flushes. "Neither can you, Ray. She's an Olympian."

Ray laughs. "Yeah, her pussy is practically made of gold."

I grind on my teeth. Found the smug-looking, granola-eating dick. He's literally eating a granola bar while we wait.

"Isn't she a virgin?" Garrett asks.

Ray grins. "Yeah, even better."

They laugh.

I don't like these shitheads anymore. Not that I had them on the *nice* list. They were in fucking limbo, and they didn't even last long there.

Akara adjusts his baseball hat. To hide his glare.

Another student suddenly opens the door from inside.

"Finally," Garrett says in relief.

We all head into the gym, but Akara and I detour towards the office. He slips me a look. "Get used to that."

"What? People talking about her gold pussy?"

Heat hasn't extinguished from his glare. "No, guys being crude behind her back. I never told her what people said during the Olympics, but the shit I heard made me want a stiff drink every night."

I grunt. "Sounds like we're gonna be having a shit ton of fun."

"I'm *banking* on it." He smiles. "See what I did there?"

"Take my name in vain, yeah." The two of us command the hallway, student athletes and swimmers parting as we walk.

Once we reach the office, Akara raps his fist.

"It's open!"

I follow my boss inside.

Coach Ryan Reed is seated behind a mahogany desk and toiling over a stack of papers. Two buttons are undone at the top of his long-sleeved floral shirt, and his light brown hair has a dramatic fade on both sides, plus he has black gauges in his ears.

He's twenty-nine.

Just like me.

I knew that before I walked in here, but if someone asked me to play *Guess This Man's Age*, I'd say he was a college student. Not a *head* coach of a swim team.

Feels backwards.

Coach Reed pries his attention off his work. "You both made it, great." Seems friendly enough. "Did you get your student IDs?"

"Have them, and we already talked with administration," Akara says with the same friendly rapport. "We just need to walk around the facility and chat with some of the swimmers."

I thread my arms over my chest. Giving off the stiff bodyguard vibe, but while Akara talks, I'm inspecting the coach's office.

Covertly.

No photos of kids or of a wife or husband. Of course we did an extensive background check on Coach Reed before today.

He's not married.

Verified and confirmed.

But he could be in a long-term relationship. Since he's an "infrequent" social media poster (mostly uploading pool pics) Ryan Reed isn't a complete open book ready for us to flip through. And I know well and good that people harbor secrets.

Whether or not he's the kind of guy who'd shove a skeleton behind a wall—that's yet to be determined. All I know is that Sulli will be around him, and it doesn't hurt to be heedful and vigilant.

At first, quick glance, he appears ordinary.

Coach Reed stands up. "I can give you a tour."

"That's kind but unnecessary," Akara replies. "It'll be easier to get a feel for the space on our own."

He wavers for a beat. His cautious stance throws me off.

What does he have to be cautious about?

"Sullivan is safe here at Warwick. The team is excited to have her on board, and so am I."

First impression: I don't like him.

Maybe it's his unbuttoned shirt or perfectly styled hair or the fact that he looks more ready to be a lifeguard on Venice Beach than a collegiate swim coach.

"That's good to hear," Akara nods, authority puncturing his words. "Her safety is our first priority."

Yes, it is.

Coach Reed smiles. "I'm just happy she chose to come here for the job. Princeton was about to reach out to her before I made the call."

Princeton. Talk about *bougie*.

Sulli would have rejected the Ivy League invite on location alone. Warwick isn't a far drive from the penthouse and suits her better, even if it's a slightly smaller college.

"Do you have the key to her locker?" Akara asks.

"Right, yeah, it's over here." Coach Reed retrieves the key from a filing cabinet and hands it to Akara.

"Can I leave this here while we walk around?" I raise my tote bag. Do not want to haul this thing everywhere, but I'm not about to toss perfectly good cups.

"Yeah, no problem." He has trouble looking me in the eye. Intimidation is just the skin we wear, but I'm damn glad I'm intimidating him.

We leave at that.

Akara twirls the keyring around his finger. The hallway is quiet as we both slow our pace to take notes of exits, entrances, and security cameras. Akara logs some of the information on his phone, while I take the old-fashioned approach and jot in a small spiral notebook.

With a Warwick University pen.

This thing writes nice. Smooth crisp ink. Simple pleasures, man.

As we pass a *Fizzle* vending machine, Akara tells me, "I'm going to ask her out."

I click the pen, a bit surprised. "You're already dating her, Akara."

He cranes his neck behind us, ensuring no one is rounding the corner. We're alone. "On a *date*, Banks."

I scratch the pen against my jaw. "That kind of *asking out*."

Concern pulses behind his brown eyes. "I'm not asking for permission—"

"You don't have to," I interject. "Take her out. She deserves to be wooed and doted on and loved, and I'm just pissy 'cause I haven't even considered *where* I'm taking her yet—and I bet by the time I do, you'll be on date number thirty-seven."

Logistics.

Never been my specialty.

But they are his.

Akara takes his baseball cap off, pushing back his hair, then fits it on to ask, "Are you supposed to come along?"

I scrunch my brows. "On your date?"

"Yeah?"

"Do you want me to?" I wonder.

He asks, "Do *you* want me to join yours?"

I lift my shoulders as an answer.

"Yeah...that's where I am too." He sighs. "Either way, I think I'd be okay with it." He flips his phone in his palm. "This is really hard to figure out. I don't know the *right* way to do any of this shit."

I feign slugging his shoulder for cursing.

He doesn't even flinch.

So I pat his back. "Survived this time."

"Every time," Akara says like a promise.

"Amen."

I can only hope.

He checks his phone, scrolling, and the strange, constipated look on his face goads me to ask, "What are you looking at?"

"Don't worry about it," he says too fast, pocketing his cell.

"Christ Almighty, I used to *love* that phrase," I say, rocking forward on my feet towards him, "*don't worry about it, Banks. I've got it, Banks.*

Now it's as ugly and grating as the face you just made two seconds ago."

He glares.

"Give me your phone."

"No," he scoffs. "This isn't a negoti—*Banks.*" He cuts himself off and raises the phone above his head after I try to steal the thing. "I love you, but you accidentally break my phone, you die."

"You are way too attached. It's like a fuckin' parasite. Clinging to you with its 1s and 0s. Where's the fucking scalpel?"

"*Banks.*"

"If Sulli were here, she'd try to cut if off you first."

"Well, she's not here." He expels a sharper breath, then rolls his eyes. "*Fine.*" Something I said does the trick. Not sure what it was, but he lowers his arm and shows me his phone. "I was doing a quick social media check."

Twitter, I see.

"Those are your notifications?" I ask what I'm staring at.

"Yep." His jaw tenses.

I skim the tweets about him…and her. And they read like this:

Sulli & her bodyguard are THE PERFECT match imo! Total stan here.

Kitsulli 4Ever!

Omg can you imagine how beautiful Akara & Sulli's babies would be? Puh-lease let it happen!!

There's no way Sulli and her bodyguard aren't dating. The chemistry is off the charts. So obvious.

Akara isn't fooling anyone. He's definitely into our Sullivan Meadows.

And on and on and on.

The public praise is hardly newsworthy. They've been rumored to be a pairing for a while, even before our trip to Yellowstone.

I push his phone back to his chest, and we scan our surroundings, then move.

Humor has already drained fast as we stop in the middle of the hallway, right next to a set of double doors that leads to the pool room.

Something serious lingers between us. Something raw.

Very quietly, he says, "I don't want you to ever feel second-best to me when it comes to her." They have history together.

They have pre-existing love.

It doesn't hurt to know or see. And I'm not living in fear that it will.

I drop my voice another octave. "Sulli has never made me feel like that." Not for one damn second, not for one fucking moment. She has only ever made me feel irreplaceable, invaluable, *worthy*. And I'm not seeking a first-place prize or a trophy.

I live for the beat of my heart, and it beats at a wild, unafraid, unfathomable pace around her.

Akara worries though. "Other people could make you feel lesser than."

He worries for the same reason my brother does. He knows I'm constantly compared to another human being as a twin. And I'm the *dispensable* one, and by God, I've already proven that fuckbag of a father wrong.

My life isn't a waste.

"If anything," I tell my best friend, "being compared to Thatcher for twenty-nine years has me prepared as hell for the day the world compares me to you." I smack his chest. "And the only people who matter to me are her and you, man. The rest can rank me at bottom two."

I don't even mind being called a zero.

To Sulli, I'm more.

To Akara, I'm more.

To my family, I'm more.

To myself, I'm everything. Hell, I'm all I have when I'm alone. I better be happy with who I am.

Akara nods strongly.

We wield a love for one another that has no words. Just a feeling. He wouldn't be so pressed about what other people are gonna think of me if he didn't care.

He squeezes my shoulder as he pushes open the double doors. The smell of chlorine hits me all at once. Eight swimming lanes are roped off in the pool. Half are filled as students practice.

To Akara, I whisper, "If you go on a date, you should put me on someone else's security detail for the night. It'll take some stress off you and actually let you enjoy the night for a change. Hell, maybe you'll be able to make it through the date without getting a phone call."

His lip quirks. "Unlikely."

It's partly my fault that my dad has been speed-dialing Akara. Couple days ago, Akara officially put me on Sulli's *permanent* detail with him.

I'm no longer a floater.

No longer the man rushing to Maximoff's detail, if Farrow receives a med call.

Change keeps me on my toes where I like to be.

This change I love even more.

Farrow's sour over the transfer, and I can't blame him when I was his best substitute every time he was pulled away from his husband's detail.

Now Maximoff will have temps.

But with my dad training temps like they're SEAL recruits, the fresh blood is looking more qualified, and Akara plans to hire more bodyguards to the 24/7 roster.

One day Security Force Omega will grow to more than just seven men, but the recruits have to get through my dad first. And I grew up with him. He's not easy.

Not in the least.

He wants *constant* communication with Akara, and I can see it wearing my friend down.

I did reach out to my dad.

Through text.

I said, hope all is going well.

He replied, it is. We should grab lunch next time you're free. Let me know when's good for you.

I sent, K.

Haven't solidified any plans to meet-up for tea and crumpets and a side dish of painful family history, and I'm not sure I'm ever going to.

After Akara and I walk a couple laps around the pool, we scope out the unisex locker room. Garrett and Ray are back here chatting, and when they spot us, their conversation dies immediately.

"Wait," Garrett says. "I thought you guys aren't swimmers."

"We're not," Akara states.

I find Sulli's new locker, and Akara hands me the key.

"Hold on," Ray says. "Why are you opening the assistant coach's locker?"

Ladies and Gents, this is the fun part. I smile as I look to him. "We're Sullivan Meadows' bodyguards." *Dick.*

Ray pales.

Garrett says, "Shit."

I click open the locker. An avalanche of stuffed animals tumbles out. I go rigid, muscles tensing. *You've got to be shitting me.* I pick up the *Sasquatch* plushie. A small plastic gold medal tied around its neck. Anger brews in my chest.

Before I became a floater, I used to protect the kid who's constantly revered for his beauty. Xander Hale never had a bunch of shitbags stuff Sasquatch plushies in his locker.

Worse, even, they're fucking with my girlfriend.

"Who did this?" Akara nails a glare on them.

Garrett smears a hand down his mortified face. "Uh, you know… the whole team? It's a welcome to Warwick kind of thing."

I narrow my gaze. "Is that the new definition of hazing these days?" I crouch down and scoop up as many plushies in my arms as I can.

Naughty list for life, the whole damn team. They're lucky I'm a bodyguard and can't incite a fight, or else they'd be on the fucking ground.

"They have gold medals around their necks," Ray says. "We're honoring her. She's a legend, man."

"We'll let her know," Akara says with a lethal bite. "But let's be clear here, don't *fuck* with her locker. You can pass that along to the team." His threat comes in clear, and I'm making an exception for the "no swearing" bet he lost.

He can curse when protecting Sulli.

Nothing says, *back off or eat pavement* like *back the fuck off.*

I trash the plushies in the nearest garbage can.

Akara relocks her locker just as Garrett and Ray vacate the room quickly, probably scared shitless they'll get in more trouble. Sulli's not a teammate.

She's their *coach.*

I dump the last Sasquatch. "Are we telling her about this? I'm asking from boyfriend to boyfriend. Because I want to." She should know and be prepared. Relying on us is fine (I'll always have her six), but Sulli wants to rely more on herself these days. It means being more aware of threats around her, more than her dad ever let her see, more than Akara did too in the past.

"From boyfriend to boyfriend, I think we should." He steps away from the locker. "They didn't seem malicious, but she can go into the job with a firmer hand if she knows they're not respecting her position."

I bob my head, agreeing.

Comms sound off. "Been surfing through fandom sites," Donnelly says with a thick South Philly lilt, "and I saw something important online."

Akara clicks his mic. "Text it to the group chat."

My phone buzzes.

"Done."

Check this link. Flag as high-risk? — Donnelly

What do I know about Paul Donnelly?

I know he's from the same town as me, and even my broke as hell family wouldn't associate with people like the Donnellys, gun to our heads.

But Akara and Thatcher told me what I've found to be true. Donnelly has the one trait you can't teach or pray for or force inside a bodyguard.

That knockout, hand-to-heart empathy.

He cares about these famous families like their hurt is his hurt. And he'd throw himself into oncoming traffic for every single one.

Donnelly wanting to flag a site means that the site is something with potential to harm.

Akara and I both open the link.

THE ROYAL LEAKS

We reveal all the truths about the American Royals. These are verified and come directly from the source.

ROYAL LEAK #1: Maximoff Hale is taking back his position as CEO of H.M.C. Philanthropies.

ROYAL LEAK #2: Jane Cobalt hired a new cat sitter.

ROYAL LEAK #3: Sullivan Meadows is on birth control.

#TodaysLeaks #omg #birthcontrol

I stare at those three leaks. All I know, for certain, is that number three is true. Don't know how the fuck this ended up on some random website.

Akara frowns. "Do you know anything about one or two?"

I shake my head. Maximoff's decision about going back to H.M.C Philanthropies has been up in the air for a while, and as far as I know,

Jane was still conducting interviews with cat sitters. I didn't think she hired one yet.

Akara's nose flares. "Could someone be making shit up?"

"How would they know she's on birth control?" I ask since this recently happened. After Akara and Sulli had sex without a condom at his gym, she wanted to be on the pill.

Her gynecologist wrote her the prescription. *I* picked up the pills from the pharmacy.

Sulli's footprint is nowhere near *birth control.* So how the hell did that leak?

"It's a good guess," Akara says tightly. "She did have a boyfriend."

I want to correct him that she *has* two boyfriends, but I can't do that in public. We're still *just* her bodyguards to the world.

I study the website. Colorful doodles of crowns, lipstick smudges, and the words *shhh!* make up a graphic header. Someone put effort into this shit.

Akara frowns and stares harder at his phone. "The thing is, if it's all true, it doesn't make it gossip."

I rake a rough hand across my jaw. "And if it's all true, how did they find out this information before *us?*"

Security's motto has always been *stay ahead of the media.*

Is the leaker even a part of the media? Who's running the site?

Akara motions me back towards a water fountain as a few swimmers climb out of the pool. I huddle closer to him as he lifts his mic to his lips. "Akara to Farrow and Thatcher, check the link Donnelly sent and confirm whether your client's leaks are real or rumor."

No surprise, Thatcher rogers up first. "Real. Jane just hired a cat sitter." My brother sounds tense. "She only told her family over the phone."

A phone leak?

Farrow comes in next. "Real."

"Redford," Oscar speaks. "The Husband is going back to H.M.C.?"

"Yeah. He already put in his final notice at the aquatic club." Maximoff teaches little kids how to swim. Guess that's ending.

Akara tips his head to me. "It might be a leak at Maximoff's workplace."

Kinda seems likely.

Oscar asks, "Kitsuwon, Real or Rumor?"

We exchange a hard look. Neither of us want to air Sulli's birth control on comms, but for the sake of letting SFO know all the leaks are real, Akara has to make that plunge into cement.

"I hate this," he tells me before he clicks his mic and tells them, "Real."

Before anyone else can interject, Akara adds, "I'm contacting the tech team. They'll trace the IP address. Until we know more, the site is flagged as a *watch*. Nice find, Donnelly."

"Thanks, boss."

I scroll through *The Royal Leaks* again. "I don't know much about gossip sites like this," I admit to my friend. I doubt it's high-trafficked like *Celebrity Crush* or *Us Weekly*. "Unless you're someone like Donnelly, will anyone find it?"

"If you're someone like Donnelly, you know how to make shit go viral," Akara says as he texts the tech team. "But there's only one post. Let's hope the leaker is either good at guessing or no one will take them seriously."

Yeah.

Let's hope.

Feels like that's where my chips are these days. All-in on hope.

16

Sullivan Meadows

"YOU ALREADY WARMED up at the barre?" I ask Beckett as he fixes his white tunic over ballet tights. His dressing room is small, complete with a vanity and clothes rack.

I sit on the extra stool. I haven't been backstage long, but I hoped to spend some time with my best friend before his performance as Romeo tonight.

Being around Beckett for so long, I quickly memorized his pre-performance schedule.

Hair and makeup. (He does his own.)

Warm-up with the other dancers at the barre.

Costume.

Take the stage.

"Yeah." He checks the analog clock ticking on the wall among ballet posters of *Swan Lake* and *Cinderella*. "I have about twenty minutes left. Never feels long enough." His yellow-green eyes land softly on me. "It's been a full week since you told your dad about your boyfriends."

He remembered. Beckett is hard on himself about using all his energy on ballet rather than family, but he is a great friend with the time he has.

Right now, my two boyfriends stand outside the closed dressing room with Beckett's 24/7 bodyguard, O'Malley. On-duty, they guard the door and give me some privacy with Beckett.

"Yep, one full fucking week." I lift my foot to the stool, hugging my leg. "And I'm nowhere closer to bridging any kind of silence. Even harder is still confronting my mom."

"I'd be shell-shocked if your mom didn't support you dating both Akara and Banks. She's a bigger risk-taker than you've ever been."

"I know," I say in a deep breath. "I hoped she'd understand me chasing after my heart, but I thought after a week, my dad would too."

I still hesitate to reach out to my mom. Her opinion will be the one that matters most. The one that soul crushes me if she expels even a fraction of the hostility that my dad did.

"It might take time." Beckett fixes strands of his dark brown hair, trying to smooth the wavier pieces down. "My dad has said that Uncle Ryke views the world through his own experiences. So he must have a harder time understanding things he can't personally relate to."

"Fucking great," I mutter, just as the door blows open.

I jolt, thinking Akara and Banks are bursting in for a security emergency, but in walks a face I'm *not* excited to see.

"Charlie." I try not to groan. His ploy to rekindle my friendship with Beckett might've worked, but he still *blackmailed* me in Montana.

I didn't fucking forget or appreciate the strongarming.

"Hello to you, too," Charlie says and gives a short goodbye wave. "Oscar." And then he shuts the door, leaving his bodyguard with ours. To Beckett, he asks, "You're on in twenty?"

Beckett affirms with a nod, stretching his arm to his foot, and Charlie lounges against the *Swan Lake* poster.

"You're staying?" I ask Charlie, bummed out. But for a second there, I thought I had Beckett all to myself for twenty awesome minutes. Selfish? Fucking *maybe*, but I miss being on good terms with Beckett and our one-on-ones.

"Don't sound so excited, Sullivan." Charlie massages his leg. His wrinkled, white button-down is half untucked in pink velvet pants like he woke up in yesterday's clothes.

"You're not my favorite person right now," I admit with a shrug.

Beckett stretches his left quad. "Told you not to blackmail her."

"Worth it," Charlie says simply.

Beckett slips me an apology. "If you want to be mad at someone, just be mad at me."

"No, I'm *done* being angry at you. I'd just like an apology from Charlie."

"You're not getting one," he states.

"On behalf of Charlie, I'm sorry," Beckett says with honesty and depth, and I sigh heavily, hating that Beckett has to make amends *for* Charlie.

That's not how apologies work.

"I guess I accept on your behalf," I say, because I love Beckett and I know he loves Charlie, and I'd rather not have a hate-fest on someone he loves right now.

Charlie is staring strangely at me. His lip is slightly corkscrewed, arms lightly threaded.

I crinkle my brows. "What…?"

"I heard you're no longer single."

Oh fuck.

"From who?" I turn fast to Beckett.

Confusion touches his face. "I didn't say anything to anyone, Sul."

Charlie answers, "I overheard Moffy and Jane before I sat down with them at breakfast."

"Breakfast?"

"At Lucky's Diner."

"Just the three of you?"

He shrugs like it's nothing, but holy fuck, they're like *really* friends now. Crystal clear evidence just keeps piling on and on, and I thought I'd be happy about Charlie reuniting with Moffy. But the powerhouse of this friendship tripod is fucking *terrifying*.

At least they're on my side.

Are they?

My roommates are all supportive but cautious which has made everything fucking awkward. These days, I spend a lot of time in my bedroom.

Now that Charlie knows the truth, I ask, "What do you think?"

Charlie tugs at his hair, glances for a brief second to Beckett, then says, "You're not ready to hear my opinion."

I bristle. "What does that mean?"

"Don't be an ass," Beckett tells his twin brother.

Charlie smiles. "My opinion is the asshole."

"More like you're the asshole," Beckett says smoothly and actually sweetly. He smiles over at his brother.

Charlie's lips rise even more. With a hand to his heart, he says, "Undisputable."

"Charlie," I chime in. "I want to hear your opinion. I can handle an asshole one."

Charlie taps his lips in thought before he says, "Only because Beckett's here, I'll let this opinion out freely, but I did warn you, Sullivan." He locks eyes with me. "I think it's great that you found love in two men. The fact that they're bodyguards—I don't really give a shit."

I sit on pins and needles. "Where's the asshole part?"

"I think to be in a polyamorous relationship *and* in the public eye, you need to be a certain type of person to survive. And quite frankly, I think you're too weak for it."

I go cold.

"Fuck you," I curse hotly.

He unfolds his arms, opens his palms. "You wanted to hear it."

"Yeah, I did," I mutter, frustrated that I'm letting his opinion cut deep. Who cares what Charlie thinks? I remember what Banks would tell me.

He doesn't know you like you know yourself.

And Akara's optimism, *We'll survive together.*

"His opinion isn't mine," Beckett suddenly says, the tone of his voice as melodic as the way he moves. "Charlie doesn't understand that you have courage and *grit*, especially towards the things and people you love, and if you love your boyfriends as much or more than you love your little sister—no one will get in your way."

I let that flood me, even as Charlie says, "Time will tell where this all ends anyway."

I drop my foot. "You know, Charlie, you have a fucking talent of making me feel like I'm at Tribal Council in *Survivor* about to get voted off the island."

"Hmm," he muses. "Are you projecting? Possibly you feel like you're not strong enough to be the sole survivor—"

"I'm not weak," I cut in. "And you're a dick."

"I am," Charlie flashes a smile. "That's the difference between you and me. I'm highly aware of my flaws."

"The ones you just let *fester* like ugly cysts that need ruptured?"

Charlie blinks. "Beckett might be right about your grit."

Beckett smiles softly at me, and after I exhale, I notice the mess of crushed Coca-Cola cans on Beckett's vanity. *That's odd.*

"What's with all the coke cans?" I ask, drawing Charlie's attention to the disaster too.

Beckett is usually very precise about his things. Plus, if our Uncle Stokes (the CEO of Fizzle) saw the coke products, he'd think Beckett has become the Judas of the family. Uncle Stokes is hardcore about marketing strategies for Fizzle.

Us promoting Coke Zero is not in that plan.

Beckett glances at the vanity, then rolls his eyes. "Leo." Annoyance coats that name. "He's been using my dressing room while his is being repaired for water damage. The asshole does *this*"—he motions a graceful hand to the coke cans—"on purpose."

I stand to grab the trash bin, but Charlie is swifter. Snagging the bin, he swipes the cans into the trash before I can, and I try not to stab a look into him.

But as Beckett's *best* friend, that was my friendship duty.

I plop back on the stool. "Does Leo know you have OCD?" I ask since it's not public knowledge.

"No," Beckett fixes his hair again with more frustration. "And I prefer it stays that way."

"It will," Charlie assures.

"Maybe Leo is jealous of you."

"You think?" Charlie says like I'm an idiot.

If I had a projectile, I'd throw it at him. *Actually.* I take off my sneaker and chuck. He dodges like I'm a child.

"Can you spell immature?"

"F-U-C-K."

Beckett laughs, then says to me, "He's definitely jealous of me, Sul. He wants what I have."

"Which is?"

"Looks, charm, talent," he says while lowering to the floor in a split and stretching forward. "He's pissed I took his role."

Beckett filled in for Leo Valavanis one night, and the company preferred his performance of Romeo over Leo's.

They switched spots.

Now Leo is his understudy. At least until the end of November. Then they go into production for the Nutcracker.

Beckett looks up from his stretch. "Leo hasn't come to terms with the fact that he doesn't measure up to me."

My lips lift. "Confidence or cockiness?" We'd ask the question all the time when one of us verged on the latter.

He matches my smile. "Both. And I missed this."

"Me too." It's been a long time since I've been backstage at one of his performances.

"Me three," Charlie says mockingly.

I take off my other shoe.

He flinches, and that's good enough for me.

Beckett laughs more, and we all chat for a little bit before Beckett zones in on the phone I toss between my hands.

"Just do it, Sul." He reaches for his foot on the ground. "You're not going to find a better time."

"After you're gone. I don't want to waste my time with you."

"It's not a waste to me." He nods me on in encouragement. "I don't like seeing you at war with the people you love."

Charlie makes a gagging noise.

I fling back, "How do you spell immature?"

"I-M-M-A-T-U-R-E," he says in point-one seconds, ending with a flat smile.

Keeping up with Charlie is pounding my head, and I find myself on automatic. Dialing a number, like I know who always gives me comfort and love.

I end the call fast. Before the second ring.

What are you doing, Sulli?

I push myself to do something more.

Bracing the phone in front of my face, I FaceTime my mom.

She answers on the first ring. "Sulli?" Her face breaks with hope and pain just seeing me, and I almost come undone. My vibrant, *gorgeous* mom is youth and sweetness and reckless inhibition, and memories crash against me of being so little and her being so young holding me as I cried over pickles.

Fucking *pickles.*

I hated all of them. Dill. Bread and butter. So fucking dumb. But Mom brushed her nose with mine and then tickled me until my tears morphed to laughs. And all my angsty, pickle-loathing feelings left me.

How good she always made me feel.

How happy I can be just seeing her, and I hate icing her out more than I've ever hated a single fucking pickle.

I wipe my runny nose. Wishing we were in the same room, but that's my fault. I could've come over and let her hug me. "I'm sorry it's taken me a while to fucking call back."

"No, *no.*" She rubs at her eyes. "Don't apologize. You can take all the time you need. I know I called too much—" Her voice cracks.

"No," I shake my head.

"I did," she nods. "I hated how much my mom hounded me growing up, and I didn't want to make you feel—"

"You didn't," I say fast. "You made me feel loved."

She exhales a tender breath. Smoke billows behind her head.

"Mom—is that smoke?"

She whips around. "Oh…shit." The video is blurry and out of focus as she deals with the crisis off-screen.

Beckett and Charlie have been talking quietly amongst themselves, but they overhear smoke and look to me.

"I think everything's okay," I tell them. "Is everything okay, Mom? *Mom?*"

"Yeah! Just burnt the quinoa." She reframes herself in the video. "Your dad has been struggling with going vegan."

Me too. I can't find the words, though.

"And I'm trying a new recipe that he'd definitely cook better than me. But I can't burn the avocado, so hey, he'll have something edible to eat."

I try to smile, but the weight of the rift still lingers. "I couldn't...I didn't listen to your voicemails."

She tucks a strand of blonde hair behind her ear. "That's okay." She nods a lot, but I can tell that hurt her.

It hurt to say. "I love you, and I'm just scared of what you have to say."

"Your dad told me everything." My mom can't keep still. She jumps on the counter, jostles the camera as I assume her feet swing. "What he did, how he reacted—it was so, *so* wrong. I wish I would've been at the quarry with you all."

"Me too," I say out loud this time.

She takes a short breath. "I don't agree with him. Your dad and I are different people, and I'll always love and support him, but that also means telling him when he's wrong."

Panic rips at me. "I don't want this to come between you and him. Please don't fucking fight over this—"

"We're not fighting," she assures quickly, then jumps off the counter. After rounding a bunch of potted plants in the house, she ends up at the window nook. "One thing I've learned about him is that you have to be patient. He needs time. That's all. In the meantime, you have me." She offers the prettiest smile, and I can almost feel her hug.

I breathe easier, knowing I haven't lost my mom. "I couldn't go through this if you reacted how he reacted too." *My dad told me to call my mom.* I realize now that he knew I needed her.

Maybe he even knew she'd support me.

"You don't have to wonder what that'd be like because it's gone, *poof*. Vanished." She mock gasps. "I never saw it. The strangeness of it all."

We share a warm smile.

And gently, I ask, "How much time do you think he'll need? Weeks, months...years?"

Goldilocks, a Golden Retriever, jumps on her lap. "I wish I could give you an answer. But the truth is that I don't know." She meets my eyes. "He just wants to protect you."

"I'm not a little girl anymore, Mom. I don't need him to fight all my battles. And me dating Akara and Banks shouldn't be a battle in the first place."

"Totally agree."

I inhale strongly, but her understanding can't completely mend the wound my dad created. Can I be at odds with my dad for more than a couple weeks? Not having him in my life is gut-wrenching. I want to tell him about my new job, and my swim times on the rooftop pool.

My mom whispers, "I love you, Sullivan. I want you to know that." Her eyes are glassed with tears.

Mine redden and burn, and I say deeply, "I really, *really* love them, Mom. It's World Series kind of stuff."

Her smile bursts across her face, eyes glass now with happiness. "It feels good, doesn't it?"

"Yeah," I say. "I believe it'll last, and that should be enough, right?"

"Indubitably," she says with a cute nod.

I'm about to update her on the coaching gig at Warwick University, but I check the time. Only a few minutes left with Beckett. "Can I call you later? To talk more?"

"I'd love that. You know I'm always here. Free. Just buzzing around. Trying not to burn food."

I laugh.

She blows me a kiss. "Take care, peanut butter cupcake."

"Bye, Mom." I blow her a kiss back.

We hang up.

"I'm not taking the piano," Charlie says to Beckett in mid-conversation. I didn't hear a lot, but I'm guessing this is about Grandmother Calloway's wedding present to their older sister. "Our apartment is crammed enough with Tom's shit."

"Jane says you play it every time you're over there," Beckett says, "so obviously you enjoy it."

"It's a nice piano," Charlie says, "that I enjoy *there*."

Beckett suddenly notices me off the phone. "How was that?"

"Bittersweet. My dad is the bitter part. Mom is sweet." My phone buzzes.

House meeting. Tonight. Required. – Thatcher

I make a face.

"What?" he laughs.

"Thatcher. Your brother-in-law is not the easiest roommate to live with. Yesterday, he made a chore list. I might've missed dish duty on accident." I grimace. "Granted, I was swimming on the roof, and I just lost track of time."

"He sounds like someone I'd actually want to live with," Beckett says.

"Let's trade him for Eliot," Charlie quips.

Beckett laughs with the shake of his head. "You would never, and neither would I."

Charlie doesn't disagree, but asks me, "What did Thatcher want?"

I pocket my phone. "I have a house meeting tonight. It seems serious, but it might just be another chore list."

A knock sounds on the door.

A girl with curly brown hair pulled into a bun and light golden-brown skin peeks inside. "Hi, sorry to be a bother. Beckett?"

"Roxanne," Beckett nods.

Charlie says a couple words in *Russian*.

Roxanne looks surprised but also in a hurry, just telling Beckett, "Curtain in three." She shuts the door, but we hear a squeaking sound.

"Did she slip?" Charlie asks Beckett.

"She's a little clumsy for a ballerina," Beckett says but also gives his brother a foreboding look. "Don't, Charlie."

"Don't, what?" Charlie knows what Beckett means.

"You promised to never fraternize with anyone at the company." Beckett stands up. "I work with Roxanne."

I chime in, "How do you know she understands Russian?"

"I told him," Beckett says to me. "Back when I thought he didn't like her."

"I don't like her," Charlie says. "I hardly know her, Beckett." He moves away from the wall. "And I would never break a promise I made to you."

But he'd blackmail *me*.

Don't be bitter, Sulli. They have a twin bond. Charlie would do absolutely anything for Beckett. And I realize outside the dressing room door, I have two men who'd do absolutely anything for me.

17

Akara Kitsuwon

Hi Mr. Kitsuwon,

I saw the "closed until further notice" sign on the door to Studio
9 Boxing & MMA Gym, and I wondered if you'd be interested
in selling? My son C.J. Bishop used to practice martial arts at
Studio 9, and as he graduates college soon, I'd like to help him
live out his dream of owning a gym and keeping the one he
loved so much alive.

At your best convenience, I'd love to chat more and
provide an offer you'll find substantial.

I GLAZE OVER THE rest of the email.

Here's my number blah blah blah *hope to talk soon.* Yeah.

I bet.

In the penthouse's kitchen, I hunch over the sink with my phone in
my fist, and even if I want to flippantly write this offer off, I can't stop
staring at the email.

A dad wants to kickstart his son's dream.

Is there poetry or symmetry in this offer? Is this what I *should* do?
This is an easy out.

The logical out.

Especially when it comes with *money*. The financial burden of Studio
9 will be gone, but so will my hand in a gym that *I* love.

The one that *I* built.

The one that I've never even considered selling.

Until now.

All of a sudden, a flat *tortilla* smacks my cheek. I cut my gaze to the left where Banks and Sulli have been hovering over bowls of guac and salsa. Jane and Maximoff made a whole "taco bar" on the kitchen counters for Taco Night.

Last I saw, Sulli was eating a vegan corn chip out of Banks' hand and giggling with the *cutest* smile—and that vibrant laughter should've taken my brain off of work.

But it didn't.

A tortilla to the face did.

They act like nothing happened, but I clearly see the tortilla lying pathetically in the sink. "What the H-E-double-hockey-sticks?"

Sulli snorts.

I straighten up, phone still in my fist. "Who threw a *tortilla* at me?"

"Me." Sulli bounces her brows. "I was testing the velocity of a tortilla. Fucking perfect projectile." She turns to Banks. "You think corn tortillas are slower?"

Banks picks up a corn tortilla. "Only one way to find out."

I point at him with my phone. "You don't know what you're about to start. You smack me in the face with a tortilla, Banks, and I'm not letting you out of here without retaliation."

"Bring it on." He chucks the corn tortilla at me.

I slip left. It splats against the forest-green cupboard, and we all explode into action. I fling the bowl of shredded lettuce at Banks' face.

He gets a mouthful of iceberg and Romaine, and Sulli pelts me with vegan chips, laughing. We're all laughing, and bowls clatter as food flies ceiling high. Ground beef splatters on the cupboards, my muscle shirt, my face, and I sling sour cream at Sulli and Banks with a spoon.

"Foul play! He's gone for the fucking dairy!" Sulli laughs.

We slip on the floorboards, slick with taco juices and sautéed onions.

Shoot.

We laugh and grab onto each other for support before we reignite the food fight. Every concern, every stress, and burden retreat to make way for the ecstasy that explodes inside of me.

I'm not thinking about my gym.

Or money.

Or SFO and security.

It's just me and Sulli and Banks. On our peaceful island together— where no crap can reach us. Where every dang thing makes sense.

With guacamole all in Banks' hair, I'd say I'm holding my own for two-to-one.

But then Banks gives Sulli a boost. Throwing her over his shoulder, she descends on me with a bowl of shredded cheese. She pours the whole thing right over my head.

Colby jack catches my eyelashes.

I grin.

"Why are you smiling?" she asks like I already lost.

She's waiting to eat my "sore loser" heart. Seeing her happy and safe, I've already won.

"Because of this," I say, and with two hands, I smear salsa on her cheeks. The light in her green eyes barrels through me.

"Banks, more cheese!" Sulli calls to her other boyfriend, who's still holding her over his shoulder.

He passes her more cheese, and after gently setting her down, Sulli is back on her feet. We slip, we throw, we laugh, and after we all nearly do the splits, we fall to the floor. Unable to stand with the amount of crap beneath our feet.

The food fight ends when we have nothing left to throw. We pant hard, our smiles softer. Leaning against the cupboards, Sulli is sitting between me and Banks.

I pry lettuce out of her long brown hair.

"Is beef juice on my lips?" she asks us. "Fuck, I don't want to taste it."

Banks reaches up and grabs a towel. He tenderly holds her jaw, then dabs at her lips. She smiles at him, and when he's done, she looks to me.

I lean in and kiss Sulli. Softly, the moment quiet and serene, and she kisses back. Feeling her lips is like knuckles rapping my heart. Creating an extra thump. Thump.

Thump.

Dang.

After we break, she turns to Banks with light swirling in her eyes.

He leans down and kisses her next.

I watch their embrace. How her legs magnetically pull towards him. How her hand reaches out for me, and I draw her palm to my thigh. My pulse feels alive. Soaring. Like this is how life is supposed to feel.

Yet, there are responsibilities I can't ignore.

Worries.

Other people.

I bang my head back on the cupboard, realizing that I let go of my phone.

That's good, Nine.

No, it's not. I can't totally let go of my promises to SFO. I can't say goodbye to every *responsibility* I have and live in some happy fantasy forever.

Even if that sounds like peace on Earth.

Anyway, I *love* my companies. Who even am I without my ambition and pursuit of something *more* in this life?

"Kits?" Sulli catches my attention. "What's wrong?" Her frown pinches her brows. "Was it because I kissed Banks after you—"

"No," I interject. "That was..." I tip my head with a growing smile. "That was hot."

Banks cracks a smile. "Tell me more."

I reach over Sulli and shove him.

He laughs.

And then Carpenter and Walrus race into the messy kitchen.

"*Fuck,*" Sulli curses.

We all spring up, but the calico cats roll in the salsa, cheesy beef combo.

Banks picks up both cats by the scruff, and a shaggy puppy bounds into the kitchen. Orion's paws skid on the sour cream, and his furry body collides into kitchen stools.

Thatcher suddenly appears.

Sulli freezes like Thatcher caught her reckless misbehavior. "Um, I'm going to clean all this up."

"We will too," I tell Sulli.

Banks nods.

She wrangles Orion. "Go find your Mommy." After a pat, the dog races away.

Banks passes the cats to the Thatcher, the Cat Dad. "Everyone already got food?"

He nods strictly. "We're all on the terrace waiting for you three before we start the meeting." The *House* Meeting that I said should coincide with Taco Night and a Security Meeting. Even though I don't live here, security issues are cropping up, which is *my* responsibility to have under control.

While Thatcher lingers, the air tenses and grows more awkward.

He won't make eye contact with me. Ever since I announced my relationship with Sulli and Banks, it's been frost and cold-shoulders.

So my friendship with Thatcher is officially on thin ice, only propped up by the fact that Banks cares about me. Otherwise, in Thatcher's eyes, I'm the guy that's orchestrating a scenario that could hurt his brother. I don't have any siblings, let alone a *twin*, so as much as I'd like to understand that kind of love, I only have what I know.

My endless love for Sulli.

My enduring love for Banks.

Still, I'm Thatcher's boss.

He's my lead.

There's one thing I know about Thatcher Moretti. He'll do his job to the best of his ability no matter what asshole he's working for.

Even if that asshole is me.

Right now, I pick more lettuce out of Sulli's hair. Thatcher's stern eyes graze us, then the wasted food.

I can tell Sulli feels like crap. Even before she tells Thatcher, "We can cook something else if everyone wants seconds. I wasn't fucking thinking—I mean, I *know* Jane put a lot of effort into this roommate meal with Moffy. I just, we just—"

"It's fine," Thatcher says coldly.

Banks glares. "Don't be like that, Thatcher. We're just messing around."

"Is that what this is?" Thatcher snaps back. "Just messing around?" His words have greater meaning than just the food fight. He's talking about our triad.

I grow hotter. "Thatcher—"

"Forget it." He leaves.

"*Shit*," I curse.

Sulli limply taps my shoulder, looking sad. Banks pulls her into a hug. She wraps up into his burly chest, and I scrounge the kitchen. Trying to find my phone.

I grit my teeth. *There it is.* In the sink. Covered in salsa and beef.

Great.

Just great.

And honestly, I'm not upset at sour cream streaks on the screen. I'm upset that my best friend is acting like the three of us are adolescent teens. Horny at Spring Break.

Spinning to Sulli and Banks, I tell them, "We did nothing wrong. If they think this is *us* just fucking around, then whatever. Let them think that, but we know it's not."

Banks takes a deep breath, nodding strongly to me.

I finish with, "I don't want to lose what we have just because they think it's us being reckless and wild for a season."

Sulli unburies herself, eyes reddened. "I shouldn't have wasted the food they made, Kits. They're not your roommates. They're *mine*, and I was fucking inconsiderate."

"It's on us too," I tell her. "Banks and I started it."

"I started it," she says. "I hit you with the first tortilla."

We all slowly smile, remembering.

She groans, "God, I don't want to love what we did because it was fucking *bad*."

Banks shrugs. "No use crying over spilled guacamole."

I smile more. "If they're that hungry, we can order more food."

"Solutions," Banks says. "Akara has them."

She exhales. "Okay. Alright…I feel better. Thanks." She gives me a smile, then Banks. "And I ditto everything you said, Kits. I don't want to lose what we have either."

Before we meet with Sulli's roommates, we clean off and try to scrub the floors, at least.

"Here's some *mapeens*." Banks throws me and Sulli dish towels.

After the floor is less slippery and we've wiped our faces, I check my phone and see the email again. Without much thought, I just say, "Someone wants to buy my gym."

"What?" Sulli frowns. "I didn't think you wanted to sell it."

"Me either," Banks frowns too.

"I didn't ever consider it."

"So why are you now?" Sulli asks.

I flip my phone, then shake my head. "Money, less headache." I push my black hair back, the strands sticky.

"We can find the money," Sulli assures. "*I* have the money, Kits."

"No," I cut in. "Save your money. Your trust fund isn't *limitless*."

"But I can invest in my boyfriend's gym."

"*No*."

"Pride," Banks says with a nod, "is gonna be the death of you, my friend."

"Metamour," I say *proudly*. "I'm your fudging *metamour*, Banks."

He almost, almost smiles.

But tension still hangs in the air. It won't escape us. Because we have more tense crap to deal with. Like the Royal Leaks.

Leaks that Banks and I haven't discussed with Sulli yet. Days ago, the website was a minor security threat, but a new leak popped up this morning.

Real.

True.

Farrow told Maximoff, who's now freaking out.

Sulli looks at the salads we grab from the fridge in disdain. Ones we left here a few days ago, but she's not curling her nose at the expiration date.

"I think I'll pass."

"You can't eat the air," Banks says. "My cock probably has more nutritional value than oxygen."

"I'll eat your cock," she says triumphantly.

He laughs.

I smile, and she adds, "I'll eat yours too, Kits." She grabs our waistbands, drawing us to either side of her, and as cute and hot as Sulli is right now, I look down and tell her, "As much as I want to fill your mouth with my cock, it's not the way."

"The way of what?"

"The way to Sullivan Minnie Meadows staying healthy."

"I know how to stay healthy," she says strongly. "I'd just rather eat the vegan chips on the floor than eat that green stuff."

Banks and I smile, and solutions, I find another one in the form of a vegan power bowl in the freezer. I pop the frozen meal in the microwave.

"Thanks, Kits," she says, "but just so we're crystal, I really do want your cocks too."

Banks touches her head in fondness, pulling her closer to him. She wraps her arms around him, and I'm smiling as the light in her eyes reaches me. It's a good feeling heading into the meeting.

Food in hand, we're ready. "Here we go." We make our way up to the patio terrace.

"Come what fucking may," Banks says. His *lets push through any hell hole* attitude is one of the few things keeping me going these days.

18

Banks Moretti

BEING MID-NOVEMBER, my nuts should be frozen hockey pucks on the penthouse's rooftop, but my sister-in-law and her bright thinking ordered patio heaters for the colder weather. *Go, Jane Moretti.*

Heaters surround the iron dining tables and the pool lounge chairs nearby where Sulli and I take seats. We smell like a bum-fuck-nowhere Taco Bell and we look like weeks' old dirty laundry.

I almost laugh at the thought.

Christ, I love this life.

Sulli isn't hurrying to shower, and she doesn't seem to care that salsa is crusted on her cheek. Still, I pick some off for her while she wipes away sour cream I missed on my neck.

For the big meeting, Akara takes front and center near the edge of the pool. He's on his phone for a hot second.

Sulli whispers to me, "Are you okay with distancing ourselves from the pack? I just don't really want to *congregate* at one table. God, look, they're looking at us."

Sure enough, Quinn, Donnelly, Jane, Maximoff, Luna, and my brother are eagle-eyeing us to fucking death. At least Farrow doesn't seem to care, and Oscar is up in New York, on-duty.

"Pack of vultures," I say lightly, putting a toothpick between my lips. A slow thump beats at my temple, the start of a (hopefully) dull migraine.

Sulli notices me shutting one eye.

"I'm alright."

"Is it the sun?" She blocks the setting sun with her hands, shielding the orange rays from bludgeoning my brain.

My lips curve. "Thanks, mermaid."

She smiles. "Are they still looking?"

I check in my peripheral. "Affirmative." After I pluck out my toothpick, I notice how her eyes descend to my lips. "You wanna give them something to talk about?"

"Fuck, *yeah.*"

I clasp a strong arm around her shoulders and dip her down to the lounge chair like a dance move. Her breath hitches as I hover over her, our feet stay on the ground, but her ankles rub against me like she wants to lie fully beneath my body.

I feel the *thump thump thump* of her heart racing against my chest.

"Banks," she rasps, and I fall into the depths of Sulli. Of how she's staring into me. Like she never wants me to drop her. Like she never wants me to leave, and I want to promise, forever, that even if it's hard, even if I shouldn't—I'm staying and holding her against me.

In another breath, she says, "Kiss me."

I bridge the space. No air left between her soft lips and mine. I kiss her gently, sweetly. She might be the crudest American princess, but I remember my manners.

And I'm not *ravaging* her in front of her family and my brother.

She smiles against my lips, kisses me back, then I whip her upward to a sitting position. Her hair flings forward, and she laughs and lightly slugs my arm. The sound abruptly dies when she sees her cousins and SFO staring. Their eyes are detonating on us.

She scoots a little, almost hiding behind my back. "Fuck," she mutters to me. "I go from being *stick it to them* to being a scared fucking turtle." She exhales a strained breath. "I need to stop turtling."

"We can help with that."

"We?"

"Akara," I call out and wave to the red *Studio 9* ballcap he's wearing. In front of everyone, he tosses me the hat.

I fit it on her. Oversized for her head, the brim falls down to her brows. "Now you can come out, Sulli."

She smiles, sitting more against my side and not behind me. I keep an arm around her shoulders.

Sulli is the first girl I get to call a *girlfriend*. The only one I've ever really wanted.

SFO always thought Akara would be with her. Hell, so did I.

I'm the interloper to some.

To my brother and Jane, I'm just the fool who'll get his heart smashed to smithereens.

With flushed cheeks, Sulli doubles-down on our PDA and clasps my hand. "You could use the hat more than me," Sulli whispers. "The sun—"

"It's not a bad migraine." I try to speak as quietly as possible.

"You promise?"

I hold her gaze. "I promise. Cross my heart—"

"Hope to *never* die," she finishes for me.

I crack a smile. "Ooh rah."

She focuses in on my dog tags.

I've told Sulli a little about my deployments. How there were sleepless, hyper-vigilant nights. How when I came back to Philly, I didn't have nightmares or traumatic stress. I had back pains and knee pains and body aches that made me feel a hundred fucking years old.

And my head pounded like I bought a marching band overseas and they decided to camp inside me.

But I know my strengths and limitations. Beat me down until I'm crawling, I'll still crawl. Being stuck in quicksand, being motionless, horrifies me.

"Hey, everyone," Akara addresses SFO and our clients. "Before I get into it, Sulli wanted to say something."

Sulli clears her throat, rotating mostly to Jane, Luna, and Maximoff, who share an iron table together with plates of tacos. Bodyguards are seated at the other one.

FEARLESS LIKE US // 163

"So the three of us had a food fight earlier and all the food is fucking gone, and if you all are still hungry, I can order from a local place or pizza. And I'm really fucking sorry."

"I'm sorry too," Akara chimes in.

"Same," I add.

"I appreciate the apologies," Jane notes, and she offers a giddy smile to me and Sulli sitting together. "As my brother Tom would say, *as you were*."

Take it back, some vultures here are more like gooses, wanting to lead chickadees into the world. Jane is happy for me like I'm a baby bird dating for the first time. And I am new to relationships, even more than Sulli, who dated the Rooster.

Only I'm not looking to be pushed towards Sulli without Akara.

I'm not sure what it'll take for people to understand that.

"Thanks, Jane," Sulli says. "Sorry, Luna, Moffy."

Luna lifts her big taco bowl. "I have enough here. I'm okie dokie."

"Artichokey," Sulli finishes with a smile.

"You-gnocchi," Luna sing-songs with a grin.

Sulli fist-bumps the air.

Luna air-bumps back.

All's right in one friendship.

She zeroes in on Maximoff.

"I'm good with my plate," he tells her with a nod, then spoons applesauce to his son on a highchair. "You're okay, Sul. Just don't let my dad see the Great Taco Slaughter. He'd convulse."

"Oh no way, I'm not inviting Uncle Lo here." She exhales another breath, like she worried they would've evicted her over spilt beef. They love her too fucking much to kick her out of the penthouse.

Akara snaps a finger to his palm. "Okay, SFO and Maximoff already know what the security meeting is about, and we're here to catch the girls up."

Sulli's shoulders drop. "God, not another fucking pervert. Please tell me no one's stalking Jane again."

The pervert. I tense, remembering the night I detained a sick fucker that security called *Sneakers*. Middle-aged, his dick out as he leered over Jane's bed in the now-burned-down townhouse.

I blink back the image.

"No one's stalking Jane," Akara assures.

Jane steeples her fingers. "And no one's stalking Luna or Sulli?"

Thatcher pipes in, "No stalkers, honey."

The girls noticeably ease.

"What then?" Luna asks, looking more at her brother. "Is it Dad?"

"No," Maximoff shakes his head. "Not dad."

Akara cuts in before the guessing grows. "It's a website that Donnelly found a few days ago. It's called *The Royal Leaks.*"

"Oh…fuck," Sulli curses.

Jane tenses, and Luna is harder to read.

"So far," Akara continues, "they've posted three leaks about Maximoff, Jane, and Sulli, and all have been true. Including the fourth one posted today."

Sulli bristles, her head swerving to me. "What leak was about me?"

"I'd like to know them too," Jane says with a raise of her hand.

We all start showing the girls. Thatcher reveals them to Jane, Maximoff to Luna, and Akara passes me his phone. I angle the cell to Sulli, showing her the three old leaks. The patio quiets except for the pitter-patter of Orion and Arkham chasing each other around the tables.

Her mouth drops. "Birth control?" Her voice is simultaneously quiet but loud. "How'd they fucking know that?"

Akara answers before I can, "We don't know yet, Sulli."

She winces, and I hug her more against my side and show her the newest leak.

THE ROYAL LEAKS

We reveal all the truths about the American Royals.
These are verified and come directly from the source.

ROYAL LEAK #1: Jane Cobalt is planning to schedule an egg retrieval surgery. She's freezing her eggs for Farrow & Maximoff Hale's future child.

#TodaysLeaks #babynews! #AnotherRoyal

"They're not even using our correct surnames," Jane says like she's investigating the article. Currently, Akara and I are coming up with an ass-load of nothing as Hardy Boys, so maybe Jane can be our Nancy Drew.

Farrow slings his head back to look at Jane. "To the public, you're always going to be a *Cobalt*, Cobalt."

"Is it true?" Luna asks Jane. "About the egg retrieval?"

Sulli whispers loudly to me, "The Seasons are tensing." The Seasons are what Luna and Sulli nicknamed Thatcher, Jane, Farrow, and Maximoff.

"Farrow doesn't tense," I tell her. "He's leaning back on his chair."

"He definitely looks concerned, though."

"It's true," Jane answers with a deep frown. "I haven't scheduled the procedure yet, and the only people who knew about the plan were Thatcher, Farrow, Moffy, and me."

Sulli freezes. "So how did this leak?" No one even suggests *The Seasons* as options. They wouldn't betray each other. Those four are close.

So close that I'd submit an application for Farrow as Thatcher's New Best Friend. Akara has been fucking ousted of the position since charades night.

Hell, maybe the fracture started even before then. When we both missed his wedding.

I tense thinking of that night.

The patio tenses thinking of the leaks. Everyone knows the answer to Sulli's "who-done-it" questions can't be a good one.

Maximoff is already sitting stiffly like he's made of iron.

"Merde," Jane curses in French.

I hug Sulli tighter while worry etches across her face. Security threats are our job to handle, but this one is a shot in the fucking dark.

We have no good leads.

My brother stands up and goes to his wife to console her. He crouches down to her chair, and they talk hushed together.

"That's what we're trying to figure out," Akara says to Sulli, taking over the meeting again. "Here's what we know, guys. The four leaks are all true. The tech team couldn't trace the IP address to *The Royal Leaks*. We have no idea who's behind the website, but every leak has one common denominator."

"Us," Jane realizes, wide-eyed.

Akara nods. "The leaks have all centered around people living in the penthouse. We think the penthouse might be bugged."

"Fucking fuck," Sulli breathes out. "Seriously?"

"It's a working theory."

"Unproven," Farrow says easily. "If the house were bugged, it's more likely a leak about you three would come out." He raises his brows at me, then Sulli and Akara.

Sulli isn't ready for our poly relationship to be blasted to the media while we're newly together. She looks like a deer in fucking headlights, and I want to protect my Bambi from being run over.

"Maybe it's coming," Maximoff says ominously.

Fuck.

Sulli says the word I'm thinking out loud.

"Right now, this site has *zero* traction," Akara says confidently, making sure Sulli hears him. "It hasn't been picked up by superfans of the famous ones or the general media. It's just another random site that no one but us *here* realizes is spitting facts."

Luna looks wary. "A site like this could go viral if someone popular boosted the link."

Donnelly says, "We're not gonna boost the link."

"Treat the site like you never saw it," Akara declares, and to the girls and Maximoff, he says, "You can check any new leaks yourself every day, or you can rest assured that your bodyguards will keep tabs."

"So what now?" Jane asks. "We find the bug?"

"We're compiling a list of everyone who's entered and exited the penthouse this month. We'll crosscheck on who could've potentially planted a bug," Akara explains, "but until then, we need to sweep the penthouse. And to *thoroughly* canvass a place of this size means we're going to need everyone to vacate for the next couple of days. Is that okay?"

Luna speaks up first. "That's good with me. I can stay with Eliot and Tom."

Maximoff gestures over to Farrow and his son Ripley. "We're going to stay with my parents."

Jane nods heartily. "Thatcher and I will head back to my parents' house as well."

Everyone turns to Sulli. Mermaid cringes a little, and it doesn't take the smartest shitbag on Earth to know she's thinking of staying with her mom and dad.

I'm here for whichever direction Sulli goes.

Jane tells her, "Beckett will surely let you stay over with him."

Sulli frowns. "I know he would, but maybe I need to go home. I can't keep running away from my dad." She looks over at me and Akara. "Would you two be okay coming with me to my parents' house?"

Akara and I share a smile, proud of Sulli for wanting to rebuild what exploded, even if it'll be an uncomfortable shitshow.

I nod to Sulli. "Pack me up and ship me out."

I'm ready.

19
Banks Moretti

AKARA DRIVES THE OLD Jeep Wrangler down Sulli's childhood street. With Triple Shield's security mansions one street over, Akara and I are familiar with this bougie gated neighborhood in Philly. I spent six years living here when I protected Xander Hale. But I can't remember ever needing to step foot into the Meadows cottage like Akara.

Been outside, sure.

Before I pocket my phone, I finally click into the unread text.

Breakfast tomorrow? I'm free at 0700. — Dad

I run my hand back and forth over my unshaven jaw. Sulli has two 24/7 bodyguards now that I'm permanently on her detail and Akara isn't going anywhere. So I could probably swing a morning off work while he's protecting her—unlike when I was a hot commodity *floater* and was twisted in every direction like a fucking gold-foiled pretzel.

Thought I'd miss being pulled and staying on my toes, but I don't.

I haven't.

Nothing beats being able to protect the woman I love. And having Sulli curl up against my chest at night is better than being stuck in New York City traffic with a Cobalt.

Reminds me that Akara and I haven't slept in our apartment much lately. We've crashed in Sulli's room. Her bed. Most of the time, we all just fall asleep together.

Ryke Meadows is gonna *love* learning that his daughter is going to bed with two men every night. Not that I plan on telling him intimate shit, but if he asks, I won't lie.

Quickly, I text my dad back a few words: Can't. On-duty tomorrow.

Any face-to-face talk might actually do damage, I've decided, and that's what I'm avoiding for Akara's sake. Separation is best. It's what my dad always wanted anyway.

He's quick to reply.

Another time then. Let me know what works for you — Dad

I send: K

He's not picking up the chill in my response because he doesn't really know me. We don't lament about the bad times or good times. We hardly ever text, and the only reason he's messaging now is because he's living in Philly again.

After pocketing my phone, I turn in the passenger seat and nod to Akara. "We're off-duty?" I need confirmation before I take off my radio. Meeting our girlfriend's parents at their home means I'm here as Sulli's *boyfriend.* Not her bodyguard.

Same goes for Akara.

"Yeah. Leave your gun in the glove compartment."

I unbuckle to sit forward and unholster my gun. "Shame. I was hoping Ryke and I would draw pistols and duel."

Akara lets out a laugh. "You want to go Wild Wild West out there, Banks, let me know. I'll buy you a cowboy hat with extra rhinestones."

"Just make it *blue.*"

"Pink," Akara jokes.

Whatever, I'd rock it. "Yippee-ki-yay."

Sulli leans forward in the back, head between our front seats. "The only duel that's happening is between me and my dad. So I'm taking that cowboy hat from Banks."

"I'd give it to you."

She's too apprehensive to smile, but she puts a hand on my shoulder and a hand on Akara's shoulder. "No more fucking bloodshed. Okay?"

"That's the plan," Akara assures.

I bounce my head, but it's better to be ready for hell than to be gut-punched when Ryke does take another swing. So I'm not expecting her dad to have warm, fuzzy feelings towards me.

Gun in hand, I remove the round from the chamber, and Sulli watches more attentively. Her dad has taken her to a shooting range before, and the gun he packed for Sulli's out west adventure, she returned before their blow-up. Only her dad owns firearms, so she's now reliant on me and Akara if we encounter another wild animal during hikes, camping, or climbs.

Can't say it's a regular occurrence to cross paths with any. Not like in Yellowstone Country.

I notice how she watches me safely place the handgun in the glove compartment. "You want your own gun?" I ask Sulli. "That way you don't have to ask your dad for his."

She contemplates for a second. "Yeah…I'd actually really like that."

Akara looks back and forth from the street to her, maybe noticing the crinkle in her brows. "Are you scared to shoot a gun after Montana?" Where she shot and killed a cougar.

"Sometimes I think I might be. What if my hand fucking shakes when I touch the trigger next time, or what if I struggle to even hold the gun?" She slides back against her seat, further away from us.

Akara catches her gaze in the rearview. "You don't ever have to touch a gun again, Sul. Banks and I are armed."

"Oh hey, I know you two will always protect me." Sulli slips her arms in her jean jacket as we close-in on her childhood home. "But I don't want to be scared of anything anymore. Not if I encounter another cougar, not holding a guy, *nothing*."

I glance at Akara. "Sounds like we need to take her out shooting."

She sits forward again. "Like…a date?" Her smile reddens her cheeks.

Akara and I exchange the briefest look that she can't decipher.

Her smile vanishes. "Fuck, unless that's not something you two want to do together. I can just go with one of you?" She sinks backwards and cringes at herself. "*Fuck.*"

Akara is smiling. "String bean—"

"Oh my God, don't *string bean* me right now."

"You didn't get rejected," Akara says with another laugh. "Sullivan."

"Well, it fucking feels like I did."

Akara asks me, "How does someone reject their girlfriend?"

"Expertly. Bastardly," I say, and then I tell Sulli, "I'd very much like to take you on a date with Akara to go shooting."

She eases, but still looks confused. "Then what was that look you gave each other?"

Akara explains, "We were planning on taking you out separately on more formal dates and it's something we've talked about with each other already. But we can do both."

I add, "That look was us saying, *let's do both.*"

Sulli's smile slowly returns. "You both talked about taking me out?" Before we respond, she adds, "I like that."

Jealousy isn't a big beast like before, and if anything, guilt comes stronger. Guilt when I spend more time with Sulli than him. But Akara and I are doing our best to communicate. Stay on the same page. Soothe any bruised egos.

"We like talking about you, string bean," Akara teases.

She kicks the back of his seat for the nickname, but she's smiling. Until we drive up to the cul-de-sac, the cottage in view under a full moon tonight.

Quaint. That's how security describes the Meadows Cottage. But that wouldn't be the first word I'd pick.

Welcoming is better.

Situated in the private cul-de-sac, the cottage looks like Hobbiton or a picture book coming to life. Foliage landscapes the house, and large mismatched stones pave the walkway to the half-glass door.

Akara parks the Jeep under the portico, and I detach my radio from my waistband, then unclip the mic cord. He keeps his radio on, in case SFO needs him.

Sulli stares out at the cottage. "Maybe I should've called."

Akara pockets the car keys. "You never needed to call to spend the night before, and there's no way your mom revoked that open invitation."

She sighs heavily. "Fuck, I wish you both could spend the night too."

I fit the radio in the glove compartment. "We'll be alright in a motel."

"Hotel," Akara corrects me.

"Whatever he says, since he's paying," I say, putting a toothpick between my lips. I give her a onceover. Tension lines her broad shoulders. "You sure you want us to see your parents with you?"

She nods strongly. "My dad will have to get used to the idea of us being together. I'm not hiding it."

The corner of my mouth lifts. She latches onto the way I look at her. With pride and love. She's someone I've wanted to stand beside. The girl who hates loneliness, who rages against sleep, who laughs and jokes and loves and screams when she needs to scream.

What I respect about Ryke is that he raised a woman like Sulli. She wouldn't be who she is without him, and while I'm not looking for his respect in return or his approval like Akara—who cares what Ryke thinks—I don't plan to go in guns blazing.

Akara isn't ordering me to *behave* or *keep your mouth shut, Banks.* For one, I'm now off-duty, and for another, I do have a filter. Can't make it in the Marine Corps without biting your tongue in half.

We unmount from the Jeep, and Akara and I let Sulli go ahead of us. Walking behind, we're dressed for a casual affair. My mom would shit a fucking brick knowing I didn't wear my best. Not because Sulli is American royalty needing to be impressed, but because these are my girl's parents who deserve my best effort.

Tonight, my best effort is an opened gray long-sleeve button-down, white tee beneath, and jeans.

Akara's best effort is a black hoodie under a red Columbia windbreaker.

"What do you want for your birthday?" I ask Akara. December 18th will be around the corner before we know it.

"That's what you're asking before we see the parents?" His breath frosts the cold air.

"No time is a bad time except the times that are good times."

He laughs into a groan, "*Dang*, Banks, just when I think you're tapped out of nonsensical mottos, you pull that one out of your ass."

"Came from my heart," I say quietly, "but you would confuse my ass with my heart."

Akara laughs, then says, "Just buy me a six-pack. What you always do."

"I can't get you what I always get you. It's different now." *Between us*, is the unsaid thing.

He holds my gaze for a stronger beat, and then the porch lights turn on while we're walking towards the door.

They know we're here.

I'm guessing we triggered their motion sensor cameras. Can't even pull off a secret arrival with modern-day technology.

My boots hit the front stoop just behind Sulli.

The door swings open.

A tall blonde with shoulder-length hair fills the doorway. Green eyes, the same emerald pools as Sulli's, are on us, then on her daughter.

"Sulli." Daisy's radiant smile pulls at an old scar along her cheek, and instantly, she draws her daughter into the tightest hug. They sway playfully side-to-side in the embrace.

When they pull back, Daisy brushes her nose with Sulli's, and I watch Sulli exhale in relief. She hugs her mom another time, and then asks, "You're not upset that I just showed up?"

Daisy frowns. "No. This will always, *always* be your home. You can show up whenever you want. I want you to." Her eyes flit to me and Akara. "And I see you brought your *devilishly* handsome boyfriends." She wags her brows at her daughter.

Sulli blushes at either *handsome* or *boyfriends*.

"Ma'am." I hold out my hand.

Daisy grins. "The formality of it all." She grabs my hand and does one strong shake, like something you'd see in *The Parent Trap* or at summer camp. "I've known you for years, Banks. You can call me Daisy—not Duck, not Duke, and definitely not Buchanan. I'm a Meadows."

She's the youngest of the Calloway sisters, only in her early forties, and tabloids say she's the sun to Ryke's shadow. I'm hoping she's doused him with fuckin' light rays and magma since the last time we encountered his dark cloud.

And I hang onto something Daisy said:

I've known you for years, Banks.

Not in the same way as Akara. I've just been that bodyguard attached to a Hale.

"Daisy," I correct. "How are you?"

"Better now that I've seen Sulli in one lively piece." Her eyes glitter against Sulli's green orbs. Daisy turns her gaze onto Akara, and her smile shifts a fraction, not disappearing completely. "Akara."

"Daisy," Akara nods. "Is Ryke still ready to rip out my jugular?"

She seesaws her hand. "It changes daily, honestly." She opens the door wider. "Enter at your own risk." Her brows wag again, and I see where Sulli gets some of her playfulness.

Sulli guides me and Akara inside her *messy* family home.

Her parents obviously aren't strict. My dad would've wrung my neck if I left dirty dishes and mugs out in the living room. Blankets are strewn messily over a window nook. Pillows are piled on a hammock (I see where her love of pillows comes from)—and green potted plants are everywhere. Even dangling from the ceiling.

I duck to avoid head-butting a hanging fern.

Hell, as much foliage exists *inside* as it does outside. With the open floorplan, the kitchen is visible from the living room and I realize no one else is here. A rerun of the original *Charmed* plays on the TV, and I only recognize the show because it's my mom's favorite.

Sulli scans the room. "Where is Dad anyway?"

Daisy rounds the kitchen counter where a mixing bowl is sitting out. "With Winona outside." She looks more hesitant at me and Akara. "I don't recommend going out there."

The dark cloud must still be a dark cloud.

"Recommendation appreciated," Akara says while pushing his black hair back and fitting on a baseball cap. We all approach the kitchen stools.

I nod a couple times. "We're not hard up to get screamed at today. We just stopped by to drop Sulli off."

Daisy gasps at Sulli, then smiles. "You're staying?"

She didn't bring a bag since her old room here still exists, clothes left in drawers. "For a couple nights, if that's okay…" Sulli breathes.

Daisy frowns, pouring a box of Crispy Rice cereal into the mixing bowl. "Of course that's okay."

"But Dad—"

"Will be totally fine," Daisy finishes. "Don't worry about him. Just live your life how you want to live it, and if that life drives you back home for a couple nights, then all the windows and doors are open for you to fly through."

Sulli smiles softly and slides onto a stool. Akara and I stay standing.

Daisy opens drawers, probably trying to find a spatula. She's constantly in motion. "You both are welcome to stay too. The more the merrier."

As soon as the words leave her lips, the backdoor opens. Bad timing is something I'm getting used to, but this just takes the motherfuckin' cake.

Ryke Meadows stiffens, jaw hardening and eyes narrowing on me and Akara. What I know about Ryke extends years back on security and Google searches on the internet.

Nothing as personal as Akara.

"Bow chicka wow wow," Daisy smiles to her husband.

Flirting isn't clearing away the cyclone that's rage-fucking over his head. "They're not staying, Dais." His voice is cement.

"A couple nights," Daisy counters. "Just while the penthouse is being cleared of any bugs." She pours Crispy Rice into the palm of Sulli's hand.

"How do you know about that?" Sulli asks, chewing on the cereal.

"Your Aunt Rose."

My brother's mother-in-law. Queen Rose is what Loren Hale mockingly (and I'd like to think lovingly) calls Rose Cobalt, but fuck, it's fitting considering she hears all. Gossip in my rowdy family would've traveled just as fast.

Ryke glares at *me*. Why the hell am I the target of his anger right now?

Maybe it's my height. Being the tallest in the room, I stick out like a beanstalk he clearly wants to chop the fuck down.

Ryke grips the counter. "I don't fucking care if the penthouse is on fire. They're not staying in our house with our daughters."

"It's okay," Akara easily slips into the conversation. "We didn't plan to stay."

"Thank you for the offer, Daisy," I add. Gotta remember my manners or my grandma would cluck her tongue all the way from South Philly.

No kidding, after my politeness, I swear Daisy mouths, *cutie patootie*, to Sulli, who I'm 100% positive whispers poorly, *hottie patottie*, back. They share a giddy smile, and Akara is near laughter, stealing Crispy Rice from Sulli's palm and throwing them back in his mouth.

Wish I could delight in my "hottie patottie-ness" but I can't.

Because Ryke Meadows is burning a motherfucking hole through my head. Murder is on his mind, and I stand guard, not shying from his glare.

His face hardens. "Get the fuck out of my house, Banks."

Akara and I share a confused expression. Since when did Akara get crossed off his hit list?

"Dad, they don't have to spend the night," Sulli says quickly. "But can they at least stay for an hour or thirty fucking minutes? Dessert, maybe? I want you to get to know them better."

Daisy twirls towards her husband. "Sounds like a great idea." She slips her husband a look, and he meets her eyes briefly.

Ryke crosses his arms. "Okay."

"Okay?" Sulli rocks forward excitedly on the stool, her elation infectious.

I smile.

Ryke sees it. "But just Akara stays. Banks can go."

It's a kick to the face—my smile is gone. I expected him to shove me out, but for a second there, I held a morsel of hope.

Sulli gapes. "What? You barely know Banks. Wouldn't you want him to stay so you can get to know him better?"

I lock eyes with her dad again. His intense stare doesn't hold a candle to my strict dad. And Sulli is right—he doesn't know me. But I know about him.

I know he's a child of a nasty divorce like me.

I know he hates blue-blooded, silver-spoon-wielding WASPs like me.

But unlike me, he grew up in the upper-class, upper-echelon of society. He attended an Ivy League with his family's money. If I had it, I'd use it too, but I'm not even fucking sure Ryke Meadows has stepped foot in the kind of places I grew up.

I talk more to Sulli. "Akara has more in common with him anyway."

Ryke drops his arms, brows knotting. "What's that supposed to mean?" He sounds antagonistic.

Be polite, Banks. "It doesn't matter, sir."

"Yeah it fucking does. Say what you mean to say."

Akara backs up and stands beside me. His friendly, concerned gaze makes me want to walk more recklessly, because I know Akara has my six. Even if I detonate this bitch.

"Cross the Schuylkill River"—sounds like *skoo-kel* from my mouth—"and you hit Chestnut fucking Hill where Akara grew up."

Also, where Farrow lived as a kid.

I point towards the northwest. "Multi-million-dollar homes that match the ones around Villanova, where *you* grew up." I lift a shoulder. "Respectfully, that's all I meant."

"Respectfully?" He cringes. "Cut the fucking bullshit."

"*Ryke*," Daisy nudges him. "He just has manners."

"No, he's a *yes, sir* kid," Ryke says to me. "Always told what to do. Can't speak his mind outright—"

"No, *sir*," I cut in heatedly, "I'm a kid who was raised by a bunch of women who taught me to never utter a disrespectful word to those older than me. Especially people like my *girlfriend's* parents. So excuse me for not cursing you to hell and back."

Ryke goes from a boil to a low simmer. "Sorry…" He exhales hotly, then looks to his wife, which helps him soften a little. "I thought you were being smart with me."

I have said "respectfully" in a smartass way plenty of fucking times, so I understand why he popped off at me.

Sulli holds out her hands like we're all standing on thin ice that could shatter at any uneasy step. "Are we okay?" She climbs off the stool, and Akara and I instantly look at her ass.

Ryke is set to boil again. "Get *the fuck* out." He points at the door.

We ignore him. "Sulli," I call to her in concern. We weren't checking Sulli out, even if she has a smoking ass.

Period blood is seeping through her jeans.

"What?" Her brows furrow.

Akara tells her, "You're bleeding."

"Oh fuck." She looks between us. "Is it bad?" She turns around so we can examine her ass better, and I'm fucking aware her dad is watching us inspect the blood stain.

Daisy mentions something about tampons and leaves for upstairs.

"It's pretty bad, Sul," Akara says.

"Really? *Fuck.*" She makes a worried face at us. "I just put a super-plus tampon in like an hour ago."

I chew down on the toothpick. "It's gotta be the birth control. You've been bleeding since you started it."

She sighs. "I'd let my gynecologist know, but she has a habit of ghosting my emails."

"I'll text Farrow," Akara takes out his phone. "He can refer you to a new gynecologist."

She tries to relax. "My periods aren't usually this fucking heavy either." She sighs. "At least the cramps have been mild so far—knock on wood." She secretly and lightly knocks on Akara's *dick* without her dad seeing.

If Ryke noticed, a blood vessel would burst in his eye, and his eyes only carry a severe case of rage right now.

Sulli turns more towards the kitchen. "Dad," she says to the stone statue that is Ryke, "at least I'm not pregnant. Fucking yay?"

He swallows hard. "You're sleeping with them?"

Akara clamps a firm hand on his mouth, looking to me like *we're fucked.*

Welcome to our knucklefuck shitshow.

Neither of us turn away or close our eyes from the train wreck.

And Sulli mutters, "Uh, fuck, I thought...I thought you inferred that when Banks said the whole thing about touching me at the quarry...*shit, fuck.*"

"I didn't want to jump there, Sul," Ryke tells her.

"Well, now I guess you fucking know that I lost my virginity." She grows a little hotter and defensive. "Don't worry, I'll spare you the details of which guy took it."

Akara and I try to hide our peeking smiles just hearing Sulli stick up for herself.

Ryke rakes a hand through his hair. "It's your body, your choice. I wouldn't tell you *who* to sleep with, and I'm fucking sorry if you thought I would." He sounds sincere and attempts to calm. But his nose flares.

He looks fucking tortured.

Who knows what's going on in his head? He could be standing there, thinking about how I'm six-seven, tall and *big* and his daughter *was* a virgin.

Christ.

I hope he's not picturing me hurting her.

Ryke exhales a rough, pained breath. "I love you, sweetie."

"I love you too, Dad." Her voice is softer.

"I'm just having a hard time…" He holds out a hand, unable to even produce the words. He seems relieved as Daisy suddenly returns with a box of tampons.

"I have these, Sulli. You can go change. I'll stay with your boyfriends."

Ryke looks like he's fighting a fucking demon just hearing the word *boyfriends*. His face contorts a thousand different ways.

"I can change later," Sulli says. "I'd rather stick around while Dad gets to know the guys better."

Ryke's nose flares again. "Banks is leaving, Sulli."

Her face falls. "I thought we went over this already? You know Banks the least."

"If you'd rather have Banks stay, then fucking fine. Akara can leave. I don't give a fuck," Ryke says, his chest rising and falling heavily. "But you can't date both of them."

"Ryke—" Daisy cringes

"Dad," Sulli snaps. "I *am* dating both of them."

"What?" Winona Meadows suddenly appears at the backdoor behind Ryke. And her jaw is on the fucking floor.

20
Sullivan Meadows

"YOU'RE DATING YOUR bodyguards?" my fifteen-year-old sister questions, lips parted and wide-eyed in all her outdoorsy beauty. Delicate faced and thimble-nosed, her dishwater-blonde hair is half up in a bun, and instead of cargo pants today, she's in floral bell-bottoms.

Winona always looks fucking cool, but ever since Yellowstone, I've been feeling more and more like her *older* sister. Like I should've always felt.

I am six years fucking older. The fear in her eyes when she heard I could've died out west has stayed with me. Maybe it's stayed with her too. I've never been the reckless one, but I'm ripping through caution tape, even when it comes to love. Dating Will Rochester was *safe*.

Dating a bodyguard is a danger zone.

Dating two bodyguards is lethal.

"Hey, squirt," I try to smile, but Nona's confusion and hurt nearly chokes the whole kitchen.

"Does everyone know but me?" she frowns. "Sulli?"

"Can we talk outside?"

"Yeah, *now.*"

As soon as I leave Banks and Akara's side, I tell them, "*Don't* leave without saying goodbye. *Please.* Just wait for me. I'll be a sec." I realize I'm leaving them alone in the pits of fucking hell with my dad—what I didn't want to do—but my mom is here.

She double thumbs-ups me. Ready to reel in Dad from potentially reenacting what happened at the quarry.

Okay.

Alright.

I can go talk with Winona. So I leave, and as soon as I reach my sister, she grabs my hand and a couple headlamps. We race outside in the cold, moonlit dark together.

I fit my headlamp on.

She switches hers, and strobes of light give us greater clarity of our surroundings: the treehouse, the glass-walled gym, the woods that travel deep into our parents' property. And greater clarity of each other. Her uncertain eyes that I hope to clear.

Winona catches the rope to an old tire swing that our dad constructed at the crest of the woods. We both fit our legs through the hole of the tire.

Sitting across from my sister, she asks, "How? When? Where?"

"It happened in Montana." I explain what I've already rehashed to my cousins, and it should be easier the umpteenth time around—but I'm still holding my breath all the fucking way through.

Our feet brush the earth beneath us, and we rotate the tire in a circle, twisting the rope above us while we talk. "You fell in love with both of them?" Nona tries to process. "I...*how?*"

"How?"

She nudges my foot with hers. "Sulli, I...I can't even *un*guard my heart for one dude. I say *one* personal thing to the wrong asshole and next thing I know, he can post everything I spilled in confidence. Not to mention, *sex*. Like, do I really want a guy to blab to his friends whether or not I shave my labia, and then, that'll end up on the internet."

I think about *The Royal Leaks*, and her fears aren't so fucking unfounded. Privacy is something Winona and I value, something our parents safeguarded growing up, and we weren't taught to brace the full impact of the world as much as the Hales and Cobalts.

In some ways, our parents gave us a real gift, a semblance of normality, and in others, we know what it's like to have some privacy, so it's more terrifying to lose it.

"I trust them," I tell Nona. "You'll find someone you trust too; I know it, squirt."

Our breath smokes the air in our silence.

We spin slowly, our feet still grounding us. Winona asks, "How do you know one isn't lust and the other is love?"

How do I describe a fucking feeling? I dip my head, the headlight illuminating my boots. Before I can form the words, Winona says, "I know you love Akara. You two were always so playful together like Mom and Dad. He'd be an idiot not to love you."

He does love me.

But I follow where she's going. "So you think Banks is the lust?" It hurts even thinking. I grip harder onto the rough rope.

She adjusts her hands on the rope too. "How do you know it's not just a physical connection?"

The words tumble out of me. "Because when I picture losing Banks, I feel like I'm suffocating, Nona. I *love* him, and I need him as much as I've ever fucking needed Kits."

Banks reached a part of me that was dying to be held, and I know Winona thinks it's a sexual part—but it's not.

He uplifts my womanhood, my independence, my strength, my soul, and Akara uplifts my drive, my playfulness, my fervor, my spirit.

I love them both for different reasons because they're different *beautiful* people, but I need and love them all the fucking same.

My spirit and my soul.

Her face downturns. "Does this mean you like Akara less than you did—"

"No," I say strongly.

"But you're *sharing* him with someone else. How can you love two guys totally, completely, the same way?"

I shake my head, the light going left and right over her delicate features. "Nothing is cut in half, Nona. The love I have for them isn't split apart and shared. They both have all of me, and I have all of them." My eyes burn, hoping she understands, *please.* "We'd feel *less* if we went from three to two. We all have *more* together. So we're staying fucking *together.*" With another breath, I tell her, "They want to be in a poly relationship over a monogamous one, like I do. They have a friendship that extends far fucking beyond me."

Winona lifts up her feet. I'm the only one keeping us grounded.

"Say something, Nona," I breathe.

Her lip lifts. "I'm trying to get it. I'm going to get it a lot better than some people, and you need more allies. You're my sister; I'll always have your back in our wolf pack." She leans forward to press our foreheads together. "What you're doing is ballsy AF, and if anyone messes with you, they have to go through me."

"Hey, I'm the big sister. That's my line."

She smiles. "I love you a waffle-lot, Sulli-Bear."

"I love you a waffle-lot more, Nona-Frog."

And with the biggest breath all night, I lift up my legs. We start to spin wildly as the rope untwists, the light of our headlamps whipping in circles as our bodies rotate and rotate and rotate.

Winona smiles. We laugh, and she says, "You have a heart-on for them."

"An affection-erection," I grin.

We lean back and howl up at the moon, and I should know not to delight in moments this too-good-to-be-true. Because all of a sudden, we hear the crunch of leaves.

Our feet drop, stabilizing us.

We go quiet.

My pulse thumps, and I consider calling out for Akara and Banks. *It could just be an animal.* Definitely not a cougar. A bobcat is more likely.

I strain my ears and hear...snickering. *Human* snickering.

Winona looks enraged. "Those douchebros." She springs from the tire swing and chases after figures in the dark.

"NONA!" I yell, jumping off the tire. Hot on her trail.

I'm older.

Faster.

And what I've learned in point-two seconds is that I'm *still* not as rash and heedless as my little sister, who'd chase after creepy fucking laughter in the woods.

"Nona, stop!"

"They're the neighborhood douchebros, Sulli!" Twigs catch our hair as we run deeper and deeper. "They live two streets over, and they've been tormenting my babes at school! COME OUT, YOU COWARDS!"

"Nona! *Fuck.*" We roll to a sudden stop as our headlamps illuminate three teenagers. They wear navy-blue Dalton swim team sweatshirts, and it fucking sucks to know there are assholes on Dalton Academy's swim team. What Moffy must've gone through, since I bailed on the normal high school experience.

They grin.

From behind my sister, I wrap my arms around Nona, keeping her from *lunging* at them. "Let's go, Nona."

"Yeah, *go, Nona.*" The tallest mimics me in a high-pitched voice.

"Fuck you," I spit out.

"Look, she's bleeding out of her cooch." They cackle loudly, and I glance down, the blood visible from the *front* now.

Fucking awesome.

"Grow up," Winona growls. "Some women have menstrual cycles. We *bleed.* What do you do? Jack off and cry over a paper cut?"

The tall one snorts. "That's all you've got, Winona?"

I cut in, "You can't be here. This is private fucking property—"

"What are you gonna do about it?" They all laugh. "Punch us? You wanna hit me, Winona? Come on, right here." He taps his face aggressively.

Nona seethes, her hands clenched in fists.

I tear her backwards.

Her voice rises. "You're so lucky my sister is here and has more sense than me."

"No, *you're* lucky, bitch."

The threat in his voice sends a chill down my spine.

Winona loses her bravado, a sickening look on her face. One that I feel, and no way am I *ever* letting teenagers assault my sister.

"Don't fuck with my sister," I growl, "and don't *think* about putting a hand on her or any of her friends."

They laugh, and the tall one says, "You think you can hurt us?"

I want to say, *yes*. I can take on three fucking teenagers. I'm that strong, but they won't take me seriously like they would Moffy.

"I have a button on my headlamp. One push and our bodyguards are called. Two pushes and the fucking cops come. I've already pushed it once."

"You're lying."

They can't see my shitty poker face in the moonlight. "I'm glad you think so. Your fucking confidence is a win for me. My bodyguards will be here in five seconds. They have our location."

The three douchebros swap a wary look. "Fine," the tall one says. "You really are lucky this time, Nona." They start into a jog and then sprint away. Disappearing through the woods, and I tug Winona in the direction of our parents' house.

She's stupefied, slow to follow until I pull harder. And then we're running again.

When we break into the grassy yard, we hurry towards the house. "You have to tell Mom and Dad."

"They've never been that sick, Sulli."

"Have they ever crept in our backyard before?" I glance backwards, glad they didn't try to follow us. Winona goes to school with them, so their names will be easy to hand to security.

"This is the first time that I know of, I swear."

My heart is still beating out of my chest. "Do you think they overheard us on the tire swing?" We were discussing my relationship with two bodyguards.

Winona looks distraught. "I don't know...Sulli, I'm so fucking sorry. If they heard anything, it's all my fault—"

"No, you didn't know they were there."

She rips off her headlamp, upset. We both always spend a lot of our energy ensuring we don't leak each other's private lives to the public. That starts with not blabbing to enemies, especially shitheads down the street.

We near the cottage.

I left my boyfriends alone with my parents. The sudden thought practically catapults me back through the door.

21

Akara Kitsuwon

BANKS ISN'T WRONG. I have more in common with Ryke Meadows. But not just because we both had money in our pockets from birth.

Ryke fell in love with the "off-limits" girl. A girl who was too young when he first met her. A girl who became his friend. A girl he chased to the ends of the earth. To protect her. Because he loved her. Because even if he never held the title or career, he was her bodyguard.

So while Sulli is outside with her sister, Banks and I face our girlfriend's parents with unspoken truths stretched taut in the kitchen.

"We can all sit down. Talk a wee little bit?" Daisy suggests with a playful smile, but her Golden Retriever partially distracts her as Goldilocks paws at the backdoor. "Goldi, you were just outside." She kneels beside the young dog, scratching behind her ears.

None of us make a move to sit.

Kitchen stools, the counter, and discomfort separate us from Ryke. His glare mostly stays on Banks, and my muscles constrict the longer he avoids me.

I'm right here.

My chest tightens. "Why can't you even look at me?" I ask him.

His nose flares, and as expected, his narrowed eyes never graze me. He mumbles something hot.

"What was that?"

He looks up, hurt in his eyes. "I'm fucking *disappointed* in you."

It stings, and I shift my weight. "You should understand," I say heatedly, "better than *anyone* how this could happen."

He glances back at the door where Goldi whimpers, then to me, he says, "You'll be twenty-eight in December…I was three years younger than you when I sat down with Daisy's father and he interrogated me. And I never thought I'd be on the other side, but here I fucking am."

"You can interrogate me," I urge. "Ask me what needs to be asked." My chest rises and falls heavily. *Come on, Ryke.*

"I can't…" Ryke's eyes redden and he looks away. "I've already put you through too fucking much, Akara." He's referring to the shouting match at the quarry.

"You think what you're doing to me now is any better?" I slip my phone in my back pocket, my whole attention on him. "I want to make things right for Sulli. She loves you, and…you know, I have no family in Philly. I only have the family I've made. My men and Sulli and your family have all been my family, and I'm *sorry* if you thought I'd never cross a line, if you thought I wouldn't—but I *did.*"

Ryke scratches the back of his neck. "Look, I'm fucking abrasive, and I'm not sure how to say things that won't hurt you."

I put a hand to my chest. "I don't care if you curse me left and right. I don't care if this ends up worse than it started because at least I know I did *something* to make it better." Solutions.

I'm hanging onto this one.

I know what it's like to try to brush rifts and awkward situations under the rug. I did that when Sulli made her confession in the funhouse.

All it did was postpone the inevitable. Me. Waking the *fuck* up.

Ryke nods, and Daisy smiles over at him. He finds something inside himself to hold my gaze. "You've been around the fucking world with my family."

"Yeah." *Around the world.* I've touched almost every continent. I've been to Thailand several times with the Meadows, only one time with my mom, and I never had the chance to go with my dad.

I regret that the most.

He never asked. Never booked a trip.

Never really wanted to go. All his family was in New York.

It's okay, Nine.

Is it?

Ryke drops his hand from his neck. "I still see you like a son, Akara, and I did consider you a brother to my daughter."

Did.

Past tense.

He continues, "I know you've been Sulli's *companion*, her best friend, when she needed one." He pauses, struggling with speaking this deep for this long out loud. "Just like my father-in-law never expected I'd fall in love with his daughter, I did, and you're right, I do understand how this could fucking happen between you two. It just does. It just did."

I inhale, feeling understood for a brief second. "Then why the disappointment?"

"You're a *trained* bodyguard. Besides the fucking fact that she pays you for those services—"

"She doesn't pay me," I cut in. "Not anymore."

His hardened face seems to soften. He soaks this in. What I'm doing to make this right for me, for her, for everyone.

He nods, but some raging thought causes Ryke to shake his head, his face contorting. "You have to know what *you* and *him* are about to put Sulli up against. It's your *job* to know."

The media circus.

The headlines.

The loss of privacy.

"Of course we know," I say strongly.

His scowl darkens. "And you don't fucking care?"

"I *love* Sulli—"

"If you loved her at all, you wouldn't do this to her."

His words ring in the pit of my ears.

"Ryke." Daisy stands. "Sulli loves them, and you're telling them to give up."

"That's not what I'm saying." He exhales a ragged breath. "Two bodyguards dating a Meadows girl…there's never been a more salacious truth. Out of decades, that takes the fucking cake. You guys say you *love* my daughter, that you want to protect her? Then one of you stays, the other needs to fucking go." He points at the door. "She can't have both of you."

"*Ryke*," Daisy says from her core.

He looks physically pained.

Silence ekes.

I scrutinize the backdoor for a beat. *Secured*, I remind myself. The gated neighborhood has 24/7 security posted at the entrance, so I didn't need to follow Sulli out into the dark.

She's been a while.

Banks is watching the door too.

Ryke smears a hand down his mouth. "Daisy and I spent how many fucking years protecting Sulli from what tried to rip the two of us apart, and you're about to throw her to the fucking wolves."

Banks chimes in, "She is a wolf, sir. She's not a little girl."

Ryke's jaw tics. "We didn't fucking prepare her for *this*. And maybe it's my fucking fault, but I expected more from you." He's looking at me. "I thought you'd protect her, not obliterate her."

She's not obliterated.

He's scared she might be. He's scared what the media will do to the girl who's largely been sheltered.

His fear is a toxin, and I'm worried about inhaling the fumes.

The door suddenly whips open.

"Dad?" Sulli storms inside, and I zero in on the leaves and twigs caught in her hair. In Winona's hair, her sister slipping in behind.

"Sulli? What happened?" I catch her hand as she bounds over, not out of breath, but her eyes are saucers. "*Sulli.*"

Shit.

Shoot.

Banks and Ryke push urgently towards the backdoor, and I'm about to follow.

"They're gone," Sulli says in a sharp breath, yanking me back to her side. "They took off, Kits."

I cup her face, seeing the dread pour through. *What'd they do?*

They did something.

"Sul?"

I'm going to kill them.

"Who?" Daisy asks her daughter, wrapping her arms around Winona.

She looks up at Daisy. "The douchebros. Kinney calls them the three T-bags: Tate, Topper, and Tristan—they all live in the neighborhood."

Ryke is murderous. For once, it's not towards Banks and me.

"Banks, check the perimeter," I order.

"Roger." He's gone.

Ryke grabs two flashlights, charging out behind Banks, and while I pull out my phone, I ask Sulli, "Did they hurt you or Winona?"

"They threatened her, Kits."

I feel my jaw clench with my teeth. "What'd they say?"

"You want the exact words?"

"If you have them, Sul."

While she thinks, I text Price Kepler with one hand.

"They said, *you are lucky, bitch.* Like they would've done something if she'd been fucking alone out there." She pants hard, distressed.

"Hey, it's going to be okay." I tuck her close, and I ask her sister, "You okay, Nona?"

"Yeah…" She looks a little rattled.

Daisy whispers in her ear and hugs her tighter.

Sulli glances down at my phone. "Who are you texting?"

"Price."

Her brows jump.

"He'll want Triple Shield guards to scout the perimeter of the cottage." In a whisper, I add, "I'm playing nice."

Considering I'd rather just call my temp guards to the job, who are more than qualified now that Michael Moretti is kicking their ass. But Price is Daisy's bodyguard, and he'll want to be informed of teenage trespassers now. Not later.

Plus, teen issues aren't in Kitsuwon Securities' wheelhouse, as Price has so often and *patronizingly* told me. Xander Hale is the only minor on my client list. He's enrolling at Dalton Academy starting in January, but until he's in school, Price is staking claim to threats around the teenagers.

The T-Bags are his problem.

As long as the Meadows girls and everyone else are protected, it's fine.

Though, yeah, my ego is a little bruised.

I know Kitsuwon Securities has better bodyguards than Triple Shield.

The door opens.

"All clear," Banks slips inside.

Ryke is right behind, shutting off the flashlights. "Did they touch you?" he asks Nona and Sulli.

"No, Dad," Nona says.

"I'll call their parents later," Daisy tells Ryke. "I think Rose has met some of them at PTA meetings."

"Fucking fantastic." He unpockets his phone. "What are their last names?"

Daisy tells him quietly.

Banks isn't lingering in the kitchen. He aims straight for Sulli, and I glance at her jeans, blood sleeping down her thighs. My phone vibrates like bullets unloading in my fist.

Messages from Farrow, from Price, from Michael Moretti, Connor Cobalt—on and on and on.

"You alright?" Banks asks our girlfriend, gently holding the back of her head.

"Yeah, the T-bags are real *D*-bags." She blows out an unsteady breath. "Fuck, *fuck*." She notices the blood in the light. "This period sucks."

Banks rests a comforting hand on her lower back, and I whisper to Sulli about how she can go change. We'll wait, but she's adamant on staying here.

"I'm not leaving you guys again."

"Did you try to hit them?" Ryke asks his youngest daughter.

"Sulli held me back. But I should've spit at them," Winona says angrily, but her arms still quake. She squats down to hug Goldilocks.

Ryke shakes his head. "You did the right thing walking away."

Winona frowns. "They might've heard me and Sulli talking about her boyfriends."

Lovely.

But I hold on to the fact that Winona said "boyfriends" like she's accepted me and Banks. I'll take any win these days.

Ryke buries his face in his hands for a second. He's not ready for our relationship to leak. Honestly, none of us are ready. We'd rather stay in *private* for as long as possible. Less stresses and voices. We're free to be happy without total condemnation.

The thing that I've learned about us is that we're not as careful as Farrow and Maximoff were. Not as careful as even Thatcher and Jane.

Charlie caught me kissing Sulli in Yellowstone.

Jane found out about Banks and Sulli around then too.

When it comes to Sulli, I've always walked a risky tightrope. But it's even riskier now that we're together. The feelings we feel are like a haze I walk into and never want to come out of.

 Sulli turns to me and Banks. "Back in the woods, they never said anything about my love life or my bodyguards, so there's still a chance they never heard a thing."

I ease. "We'll keep an eye on headlines."

Nona rises to her feet. "I'm going to Vada's to study. Is that okay, Mom?"

"I can take you," Daisy says.

"No, I can," Ryke cuts in.

"No, I have this." Daisy rests her hands on his waist. "I love you to the moon and back, Ryke." She loops her fingers in his waistband, rising on her toes to kiss his cheek. "You should stay and talk more with your daughter's boyfriends."

Ryke glares at the wall, but his gaze softens on his wife. "I fucking love you too, sweetheart."

Daisy grabs Nona's hand. "Onward and out."

As they leave, Ryke takes over what Daisy left unfinished. He sets a saucepan on the stove. "Akara, can you grab the fucking marshmallows from the pantry?"

Sulli begins to smile, more hopeful, like maybe we buried the hatchet. But I'm pretty *dang* sure the blade is out in the open. Sitting between us. Waiting for someone to grab and hack.

"Yeah, sure." I give Sulli a look to lower her expectations on my way to the pantry.

She nods understandingly. Her smile is gone.

Disappearing, I text Price back and find a bag of *Dandies* marshmallows on the shelves. The silence is skyrocketing the level of awkwardness. Astronomically.

And I'm not even out there.

When I return, I rip open the bag. Sulli has an even sadder face, and I toss a marshmallow at her. It bounces off her forehead. Coming close, I catch the marshmallow before it hits the ground.

A softer smile plays at her lips.

She tries to grab the *Dandies* from me. I raise the bag over my head. "Uh-uh."

"*Kits.*"

I grin.

"Fucking A," Ryke growls. "Not in front of my fucking face."

I stiffen.

Ryke pinches his eyes. "*Fuck*, I sound like my brother." He throws a dish towel and sighs heavily. His back is turned to us while he's sorting through his own feelings.

I hold out the marshmallows to Banks, who takes one, just to put in Sulli's mouth. She grins up at him, then tries to feed Banks a marshmallow.

He has to bend down to her.

When Ryke turns around, he's missed that interaction, and I hand him the bag.

Ryke takes it roughly. "I'm still waiting for one of you to leave." He looks between Banks and me. "That hasn't fucking changed."

"You're going to be waiting all night," Sulli tells him.

His nose flares. "By the time these Crispy Rice treats are fucking baked. One of you is gone. That's the best deal you're getting all night."

"Deal," Banks and I say at the same time.

Sulli pulls her hair up in a messy bun. "I guess I should take what I can get, right? The alternative is you punching them."

Ryke grimaces. "I don't feel good about that, Sul." He runs a hand against the back of his neck. "I'm not fucking proud of it."

"We don't blame you," Banks says. "We know you were just trying to protect Sulli."

"I'm still trying to protect her. Something I don't fucking believe you two are trying to do."

"That's not true," Sulli cuts in.

Ryke takes a breath. "Look, I don't think Akara and Banks have your best fucking interest at heart. If they did, they both wouldn't be with you." He sets his glower back on *Banks*. "I changed my fucking mind— one of you should really leave before this gets any worse tonight."

"I'll go," Banks says the words first.

He backs away from Sulli.

22
Banks Moretti

LAST THING I WANT IS TO continuously add more friction between Sulli and her dad. They have a chance to repair things these next couple days, and if it takes me getting out of everyone's hair, so be it.

She tries to catch my wrist, but I rest my hand against her cheek. "I'll see you tomorrow, mermaid."

"Promise?"

"Promise. Cross my heart, hope to never die."

Her lips try to rise.

I almost lean in and kiss her, but Ryke's glower has torched to volcanic levels, so I back the fuck away. And I leave.

Cold wind hits me from the outside, and I dig in my pocket, feeling a pack of cigarettes. I scan the moonlit cul-de-sac. Threat still at large.

You'd think I'd feel like utter shit leaving Akara with Sulli and her dad. *The one true boyfriend to rule them all.* But I feel light. Happy, even. For once, I could give him something. A win. And hell, Akara Kitsuwon needs a win more than me these days.

"Wait up!"

I wince at the sound of his voice, and when I rotate, I just shake my head. "You dumbass," I say to Akara and let go of the cigarettes.

He wraps an arm around my shoulder mid-step on his way to the driveway. He propels me with him. Not missing a beat. "How am I the *dummy* when I came to keep you company?"

"I don't need any company," I say. "I need you to get your ass back inside there—" I shrug his shoulder off me, but we're already at Booger.

Akara twirls the keys, then unlocks the door. "I'm not going back without you, Banks."

Slinging my head back, I let out a long cantankerous groan. "Mother of Christ. You're so fuckin' diehard SFO, you can't even see that you're hurting *yourself* in this—"

"So what if I am? I'm the boss. You're my responsibility. I take the hits."

"You have a chance to be alone with her—"

"Not at your expense," Akara cuts me off, twirling the keys again but slower. "Ryke shouldn't see you as the *dispensable* one."

Dispensable.

He doesn't even know the full brunt of what my dad said to me the night Skylar died, and still, he's looking out for me.

How the hell does Akara think he's the *bad* guy when he's been so good to me?

"That's the thing, Akara, I don't care how the fuck Ryke sees me. I don't even agree with half of what he said. Daisy was making more sense." I lift my shoulders. "I don't need her dad to like me—I need him to fix what he broke with Sulli, and they can do that with *you* there. Not out here freezing your nuts off with me. So go." I shove his arm.

He wobbles and glares.

I huff, and our heads turn as floodlights from a security vehicle shine on us.

Price must be here.

We share a tense look and squash our fight. I'd rather end things short than have a run-in with Triple Shield, and Akara must feel the same.

"What'd Sulli say?" I ask him quietly.

"She wanted to come with us." He hangs onto the edge of the door. "I told her to stay. Talk with her dad. She may not get another chance like this."

I nod, feeling the same.

Just as Price rolls up to the curb, we climb into Booger. Akara gives him a polite wave on our way out of the neighborhood. As far as we know, Triple Shield doesn't have a clue about our relationship. Not about to spill those beans tonight.

We make the short drive to the hotel. It's late. Sun set, and tomorrow we'll have a full day of destroying the penthouse top to bottom in search of any bugs. I'm just looking forward to getting some shut-eye tonight.

My back is fucking killing me.

At the front desk, I stretch my arms backwards, and Akara pulls out his wallet. "One room for tonight."

The receptionist clicks on the computer, barely looking up from the screen. "King or two queens?"

Akara glances at me for a split-second.

Gun to head, my initial reaction is *king*. We've been spending almost every night in Sulli's bed together. She's been on a monsoon period, and all we've done is curl up against her.

And every night, I keep thinking I should've been in a relationship sooner. I love just *holding* Sulli in bed more than I've ever loved a one-night stand.

Then again, she's the only girl I've ever wanted to hold all night long.

I curl my hair around my left ear, then right. How strange will it feel having a bed all to myself? But Sulli is gone, and Akara and I—we're not *physically* intimate with each other. Should that make a difference?

"What do you think?" Akara asks me for advice.

Screw it.

"I'd get the king," I tell him.

Akara nods to the receptionist, "The king is fine."

Again, she's superglued to the computer as she collects his credit card.

Entering the elevator, quiet stretches. I turn my head, half expecting to see Sulli standing between us. Her absence leaves a crater.

A fucking abyss.

An emptiness that I hate. It makes me want to be less and less alone. Akara sees the same space where she'd be, and his gaze lifts to mine.

We're friends. The two of us will always be friends, but I can't deny that the three of us share something I can't quite explain. None of us really can.

I dig in my pocket. Not for cigarettes.

Really, I want to smoke, but Akara, just being here, is helping me dick-kick my vice. I don't want to smoke in front of him.

Instead, I pull out a travel-sized Tylenol and pop two without water. Swallowing hard. Christ, that sucks.

Akara tenses. "You have a migraine?"

"No, I fucked my back running around the woods." I arch my aching back with a wince. "Don't ask me what I did because I don't know."

"Migraines, back problems, anything else I should know?"

"I have a suspicious looking mole on my ass. Wanna check that one out too?"

Akara fits his baseball cap backwards. "For your health, yeah."

"I'm not going anywhere, man." Our gazes are latched, almost in challenge. Me saying, *I'm fine.* Him saying, *you better be.*

The elevator beeps.

After a short walk along the hall, Akara unlocks the hotel room with a swipe of the keycard, and I close the door behind us.

"You can take the shower first," he says. "I have to make some calls."

"To my dad?" I pull off my shirt.

"He's one. Yeah. And then I have to call a team who deals with surveillance technology and make sure they're still available tomorrow to help sweep the penthouse."

How he juggles all of that and still stays upright, I don't know. I couldn't do it. "Anything I can help with?" I ask him as I step out of my jeans.

He's already dialing a number. "I have it. You shower."

Don't need to be told twice. Leaving him in the bedroom, I head for the warmth of the water. When I finish up, I dry off and tie a towel around my waist. Once I exit into the room, I hear Akara on his phone.

"Yeah, it's nine thousand square feet." He sits on the edge of the mattress, his windbreaker and hoodie off, just in a Studio 9 tee. He sees me and stands up. We pass each other as he heads to the bathroom. "I'm aware it'll take more than a day." He shuts the door.

Hell, I feel alone.

I wonder if this is how Sulli feels when she's alone with Akara. Or if she's able to help him pull away for a second. It's not even his fault.

It's the job.

A time-suck that's sucking him dry.

I change into gray boxer-briefs, hop into bed, and scroll through the TV channels. Battle Ring, a pro-wrestling show, wins out, and I watch a couple of guys tussle against the ropes. When the smaller guy lands his finisher, Akara exits the bathroom, towel wrapped around his waist.

Cellphone in his hand.

"Alert the press," I say. "He's off his phone."

Akara throws up a middle finger my way.

I smile. "You masturbate with that hand too?"

"I sin with my left," he says seriously, waving his other hand. He eyes me up and down. "You?"

I hold up my right hand. "I swear to tell the truth and nothing but the truth."

He lets out a short laugh, his smile rising.

"Truth: I used to do it with my left hand, but I popped my shoulder out in boot camp. Been doing it with the right ever since."

"Too much information." He changes into a pair of boxer-briefs quickly, and I get a nice view of his bare ass. "Or as Sulli would say, TMfuckingI."

"Yeah, I miss that girl, too," I breathe out.

"It's the worst when she's not around," he agrees as he climbs into the king-sized bed.

Spacious room lies between us, and I'm not sure how much I like the emptiness. I pound a pillow next to me, where she'd be, but everything in my head feels disconnected to what I'm actually feeling.

I shove the pillow onto the floor.

Glancing over, Akara is on his phone, the light illuminating his features. And then he rests his cell on the nightstand.

I lie back, getting more comfortable.

Akara lies back.

We're staring at the ceiling. The air eases, and there's nothing weird about tonight to me. But where's his mind at? "You wish I said *get the doubles*?" My head rolls to the side on the pillow, and his gaze catches mine.

"No," he says quietly. "I didn't want to be alone tonight."

Alone.

We could have been in the same room in different beds, and not been technically alone, but I know what he means.

It's a feeling we're both trying to combat like we're on home base swinging at fast balls. Loneliness might be all three of our kryptonite.

We end up lying closer. Pressed up side-by-side. Feels better now. Not complete. But better.

"Get some sleep, Banks," he tells me like an order. I want to say the same thing to him. I almost think I do, but I can't be certain before sleep grabs me and doesn't let go.

23

Sullivan Meadows

FUCKING ZILCH. NADA. Nothing.

That's what security and a professional surveillance team found at the penthouse after two full days of sweeping for bugs.

I trust my roommates. I trust security and my fucking family. No one that I love would create a gossip website and leak our private lives.

It makes no sense to me.

We have less strangers coming in and out of the penthouse than Beckett has in his Hell's Kitchen apartment. From cleaning services, to a private chef, to the boozy ragers Tom and Eliot have thrown—*they* should be the ones with their secrets blasted online.

Not that I'd wish that on them!

God, I just hate that being so cautious still leads us here. The universe is a pigeon taking a giant, steaming shit on our heads, and no matter if I'm holding an umbrella or wearing a hat, I still have to deal with the pigeon crap.

Akara showed me the list of "suspects" that have entered and exited the penthouse recently, and he circled the high-threat ones.

Delivery men dropping off a piano.

Delivery men dropping off baby clothes. (For Jane, another gift from our grandmother, even though Jane never said anything about trying to have a baby to her.)

Cat sitters that Jane interviewed.

Grandmother Calloway.

Personally, Grandmother Calloway is at the *very* top of my You Stink Like Dirty Old Socks & Suspicion list. But she's professed innocence to SFO, my uncles, aunts, and parents. The surveillance team tore apart the baby grand piano.

No bugs.

They even rummaged through the expensive onesies and bibs she bought Jane.

Again, no bugs.

If our penthouse isn't wire-tapped with microphones and secret recorders, then someone in the inner-circle is blabbing to an untrustworthy fucking *mole*. Like how Audrey Cobalt sent the Hot Santa Underwear Contest video to a friend, who leaked the clip of SFO strutting around in next-to-nothing.

But Jane and Moffy are so careful—it's hard to imagine they'd tell the wrong person about Jane's egg retrieval.

And then two new leaks dropped on the website today.

THE ROYAL LEAKS

We reveal all the truths about the American Royals. These are verified and come directly from the source.

ROYAL LEAK #1: Sullivan Meadows is trying to be vegan for her sister.

ROYAL LEAK #2: Thatcher Moretti had an older brother named Skylar who died at 15.

#TodaysLeaks #sisterbonds #brotherbonds #DeathInTheFam

I'm not that impressed the mole thinks my being vegan is some sort of "salacious" leak. What I find more in-fucking-furating is the fact they announced Skylar's death like some super juicy secret.

Skylar Moretti was a real person with people who loved him and still hold love for him. He shouldn't pop up on *The Royal Leaks*.

SFO is concerned how Thatcher's now a name on the gossip site without Jane attached. If he's considered *royalty* by marriage, then Farrow is too. Fair game to be exposed to the world.

It's another checkmark in the Reasons Not to Date a Hale, Cobalt, or Meadows category. I worry about my relationship leaking even more. Everyone is fretting about how I'd handle the media pressure, but my boyfriends grew up totally out of the spotlight.

I don't want the loss of privacy or Negative fucking Nancies to take a toll on their mental health either. But fear of the danger ahead isn't depriving me of the greatest *love* I've ever experienced.

Fuck fear.

Fuck the media.

Fuck the dirty mole.

My stopwatch goes off, jolting me from my thoughts.

I see the time and Garrett Winthrope still swimming the backstroke in his lane. His flutter kick has improved since day one, but his body roll from side to side has major issues. His head should be steady and still, and right now, he looks like a bobblehead dunked in water. On a clipboard, I jot a note next to his name.

NEEDS TO ISOLATE HEAD WHILE SHOULDERS AND HIPS ROTATE - BACKSTROKE SUCKS.

He's definitely not in contention to qualify for the Olympic team.

Being fucking frank, only two people here are good enough to make it. Frankie Hansen taps the edge of the pool and pulls off her goggles. A *Warwick* swim cap hides her platinum blonde hair. "How'd I do?" she asks Coach Reed, who's keeping track of her times.

"Four seconds faster than your last lap. Good work."

She frowns, water dripping down her fair, white skin. "Yeah, but how far from the record?"

He winces. "Still fifteen seconds behind."

She blows out a frustrated breath. Know that feeling. Her eyes flit to me, catching me staring.

"Oh hey, you'll get there," I encourage. That's what coaches do after all, right?

She smiles a little. "Really? You wouldn't mind me beating your record?"

My stomach flip-flops. *Yes, I would very much fucking mind all my hard work being destroyed in just a few years.* Those words stay at the back of my head. I'm a coach now. Encouragement over pride. That's what my dad told me when we chatted at the cottage.

The two days I spent there, we actually had good talks…about swimming.

Yeah, I was a fucking coward and we avoided all conversation about Banks and Akara. I just really wanted him to know that I was doing well *on my own.* Boosting up my independence felt more important. Like a steppingstone into him being cool with my boyfriends.

"If you can beat my record, you'll qualify without a doubt," I tell Frankie, skirting around her question. "So it's a good goal to fucking shoot for."

She smiles wider. "Thanks, Coach Meadows." She hops out of the pool to take a start again on the block.

I suck in air tightly through my nose. Why does it feel like baby rhinos are kicking me in the gut? My eyes graze the blue water, the lanes, and empty stands. Chlorine floods my senses in such comfort and familiarity. I remember Disney's *The Thirteenth Year* and the weekend Moffy and I watched the swim movie five whole times.

While Luna couldn't wait to turn eleven to be sorted in a Harry Potter house, I couldn't wait to be thirteen and see if I'd grow gills and a fin.

Taking in Warwick's aquatic center for another moment, I imagine people filling the stands, chatter echoing off the glass dome, the sound of "take your mark" and the beep, the cheering and splashing, and I almost feel like I'm back home.

The pool tries to beckon me closer like I'm starved for an unquenched feeling. Being so close to the water and not swimming is harder than I expected.

I'm stuck here. On the sidelines with a clipboard in hand.

Also, the wild animals kicking my gut keep on kicking. Literal pain cramps my lower abdomen, and I squeeze my eyes shut. *Please don't be menstrual cramps.*

Please don't be cramps.

After seeing a new gynecologist, the doctor prescribed me a new brand of birth control, and I'm banking on this being the magic fucking pill.

I blow out a measured breath and try to ignore my contracting muscles.

Where I stand, another swimmer pops up from their lane. I click my second stopwatch, and my eyes bug at the time. Holy fuck.

"You're fast," I tell the twenty-one-year-old. Ravi Chawla climbs out of the pool, water beading down his reddish-brown skin and lean abs. He pulls off his goggles to try and read my stopwatch, but water gets in his eyes. He rubs at them.

"Yeah, but how fast?" Ravi asks. "Like Kingly fast or qualifying fast?"

I snort. "Qualifying fast. No one is faster than Kingly."

He lets out a heavy breath. "Come on, someone has to knock him off his throne."

"You think it's going to be you?" I size-up Ravi. He's tall with a good-sized wingspan for swimming, but he lacks Kingly's size 15 flipper-like feet.

"Yeah, it's going to be me, Coach Meadows. Watch it happen." He stomps towards the starting block. Coach Reed watches him and then rotates to me.

Shit.

Ugh, I might have fucked that one up.

I back up a little and bump into Akara. "Sorry, Kits." I tap the clipboard to his arm.

He smiles, and I notice Banks right next to him, a shadow of a smile playing at his lips. I start to smile back, but cramps come knocking full-force.

"Banks," I whisper into a slight wince.

He rests a hand against my shoulder blades. "You feel alright?"

Akara studies the way I cradle an arm around my lower abs. "You have cramps?"

"Yeah," I say tightly in pain and try not to draw attention from the swimmers or Coach Reed. "Banks, do you have any pain meds on you?"

He digs in his pocket and hands me a bottle of travel-sized Advil. Their concern bears down on me, and I wish I could draw into them. I wish I could hold on to Akara's arm and sink into Banks' chest. Imagining that physical comfort is good enough for now.

Akara goes and grabs my water bottle.

Banks keeps that comforting hand on my upper-back. "You need to go home early?"

I shake my head, watching Akara hurry back as I say, "I might be too unfiltered to be the best at coaching, but I can't bail on my job. It'll give the locker room a reason to call me a princess."

"They call you a princess, just tell them you're the fucking Icebox. No one messes with you." He almost, almost affectionately draws me in, his hand nestled in my hair for a blip before he lets go.

My heart soars. *Becky the Icebox.* Our *Little Giants* talk in Yellowstone Country comes crashing back into me.

"What's the Icebox?" Akara asks, handing me the water.

Banks makes a confused face at *me.* "You never watched *Little Giants* with Akara?"

I go red and throw back the pills with a big gulp of water.

"What's that look for, Sul?" Akara asks, scrutinizing me with his playful smile. "I know you couldn't have been embarrassed to watch a kids movie with me." He tells Banks, "She made me watch *The Little Mermaid* a hundred times until I said mermaids are real."

"It wasn't a hundred fucking times," I refute, trying to keep my voice down. "It was *eight* times, and you mumbled the words." I shove the water back in his chest.

Hard.

He grunts.

I grin.

He shakes his head, smiling. "Tell me. If you like this *Little Giants* movie, why not let me watch it with you? I've seen all of your favorites."

I shrug tensely. "Maybe I was afraid."

His smile begins to fade. His eyes flit up and down me. "Afraid of what?"

I never intended to tell Akara this, but maybe I should. "That you'd love the part where Becky the Icebox drops her football gear and becomes a cheerleader. That you'd want the cheerleader," I say hushed, "and I guess I never wanted to know the answer…because then it felt like you would never be attracted to me."

He looks confused, shocked, and he glances cautiously to the swimmers in sight, then whispers, "Sulli, you're *hot*."

I can't help but smile. "Yeah, I know you think that now, but back then, if we watched *Little Giants* together, who would you have picked? The football player or the cheerleader?"

His gaze cuts along the pool.

I go cold. "Yeah." This is why I never fucking wanted to know. I'm about to leave, go back to work, but Akara catches my wrist.

"Sulli—"

"It's fine, Kits. You can like girly girls. I'm not trying to bash them or anything." *They're just not me.*

"Back then, I would've chosen the cheerleader," he admits, "but not because I would've liked her more."

I frown, not understanding.

He explains, "If this Icebox chick even remotely reminded me of you, I wouldn't have picked her in front of you. I wouldn't have wanted to tempt anything there, between you and me."

He wanted us to just be friends.

He liked it that way.

Our friendship meant too much to Akara to put it in jeopardy, but I can see now that he's glad we rocked the fucking boat.

I look between Akara and Banks, smiling. And fuck, I need to stop chitchatting with my boyfriends while I'm working.

Swimmers really will start calling me a princess for paying more attention to my bodyguards than to them.

Luckily, no one has tried to haze me after the Sasquatch plushies. A hazing that I was not a witness to. Banks and Akara must've really intimidated them.

"I have to get back," I tell them, waving the clipboard.

I love having Banks on my permanent detail, and I cherish the times where Akara joins him. Having both guys on my duty at the same time doesn't happen as often as I'd hope (I'd want all the time—I'm fucking greedy), but Akara has attended every swim practice so far.

I think he has flashbacks from my Olympic training days, and he doesn't want to miss this.

"If you feel any worse, let us know," Akara says.

"Aye aye." I fist-bump him, then bump Banks' knuckles. Right when I turn towards the lanes, Coach Reed approaches.

Oh fuck.

I'm usually 100% concentrated.

Knowing my focus slipped at work is embarrassing. My face is hot, and I flip fast through my pages of notes for the swimmers.

"Sullivan," he says.

"Sulli," I correct like I have since Day 1. "Do you need my critiques?"

"Later, I'd love to look over them with you."

"Great." I let the pages fall flat on the board.

"That was amazing work with Ravi." He jabs a thumb towards the lean-cut swimmer who dives off the block.

"Really?"

"Yeah, I haven't seen him that motivated in months." He hugs a binder of his own. "We should talk about strategies for Ravi and

Frankie. I know you have experience when it comes to qualifying, and since the Olympic Team Trials are in June, we'll need a rigorous training schedule to make sure they both make the team."

"Agreed." I can do this. Maybe my goal isn't to land on the team, but helping someone else make the cut has to be equally rewarding.

Coach Reed smiles, absentmindedly touching his black gauges. "How about Michelangelo's Pizza at nine?"

"Works for me."

"See you tonight, Sullivan." He leaves for the office just as practice ends.

I'm in charge of giving out more pep talks (shitty ones) and then I hand out a workout plan for each swimmer, modified personally by me to focus in on their weaknesses. Pain meds kick in, my cramps milder and easier to push aside.

"Do these at home before the next practice," I tell the team.

Ravi reads over his sheet. "Seriously? Flutter kicks?"

"It'll help your core and boost your endurance, which you're lacking."

"My endurance is better than everyone's here," he refutes. "I'm not lacking anything."

He's being a cocky a-hole, but I get his complaints. He's the hardest working male swimmer at Warwick. Stays late, comes in early. But if he wants to be the fucking best, he has to realize he's not the best. There is always someone behind him, chasing after his records.

I try not to glance at Frankie, who's chasing after mine.

"Your endurance isn't better than your competitors outside of Warwick," I tell Ravi. "You want to swim the 1500 meter freestyle? You can't gas out after five-minutes, *which* you did today."

He studies the sheet more.

"Any other complaints?'

He mumbles, "No."

Frankie smiles brightly. "Looks great, Coach Meadows!" She practically hop-skips to the locker room. That's unsettling.

The team departs, and Akara and Banks follow as I grab my gym bag off the stands. I've already asked my boyfriends not to carry my bag for me.

Not because of secrecy or anything. Bodyguards often do carry shit, but at work, I want to stay professional and as normal as possible. Most people don't have bodyguards at their beck and call. And I want to be treated like a coach and not like the famous Olympian.

I sling the strap over my shoulder and spin to them. "Is it weird I relate to Ravi more than Frankie?"

"No, because you are more like Ravi," Akara says while we all walk to the exit. "Motivated by tough love."

"I wish I could understand her though. She's going to be on the same women's Olympic swim team that I was on…if she makes it." I shake my head. "She *will* make it. Of course she will." Why does that toss my stomach? I'm her coach…a horrible coach.

A jealous coach?

Akara pushes open the doors.

Unlike my cousins, no hordes of paparazzi wait outside of my workplace to pounce on me. There's just Earl from a sports blog. He frequently shows up to catch me leaving.

"Hey, Sulli! How was practice?" he calls out, notepad in hand.

Akara and Banks both sidestep and block him from approaching too close.

"Pretty good," I reply, walking a short distance across campus to the nearest parking lot. "Top secret though."

"One of these days I'll get that interview!" Earl yells because he doesn't ever follow me to my Jeep. He stays a respectable distance.

I don't know…I kinda like Earl.

I smile as I climb into the backseat of Booger. Only when the doors shut—Banks behind the wheel and Akara in the passenger seat—do I sense a long, drawn-out silence.

Weird, *awkward* silence that has no origin.

Does it have an origin?

Did I miss something?

"Are you two mad at each other?" I ask tentatively, trying not to panic. *What the fuck happened?*

24
Banks Moretti

"WE'RE NOT FIGHTING, SUL," Akara says while glaring out the windshield. "I think Banks and I are on the same page on this one."

Yeah.

We were *right* fuckin' there. Side by side. Witnessing something at the pool that whiplashed me to the day where we watched as Will Rochester hit on Sulli at the Avondale Club. *Good for her,* I should've thought back then. *She has an admirer.*

That wasn't coursing through my head today.

I was thinking other things.

Who is this fuckbag?

What's he doing?

Why isn't that me?

I start up Booger with heat in my chest, then I tell Akara, "I'm not Sherlock fucking Holmes, but I swear Ryan Reed just asked our girlfriend out."

"Yep." Akara stews.

Sulli chokes on shock, then slings herself forward, head between our seats. "What? He just asked me to a work dinner."

"To Michelangelo's." I tighten a hand on the wheel.

"Yeah, a pizzeria."

Maybe it's nothing to Sulli, but I couldn't afford a bill at Michelangelo's growing up. If that's the kind of place you shoot the shit with coworkers, then fuck me two ways to sundown, is everyone wasting their paychecks on overpriced, overhyped cardboard?

Akara flips his phone in his hand. "I don't like him, Sul."

"You don't like a lot of the guys who interact with me," Sulli reminds him. "And I don't think all of them have hit on me."

"I like Jack Highland," Akara defends.

"You *hated* him at first," Sulli retorts.

He's digging himself in a hole.

"What about me?" I ask Sulli. "You think my judgment is clouded by jealousy?"

Akara shoots me a look. "I thought you were on my side, man."

"I am—"

"*Whoa,* when did we make sides at all?" Sulli frowns, like she's being left out.

I almost smile. Good grief, my heart wants to fly out of my body and kiss her. "A side that exists is the one where we're protecting you."

Akara rotates to her with suggestive eyes. "And the one where we're playing with your pussy and tits."

Sulli lets out a breathy, "Fuck." She leans closer to him, and his fingers graze her cheek before he kisses her lips.

Can't see much more. I keep my gaze on the road.

Akara settles back in his seat. "And Banks is just as jealous as me, don't let him *fudging* fool you."

I almost crack a smile, but talk of fucking Sulli only makes me more protective. A territorial expression crosses Akara's face. We're in a *closed* triad. It's not welcome *two,* come *all.*

I glance at him. "The Rodent thinks she's single."

"He's going to make a move on her tonight," Akara says tightly.

"The Rodent?" Sulli makes a face at us. "How long have you been calling my coworker a fucking rodent?"

"After the first day," I confess.

"We don't like him, Sul," Akara repeats.

She leans back, fingers to her lips. "Yeah, you said that already. But just so it's crystal, the only rodent is the *mole* leaking our private lives."

"Hey, we hate that rodent too," Akara says lightly.

Sulli contemplates everything for a long moment. "You really think he was flirting with me? I don't see that at fucking all."

I drive onto the freeway. "No offense, but you could never tell when Akara was flirting with you either."

"But he's *Kits*." Confusion scrunches her face.

Akara grimaces. He's beating himself up right now. It's his fault she can't tell when guys are hitting on her unless they do it with a fucking sledgehammer.

Sulli draws her legs to her chest. "Coach Reed asked me to go over some swim strategies. If he were asking me out, don't you think he'd end with, *it's a date?*"

Akara scratches his neck with his phone. "What if we are wrong, Banks?"

He's just feeling guilty. In his gut, Akara knows the Rodent wants in our girlfriend's pants.

"I'd bet my next paycheck he tries to take her to his place after dinner." Even saying the words churns my stomach. Imagining his hands on Sulli is actually making me *physically* nauseous.

"I'm not taking that bet," Akara says, adjusting in his seat. Uncomfortable at the scenario too, and he fists his phone tighter.

"Good, 'cause I don't want it to be true."

Sulli frowns deeper. "What if he does hit on me at the restaurant? Should I not go?"

I ask, "What are you leaning towards?" I want her to make up her own mind. Figure out what she wants to do first. It's not something for us to decide.

She sits forward again. "I want to respect you two, but I also don't want to run from what could just be a work meeting because I'm afraid. I think I can fucking handle myself. If he makes a move, I say *no*."

Alright, alright, alright.

I nod.

Semper Gumby.

Always flexible. Ready to repel a rodent if the night turns bad.

While I drive, Akara turns more towards Sulli. "We'll be at the restaurant on-duty, so if you're uncomfortable and want to bail early, just use a code word and we'll make an excuse for you to leave."

"Banana peppers," Sulli says fast. "No wait, let's go with something less disgusting."

We laugh.

Akara snaps his fingers. "Spinach."

She shoves his arm with a smile. "Kits. I'm being serious."

"So mushrooms then."

She grabs his hand on the middle console like they're about to arm-wrestle. "Cinnamon rolls, and you *both* better remember it."

I tell her, "We'd never forget."

Sulli begins to smile and the light in her eyes lifts to me. Akara tickles her armpit. She squeals and slugs him hard.

He winces.

"Oh fuck, sorry."

Akara is about to reply, but my phone rings. I check the Caller ID. *Have to take this one.* Answering the phone on speaker while I drive, I say, "Hey, Cinderella."

Thatcher makes a gruff noise, not in the mood for my jokes. "I'm calling about the leak, Banks."

Sulli and Akara go still as they listen in.

I rotate the wheel. "We're really doing this now?" I wonder, no desire to dig into our past. Definitely not over the fucking phone.

"Yeah, we are," he says sternly. "Someone is leaking private intel about *my wife*. About your girlfriend. We either do this now or we wait down the fucking line when it's too late."

I stare hard, unblinking. "You're on speaker. What do you want to know?"

"Did you ever tell anyone about him?"

About Sky.

All I hear are the tires bumping along the freeway.

"Yeah." I pause. "I told Sulli and Akara."

Thatcher is quiet.

I wish I could see his face. Is he shocked that I'd rip those words out, recount that night, and say them to someone else when we can barely talk about Sky? Or maybe he's realizing how much I love her and him. But I end up saying, "You know they wouldn't leak anything."

"I know." He takes a beat. "I told Ben."

My jaw hits the steering wheel. "Ben Cobalt?"

"Yeah."

Thatcher got *really* close to the family he married into. I've tried not to yearn for tight bonds with Sulli's parents and sister because they *love* Akara. Loving him doesn't mean they can't also love me, but our friends and family keep acting like one of us needs to fall for the other to rise.

Jokes on them, I'm not falling.

I want more for my life, and why the hell can't I be the phoenix? Rising up next to the girl I love.

I focus more on the road and Thatcher's admittance. *Ben Cobalt knows about Skylar.*

All this time, I thought my brother only ever told Jane. My lip curves upward. Proud of him for being able to open up. Not shocked he's never confessed this until now. Our heart-to-hearts about Skylar last seconds and end with me pissed off—if they occur at all. Hell, we're only sharing now because we want to protect everyone.

"Anyone else?" I ask while I have the chance.

"I think Farrow and Maximoff know about him, but they never asked me more."

My eyes narrow in confusion at the freeway. "How did that happen?"

"Tony told them back when I was fake-dating Jane. We were at the bingo hall on a double date, and he made a big scene about how they didn't know my own brother existed."

I boil. "I'm glad you never told me because I would've knocked him on his fuckin' ass."

"I tried."

I nod, believing it. Farrow must've stopped him. "So Tony Ramella and his big mouth have been known to spread information we want kept private."

"He's also in the inner-circle." He's a Triple Shield bodyguard and protects Connor Cobalt. "But it'd be career suicide. He has no clear motive."

"Money, Thatcher," I say. "That's motive enough." Tony is the least selfless bodyguard on the damn roster. He's in this job so he can boast about protecting celebrities. All arrogance and pride.

"I'm just trying not to let *our* dislike of Tony affect our judgment."

For fuck's sake, why is everyone's judgment being questioned today? We hang up with no real resolution, and I look to Akara, who heard everything. "What do you say, Hardy Boy? Is Tony Ramella a suspect?"

"He is now."

25

Akara Kitsuwon

THIS IS DEFINITELY a date.

Sulli almost walks out when we arrive, as she whispers to me and Banks, "Fuck, I'm *severely* underdressed." Michelangelo's Pizza is upscale. White tablecloths kind of *upscale*. Waiters even splay cloths over their arms and pour sparkling water in wine glasses. An oil-lit candle and single red rose sit on each intimate-sized table.

Intimate.

The word burns my retinas.

Banks frowns at Sulli. "Wait, you didn't know Michelangelo's is fancy?"

"I thought it was a fucking *pizzeria*," she whispers pretty loudly. People are looking, and I shoot them glares to *stop* looking. She wedges herself more between me and him to hide at the entrance. "Like a sports bar with arcade games in the back. Not *this*."

We try to conceal our girlfriend between our bodies. Just until she decides whether she wants to bail or not. Comms hum in my earpiece, no big chatter tonight. Banks and I scan the restaurant from afar, and I tilt my head to him. "You knew Michelangelo's is fine dining?"

He lifts his shoulders and whispers, "I thought everyone fucking knew that, including *you*."

I whisper just as heatedly, "There's practically a thousand pizza joints on this side of town." I barely pause. "And another thing, Sulli's wearing jeans and a jean jacket—and you didn't think she couldn't have known?"

"I didn't think she cared about dressing up," Banks whisper-hisses. Yeah, we're *hissing* under our breaths, both riled up and pissed. More so at the fact that we're about to chaperone our girlfriend on a formal date with another dude.

When *we* haven't even taken her to a place this ritzy.

My ego would be more battered if I weren't concerned. The Rodent is totally unprofessional for asking Sulli to meet him here—and yeah, I might have no room to talk about professionalism, seeing as how I took my client's virginity, but I'm not in business with Sulli.

We're not coworkers.

And Ryan Reed is her *boss.*

The power imbalance is screwy, and I want to whisk Sulli away. Like Banks, though, I recognize she's struggling with her independence. Rescuing her before a fall is what I've done, and I can't do that as often anymore.

"No fighting, okay." She grabs onto our biceps with a loose hold. "I wouldn't care being undressed, but this is supposed to be for work. Adulting means looking professional, right?" She zeroes in on our wardrobe choice.

Banks and I opted for the black pants and black button-ups, a staple for security at night. If I'd known that I would fit in more than Sulli, I would have just worn some gym shorts for her.

She shrinks. "You two are way more experienced at adulting."

Banks smiles down at her before hawk-eyeing the space. "We have been adults longer."

"Yeah, I am twenty-seven," I point out.

"Twenty-nine for me," Banks says.

I let out a laugh. I'll only be a year younger than him soon.

"I like suits," I remind Sulli since she sees me in workout clothes more than anything. "You like what you're wearing. Inhale some confidence, string bean."

"Yeah, you're right." She stands taller, her full six-foot height. "Except about the string bean part."

We're both smiling.

"Incoming," Banks whispers.

The Rodent pushes to the hostess stand, seeing us at the entrance. He must've been seated already out of view. He's wearing a well-tailored, navy blue *suit*.

"Sulli, I'm over here," he smiles and ushers her past the hostess.

But I come out in front and tell him quietly, "Wherever you're taking her, we need a table beside your table for security."

Under most circumstances, I work this out in advance with the initial reservation. I would've called the restaurant, but it slipped under my other obligations.

Like a three-hour phone call with Connor Cobalt. Trying to stop the leaks and shut down the website is a top priority, but I hate that it's distracting me from being all there for Sulli.

I should've handed the task off to Banks. *He's here.* He's her permanent bodyguard too. He's more than competent, but I'm still gripping onto her detail.

Let go, Nine.

Let go of work or of her?

I shake the painful thought, just as the Rodent says, "Uh, sure, yeah." He pales a little. "I think we can manage another table."

"Great."

He speaks with the hostess, and after slipping her a…hundred? Banks' head whips to me. *Saw that*, I nod to him.

Sulli didn't.

"This way," the Rodent gestures Sulli to follow.

She decides not to bail early. Trailing after him, she tells us, "Smells fucking good."

He overhears and thinks it's for him. "The vegan zucchini pistachio-crusted pizza is"—he mimes a chefs kiss—"you'll love it."

I whisper to Banks, "Doubtful."

Sulli is cringing at zucchini.

And no wonder we couldn't see Ryan Reed from the entrance. A *reserved* sign adorns a private table for two. In a backroom with even dimmer lighting and crystal chandeliers.

I'm a little annoyed.

Okay, a lot annoyed.

"Stay frosty," Banks whispers.

"My eyes aren't leaving him, trust me."

Banks and I settle at our own table for two, only a few feet away. Not in arm's reach of Sulli but in earshot. And the *intimate*-sized table looks comically tiny between us.

We watch as Sulli sits fast, too fast for Ryan Reed to pull out her chair.

"I didn't look this place up," Sulli admits, grabbing the flower vase. She stretches an arm for us to retrieve the red rose. The Rodent looks alarmed at her fast pace, and before I can stand up and take the flower, a nearby waiter swipes the vase from her hand.

"Thank...you," Sulli trails off as the waiter disappears. She sets her binder on the table. "I just needed more fucking room."

Banks and I share a smile.

"It's no problem." He leans back, unbuttoning his suit jacket.

She opens the binder. "So I just thought *pizza* and figured we'd be at a bar or something."

"Would you have rather gone to a bar?" he frowns. "I just thought... you're *you*. You probably want the best. Since you are the best." He flashes a smile.

Banks casts a cold glare on him.

My muscles sear. Very quietly, I say, "Why in the *fudgesickle* is her boss flirting with her?"

He crosses his arms over his firm chest. "Let me know when I can punch him."

We're not too inconspicuous about glaring. If this guy spots a threat or warning from us, *great*. He deserves both.

Sulli shifts in her chair. "We're already here; it's fine. Can we just talk about swimming?"

26

Sullivan Meadows

"WE HAVE ALL NIGHT," Coach Reed says. "Let's order some apps first."

This douchecanoe really isn't taking any of my hints. I might as well attach stink bombs to them and fling them at his face. "As long as we discuss swimming, I'm game for apps."

He gives me a short nod. "Of course."

I sit stiffly, hands on my binder. *I can get through this situation without help or running away.* I need to prove this, mostly to myself. Plus, I'd really like to go over the students' swim times and strategies. Acing my job means everything to me. I haven't touched gold in a while, so I want this win.

Coach Reed removes his suit jacket and fixes the cuffs to his white button-down. "You look great tonight, Sulli."

Okay, my boyfriends definitely hit the bullseye. This is a date. Fucking *ugh.*

My face scrunches up like someone waved broccoli in front of me. "Coach Reed—"

The waitress pops in, cutting me off. "Can I start you off with a beverage?"

While he orders, I steal a glance at Akara and Banks' table. They're in earshot of us, and they're glares could erupt volcanoes. I'm sure they've heard him flirting. I am *not* flirting back. I'm just trying to reroute this train, so that I can talk about *swimming.*

Coach Reed peruses the menu. "We'll do your Cab from Napa."

"Oh no, not me." I wave a hand to the waitress. "Water is fine."

He frowns. "Would you rather do a martini? Beer?"

"I'm not drinking tonight. This is a work thing." *A WORK THING!* I scream in my head. Seriously, I'm seconds from yelling out loud.

"Come on, one glass of wine won't hurt."

The waitress must sense the awkward shift because she gives me a sympathetic look before turning to Coach Reed. "Sir, I don't think she wants anything to drink."

"I don't," I say, and give her a small smile. *Thank you.*

She nods back. "I'll come back in a few more minutes to grab your food orders."

Coach Reed slouches a little in his chair. "Sullivan—"

I cut him off. "Coach Reed," I snap, hot with annoyance. "I'm only here for work. I want to make it crystal clear that this is *not* a date."

Words. I've found them deep in my core, and I'm so fucking glad I didn't stumble over them. I think about how proud my mom and dad would be of me, and my carriage rises tenfold.

Coach Reed nods. "You're right. The signals got crossed. I thought it was clear I was asking you out." He winces harder. "I'm sorry I wasn't more upfront."

I take a tight breath and scoot my chair back. "Can we just talk back at the gym?"

"Yeah, of course." Coach Reed places his cloth napkin back on the table.

Akara and Banks stand up at the same time as me, and the tension in the air strains. Their glares are *cemented* on Coach Reed, and I'm lucky they didn't intervene at any point on my behalf. They knew I had the power to work this out myself.

"Bye, Sullivan," Coach Reed says.

Before I leave the room, I say, "It's *Coach Meadows.*"

Akara plants a hand on my shoulder. "Take her to the car," he whispers to Banks.

I feel Banks' hand on the small of my back, and he's already guiding me out. Away from the private room. Akara doesn't follow. I stop suddenly, glancing back as the door to the private room swings closed. "What is he doing?" I ask Banks.

Banks doesn't even look over his shoulder. "Having words with The Rodent."

27

Akara Kitsuwon

I HATED EVERY SECOND of watching that interaction. It was hard not to swoop in, but I'm proud of Sulli for sticking up for herself. And as her security, I need to make sure Ryan Reed won't be a bigger threat down the line. I wait for the door to the private room to swing closed before I turn back to the coach.

"What are you still doing here?" Coach Reed asks me.

I remain standing. Towering. I may not be six-seven like Banks, but I can hold my own when it comes to intimidation. "I want us to be clear," I tell him. "That you won't be asking Sulli out ever again. Don't even think about making a move on her."

Coach Reed leans back in his chair, frowning. "I told her this was a misunderstanding, and I meant it."

"Good," I nod. "So there isn't any more misunderstandings, I need you to know something. Something that will stay between you and me per the NDA you signed."

Curiosity blankets his face. "I won't tell anyone anything. Sullivan is a part of Warwick University now, and if she helps Frankie and Ravi get on the Olympic Team, that looks good for the school. And it looks good for *me*, since I'm the one who recommended her for the position."

That's good to know.

Honestly though, I don't care if he blabs this to the whole world. That risk still exists no matter what he signs or what he says to me.

Right now, all I want is to make sure he doesn't think Sulli is free to be asked out or set up. She's taken.

"Sulli isn't single," I tell him, unleashing this truth in one blow.

He leans back, dumbfounded. "Why didn't she say anything about that?"

"Because she's dating Banks, her bodyguard, and it's not something she wants out in the public. You can understand that, right?"

His brows rise. "Yeah...wow. Yeah, of course." He nods for a while and stares haunted at the table. "So Banks..." He looks to the door where Banks left, and worry crests his eyes. "He's not going to have any hard feelings, right? I just don't need a pissed off Roman god trying to smite me down."

Roman god?

I almost laugh.

I lift a shoulder. "Don't hit on her again, and you won't have to find out."

Coach Reed nods. "Yeah, thanks for the warning. I appreciate it, Akara."

My stomach tenses. I don't want to be on The Rodent's good side, but I have a natural habit of trying to deescalate situations. To remove the fire out of a fight.

I leave the private room with weight bearing down on me.

I told Ryan Reed that Banks and Sulli are dating. That realization hits me all at once.

Good.

I'm tired of all the Kitsulli praise when Sulletti gets crickets. A part of me hopes Coach Reed blabs to the wrong person and this ends up online. Maybe Tumblr will make Sulletti fan pages. Maybe Banks can come out on top for once.

I make a pitstop at the hostess stand. "How can I get my hands on three pizzas? One vegan?"

"Right now?" she asks.

"Right now." I open my wallet.

Down three-hundred later, I'm walking out with three large mystery pies. We parked in a deck around the block. Once I'm on P3, the floor deserted, I open Booger's passenger door and realize Sulli and Banks are in the backseat.

"—I'm more used to being everyone's *buddy* and pal, not being the girl that gets hit on," Sulli says, mid-conversation with him.

"Guys were probably interested in you. You just didn't notice."

"Like you?" Sulli asks, then sees me. "Kits." The look in her eye says, *come here.*

Keeping the pizza boxes on the passenger seat, I abandon that side and slip into the back with them. Sulli sprawls lengthwise across our laps. With her ass on me, her legs rest on Banks.

"Hey," I whisper, cupping her face. "You okay, Sul?"

She nods strongly. "I feel good that I didn't run away. At least he knows now that I'm not interested in him."

Banks rubs her legs.

I ignore the knot in my stomach that's pushing me to tell them what I said to Coach Reed. I don't want to. They're going to be pissed, and I'm not breaking this moment for anything. I tell Sulli, "You adulted so hard back there."

Her lips lift, matching mine. "Thanks for letting me stand my ground." Her eyes fall to Banks. "Both of you."

"Anytime, mermaid."

"Oh hey, and I didn't have to use any codewords tonight. Another success." Her head swings to me. "What'd you say to him anyway? Banks told me you were having *words.*"

"I told him not to hit on you again." It's not a lie, but it's an omission of the complete truth. It's good enough. "And he won't," I assure Sulli. "He touches you, he's dead."

Sulli nudges me like I'm overly dramatic.

I playfully cup her ears. "She thinks I'm nice."

"She's not wrong," Banks says, surprising me.

Sulli sniffs the air. "Is that...pizza?" She leans forward, nearly crawling into the front. "Kits!" She brings the pizza boxes to the back. "My hero."

"*My* hero," Banks combats. "How the hell did you swing this?"

"How I swing most things."

"With your fists?" Sulli says, like that can't be right.

"With his words," Banks counters confidently.

"With my money," I say.

"Take it back," Sulli tells me. "We don't want it."

Banks closes the top.

"Come on. You're both starving."

"Let me pay you back then," Sulli says.

"No, it's a date."

"Akara and I can split the cost," Banks adds.

"Wait…" Her brows spike. "This is a date?"

"Yeah, why not?" I eat a slice of plain cheese. "It's a drive-in without the movie."

Her lips rise.

Banks smiles off her smile, and soon, they're both digging in. With our girlfriend lounged across us, we bite into pizza and talk about the best toppings, which veers into a thousand other directions. Donuts. South Philly. Mermaids. Disney movies. Gyms. Muay Thai. We laugh and smile and laugh harder, and I'm so *dang* happy with them.

Just crammed in the backseat of an old Jeep. Eating three-hundred dollar pizza. Even after the painful moments, the saddened minutes, we find joy together.

But behind that feeling, I'm holding my breath.

If you loved her at all, you wouldn't do this to her.

Ryke's declaration is still ringing in my head.

28
Sullivan Meadows

EVER SINCE NO BUGS WERE FOUND, we've been back at the penthouse. This morning, Akara spots me on a weight bench in the penthouse's home gym. Love my old bench in my room, but the home gym has a fuck ton more plates, and I'm going heavy today. Using all my strength in my core and arms, I heave the barbell overhead.

Last one.

I finish strong.

Akara takes the bar and sets it in the holder.

I grin. "Top that, Kits."

Banks smiles while doing bicep curls. He rarely uses a mirror. Just faces me while he works out, and I didn't realize how much I'd love being in the gym with both guys. Distractions always felt like poison to progress, but I'm willfully chugging this poison.

Being around a shirtless beefcake and a shirtless dreamboat is the pinnacle of eye candy. Akara's washboard abs and Banks' six-pack glisten with sweat.

Akara is quick to say, "Lest you forget, *Lady Meadows*, I can still lift twenty-pounds heavier than you."

While I grab my phone, I motion to the plates. "Put twenty more on. Let's go."

"No quit in her," Banks says, curling his heavy hand weights.

Akara smiles. "That's how I like her best."

"I thought you liked me best naked and against you?" I say, hearing the smokiness in my own voice. My lips rise as Akara gives me a clear onceover.

Banks drinks me in too, and I'm finding greater footing in the realm of flirting. As I straddle the weight bench, I open my legs wider for Banks. He looks at my pussy.

Today is one of the few mornings where cramps aren't annihilating me. We're all sweaty, pheromones swirling in a primal state of existence, and I hope they both rush forward and just take me like I'm too fucking hot to ignore.

Just as Banks sets down his hand weights and Akara moves closer, their cellphones go off with a *knock knock* sound.

I go eerily still.

Every SFO bodyguard rigged their phones to notify any *Royal Leak* updates. *Knock knock* is the tune they all chose. My phone already in hand, I quickly open and refresh the website.

THE ROYAL LEAKS

We reveal all the truths about the American Royals. These are verified and come directly from the source.

ROYAL LEAK #1: Close family members call Maximoff, Farrow, Jane, and Thatcher "The Seasons" collectively.

#TodaysLeaks #WeStanTheSeasons
#SummerWinterSpringFall #winteriscoming

"Fuck no," I gape at my phone, realizing the awesome name that Luna and I came up with for our cousins is going to be desecrated by media and trolls.

I almost chuck my phone.

29

Banks Moretti

EATING CHOW AT WARWICK with Akara and Sulli, I found a new love. College dining halls. All you can eat lunches? Pizza oven, hoagie station, a fucking sushi bar—sign me up for the meal plan. (Akara already did.)

With a mountain of food on my plate, students give me side-eyes like I'm eating for twelve.

I'm a big guy, leave me the fuck alone. At least I'm not my brother, shoving lunchmeat in my pockets. Although, almost a year ago now, security *thought* I was the lunchmeat-pocket-eater.

Still makes me smile.

As Akara steals and eats the cherry tomatoes out of Sulli's salad for her, I scarf down a burger.

Knock knock.

I glare at my phone, then the ceiling. Couldn't wait until I finished my food? Wiping my mouth and hands with a napkin, I pull out my phone.

Akara and Sulli do the same.

THE ROYAL LEAKS

We reveal all the truths about the American Royals. These are verified and come directly from the source.

ROYAL LEAK #1: Luna Hale, Jane Cobalt, & Maximoff Hale made pot brownies.

#TodaysLeaks #holypot #CanWeSayScandal?

Sulli chokes on a lettuce leaf.

Akara pats her back, and she spits out the lettuce.

"Drink this." I pass our girlfriend a water.

Once she clears her throat, she takes a gulp, then shakes her head, "When did they make *pot* brownies? They had to have made them, right?"

"Yeah." Akara tenses. "These have all been real."

"Maximoff Hale made pot brownies?" I say with disbelief. "Seems far-fetched to me." He's sober concerning alcohol and stays away from weed. Except that one time I heard he accidentally ate an edible.

"It didn't say he ate them," Akara points out.

Gotta stop the leaks.

Security meetings are now daily and sometimes taken via FaceTime. We're all waiting for the mole to slip-up. Post something that might greater identify who they are. We've been dissecting the leaks to figure out the origin.

Everything is still pointing to the penthouse.

Akara and I hawk-eye the dining hall. Students start eyeballing Sulli more and more, phones in their possessions. Leaning into their friends, cupping hands to ears, they whisper.

"That's not good," Akara breathes. Slowly but surely *The Royal Leaks* gossip site is gaining traction, especially at Warwick where Sulli's existence on campus is well-known. Students love snapping photos and video-recording her from afar. Like an A-list celebrity spotting.

At the moment, a girl with glasses not so furtively records Sullivan looking downtrodden. Sulli's bummed expression is one I've seen before.

She has FOMO.

Fear of missing out. Or Sulli's version: Fear of Missing Every Fucking Thing.

"Sulli?" Akara nudges her side, noticing too. "They could've made the brownies while you were at work."

"Or while I was hiding out in my room." She sighs, "I just hate that it's so awkward between me and them that they wouldn't even *invite* me to make pot brownies."

Before either of us can respond, a student shouts, "HEY, SASQUATCH, YOU HAVE ANY POT BROWNIES?!"

I glare colder at that shitbag.

Akara glares hotter.

Sulli moves her chair forward, pressed up against the table. Understanding what she wants, we move our chairs further backward. Our bodies create a barrier behind her and block Sulli from onlookers. She shelters herself in front of us and mutters, "Fuck the mole."

30

Akara Kitsuwon

DISCO LIGHTS FLASH on the wooden skate rink, closed for a private event.

As per Oscar's party invites, everyone is wearing their "Long Beach, California" best. Floral shirts, cut-off shorts, fanny packs—we look more like 80s beach babes, but hey, we tried for Jack Highland-Oliveira's 28th birthday.

Which is strangely exactly one month before my birthday. Before he married Oscar, we actually talked about combining our birthdays into one party—we both share a lot of the same friends and it seemed better to do one party instead of two—but now he has a husband who wanted today to be all about him.

Hey, I get it.

I'm not a big *birthday* guy. So less is usually more for me anyway.

Hand-in-hand with Sulli, we skate easily into the barrier where Banks is struggling. At first sight, you'd think he's clumsy, but he's not. He can stand still, on guard, like an unbreakable wall. Just put wheels on his size-15 feet and his balance goes in the *crapper*.

"Leave me," Banks says, his skate almost slipping out from under him. He grabs onto the side. *Dang. Banks.* I almost laugh.

"Never," Sulli says strongly, hunched a little forward from a bout of cramps today. (I really hate when she's hurting.) Clasping Banks' hand too, she declares, "I leave no fucking boyfriend behind."

I tease, "You better only have two."

"Hardy har—"

Knock knock.

Knock knock.

Great.

Just great.

The notifications hit multiple cellphones. Donnelly glides on his skates while taking out his phone. He's wearing the shortest cut-off shorts. His white ass is hanging out.

Oscar, Farrow, and the rest of SFO pull out more phones. Clients even take out their cells, but Sulli peers at mine. Selfishly, I'm thinking, *just not Sulli.*

Just not Sulli.

I don't doubt for a second Farrow is hoping it's not Maximoff, and Thatcher is hoping it's not Jane on the receiving end.

THE ROYAL LEAKS

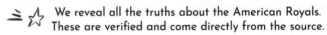 We reveal all the truths about the American Royals. These are verified and come directly from the source.

ROYAL LEAK #1: Sullivan Meadows had heavy, nonstop bloody periods and now has daily cramps.

#TodaysLeaks #SharkWeek #crampycramps

"What the ever-loving *fuck*?" Sulli is squeezing our hands to death.

Jane skates closer, then waits as Sulli turns more to Banks and me. Our girlfriend's face is beet-red as she whispers, "I didn't want the other bodyguards, let alone the fucking *world* to know about the bloodbath between my legs."

I glare at SFO to stop staring.

They drift further away on skates. All of Omega looks concerned. Oscar has an arm around Jack, and his gaze softens on Sulli.

Oscar is even less amused by *The Royal Leaks* as they're sincerely stressing out the people we dedicate our lives to protect.

In this case, it's stressing out my girlfriend.

"Is everyone looking over here?" Sulli asks.

"No," Banks lies. "They're just looking at Akara. He has a fucking booger."

Sulli snorts into a laugh.

I smile, happy to hear that sound, even if it vanishes fast. I whip out my phone and text Connor Cobalt about the recent leak. "I'm telling Connor to look into your new gynecologist. She might've broken the NDA."

Sulli winces, "Fuck, I should've just gone with Farrow as my doctor for the birth control."

"We don't know if she's the mole. We're just covering all the bases." I pocket my phone. "We talked about your period *at* the penthouse too."

"You still think the penthouse is bugged?" Sulli frowns.

"It's all-clear," Banks reminds me.

We're missing *something*.

I know we are.

31

Sullivan Meadows

PHILADELPHIA EAGLES GAME. A sea of midnight green packs the football stadium. Second quarter, and the Eagles are tied with the Giants. Football season reminds me of my dad. We'd always go to at least one game together every year, and we shouted expletives and cheers until our voices were hoarse on the ride home.

Banks says football reminds him of his dad too. They'd throw the ball back and forth when he was a kid.

Today could be somber with memories since my dad and I aren't at the best place like we were back then. I know he wants me to choose *one* guy. He made that fucking crystal when he wouldn't let both stay at the cottage.

But romance is in the air. Alleviating bad fucking feelings. Banks bought me a veggie hot dog, and Akara fits a new Eagles hat on my head.

No strangers in the stands know we're together, but it's not that unnatural for Akara to be playful with me in public as *just* my bodyguard.

I glance down our row. Jane, Thatcher, Farrow, Maximoff, and their son Ripley are here. The 10-month-old has headphones to block out the noise. I have pics of my mom and dad doing the same thing for me at football games as a baby.

Seeing Moffy bring his son everywhere reminds me so much of my childhood.

Again, I try to shake the nostalgia.

This outing wasn't my idea. Jane suggested we all take dates to an Eagles game together, after I expressed feeling left out when they cooked pot brownies. (Apparently, they made them for Eliot, who was gifting them to a friend.)

Jane made sure to include both of my boyfriends. But she still asked me, "How are things going with Banks?" Like she fears I'm seconds from breaking up with him.

Still, it's fun being here with my cousins and their husbands. All of our significant others are bodyguards and on-duty. Mics on their shirts, cords running behind their ears to their earpieces. Every now and then, I notice how they scan the crowds more than the field.

Eagles intercepted!

I sit forward, attention back on the game.

Fuck yes!

Eagles nail a touchdown! We all jump from our seats and hug. I holler and smile, and Banks shouts, "Go Iggles!"

Akara almost, *almost* wraps an arm around my shoulders but remembers not to and then throws his arms in the air, clapping over his head.

"Smooth," I tell him while we take our seats.

"The smoothest."

Halftime comes, and the jumbotron shows footage of sports fans. Quickly, the footage changes into the dreaded fucking *Kiss cam*.

And suddenly, I'm staring at my horrified face on the screen. Green streaks are painted on my cheeks, and the Eagles hat shades my eyes. The camera frames me and *Akara*.

His kissable lips are on screen. He runs a hand through his black hair, and girls go, "*Aww*," behind me.

This can't be fucking happening.

"Kiss, Kitsulli, Kiss! Kiss, Kitsulli, Kiss!" the chanting begins.

Akara acts cool, slipping a sweet smile to me. More *aww*s and shouts to *kiss him!* surround me. If I kiss Akara in public, I'm solidifying my relationship with him and denying the one with Banks. Unless I kiss both of them, but I'm not confirming my relationship on a fucking Kiss cam.

Some guy is sitting in a camera booth, controlling this outcome, and he's not dictating the next part of my life.

"KISS, KITSULLI, KISS! KISS, KITSULLI, KISS!"

Akara tilts his head and tugs at his mic cord to the camera, showing he's a bodyguard. Not a boyfriend, but the shouting never stops and the *Kiss cam* stays on us.

Maximoff and Jane are trying to wave the camera away.

The camera zooms *in* on me and Akara.

"Fuck," I curse, seeing my lips mouth the word on screen, no sound. And I'm so fucking awful at being coy because I look to Banks.

He tries his best not to make eye contact, but the camera zooms out. I'm staring between Banks and Akara, and the sports fans who also happen to be Kitsulli fans—or at least, fans of my family—begin muttering.

Banks gently elbows me like, *go kiss Akara.*

"No," I whisper to him, realizing the camera is catching me mouthing the word *no.*

Banks holds my gaze for a beat.

I'm *not* doing that to Banks. The world already loves me and Akara together, and I'm not pushing him deeper into the shadows.

Banks peels his eyes off mine and does Akara's maneuver, tugging at his mic cord to show he's on-duty. A bodyguard, not a love interest.

I shake my head at the screen and point to Jane on the other side of Thatcher.

The camera literally goes side-to-side, as though shaking its mechanical head at me.

Alright.

You want a Meadows girl on-screen. You've got a Meadows girl.

I flip off the camera with two fingers.

And like lightning, the footage switches to a more PG-friendly person. "Yeah, take that!" I shout.

Akara and Banks laugh.

The Kiss cam hasn't traveled far. Maximoff and Farrow fill the screen, and the crowds chant, "Kiss, Marrow, Kiss! Kiss, Marrow, Kiss!" And the *awws* are even louder, especially as they move in together, Farrow's hand taking Moffy's jaw, and Moffy gripping the back of Farrow's skull—they kiss with tender affection.

Fireworks literally go off in the stadium, lighting up the sky.

That could've been my kiss.

I dip my hat over my eyes and mourn what could've been an epic kiss with Akara and Banks. Yet, the world sucks, and they'll freak out over a poly relationship.

Or am I the one who'll freak out over the world's reaction?

My family's doubt is creeping in like an ugly monster.

I bite into the rubbery veggie hot dog.

Knock knock.

Knock knock.

Banks and Akara's phones sound off on either side of me.

"No," I groan.

I peek over at Akara's phone since he's faster with a cell.

THE ROYAL LEAKS

  We reveal all the truths about the American Royals. These are verified and come directly from the source.

ROYAL LEAK #1: Sullivan Meadows is no longer on birth control.

#TodaysLeaks #begonepill #noprotection

"Oh fuck," I mumble with a mouthful of wiener.

The hot dog sticks to the back of my throat. I cough and wash it down with Akara's Fizz Life. *Fuck*, I need to stop eating while I read the leaks.

Akara is angry. He pockets his phone with molten, slow heat, and Banks is grinding his teeth.

"Is everyone looking at me?" I mutter, dipping my hat further down and sinking in the chair.

"No," Banks says unconvincingly, because he sounds frostier.

I'm not embarrassed about my birth control woes. I just feel… exposed. Being on the *We Are Calloway* docuseries has helped me be more front-facing to the world, but *I* decide what airs and what ends on the cutting room floor.

I've had no mental or emotional preparation for my personal health to be a world-wide talking point. And so yeah, I'm sinking in my seat.

Peeking up from my hat, I notice Banks and Akara glancing down at me like they wish they could console me better.

I also notice Maximoff and Jane whispering and then flashing me concerned eyes. Are they fretting over how I'm shying from these *small* leaks, while a leak about my relationship with two guys would be so much *bigger*?

Sit up, Sulli.

Scooting upwards, I try to show that I'm fine.

Utterly fucking fine.

"You just went off birth control *this morning*," Akara whispers to me and Banks. "And we talked about it in the penthouse."

I remember how both guys were really supportive when I said I want to take a break from birth control. I hate how it's fucking with my hormones. Cramps left me immobile some nights, and I'm not thrilled about jumping into another hellish side effect with a new type or brand.

"Should we try to stop talking about private stuff at the penthouse?" I ask them.

Akara twists on the cap to the Fizz Life bottle. "That's easier said than done, and we're still not positive it's the penthouse, Sul. At this point, the mole could have way more leaks they're sitting on too."

It's terrifying to think that the mole could be holding onto the news about me dating two bodyguards and just waiting for the "right" time to leak it.

The mole is starting to feel like the three fates, passing around a pair of scissors, about to cut the string to my destiny.

I never really read much Greek mythology, but Beckett likes those tales. I text him my thought. But I doubt he'll text back. He rarely does after a one-night stand broke her NDA and leaked his texts.

So I'm not surprised when he calls me.

"Hey," I answer over the loud cheering as the football players take the field. Third quarter.

"Can't talk long." Classical music plays in the background, and I almost want to put the phone to Akara's ear. He always says being at the ballet makes him want to punch something.

The soundtrack to the Nutcracker being Akara's fight jam is what makes me smile randomly in the middle of the night.

"I'll take short!" I have to shout over the crowd.

"The fates don't cut the string for your destiny. When they cut the string, they're determining your moment of death."

The absurdity of it all. I start to laugh, like my body doesn't know what else to do.

32

Akara Kitsuwon

KNOCK KNOCK.

"Son of a bucket."

No one is around to hear me censor myself. I slow my motorcycle to a gas station and pull up next to a pump. Pulling off my helmet, I have a phone mic in my ear.

My Honda CBR1000R already has a full tank, and I drop my feet on either side to the cement. This bike is worth way more than what I paid. I wrecked it a long while back, and when Banks fixed it for me, he removed the fairings and turned it into a street fighter.

I ride my motorcycle when I can, and I just got back from interviewing a manager for Studio 9. Didn't like Bart. He seemed too air-headed in person.

I thought *that* was going to be the worst part of my day.

Now I'm popping up the gossip site.

THE ROYAL LEAKS

We reveal all the truths about the American Royals. These are verified and come directly from the source.

ROYAL LEAK #1: Banks Moretti hates his dad.
ROYAL LEAK #2: Charlie Cobalt is skilled at the piano.

#TodaysLeaks #daddydrama #CanWeSayProtégé?

My expression flatlines like a dead pulse.

These are two new names on the site. *Banks*. I breathe in heat even though the air is cold as winter nears. I didn't want Banks on there.

I know their relationship is strained, and Banks is more likely to curse out his dad than praise him. But he said he's making some progress with his dad. They're texting each other more.

How will Michael Moretti react to this leaking?

I tense and try to let go of that so I can concentrate on details.

Charlie doesn't live at the penthouse, but he's been playing piano there. I type these deductions into a note file on my phone.

Who is the mole?

Pocketing my phone, I fit on my helmet and ride off. Hurrying to get home to Sulli and Banks.

33

Banks Moretti

"WHAT YOUSE DOIN' OVER here pouting for?" a cousin laughs like I'm sulking in a fucking corner after the leak two days ago. It's Thanksgiving.

I'm out in the open at Uncle Joe's row house, a beer in hand. Turkey is in the oven. "Give me a fuckin' break, Vito," I say with a hard swig.

"So you're not gonna talk to your dad then?"

"So you're gonna keep standing there with your foot on your dick?" I shoot back.

Vito clucks his tongue and waves an angry hand at me. "Ah, vaffangul'."

"Yeah, fuck you too, you scustamad'."

"Hey, hey, *Banksy*," my mom says in surprise at my anger, and Vito, that fucking coward, leaves as soon as a woman approaches.

"Hey, Ma." I swig.

She takes my hand. Hers are rough like mine, from working on cars for longer than I've been alive. "Let's go talk, huh? Come on."

I follow my mom into her brother's bedroom. Small. Smells stuffy and a little like black licorice.

That's the smell of anisette, genius.

Uncle Joe loves drinking anisette, especially around the colder holidays.

"What's goin' on with you?" she asks straight out, arms crossed.

"Other than me hating Dad?"

Her gaze softens. "He called me, you know."

I frown. "What'd he say?" I sip my beer, tensed.

"He asked about you—whether you still like hockey. He was thinking of buying tickets to a game for you and him."

I stare at the shot glasses on my uncle's nightstand. "I've never liked hockey. That was…" *Skylar.* I swallow hard, unable to say the name.

"I know." She lifts her shoulders in a shrug. "I told him as much."

"Ma, you shoulda hung up on him if the first thing outta his mouth wasn't a fucking apology."

She gives me a no-nonsense look. "I've stopped expecting things from that man a long time ago." Her eyes drift over my angered expression. "You should talk to him. He's still your father—"

"He's a terrible father—"

"He's trying for you." She rests a hand on my arm. "I know what grudges are like in this family. They eat from your core and hollow something out. Don't let it get so bad it can't be filled up again."

I think for a second, lifting my beer to my lips. "I'm not saying yes, but I'm not saying no."

She rolls her eyes with a smile and reaches up to touch my jaw. "I love you, Banksy. Don't be a gabbadost' like half the men in this family. We have enough of 'em."

I'm not as big of a hardhead as Thatcher, that's for sure. I glance back at the door. "All the family knows about me hating dad now?" I ask.

"They already knew."

Right.

I finish off my beer. "Except now I get to hear an earful from my cousins."

If it were up to me, I'd be spending Thanksgiving with my girlfriend. But I wasn't invited.

Neither was Akara.

Ryke knew if he left one of us out, Sulli wouldn't show, and he wanted to spend Thanksgiving with his daughter. She wanted to spend it with us, but this was a good opportunity for them to work things out.

And even if I wanted, I couldn't invite Sulli to my uncle's house. No one knows we're together, not even my mom.

She waves a hand like my cousins are full of shit anyway. "Ignore 'em."

For a second, I contemplate telling her about me and Sulli and Akara. "Ma," I start.

Knock knock.

Fuck me sideways and back to fucking *hell* again. I dig irritably in my pocket.

"What's that noise?" she asks.

"An alert for The Royal Leaks." I open the website.

THE ROYAL LEAKS

We reveal all the truths about the American Royals. These are verified and come directly from the source.

ROYAL LEAK #1: Thatcher & Jane are trying to have a baby.

#TodaysLeaks #GetItOn #oooohbaby

I smile, liking this one, even if the news should've been aired with their permission. I show my mom.

She gasps into a big grin and pats my chest.

I wrap an arm over my mom's shoulders. "Someday soon, you're gonna be a grandma."

"You're gonna be an uncle."

"Uncle Banks." I nod, liking that for me.

The door flings open. "Gloria!" my aunt shouts. "Did ya see?!" More shouts of excitement pitch the air behind her. Uplifting my Thanksgiving.

34

Sullivan Meadows

I PEEL A GREEN CUPCAKE decorated like an alien head and just sniff the frosting. Contact sugar high. It smells fucking divine. *Bet it tastes even better.*

I'm salivating.

If Winona didn't recently profess to being so proud of me for still being vegan, I'd deep-throat this birthday cupcake right now.

I sink deeper on a teal beanbag. In the penthouse's game room, we pushed aside the pool table to make room for several beanbags and a projector screen.

The *Star Wars* movie marathon isn't enough to distract my cravings, and I already gave Luna her 20th birthday present: a new beaded friendship bracelet and a nonfiction book about life in the universe.

"Thanks, Sulli." We fist-bumped and then hugged. All seemed to be going okay. Except, now I'm a beanbag behind Luna, Moffy, and Jane, and I catch Luna passing her brother a note.

My ribcage tightens. *They're not leaving you out, Sulli.*

The insecurity rises tenfold as Maximoff unfurls the notes and reads, angling his body away from me.

Fuck.

Why would Luna pass a note? Couldn't she just talk to Moffy? What if she's deliberately trying to keep something from me?

I sink even further down my beanbag. Sufficiently no longer interested in the alien cupcake, I set the baked good aside.

Glancing to my left and right, I expect to see Banks or Akara. To seek shelter in the fact that they're with me and they leave me out of nothing. But most of SFO are in the library, currently in a security meeting.

So it's just me, Luna, Jane, Moffy, and Moffy's son. Baby Ripley is curled up on a beanbag with Arkham, the furry brown Newfoundland puppy. Luna's black-furred Newfie has been chasing a calico cat around the pinball machines.

And then Luna's best buds, Tom and Eliot are en route to join the movie marathon, driving from New York, and Luna already had a birthday dinner with her family at the Hale house.

Moffy stretches further over and whispers to Luna.

She nods.

I cage breath as Moffy passes the note to *Jane*.

They are leaving me out. I'm the only other one in the fucking room. Hurt courses through me for a full minute, just watching Jane peer at the note, and once she's done, she nods with certainty to Luna. And then…

And then she passes the note to me.

Shock parts my lips, and Jane waves the note because I'm too frozen to take it right away. Unfreezing, I retrieve the note and feel Moffy, Luna, and Jane eyeing me. They even scoot a little closer, and I'm totally fucking confused until I stare at Luna's handwriting in neon gel pen.

> In case the penthouse IS bugged, can we make a pact tonight? No one talks about my hookup with Donnelly out loud in the penthouse. My dad will kill him. My one birthday wish is for him to stay alive & not get fired.

I relax, understanding why the secrecy with the note. We're *in* the penthouse right now, and she can't say any of this out loud.

I nod to Luna and mouth, *I fucking promise.*

She begins to smile, then puts a hand in the middle of our circle. Her big brother puts his on top of hers, then me, and finally, Jane.

We explode our hands up.

Knock knock.

"No," Luna and I moan in pain at the fucking *leaks.* We're so over these incoming tidal waves.

Moffy has the same *knock knock* alert on his phone as SFO, and he opens up the website before I can even grab my cell.

His cheekbones sharpen. "Luna, wait—"

She's already looking, and I peer over her shoulder to read.

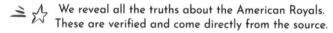

THE ROYAL LEAKS

We reveal all the truths about the American Royals. These are verified and come directly from the source.

ROYAL LEAK #1: Luna Hale writes tentacle porn.

#TodaysLeaks #omg! #scandalous

"Oh my God," Jane breathes, wide-eyed.

"That fucking mole," I mutter. "On her *birthday* of all days. It's fucking cruel."

"Oui," Jane nods.

If the penthouse is bugged, I hope they've heard how much I've cursed them to Satan's anus.

"Luna?" Moffy says a little softer, his hand on her shoulder.

Luna is superglued to the screen. "You think Mom and Dad will be freaked out?" She looks up at her big brother.

"I think they're going to ask questions, but what you write *isn't* wrong, Luna. They'll understand that."

"The world won't," she mutters. "They'll just keep saying I'm a sex addict like Mom." She shrugs. "People suck, though. What's new?" Luna is jaded towards bad things happening.

I wish we could instill more birthday magic. My mom has a staple theory above most theories.

Cake fixes everything.

"Cupcake?" I ask Luna, holding my uneaten one out to her.

"Thanks, Sulli." She licks off the icing.

The door swings open. SFO come swooping back into the game room. Concern lines their faces, knowing exactly what just leaked. Everyone falls silent as they trickle inside.

Chewbacca's Wookie noise pitches the air from the TV, and Luna mimics it almost perfectly. She adds a couple R2D2 beeps in at the end. It doesn't do much to quell the tension in the room. As soon as she's done, silence befalls for an awkward beat.

Akara cuts it and tells Luna, "Hey, I'm sorry this happened, Luna. I promise we're working on it."

"I know." She shrugs, then wobbles to her feet. To everyone, she asks, "Thumbs-up if you want a Jell-O shot. Jane made them."

My thumb goes up, along with Banks and several others. Akara must have business calls or something because he keeps his hand down.

Luna pockets the note about Donnelly, and the tattooed, chestnut-haired bodyguard keeps his thumb up for Luna. Close to each other, he uses his thumb to pick an eyelash off her cheek. "Make a wish."

"You make it. I'm not as lucky."

35

Akara Kitsuwon

"SHE *REJECTED* AKARA Kitsuwon in front of an entire football stadium of people, not to mention everyone watching in sports bars and at home, Cathy."

"We have to give Sullivan Meadows some leeway here. She's *shy* in public, and the pressure couldn't have been easy to handle. Like you said, Jackie, she had *millions* of eyes on her."

"Come on, you saw her look over at Banks Moretti."

"She denied him too. That's all I'm saying."

I pull my AirPods out, done listening to a segment of 97.2 *The Fix*. Sulli texted me the radio clip with sad face emojis and I didn't mean to reject anyone. I'm sorry, Kits.

With a pang in my chest, I quickly text Sulli back: you don't have to apologize. I didn't expect you to kiss me, Sul. It was an impossible situation. And the Kiss cam shit will die down soon. It's only been 10 days.

She's put a lot of pressure on herself to be fair and equal to me and Banks, and she's better at it than she even realizes.

Sulli also isn't a dig-for-audio-clips kind of client. *Apparently*, the girl squad overheard the radio station, and Winona sent Sulli the video, asking what she should tell Kinney, Audrey, and Vada.

Speculation has been swirling among the teenagers and the Cobalt brothers. They've been left out. Until today, when Banks, Sulli, and I gave the *go ahead* for certain family members to tell others. Before they start taking sides, it's better they know that Sulli is with me and Banks.

Winona told the girl squad.

Beckett told his brothers.

And Maximoff told Xander.

We didn't need to give Sulli's parents the *go ahead* to tell Rose, Connor, Lily, and Loren. They had already told them, and mostly, I'm unsurprised. Ryke has been pissy and moody, and I'm sure Loren Hale asked his brother, *what's wrong with you, bro?*

I can only imagine his response.

My daughter is dating two fucking bodyguards, that's what's fucking wrong.

Phone buzzing in my palm, Sulli texts back a fist-bump emoji.

I'm slugging you virtually for cursing virtually — Sulli

I did curse in text, didn't I?

I smile a little, but just in case she's still letting the situation dig under her skin, I send my girlfriend about four dorky emojis. Kiss face, tongue sticking out face, an eggplant, then an okay hand.

She texts the water emoji, signaling wetness.

My lips keep rising, and I want nothing more than to just keep texting Sulli. To forget about all the troubles that pile on and on my plate. Today, I'm currently digging through the main course with my men.

And I've just dipped out on them—for a *brief* second. I just had to text her back and listen to the radio clip in private.

I'm in a bathroom inside a swanky Philadelphia clothier, specialized in suit and tux fittings with on-site tailors. Salt scrub is in a dish next to the marble sinks, and if Banks comes in here, he'd be grunting at the pretentiousness of it all while *using* the salt scrub.

As I rotate to head back to the guys, the door opens, and my chest rises, half-expecting, half-hoping to see Banks walk through.

Instead, his twin brother comes in.

Thatcher barely acknowledges my existence. He's my *best* friend. And our friendship has already gone through the ringer once and come out bruised but whole. Now, it feels different.

Like I'm losing him completely.

Like there's no way back.

There's always a way back, Nine.

My eyes burn. I don't know if that's true. He's drifting closer to Farrow, and I'm drifting closer to Banks, and maybe there's no avenue where we rebuild the bridge that I burned between us.

Before Thatcher reaches a urinal, I call out, "You want to talk about this?"

Craning his neck over his shoulder, he looks back at me. "You already know how I feel."

I massage my hands, breath tight in my lungs. "I'm not trying to hurt your brother. I love Banks."

Thatcher turns slightly, expression incensed, pained, *protective.* "If you loved him at all, you wouldn't do this to him."

It's a gut punch.

I nearly stagger back. Hearing those same words that I heard from Ryke now come from Thatcher—it almost kills my resolve.

I shake my head tensely. "Sulli *loves* Banks more than you understand—"

"She'll never love him like she loves you, and you know it," he interjects with heat.

"Why?" I glower, my chest rising and falling in rapid succession. "My history with Sulli doesn't change the fact that she *needs* him. This doesn't work without Banks."

Thatcher is disbelieving. "You're saying you and Sulli can't be together without him? You're saying down the line, when things get messy, you won't realize it's *easier* with just you and her?"

"I don't give a crap about what's *easy*."

"That's *easy* for you to say. You won't have it that hard. You're the fan favorite, Akara. And my brother…" His eyes redden with emotion. He jabs a finger towards my chest. "…my brother deserves *more* than coming second to you, to me." He pushes his finger to his own chest, then motions around the bathroom. "And to anyone in this fucked world."

I nod, eyes stinging. "We agree on that."

"But you won't do a damned thing about it. That's how I know you don't love him." With that finality, he turns his back on me.

His words eviscerate me. Like a blade in the chest, I'm exiting the bathroom wounded, and I do my best to pretend like I'm *peachy*.

Not bleeding out at all. With a deep breath, I get my crap together. I have a meeting to lead and a tux fitting scheduled for every bodyguard.

Back in a private fitting room, racks of designer suits hang in wooden cubbies. Wreaths hang on the store's windows, and outside, snow flurries catch in the breeze.

December has arrived. Classic Christmas tunes are even playing softly in the background.

Warm inside—Banks, Quinn, Donnelly, and Farrow lounge on leather furniture while Oscar is on a circular platform facing mirrors. A tailor wraps a tape measure around his bicep.

"He's giving it that extra flex," Donnelly jokes.

"I don't need to give it an extra *anything*, Donnelly," Oscar says, "I'm just this hot." He flips curly pieces of his hair with a head-jerk. "Tens across the board."

"Keep talking to the mirror, Oliveira," Farrow calls out, "it still doesn't like you back."

Donnelly laughs.

Oscar smiles, "Aw, fuck you, Redford."

Farrow's smile stretches.

Glad that the Yale boys are having a grand ole time. Seriously, I am. I like when Omega isn't being torn apart with in-fighting. In the past, the biggest rift came from the Oliveira brothers. Now they're closer than ever.

The only giant sore spot is me and Thatcher.

But it won't change our team and trust. All seven of us together have always been less dysfunctional than we are *functional*. We work better than just *okay* together. Of all the bodyguards I've stood beside in the past, this collection of men is the best.

I never hesitated or second-guessed going to bat for them during our days in Triple Shield. I wouldn't hesitate or second-guess now.

Standing up front near the tailor, I tell everyone, "Once Thatcher is back, we'll need to go over a potential new shakeup, guys." I sober the room, but I have to return to business. We're no closer to finding out the mole than we are discovering life on Pluto, but we still have housekeeping issues.

Baby needs a bodyguard.

Banks bobs his head, but his brows pinch at me like, *you alright?*

I nod to him. Still, my chest is tight.

I snap my finger to my palm, and I gesture to Farrow. "Is Maximoff excited about the Winter Festival?" It'll be the first charity event he's hosting as CEO of H.M.C. Philanthropies again.

"More or less," Farrow says with the tilt of his head. He starts to smile. "It's a big deal for him, and if we could all just try not to fuck that up, that'd be great."

"He's looking at you, Donnelly," Oscar quips.

"Coulda sworn he was staring at Quinnie."

"Me?" Quinn smiles. "I'm the least likely to instigate drama."

"Careful what you say, bro." Oscar says, "Drama's gonna come bite your ass."

Farrow lifts his brows at Quinn. "Didn't you fight your brother at the Charity Golf Tournament?"

His face drops. "Alright, I take it back."

Donnelly laughs, and I loosely cross my arms. *Waiting on you, Thatcher.* The tailor starts to measure the length of Oscar's leg, and another consultant approaches me.

"Mr. Kitsuwon, you want to go with the Brioni collection for all of them?"

"Yes. Same color."

"Black?"

I nod, and I hand him my credit card. "Take care of it now, discreetly."

Tickets to the Winter Festival sold out in five-minutes, but to reinforce security, the ticket holders are wealthy patrons. Not just the average Joe off the street. *Socialites.* So Price Kepler informed me that his men will be arriving in tailored Tom Ford suits.

Some of my guys have been wearing the same Hugo Boss suit for over six years. Dirty, holes in the knees, and scuff marks on the legs—I can't let SFO arrive looking *less than* Triple Shield.

Not with well-to-do *gossipmongers* there.

I have a brand to maintain.

So I sold my streetfighter bike last night. Banks was pissed, especially since it barely covers half the cost of the designer suits. I'm charging the rest.

"Of course, Mr. Kitsuwon." The consultant leaves for the register outside the fitting room.

I breathe in and eye the suits in the wooden cubbies.

My gaze softens, remembering my dad.

He'd bring me to his personal tailor, and I'd watch him stand poised in Cesare Attolini, Oxxford, Brioni, and other high-end suit brands. He taught me about the super number of wool, peaked lapels vs notched, and the classic choice of a two-button jacket.

SFO couldn't care less about those details. They're just happy to have a day to unwind with the entire team. Temps guard their clients, and my mic is loose on my collar in case I'm needed.

"The lil elf knows I'd never ditch him," Donnelly says about his client. "We're buds—"

I give him a look. He's not supposed to get too close to Xander.

"But *not* buddies," Donnelly says quickly, seeing me. "We're just normal bodyguard and client. No cap."

Quinn frowns. "No cap?"

"Means *no lie*, bro," Oscar explains.

I reply to a few emails while I wait for Thatcher. Partially listening as the conversation changes among SFO.

"The leaks have to be coming from someone in the family, right?" Quinn asks, unscrewing a cap to a water bottle. "I mean, Audrey was responsible for leaking the Hot Santa Video. Anyone talk to her?"

Oscar has his arms out as the tailor (who signed an NDA) takes wingspan measurements. "How would Audrey Cobalt know half the shit on that website, little bro?"

Quinn shrugs. "Maybe she's butt-dialing Jane and listening in on accident."

"That's not happening," Thatcher suddenly says, coming into the room. Will he look at me as he goes to sit beside his brother?

That'd be a big overwhelming *nope*.

Awesome.

"Okay, guys," I begin, wanting to take my mind off Thatcher and Banks and Sulli. Best way to do that is *work*. I open my mouth, and—

Knock knock.

We tense as all seven of our phones sound off.

"Who's there?" Oscar jokes.

"Howie," Donnelly replies.

"Howie who?"

"Howie gonna catch this dick?"

Oscar takes out his phone. "Throw them big dick bait. Redford attracts big dick energy."

"He is big dick energy," Donnelly says.

"Takes one to know one."

"Oh my God, shut the fuck up," Farrow says while he's trying to read the post.

I try to focus on the website, but something Oscar said is flicking on a light bulb. But not the part about Farrow and big dicks.

THE ROYAL LEAKS

We reveal all the truths about the American Royals.
These are verified and come directly from the source.

ROYAL LEAK #1: Ripley Hale needs a bodyguard. Uncertain about who that'll be.

ROYAL LEAK #2: Farrow Hale found a used pregnancy test in the penthouse.

#TodaysLeaks #WhoIsPregnant? #solvethemystery

I go still.

Someone overheard me talking about Ripley, but I can't recall which room I said *baby needs a bodyguard* in. But that's not the biggest shocker. We're all looking at Farrow.

His eyes are narrowed on the phone. "See, this is fishy as fuck."

"Why?" I ask.

"Because I found a *negative* pregnancy test on the bathroom counter, and I said, *it's negative* to Maximoff."

"It was Jane's," Thatcher informs us.

Farrow lifts his brows. "So why did the mole leave that shit out?"

It's half the truth. "To stir up drama," I say aloud.

Now there's certain to be speculation about which girl is pregnant in the families. And *recently,* a leak stated that Sulli went off birth control.

I push my hair back.

Banks says, "Sulli is being set-up."

Thatcher looks to his brother. "Media could predict *Jane.* One of the leaks is about us trying to have a baby."

Banks bows his head, looking upset at either situation.

The same weight bears on the back of my neck, but I have to keep my head upright. To the tailor, I ask, "Can you give us a few minutes?"

He nods and shuffles away.

"That knock knock joke," I mention, "what Oscar said before about big dick bait—he was onto something."

"I always am," Oscar notes.

Farrow's brows arch like I've lost my mind. "It was a knock knock joke, not a guide to the end of a rainbow."

"Go with me here, Farrow," I say, running my thumb over my knuckles. "For the first time, the penthouse was just specifically mentioned in a leak, and the tagline hasn't changed." I quote, "'These are verified and come directly from *the source*.' Everything still leads back to the penthouse, and we need to ensure that's the origin. We can bait the mole."

"With Farrow's big dick energy," Donnelly says.

Everyone laughs, and Farrow rolls his eyes with a slight smile.

"No," I say. "With lies. We have a fake conversation in each room of the house, and we see which lie leaks. Then, I'll have surveillance come back and sweep the room."

Oscar nods confidently. "Now, I like this."

"I hate this," Thatcher declares off-the-bat.

"Me too," Farrow says. "What lie do we plan on casting out there that'll impact our clients? And who do you want to lie because I swear, Akara, if you say *Maximoff*—"

"It can be about me," Banks pipes in.

All eyes swerve on him.

"I'm the only bodyguard who's on the website that has no connection to anyone else," he explains. "As far as they know, I'm not dating Sulli."

"That we know of," I say and shake my head vigorously, not wanting Banks to sacrifice himself, but Farrow is right, I can't choose a client.

And I'd put myself out there, but the mole hasn't targeted me, the Oliveira brothers, or Donnelly yet. They may never.

Thatcher ends up saying, "Jane and I will do it. She'll want to be the one."

"Are you sure?" I ask him.

He nods. "Positive. We can handle the blowback."

Banks slips him a side glare like that was a shot at Sulli.

He shakes his head to his brother like it wasn't, but yeah, that felt personal. "Jane and I will come up with a list of lies," Thatcher says, "and we'll make a plan for each room."

"Thank you," I tell him.

He nods back, a small recognition that beyond our rift, we're still here for these families and for each other.

I'm about to address everyone again when another tailor speaks louder from the back. "I'm sorry, Mr. Montgomery, but we're going to have to order extra fabric to fit your…well, all of you really." The tailor returns with the new 24/7 bodyguard.

Security Force Omega is now officially eight men strong.

The tailor gives Gabe Montgomery a sympathetic look and leaves him in the fitting room with us. Stocky, blond-haired, and only twenty-two like Quinn—Gabe is by far the most muscular bodyguard in my fleet.

"They really did you like that, Monty?" Donnelly asks.

"They're just jealous of these guns." He kisses his bicep.

"No one's jealous of your honey baked hams," Oscar tells him.

Gabe smiles. "It's Thanksgiving every day over here."

The guy might not be the brightest crayon in the box, but he's fast for his size, intimidating at first glance, *and* he aced all of Michael Moretti's training.

After a lot of consideration, I promoted him to the full-time roster as the floater. He has Banks' old position. And he's been doing well as Jack Highland-Oliveira's part-time bodyguard.

Gabe is also a key element in my grand master plan.

I clasp my hands. "Okay, guys, the reshuffle." I motion to the most tattooed bodyguard. "I've talked with Farrow about potentially assigning a full-time bodyguard on Ripley."

"Potentially," Farrow emphasizes.

I nod and explain to everyone else, "He talked with Maximoff, who's open to the idea." I nod towards Farrow to elaborate.

"Wolf scout likes roadmaps and not a vague picture of what that'll look like. He also cares about *who* you're reshuffling to make this work."

Which is why I couldn't go for the obvious pairing. Pull Donnelly off Xander and pair him with Ripley. It makes the most sense and alleviates the tension between Donnelly and Xander's dad.

But Xander likes Donnelly.

Xander is Maximoff Hale's younger brother.

Maximoff wants what makes Xander happy.

This was a logic puzzle that I think I nailed. "I'm sending you a written proposal for Maximoff to read over tonight," I tell Farrow, "but I wanted to run it by everyone here first."

They all listen carefully.

"Quinn will be transferred to Ripley's detail. He mirrors your style of guarding, Farrow, so he should be the best fit to protect your son."

"And Luna?" Donnelly asks before even Quinn.

I stare into him. Why is he asking about Luna? I have a weird feeling, knowing Luna is sheltering some kind of secret that we shouldn't know. And he was the most vocal about the "tentacle porn" leak.

Please tell me they didn't fuck.

Banks is eyeing me, then Donnelly too.

I wanted to solve the mystery, but not if it's leading me *here*. I could ask him outright, but I almost don't want to know now.

Shit.

Shoot.

Whatever the heck.

"Gabe will be transferred to Luna," I tell everyone.

"Sweet," Gabe says into a nod.

Donnelly goes quiet.

Farrow lifts his brows. "And you're back to not having a floater." He prefers having a floater on SFO so temps aren't on Maximoff during med calls.

"Hopefully soon, Michael Moretti should have another temp ready to transition to full-time and they'll become the new floater. How does that sound?"

"I'm game," Quinn nods confidently, knowing this is a harder task and a bigger challenge. He looks to Farrow. "I'd protect Ripley with my life, Farrow. I'm good with kids."

"He is," Oscar advocates. "Babies and puppies love my bro. He's a perfect fit."

Farrow thinks for half-a-second. "I need to talk to Maximoff."

I nod. "Get back to me when you can. Until then, everyone stays where they are, but the reshuffle is all in the plan."

All in the plan.

The grand master plan.

Let's just hope nothing fudges it up.

36

Sullivan Meadows

NESTLED IN THE BACK of an iconic red sleigh, I snuggle up under a furry gray blanket. Bells jingle-jangle as a horse trots along a circular path around the Winter Festival. A heavy snowfall last night in Philly has made tonight a winter wonderland.

As the sleigh ride circles the festival, I soak in the romantic atmosphere. Snow and icicles coat tree limbs in a majestic, Disney-like setting. I've gone from *The Little Mermaid* to *Frozen* in a blink. Bulbed lights are strung along branches and trunks, and carolers sing classic holiday songs.

Around the glittering lights, kids and adults sip hot chocolate and eggnog. Sledders laugh as they whiz down the biggest hill in the distance. Others build snowmen in a contest for the Winter Fest trophy, and I see smiling families as they slip into a warm tent, full of holiday arts & crafts like ornament painting and gingerbread making.

Moffy outdid himself with his comeback.

I inhale the crisp air and eye the twinkling stars on the clearest night. When I peek beside me, I smile even more.

Unbeknownst to the guests here, I'm on a *formal* date.

Akara asked me out, and even if he's on-duty, I haven't stopped smiling, especially as I sneak glances to my left. He's underneath the same blanket, his hand subtly on my leg and dipping closer to my inner-thigh.

I warm at his touch.

Kits looks beyond dapper, like he stepped out of a *Vanity Fair* fashion shoot with a black-tie theme. He's always rocked tuxes and suits, but this one fits him like a million dollars. His smoldering gaze carries light and a twinkling smile as he sneaks glimpses of me too.

"I'm properly dressed this time," I tell him since I'm wearing a glitzy silver jumpsuit and furry cropped jacket. Cold nips my cheeks, but a white pom beanie warms my ears. Moffy told me the guest list is mostly familiar families in the charity circle. Basically, the kids we grew up around and their parents. Socialites galore. But I really wanted to dress up for my date. Not really for anyone else.

Akara leans closer to whisper against my ear, "You look beautiful." I start to smile more, and then he adds, "String bean."

I elbow his side.

He laughs into my hair.

"Oh my gosh," a teenager gasps to her friend as they stand in a line for hot cocoa and cookies. They stare right at the sleigh, at me. At Akara.

At us.

Together.

Her friend whips out a phone to snap photos, and we sort of draw a reasonable distance away.

In front of us with reins in hand, a man on the bench hardly notices the attention we attract. His back is faced to us, and he keeps guiding the horse forward.

"I knew they were together," she says too loudly as the horse trots past them.

I ache to shout, *I'm also with Banks!* He's not assigned to my detail tonight, which is why I'm on a one-on-one date with Akara.

Before guilt or weird feelings dampens the mood, I turn back to Akara and pull the blanket up to my chest. "My dad took my mom on a sleigh ride," I tell him, "out in the snowy woods. It was before I was born." I smile more, remembering the story well. "My mom said it was one of the most romantic things my dad has ever done for her."

Akara smiles, his eyes glittering on me again. He tells me, "My dad was always the romantic one with my mom. He'd go the extra hundred miles. Flowers, just because. Love notes under her pillow. Poems— dang, he wrote so many poems. I have none of that in me." His smile slowly fades in thought. "I should do more for you. Flowers, just because. Poems—"

"No," I shake my head. "That's not totally you, Kits."

His breath smokes the air as he asks, "What am I then?"

"You're the guy who eats the veggies that I fucking hate, just so I don't have to stare at them, the guy who goes out of his way to find me donuts and cupcakes, on more than just my birthday. The guy who tosses my hair in my face to make me smile, the guy who steals my gummy bears and arm-wrestles until my bicep is sore, the guy who races after me every time I say *go*. You're Kits. *My* Kits."

His chest rises in a deeper breath. He holds my hand under the blanket.

Softly, I say, "And my dad isn't the 'just because' flowers type either. Their romance was always in the adventures they took together." I feel his thumb brush over my gloved knuckles. "Plus, today is *your* birthday. I should be *wooing* the holy fuck out of you."

He laughs. "You already are wooing the holy *cow* out of me, Sul."

Smiling, I edge closer to his side. Up against each other more.

His smile softens. "Birthdays aren't always easy for me."

I squeeze his hand. "I know."

He squeezes back and eases against the sleigh.

His dad passed away on December 17th. Only one day before Akara's birthday. His dad never saw him turn eighteen. In past years of celebrating Akara turning older, I can tell memories of his dad linger and drift around.

"I love that you wanted to spend your birthday on a date with me," I mention.

"It's already been the best birthday."

I snort, like he's full of it.

"I mean it, Sulli."

The snowy festival and lights fall to my peripheral as Akara takes total center focus. I'm his main focus too.

I can't stop staring at his kissable lips.

He keeps looking at mine.

Kiss me, Kits.

He can't.

Not here. We divert our gazes as thunderous applause sounds from a professional ice sculpting competition.

Akara leans up to the sleigh driver. "Sir, can you stop up here?"

"Sure thing." The sleigh slows to a halt. "You two have a good night."

"You too," I tell him.

Akara jumps off, then extends a hand to help me down. I could jump to show off, but any excuse to touch Akara, I'm swimming my fastest towards, like the Olympian I am. With a bigger smile, I clasp his hand, and I step off the sleigh. "Where are we going?"

"On an adventure."

Something bursts happily inside me.

Take me, Kits.

He's quick to lead me while I trail behind his assured footsteps. He's reaching back, and his fingers are hooked with my fingers in a breathless embrace. This is what a bodyguard would do in a jam-packed crowd, but we're not weaving through bodies.

I realize he just wants to hold my hand like I want to hold his.

After a pitstop where Akara buys me spiked hot cocoa, he guides me towards the entrance to a snowy garden. Green hedges are snowcapped and form a wonderland maze. Butterflies flap wildly inside me. Have I ever been anywhere *this* romantic?

If I have, I shirked romance away. I focused so much on my goals that I never breathed in the atmosphere, but tonight, I'm zeroed in on *love.*

My face hurts from smiling.

We stop at the garden's entrance, and I sip my hot cocoa with gloves way too big for my hands. The black leather is identical to Akara's gloves.

Earlier tonight, I saw Banks and threw a snowball at him with bare hands. Akara pelted him too, and my fingers went numb.

Banks lent me his gloves for the night.

I love him.

And I utterly fucking love the man standing in front of me. Both can be true. Both *are* true.

Akara steps closer, and a sliver of air between us is aching to be closed. When I drop a hand, his hand dances inches away from mine. Our fingers are charged with electricity.

He brushes his fingers against my fingers before fixing his comms mic. Our eyes latch. Energy zips from my fingertips, up my body, and into my heart.

"Kitsulli!" A young girl in puffy pink earmuffs waves a hand to us, then nudges her cluster of friends and points.

My stomach tosses. I haven't felt *this* exposed since the football game, and maybe even the carnival fundraiser. I'm very attuned to the staring all of a sudden.

Out in public, the whole Kitsulli rumor is less like a whisper and more like a banshee cry.

As I brush off the girl with zero response, her shoulders droop, dejected. To her friend, she says loudly, "Jane Cobalt would've waved back."

Fuck.

I'm not Jane.

I can't easily make myself available to strangers. Especially when these people are fans of only one guy and not the other.

Akara sees me shrink into myself, and he takes a slight step *away* from me but *around* to block the girls. He's quelling the rumors, but the distance hurts, still. I just want to enjoy being with Akara without all the other bullshit attached.

I want to go back to the woods.

Back to our island.

Am I going to feel like that every time we're out with strangers?

"Sulli," he breathes out my name, seeing my hurt.

"No, you're doing the right fucking thing," I affirm. *Kitsulli* doesn't include Banks, and the ship I want to sail involves both men.

Akara stares at my oversized gloves as I hold a mug. "Are you okay that Banks isn't on your detail tonight?"

I nod, "I understand why."

To support Moffy, Xander Hale left the comfort of his home for the Winter Festival. Whenever Xander braves events of this size, it's a *major* ordeal. Most of the squeals I've heard tonight have been over him.

Akara made the call to put a second bodyguard on Xander, so my little cousin has Donnelly *and* Banks. He could've put the new floater *Gabe* on his detail, but Gabe is protecting Maximoff while Farrow is on med-duty for the event.

What time I do have with Akara lately is precious and not always endless. He's juggling a lot this year, and I just cherish every little moment with him.

I tell him, "I really like that you both want to take me out separately too." I sip my cocoa. "And I like how the three of us were together earlier. It's just…"

"Euphoric," Akara says with rising lips.

"Yeah." I smile back, and I don't think—I just feel the words as they reach me, "Like a hug and a laugh when you need it most." *That's how we are together.* It's perfect effervescence, but no one can see that or feel that but us. "Anyway, I think the three of us would've broken the weight max on the sleigh if we rode together."

Akara laughs. "We definitely would've. It'd come crashing down."

"I'd roll into the snow."

"Banks would throw you over his shoulder."

"And you'd take my face in your hands."

We've drawn even closer.

"Kitsulli!"

I check my surroundings. *Oh fuck.* The young teens have grown in number, gathering in a group around a fir tree and iron benches. *Winter Festival* banners sway in the chilly breeze near them.

I've been warming myself with the spiked hot cocoa, and as anxiety rushes through me, I down the whole mug in a couple gulps.

Akara watches me. "Sul? You okay?"

I swallow hard and then accidentally let out a soft belch. *Fuck.*

"Lady Meadows," he says into a smile. "How very courtly of you."
He looks at me like I'm the most gorgeous thing in the garden. There
is no *friend zone* in those eyes. I'm more to him, and I inhale strongly like
I'm trying to breathe in the moment for eternity.

And then I touch my lips, pretending to be more of a lady. "Pardon
fucking me."

His smile widens.

I sway a little, buzzing from the alcohol.

His humor instantly shatters. "Sul." He actually does reach for my
hand this time. Our fingers touch and the intensity of the moment *in
public* races my heart and quickens my breath.

A wave of shocked gasps comes from the Kitsulli crowd.

I flinch.

Akara drops his hand again.

I swallow hard as my nerves ratchet up. "Maybe we should get more
hot cocoa," I suggest with a tip of my mug. "I'm all out."

Akara stares at the mug for a beat too long.

"Kits?" My stomach knots.

His eyes flit to me, concern outlining his brown irises. "You feel
okay?"

"Totally," I nod, hoping he can see that I can handle alcohol now.
The pass-out phase is long gone. Feels like it hasn't happened in *forever.*
"Just warm and fuzzy. I could probably have another." I like this floaty
feeling and how the knot in my stomach untwists.

Two mugs of spiked hot cocoa and my nerves will be obliterated.
Those people pointing and staring and making the wrong assumptions
about my relationship won't be able to cross the barrier I build. That
magical barrier allows me to not care about them.

I just don't want to fucking care.

I want to be unbothered. Unaffected.

Akara tilts his head to the maze of snowcapped garden hedges.
"One time through and then more hot cocoa?"

"Deal." I follow him into the maze just as someone shouts at the
top of their lungs, "XANDER, LOOK AT ME!"

The distraction (albeit, not great for my cousin) does grant me some reprieve from the Kitsulli crowd. No one traces my footsteps into the maze.

Our boots crunch the snow, and I slip in front of Akara and walk backwards while he follows.

His brows rise. "I'm supposed to be in front of you, Sul."

"Beat me then," I say in challenge.

And I take off. Sprinting through the hedges. He's fast, but I'm faster. Darting around the green hedges. His hands catch my waist but slip off. Laughter tumbles from my lips. The air is cold, and the twinkle lights dance above us.

The alcohol drives warmth through my blood, and my head dizzies for a second. When I round a corner of white rose bushes, I trip on my own pantleg. Before I tumble face first into snow, Akara grabs me around the waist.

His hands firm.

His body hard.

He pulls me back towards him.

I'm breathless. Windblown and tidal swept. He's the dreamboat shielding me from the rip current.

His lips brush my ear. "Caught you." His voice might as well light my sex drive on fucking fire. Heat bathes me in an instant.

I tilt my head back against his shoulder to look up into his eyes without breaking from his hold. "Wild things aren't meant to be caught," I breathe.

His eyes caress mine. "You're not a *thing*."

"Then what am I?"

"Mine," he says. "*His*." His lips hover against my ear once more. "Ours."

My heart beats harder in my chest.

Kits places a hand on my collarbones in desirous affection. Longing pools between us like a raging ocean. "You're right about one thing," he whispers.

"What?"

"Wild *creatures* aren't meant to be caught," he says. "But they do choose their home."

My heart thumps. "Is that why we all chose each other?"

"I'd like to think so," Akara says with another rising smile.

Carolers hum in the distance, and the scent of roses permeates around us. Melodic and heady, we start to sway. His hands still holding me tight to him. Mine pressed atop his.

"Happy Birthday, Kits," I say as I spin to face him, and after digging in my jumpsuit's pocket (yes, it's fucking awesome and has pockets), I hand him a tiny, wrapped gift.

He smiles. "Let me guess." He feels the package. "A friendship bracelet." It's my go-to gift for him, but he's wrong this time.

"Not a friendship bracelet."

His brows crinkle. "Feels like a friendship bracelet to me."

"Just open it," I say impatiently.

He rips the paper and shakes out the red bracelet into his palm. I strung lettered beads into the braided strings, and the beads spell, *I love Sulli.*

"It's an *I love you* bracelet. Totally different."

He laughs into a brighter smile. "It's my favorite gift of yours."

"Yeah?"

He steals a kiss on my cheek, featherlight but lasting. The heat of his lips rushes down my body. Our fingers hook again, and in his other hand, his thumb brushes over the beads. His eyes soften with a sort of sadness. "I can't wear it yet, Sul."

"Oh, I know," I breathe. "You can hang onto it. Banks is getting his in June for his birthday." And I'm betting we last that long and longer.

I'm not picturing a world where we end.

"Let me guess again. His bracelet is *blue.*"

"Correct this time. You're one for two—" I'm cut off by a sudden voice.

"This way! I think the fountain is over here!" The stranger's shouts sound like a gunshot in the night.

We jolt away from each other—just in fucking time. Festival attendees slip into our section of the maze.

"Whoops, sorry." A tall, skinny boy with an orange scarf apologizes quickly, eyes darting from Akara and me like he interrupted an intimate moment. The girl behind him giggles against his back.

"Nothing to be sorry about," Akara says casually. "If you're looking for the fountain, it's three more rights."

"Thanks," the boy says before grabbing the girl's hand and tugging her in that direction.

Akara pushes a hand through his hair, more edged. "Sorry, Sul."

"No, it's okay. At least they didn't shout *Kitsulli*. Maybe they didn't recognize me. Or they could just think we were having an intense conversation."

He nods once, his focused gaze drifting back to where they left.

I think of something. "You memorized this maze, didn't you? For security."

A smile plays on his lips. "Is that a problem?"

"No, but I'll think better next time than to challenge you to a race in a maze that you've fucking memorized," I say. "It's not a fair start."

He places two hands on his chest. "I need all the help I can get if it's a foot race against you."

"You don't want to beat me fair and square?" Why am I drifting back towards him? Why can't I stay away? I stare up at him in challenge, and our hands brush again.

He looks down, longing stretching between us. "Lady Meadows, no one can beat you *fair and square*."

My heart thumps again.

Chatter grows stronger at the entrance of the maze. The moment is about to skid to a screeching halt. "Cumbuckets," I sigh. "There's no privacy here, is there?"

"We can find a place." Akara clasps my hand and leads me towards the exit. The way he cups my hand is less romantic and more professional-looking.

Outside the maze, we start to pass the hot chocolate and eggnog huts again.

"Sulli!" Jane carries two hot cocoas with Thatcher out in front as her bodyguard hubby.

"I wondered where you went," Jane says, her cheeks rosy. "I just saw your sister a little while ago. All the girls were making snow angels near the sledding, and Winona wanted to take pictures with you before it gets late."

"I'll go find her in a minute."

"Here." She passes me the extra mug of cocoa. "It's spiked, so beware."

"Thanks," I say, grateful for the warmth and more liquid to build that magical barrier.

Behind us, I hear Thatcher say, "Happy Birthday."

Akara nods in thanks, but the tension is thick between them. They barely look at each other. Jeez, that's not fucking good. I wince a little. My mom has a lot of theories about friendships, and I'm starting to believe a new one:

When one friendship is healed, another explodes.

"Where's Banks?" Jane asks me. "I thought you'd probably stick around him too tonight while he's on Xander's detail."

My stomach drops. "Uh, I'm…" *I'm on a date with Akara.* Will Jane understand? Fucking doubtful. She'll think I'm not being fair to Banks, when we all agreed to sprinkle in one-on-one dates.

"We're headed his way," Akara says, coming in with the save.

"Speaking of Banks," Thatcher says, more to Akara than us, "I don't know if he mentioned, but he'll need a Friday in January off-duty. We're going to a Flyers game with our dad."

Akara is as shocked as me. "Banks is spending time with his dad? At a hockey game?"

"He said he'd go," Thatcher tells us. "It surprised me too, considering the leak and what he's said to my brother in the past. Banks hasn't gotten over it."

Oh no…

Akara doesn't know what Michael Moretti has fully said, and I'm not at fucking liberty to divulge any of that information. But I think it should come from Banks.

Not Thatcher.

"Thatcher," I start.

Akara is already talking. "About him being the dispensable one?"

I down most of the hot cocoa in a few gulps, and Jane so sweetly places a full mug in my hand like she knows chocolate is the bomb-dot-fucking-com during intense situations.

Even better spiked.

I wash down a new bout of nerves.

"Yeah…" Thatcher scrutinizes Akara for a blip and maybe my unease. "You know the full context, right? Banks told you before you hired our dad?"

Akara frowns. "Just that those were the last words his dad said before he left."

"Banks said nothing else?"

Akara's head whips to me, looking for answers.

I have them.

My stomach twists in a billion knots. "Kits," I breathe. "Banks should tell you himself."

Thatcher grinds down on his teeth. "The three of you aren't on the same page? How is this going to work?"

Okay, it might not be an A+ showing for our triad, but we're new to this. We're not fucking perfect! We didn't pretend to be. And why do we have to keep proving ourselves to *everyone*?

Akara has a hand on his forehead, distraught. "What am I missing?"

37

Akara Kitsuwon

SULLI WANTS ME TO WAIT for Banks to reveal the entire truth, but if it were up to him, it'd *never* happen. He'd rather go die on a sword than slit one across the back of my knees and throat.

"Dammit, *someone* tell me the truth," I curse with fire in my chest. "We all know Banks won't."

Sulli must not have the heart to slug me for the curse word. Her conflicted gaze travels to Thatcher and to me. Jane takes Sulli's hand in hers with comfort and support.

I don't want Sulli to break a promise to Banks, so I drill into Thatcher. "I need to know. This goes beyond our friendship with each other. I *hired* your dad. If there's a conflict of interest…?" I trail off seeing some sort of pain in Thatcher's eyes.

His brows knit together like he's staring at the sun. "I thought he would've told you."

Tell me.

Tell me.

Please, dammit, tell me! I'm nearly rattling with adrenaline and dread. "*Thatcher.*"

"The night…" He struggles to even say the words.

Jane helps. "The night Skylar passed away."

Thatcher nods once, then finishes, "My dad wished Banks were the one who died that night, and he wished it out loud. To him."

My head goes numb. Body goes numb.

Michael Moretti wished Banks *dead*. He told him he wanted him *dead*. I know death. I've met death as a teenager, and to think a father could wish that on a young son after Banks was suffering from the loss and pain of losing his brother...

I hate Michael Moretti.

I *despise* him.

I'm *sickened* at the thought of having him even near Banks. How Thatcher is okay with that for his twin brother, how he can so easily forgive—maybe he's better than me. Maybe he's too good, but I'm not putting money or my company above Banks.

Michael Moretti can go, and I need to find Banks. *Now*.

38

Banks Moretti

"NO, YOU CANNOT TOUCH HIM," I say for the umpteenth time tonight. Jesus, you'd think they'd understand I'm not in a museum asking them to keep their hands off a fuckin' marble statue. This is a living, breathing *sixteen-year-old* human being.

Who currently has his hoodie drawn up as he packs in the midsection of a strange-looking snowman. "Sir Frost Squall of the Northern born," Xander decrees to his friend. Easton Mulligan works on the head and places gum drops in circles for eyes.

He's giving their snowman four eyes, no kidding. "Frost Squall, the *all*-seer," Easton says, "part of the elite Northern born who can spot battles three lands away."

Xander smiles over at the pale, dark-haired boy. Easton still looks like a teen vampire, but in the past year, he's had a growth spurt. Not so much in height but in build. He's still lean but less scrawny, which makes Xander look like a twig next to him.

I smile, knowing their friendship hasn't sputtered out into nothingness.

"Back up," Donnelly barks as he sidesteps in front of another young girl who wears a Gucci beanie. Every kid and teenager here are either the child of a socialite or a friend of the Hales, Meadows, and Cobalts. I'm betting this girl's parents are schmoozing other adults and totally oblivious their daughter is bothering Xander Hale and his security.

"I just want a selfie," she whines.

Xander flinches and tries to obstruct himself from view with the snowman. Easton notices and stands on the other side of Xander to fully conceal him.

"Not tonight." Donnelly keeps his arm out, and when this girl tries to duck under him, I block her with my own body.

She rams into me, hard enough to fall back on her ass.

Tonight is a clusterfuck, and my raging migraine isn't helping. I chew on a toothpick to try to ease the thunderstorm banging against my temple. But the only thing that's going to help is being away from these screams that verge on excited, overwhelmed *cries*.

"Back up," I snap angrily. Fire must be coming out of my fuckin' eyeballs at this point because the girl skitters back, grabbing her friend's hand in the process.

Donnelly gives me a look of gratitude. "Bet you missed this."

I lift a shoulder and we both steal the briefest glance to Xander. He's packing in more snow with Easton helping at his side. Quieter, I tell Donnelly, "I like seeing the kid happy."

He smiles. "Ditto."

"You've done a good job with him."

Just as I say the words, Xander asks with a smile, "Hey, Donnelly, we're trying to figure out what's cooler: Sir Frost Squall with an extra foot for speed and swiftness or an extra hand for dexterity and...*other* things." He's grinning.

To jerk off.

He means to jerk off.

To be sixteen again.

Donnelly is better than most at talking and maintaining a safe perimeter. While he waves a hand in reprimand to a girl who nears, he tells Xander, "Why not both?"

Xander looks to Easton.

Easton shrugs. "Sir Frost Squall is twice skilled on hand and foot?"

"Awesome," Xander smiles, and they get to work on the geekiest snowman in the contest. They've been meticulous on their work and also interrupted an ass-fuck number of times, so most families and teens have already finished.

Dozens of snowmen are staggered around a few trees, branches lit with multi-colored lights and decorated with ribbons. I spot mostly classic snowmen: scarves, top hats, and button noses. Only a few have character like Xander's fantasy creation. The Harry Potter snowman is lopsided with a touch of scoliosis, and the punk rock snowman is losing its head.

I'd say Xander might actually have a shot here, but Sir Frost Squall is more like Sir Blob Squall.

You'd think he was a professional snowman-maker the way a crowd has formed. Girls are crying. Literal tears run down their cheeks like they're breathing the same air as the pope. They snap pictures and call out his name.

Donnelly and I extend our arms out to fortify a barrier and keep them from encroaching on Xander's safe space. Cold pricks and numbs my bare hands, but my mouth curves upward, remembering my gloves on Sulli's fingers.

Xander pulls his hood down and runs a hand through his thick hair. The entire crowd *erupts* in a wave of *awws*. He flushes before pulling his hoodie back over his head.

Donnelly follows my gaze and whispers to me, "Only hope for the lil elf was puberty makin' him look like a toad."

"Yeah," I whisper subtly back. "That didn't go down well." Puberty was more than kind to Xander Hale. He was ethereal-looking as a preteen, but the older he's grown, the more pronounced his features have become. Sharp cheekbones, bottomless *expressive* amber eyes, a tall, lanky build, and model-worthy looks all add up to Tumblr and TikTok fans being obsessed with him.

The fact that he's been venturing out more only adds to the online craze.

Maximoff cuts through the crowd with ease, even as they fawn over him and tug at his jacket and belt loop. Gabe is having trouble keeping up with the American prince, who acts like his own bodyguard, but Farrow is right next to Maximoff and volleying grabby hands away.

I don't spot Baby Ripley, which is more unusual seeing them without him. They must've let Lily or Loren look after their son.

Donnelly and I let them pass through into Xander's safe zone.

"How's it going, Summers?" Maximoff smiles at his brother. He's been checking in on him all night, and Xander lights up every time his big brother comes around.

Xander smiles back and motions to the snowman. "Sir Frost Squall of the Northern born."

Maximoff looks impressed and happy. "What's the fourth eye for?"

"He's an *all*-seer." As Xander explains, a stabbing pain shoots in my temple.

I break the toothpick in half and spit it out.

My head pounds harder, then duller.

Gotta get this checked out.

My migraines haven't been that bad lately, but I remember the promise I made to Akara and Sulli. There's only so long I can stall on looking into my health.

I wonder what those two are doing right now. My brain auto-fills with images of them making out by an ice sculpture. Lip-locked, threaded together. It's what Akara deserves after all the shit he's been dealing with, and maybe I'll ask for details later. For my own personal spank bank.

I subtly massage my head, then hold out a hand as a crying girl blubbers, "I…I have to see him, *please*. Xander. *Xander.*" She sniffles.

Donnelly winces a little at her tears. He's already let one girl use his shirt to wipe up snot.

"Banks!"

No.

No. That is not Akara Kitsuwon's voice I hear.

My anger already folds in on itself as Akara and Sulli bound over to me. Like Maximoff, they push their way through the overzealous teenyboppers. But Xander's fans and Sulli's fans don't normally overlap, so none of the girls give her a second glance.

Making their pursuit a little easier, they reach me in no time.

Akara quickly says, "Gabe take Banks' position."

What?

"No," I snap, immediately defying my boss. My eyes hot on Akara. "It's your birthday." I say the word *birthday* thinkin' it'll mean something to the guy who's been cradling work like a newborn baby. Silly me. Sillier even, I know Akara isn't big on birthdays the way some are. Because of his dad's passing. But today was perfect for him.

A Winter Festival in formalwear *on* his birthday.

Perfect for a date.

Perfect for romance.

Hell, I'd take it if it were offered to me, so why is he being such a dumbass and turning this shit down?

"Two more temps are behind me. They're joining Gabe to maintain the perimeter."

Sure enough, I see two security guards shouldering their way through the crowds to reach our position.

With heavier breath, Akara says, "We need to talk."

Gabe makes a wincing sound like I'm in trouble with the boss. He takes my post, so I can back up from the barrier of crying girls.

I didn't consider this might be a work issue. I frown heavily, rewiring my emotions. "Is this about security?" I ask Akara while he motions me further away from Sir Blob Squall and the Hales. With Sulli at our sides, we all journey several meters to my ten, soft snow underfoot. I sink with each step.

And then we stop.

Standing among the classic snowmen, Sulli glances cautiously between us.

"No," Akara says, "this is about *us*."

Us.

The lack of shrill screaming over here is increasing the thunder-fucking throbbing in my head.

I grind down on my teeth. "What about us?" I ask, but as soon as I say the words, I notice Thatcher and Jane joining the safe zone that Donnelly, two temps, and Gabe create.

My brother and his wife are watching us.

I frown deeper. What the hell is going on?

Sulli takes a hearty swig from a mug. I stare at that, too. Don't know what she just downed, but I'm guessing *liquor* by how she sways unsteadily.

I feel like I've missed a lifetime and it's only been a few hours.

"I'm gonna…" Sulli jabs her thumb towards her cousin. "Give you guys a moment to talk."

I'm about to tell her to stay, but she's faster than my tongue.

Akara inhales a sharper breath, watching her leave. "She's on her third cup of spiked cocoa in less than an hour. I haven't seen her drink this much, this fast…ever."

More rigid, I hardly move a tensed muscle. "You don't think she's trying to have a good time?" From the concern compounding in his eyes, I see it's more than that.

"She hates the attention from the Kitsulli shippers," he explains. "I think it's getting to her. Normally, she'd brush it off but…" His gaze hits mine.

I grimace. "She's feeling bad *for me*."

He nods.

I rake a hand across my unshaven jaw. "Well, what's the solution? Telling the world we're a triad isn't going to turn off the spotlight."

Akara lightly pounds a fist into his palm a few times, anxious. Pent up with emotion that I can't name yet. "That's not what I need to talk to you about."

"Then what?" I nod to him.

He pushes back his hair and lets out a strained breath. "I know about your dad."

I don't blink. "Say again?"

Akara steps forward with something raw barreling through him. That pushes against me like a two-handed shove to the chest. "Thatcher told me everything."

My brother.

The guy who usually is more tightlipped than me told Akara the one secret I didn't want him to know. I can't tell if the knife is wedged in my back or if it's deep in my chest and I was just too dumb to notice it.

"Well…" I breathe, a rock in my throat. "That's not where I thought tonight was going."

Akara never looks away.

I'm just as unblinking, and our staring contest is one of pain and unbearable things. And I should break our gazes, but I'm not one to cower. I'm standing strong, even long after I'm buried and gone.

Akara barely stirs as he says, "I'm firing him. Tonight. He's done."

"No." My face screws up. "*No.*"

"Banks—"

"Don't be a *stunad*. My dad is the only thing keeping your head above water right now."

"He wished you had *died*," Akara snaps back, veins protruding in his neck. "I can't keep him on my company—on my *payroll*—knowing he said that shit to you." His eyes are bloodshot.

Mine sear. "That's *exactly* what you're going to do. End of story." I walk away, needing this conversation to end. Needing this resolution to be cemented. Akara can't drive his company into the ground for me. Not gonna happen.

"No—" Akara catches my bicep, drawing me back. "This isn't over, Banks."

I swivel around on him. "It's *over*," I combat. "You're not doing this for me."

"It's for *me* then," Akara says tightly. "I can't have this on my conscience. What he said to you, it's unforgivable. You knew that, and that's why you didn't tell me. You knew how I'd feel about him afterwards. You knew it'd make me want to throw him back to California. And the things I want, I *gun for*. I'm not letting him stay."

I grit down, pissed beyond belief. He's throwing his entire firm in the shitter. For what? For me? For my *feelings*? What about everything he's ever worked for? I take a step like I mean to walk away, but I swing back to him and growl out, "Don't do this, Akara. Not for me."

"Why not for you?"

I want to throttle him.

He wants to throttle me.

We're glaring, and Akara breathes, "I did it. It's already done."

Torment explodes in me, and I push Akara hard. Like he saw it coming, he grips my suit jacket, and we wrench and pull with the same raw frustration embedded in our wrenching-and-pulling words. And we crash into a snowman. Cold rips through me, and we land hard, wrestling underneath the mound of snow and a top hat and carrot. I don't want him to fall on a sword for me.

He doesn't want me to take the sword for his company. Our crossroads are met with fists and sweat, and we pass blows. Knuckles in jaws, in abs, and he's a better grappler, pinning me down beneath his body, even though I weigh more.

"KITS!" Sulli yells. "BANKS! STOP! FUCKING STOP!"

I barely hear her over my own frenzied pulse. Barely see anything but Akara and the snow. We grip and pull and wrench and *pull*. "Why can't you care about yourself?!" He screams at me through held-back tears.

Those words throttle me in the gut.

I don't know why.

I'm second best.

I'm dispensable.

I should have been the one who died.

All those things I know aren't true but have been scarred onto bone buried under flesh. Because for most of my life, I've lived for the short time. Not for the long time or the everlasting time. But the briefest moment and second in time.

Because I never thought about myself like he's thinking about me. Like she's thinking about me.

Through glassed and searing eyes, I yell back, "You *need* him!"

"Not more than I need you," he sneers before crawling off my body, and though every sore muscle in my body is screaming at me to collapse on the snow, I can't.

He can't.

Tunnel vision expands, and we notice the chaos we resurrected. Teenyboppers aim phones at us, recording our brawl into deceased Frosty the Snowman, and Maximoff has his arms around Sulli while she tries to run towards us.

"Let me stop them, Moffy! I can fucking stop them, please!"

Quickly, we scramble to our feet, just as Farrow wedges himself between us and extends his arms. "See, what we're doing is *not* this. *Not* here." Heat drills his glare onto me, then Akara. "Whatever's going on—"

"Oh my God, they were fighting over Sulli!" a girl cuts him off and shrieks like it's the cutest thing in the fuckin' world. We did kinda fight over her. But not tonight. She has that wrong. I can't see her among the crowd near Xander.

Oscar jogs over to us, and I notice Charlie Cobalt has joined Maximoff and Jane who speak to Sulli. *Fuck Charlie.*

That's crossed my mind more than once. Every time I see him— being real here.

He called my girlfriend *weak*.

Sulli told us.

We're all constantly looking from our clients to the crowds to the temps.

"Everyone's saying you two broke out in a fight," Oscar motions to me and Akara. "They're wrong?" He sees Farrow's knife-cutting gaze and then says, "Fuck me, they're not wrong?" Oscar stares at Akara like he's never seen him before.

"It's over," Akara says and glances at the crumpled snowman with remorse. To Farrow, he adds, "I'm sorry. I want to apologize to Maximoff too—there's no excuse for what just happened."

Farrow frowns, disappointment in his face. Akara is supposed to be the best of us, the example we follow, and the one he leads by.

Here I am, just wanting Akara to put Kitsuwon Securities first, and now I've fucked up his standing with SFO. How they see him. How they respect him—I know that means somethin' more to him than I'll ever know.

"It's on me too," I cut in.

"No," Akara shakes his head. "I'm your boss. I knew better." He pries out his earpiece for a second. "Banks."

"Yeah?"

"We have a two months' pay-cut and mandatory weekly therapy."

Farrow almost smiles.

Oscar is grinning.

Respect isn't all lost, thank the Lord.

I nod to Akara, accepting whatever punishment he gives me.

"Welcome to the club," Oscar pats Akara and me on the shoulders. When the Oliveira brothers threw punches at the Charity Golf Tournament, Akara let them off with the same penalty.

"Not a club I wanted to join," Akara says with a slight smile that vanishes too fast. He's eagle-eyed on something.

We all rotate to look. Near a lit tree, several Triple Shield bodyguards are snickering at us like we're a bunch of jokes. Like we're the rookies. Hell, I've *worked* with those same bodyguards who laugh now, and they're not perfect. When push comes to shove, I'd still have their backs.

We're tense.

"Kitsuwon Securities 1 – Triple Shield 3," Oscar says the new tally we've been keeping of wins. And we just fucked it.

"Dammit," Akara curses under his breath.

I lightly tap my knuckles to his shoulder.

His lips nearly rise.

And then Sulli runs over to us. Her long legs pumping like she's racing against a clock. Though, she's still unsteady on her feet, teetering a little. Farrow and Oscar leave us, and Akara catches Sulli around the waist before she crashes into my chest.

"What the fuck?" she curses at us, concern welled up in her eyes.

My dumbass almost reaches out to touch her head in gentle affection. Flashes of cameras still ignite at the other end of Snowmanville. Not sure if they're capturing pictures of Xander or of us.

I'm a bodyguard here, and she's a Meadows. Nothing more.

"You know what that was like…watching you two physically *hit* each other?" she asks as Akara lets her go, then she slugs my arm and turns, slugging his arm. "It felt like that, but ten million times *worse*. And why are you two smiling at me?!"

'Cause I love her, but I have to pocket the words for later. "Maybe your cousin should've let you intervene sooner. All the anger in me just died."

She smiles.

"Sulli the Peacemaker," Akara says, smiling too.

"What if I want to be Sulli the Fighter?"

I remember Donnelly's response to Sir Frost Squall's appendages. "Why not both?" I ask her.

She looks from me to Akara and smiles even more. She has both of us. I have both of them. Akara has both.

We all have each other.

Knock knock.

Knock knock.

"Fucking *fuck*," Sulli curses. "I don't even want to look."

But Akara and I have to.

We pull out our phones and read the newest bomb-drop.

THE ROYAL LEAKS

  We reveal all the truths about the American Royals. These are verified and come directly from the source.

ROYAL LEAK #1: Maximoff Hale bottomed for Farrow last night.

#TodaysLeaks #Sex&Tell #DoTheDirty

Sulli is wincing. "It's fucking bad, isn't it?"

I turn and notice Farrow whispering in Maximoff's ear while Xander is about done with the snowman. And Maximoff is expressionless. Like he's been frozen in a chunk of solid ice for decades and hasn't thawed out yet.

"It's Moffy?" Sulli guesses.

"Yep." Akara tenses. "Something about his sex life."

"*Fuuuck*," Sulli draws out. "He's so private about that…oh no." We all watch as Maximoff speaks to his little brother, then walks up a small slope towards the gardens. Farrow at his side, they're leaving for the only semblance of privacy at this event. The hedge maze.

"We have to find this *fudging* mole," Akara says, glaring out in the distance.

"If only it were a mole made out of fudge," Sulli says with a nod, "then we could just melt him. Stick him under a fucking lamp, and *bam*. He's chocolate syrup."

Her joke alleviates the bad news, and we all share a small smile. With simple understanding, we all try to rebuild the demolished snowman for Maximoff. The proceeds tonight are going to LGBTQ+ homeless youth, and I'm feeling even worse about the fight. Not to mention, we might've fucked someone's chances at a Winter Fest trophy.

I crouch down, fingers numb as I work on the snowman's torso. They've both dropped to their knees, and she asks, "Is the fight over then?"

"We'll be done fighting as soon as Akara hires my dad back—"

"I haven't fired him yet," Akara admits, packing in snow.

I glower. "But you said—"

"I lied."

"You fucker." I gather a fist of snow but think better than to throw it at his face.

"Hey, good call," he compliments with a pat on my shoulder.

"Is that supposed to kill my anger?"

"No, but maybe Sulli will."

I expect her to respond. *Nothing.*

We glance over at a quiet Sulli. Fingers pressed to her lips, she stares off. Her face has gone pale.

I reach over to Sulli fast, arms curving around her body. Someone had way too many spiked drinks tonight.

"We need to get her home," I tell Akara.

He sees what I do. "Carry her," he orders.

Easiest command tonight. I scoop her up in my arms. Standing with Sulli, I cradle my girlfriend and whisper, "Close your eyes. Breathe through your nose."

"Everything is spinning," she whispers, hand to her face. "People are fucking staring, aren't they?"

Camera flashes *click click click*, and Akara by my side, we move out with urgency to the parking lot. We don't slow.

Maybe the fact that *I'm* holding her will subdue some of the Kitsulli rumors that've been annoying Akara and Sulli. Maybe that was Akara's plan all along.

39
Sullivan Meadows

BACK AT THE PENTHOUSE, embarrassment roasts me. *Why'd I drink so fucking quickly?* I sip my third glass of water, a couple inches away from Banks and Akara and their towering, intimate concern. How *concern* can be so intimate—I've never known until now, under their caressing gazes that sweep and stroke me head-to-toe.

They're definitely *men.*

So quick to take care of me.

They lean against one side of the kitchen counters, and I rest against the island, facing them. Cheeks are singed from more than regret, I feel my inexperience and the youth of my age. They're twenty-nine and twenty-eight to my twenty-one years of innocence in some facets of life.

But the longer they tower, their eyes stroke, they *care*—the more I blaze under attraction. How sexy they are…I feel beloved. Fucking coveted. A girl they've chosen to carry home and make feel better.

"How's your head?" Banks asks sweetly. "Still spinning?"

"No more spinning. I'm not really tipsy anymore…I think the crackers helped." I keep roasting. Pulling off my pom beanie, my hair must be sticking up every which way but I don't try to flatten the strands. Why is it getting harder to hold their gazes? "I'm really sorry we had to leave the festival early. Especially on your birthday, Kits."

"Hey, you don't need to keep apologizing, string bean." He presents me a classic Kits smile, sparkling his eyes. I prefer their smiles over the fists that were flung earlier tonight. Warmly, Akara adds, "I'd rather be here right now than there."

"Really?"

He smiles more. "Here is where you are, Sul."

My lips rise, and I glance between Akara and Banks, their smiles so different—yet, they have the same overwhelming effect on me, swelling my heart out of my body.

"Thanks," I say to both of them. "For being here with me. I mean, I know you kind of have to be, but thanks for choosing to be, too." I blush at the intensity of the attraction, at their gazes that try to devour me.

Devour me, I dare you. I want to scream the words, but I stay an arm's length away.

"I'm not going anywhere," Banks promises.

I'm not on a period, I almost declare. But they start asking more questions:

"Do you feel nauseous?"

"You need more crackers?"

"You wanna lie down?"

After answering each one with a peeking smile (God, I feel like such a lovesick puppy), I just say, "I'm okay; I'm okay." To shake their concern that comes in each sizzling beat, I switch topics off me. And to something that *I'm* concerned about. "Are you two going to talk about what happened tonight between you guys?"

Even though I'd love to bury their fight into the ground, I don't want them to use me as an excuse to avoid their feelings.

Akara and Banks both give each other hesitant looks.

"I can be a pretty fucking great referee," I tell them. "If one of you looks like you're going to punch the other, I'll just jump between you two."

Akara assures with a rising smile, "We're not going to punch each other."

"But feel free to jump in between us, mermaid." Banks opens the space, and Akara gestures to the spot between their bodies.

The goal post is there. Calling out to me. I'm craving, begging, *aching* to be sandwiched between Akara and Banks, but knowing they're okay means more to me than the longing.

Ripped and tattered suit jackets are splayed over kitchen barstools. Their clothes took a worse beating than their bodies. Akara lost a button on his button-down, and their white shirts are stretched and torn from pulling each other.

All the money Kits spent on their designer suits is down the drain.

"But what happened back there then?" I ask. "Because it looked like fist-fighting to me."

Banks cocks his head to Akara. "She has a point."

I lean my ass more against the counter. "I don't like when you two fight."

Akara nods strongly. "Then we can solve this right now." He turns to Banks. "Give me a reason not to fire your dad that has nothing to do with me or my company."

Banks stares hard at the kitchen countertop. "My dad wants to make amends with me...and as much as I don't want to give the bastard a chance, if you fire him, it'll close all doors to that."

"But you don't want to make amends, so what does it matter?"

Banks lifts a shoulder. "Maybe I'll change my mind. Someone taught me that forgiveness can be hard, but it could be worth it in the end." His eyes are on me.

Forgiveness. It's a struggle that I'm still struggling with in terms of my dad. And where I stand in terms of Banks' dad is in the direct fucking middle. I can't take a side. One hurts Akara and one hurts Banks. I wish there could be a perfect option, and maybe there will be with more time. Right now, this is all they have.

Akara looks conflicted.

"*Please*," Banks emphasizes. "I'll fuckin' beg and it won't be cute."

Akara and I begin to smile, and then Akara lets out a heavy sigh, "Shoot, Banks—you know how hard it is to stay mad at you?"

Banks' mouth curves in those almost-smiles. "Is that a *yes, you're keeping him?*"

"Yeah. But the moment your dad says one snide thing to you, he's gone."

"I'm good with that."

I smile wide. "You both are kinda fucking hot when you're compromising."

"Kinda hot?" Banks laughs, his eyes making sweet fucking love to me.

"Understatement of the century," Akara smiles, giving me a sexy onceover.

I burn up in my glitzy silver jumpsuit. *Take it off.* I imagine myself stripping bare in front of them, but I don't yet.

My gaze pings around the green cupboards and fridge. It's just us three here. Despite the fight and newest leak, my roommates are still at the charity event, hopefully having a rad time. I ask, "Nothing anyone said in this kitchen was recently leaked, right?"

"Yeah, theoretically, the kitchen is clear," Akara tells me, his hands loosely gripping the counter behind him. Banks has his buff arms threaded casually over his chest.

I try not to check them out because I am interested in how secure the penthouse *really* is. "What do you mean theoretically?"

"Play music," Akara insists.

I grab my phone and switch on my most-listened-to playlist. "MMMBop" by Hanson is the first song and becomes decently loud background noise. "Is this supposed to drown out any mics?"

"Theoretically," Akara says.

I cringe. "I'm not sure I fucking like *theoretically.*"

Akara smiles. "I have a gut-hunch, Sul, but there is no solid evidence to support the penthouse being bugged. We've swept this entire place over and over, almost daily at this point." He also reminds me that the ploy for Thatcher and Jane to spread lies in each individual room didn't go down well.

None of the lies were leaked.

Banks thinks they were too mild. Things like *Jane Cobalt refuses to attend her brother's ballet performance tomorrow night.*

For the most part, the mole likes *salacious* headlines. But to construct a salacious lie could hurt Jane, and I'm glad they didn't go too far. Even if it could've helped catch this asshole.

Everything points towards one of my roommates leaking info to a mole. But that can't be right. Moffy, Jane, Luna, Thatcher, and Farrow would *never*. Some of the leaks are things *they'd* never even want blasted to the media.

They have zero fucking motive.

So I understand why Akara is still set on the "bugged" theory, even if there isn't evidence. No mics. No cameras. Nothing.

"You wanna stay somewhere else?" Banks asks me.

We've had this talk a lot. Months ago, I would've run away from the penthouse at the mere sniff of a mole, but I have something to prove now. Moffy and Jane and Luna will stay no matter what, just like they stayed when a stalker *entered* the townhouse that burned down.

Leaks aren't making them flee because "it's just our life," Maximoff will say. They deal with the consequences of being born into fame head-on, and even if it's smarter to leave, I need to stay.

They won't believe I can handle the heat if I go hide out in a hotel room.

"I'm not leaving," I say, cupping the glass of water. "This is good training, anyway. The heat of the leaks is like mini-explosions, and it's preparing me for the big one."

Our poly relationship.

"The big one isn't happening anytime soon," Akara assures. "We want to give you more time."

"I want more time for all of us," I admit softly. "So what do we know about the mole?"

Banks curls hair behind his right ear, then left. I love how cute he is when he does that right and left hair-tuck maneuver, but sometimes I worry he does it more often when his head is hurting. "They probably have money," he says. "Either they hired some tech wizards or they are a fuckin' tech wizard in their parents' basement."

Akara explains to me, "None of our people can trace the IP address. Not even Garrison Abbey could hack through the firewalls."

So the mole could be a rich mogul or a fifteen-year-old online troll? Two totally different ends of the spectrum.

Fucking *ugh*. We're nowhere close to finding them. "Jane said the leaks are starting to appear on *Celebrity Crush* as headlines."

They both nod, and the sinking realization stays with me. These truth-bombs are gaining real traction every single day.

"February 4th," Akara suddenly says.

I frown at the familiar date. "What about my birthday?"

His muscles tighten. "That's when I think the mole will leak our relationship."

"Fuck," I mutter, "wait, how can you even predict a timeline?"

"We're pretty positive they've been holding onto private info and choosing the worst timing to leak it."

"Worst timing for us," Banks chimes in, "but *best* timing for them."

"Luna's birthday," I realize, "they leaked her writing tentacle porn. And tonight, they leaked Moffy's sex life during the Winter Festival." His big hoorah back into H.M.C. Philanthropies, they purposely ruined. I see red. "What scum of the fucking earth."

And now, Akara thinks they're waiting on a specific, special day to implode my life.

My 22nd birthday.

Banks says, "Now we have a deadline to catch this fuckbag."

February 4th. More than a month away.

Akara nods, "We can do it."

Banks nods back, confidence flowing and rising up in the kitchen. I breathe that certainty in like the sweetest, most extraordinary perfume.

Bathe me in it.

Yes, fucking please.

With a racing pulse, I unzip the side of my jumpsuit. The fabric slips down my body and pools at my bare feet. Bra and cotton panties only, their desire touches every inch of my tingling flesh.

And then they look to each other. I hope they're thinking, *let's fuck her.*

I consume the moment with thirst and greed. Who's coming for me?

Banks breaks from the counters, his stride so long—he only needs to take one step before pushing up against me, our legs interlacing. His chest presses up against my body.

Oh my fucking God. His large hand sheathes my cheek while his other palm clasps my ass, his fingers slipping beneath my cotton panties. I'm drowning in his hungered gaze and the roughness of his hand enveloping my jaw and cheek.

Like a cannon blast, he swiftly dips his head and kisses the holy fuck out of me. Our tongues meld, my head dizzies, and my palms journey over the planes of his muscles. His movements are fast and ravenous like mine, but I'm not the experienced one guiding us to the ascent. I'm second on the rope, the one keeping up with his route.

I like it that way.

Lips stinging, Banks lifts my butt onto the kitchen island. He pulls until my ass is on the edge. Legs spread around his waist, he pushes forward in a deeper kiss, and I whimper against his mouth.

"*Christ.*" He lets out a rough, husky sound of pleasure, and then he pushes my back flat against the cold counter. "Want her here?"

"Yep."

Holy fuck, that was Akara.

I'm doubling-down on the fact that their communication is *hot*. Times infinity when it's about me.

"Fuck," I breathe, watching Akara saunter to the other side of the island near my head. I actually dip my head backwards over the edge, staring at his bulge upside-down.

His lip rises, seduction in his eyes. He's the smooth operator.

Banks is the rough handler.

I love them both absolutely, totally, unequivocally.

His two palms slide down my cheeks, tingles shooting in every nerve-ending. His fingers slip to the back of my skull. He lowers his head, and my heart double-beats. His lips meld against mine in a sensual, leg-shaking, upside-down kiss, and at the same time Akara makes out with me, Banks tears off my panties.

Their movements become fast and ravenous, and I'm loving this speed.

Akara lifts up my shoulder blades and snaps off my bra. He slips the straps off my arms, and his mouth travels against the nape of my neck, then up the curve of my soft breast. His destination is my perked nipple where he sucks and nips and kisses. Electricity zips through me.

Banks' hands chart a course down my thighs, teasing towards my pussy.

I pulse and writhe. "Banks," I rasp, wanting him to enter me. I look up at Akara. "*Kits*, tell him."

They're both smiling and kissing different, tender places of my body.

"Tell him what?" Akara whispers against my nipple. His warm breath tickles the sensitive bud, and I grow wetter.

To Banks, I say, "Come inside me. Not *cum* come. Don't shoot a load without a condom—just…put your cock in me." God, I'm so fucking ineloquent, but my choice of words didn't kill the mood. It did the opposite.

Their eyes and hands and lips hunger more for me, brushing against my flesh and tormenting my need. My playlist switches to the song "Who Do You Love" by All Saints, and heat builds tenfold. I've always thought the lyrics are about choosing between two men, and I drown into these feelings, the music, and I want to shout, *when the ship goes down, I choose both of them.*

"Okay?" I ask them as I reach behind me to grab Akara's waist.

He takes my wrists in his hands, not letting me. "We'll take your demand under consideration." His voice is so fucking sexy.

Akara smiles like he can see how much this moment is pummeling me.

Tear me to pieces.

Ravage me.

I'm wolfing them down, even with my limbs in their possession. Banks raises my legs to his shoulders, and I'm totally exposed for him as his lips voyage to my heat.

I feel Akara watching my breath go uneven and ragged. "*Fuck*," I pant as Banks kisses my inner-thigh, teasing.

I jerk in Akara's grip, and he sinks a kiss against my neck, collarbone, *nipples*. The more he toys with my nipples, the more I ache and pulse.

"I can't…" I nearly cry, my body so alight with feelings. My back arches off the island counter, and Banks eats me out like I'm sweet, glorious candy. Sucking, kissing, my clit is happy and thrumming along with the rest of my body.

"Feels good, doesn't it?" Akara whispers against my ear, bent down so he can reach me. "You know how beautiful you are, Sul? You feel how much and how *badly* we want you?" My hands that are in his possession—he takes one and places my palm on his bulge.

Hard as a fucking rock.

For me.

Fuck yes.

I throb, and Banks' skilled tongue flicks and sucks and makes my legs quiver against his shoulders. "Fuck," I cry out. "*Kits.*" He's too far away. Akara kisses my cheek, then lips, then lifts me up partially so I can watch Banks between my legs.

I'm in a heady state of fucking bliss.

Two experienced guys are on the end of my rope, and even if they're leading, we're all climbing together.

Banks and Akara make eye contact. Which means something is about to happen. Adrenaline courses through me, and right as Akara lets go of my hands, Banks suddenly pulls me towards him and brings me onto his shoulders, front-facing.

I gasp, my hand pressing to the ceiling—that's how fucking high up I am. My heat is still against his lips, ankles hanging against his back.

He kisses my pussy, and only with two more tricks with his tongue—I hit a peak and twitch against him. "*FuckfuckBanks,*" I cry out, toes curling.

I grip his hair, and while I gasp and catch my breath, he waits and then slides me down his body. He holds my ass for an extra beat.

And then carefully, gently places me on the balls of my feet.

Thank fucking God no more tsunami periods or debilitating cramps. I missed *this* with them. Pleasure, arousal, physical attraction that can be satiated with lips and touching and hopefully something harder. Firmer.

Deeper.

Akara picks up my clothes, then messes up my already messy, wild hair while Banks has his arms around me. I lean against his chest and face Akara, naked.

His eyes are still drinking me in.

They're not finished.

"That was…" I start to tell them how *amazing* I'm feeling and a round two is needed, but we hear dogs.

Orion and Arkham bark and pitter-patter to the front door.

Someone must be coming home, and I'm bare in the kitchen. Totally naked. "To the bedroom," I tell my boyfriends before anyone can catch me in my birthday suit. I grab the box of vegan crackers and phone, keeping the music on.

"You lead the way," Banks tells me. "It's one of the few opportunities you get to be out front."

I munch a cracker and walk backwards. In fucking love with how they prowl after me. "Not true. Ask Akara who won the race through the maze." We're a short distance to my room, so we're not running.

Akara sidles next to Banks, and Banks casually throws an arm around his shoulder. Akara smiles and says, "Sulli, I distinctly remember you almost face planting during that race."

"Lies," I tell Banks.

"Truth," Akara refutes.

Banks' lips draw in a shadowy smile. "Now who do I trust more?"

"Me," I say at the same time Akara does.

Banks laughs. "We're gonna have to test this one."

We slip inside my bedroom, and Akara locks the door, then tosses my jumpsuit, bra, and panties on my weight bench.

"How?" I ask Banks. "Trust falls. I'll catch you." I set the box of crackers and phone on my dresser so I can outstretch my arms.

"I don't doubt you're strong, but you're not catching my six-seven ass." His hand slides to the back of my head, cupping me gently. "I was thinking of something a little different."

Still wet, still burning up with eager desire, my brain whirls with wild thoughts. "My mouth. Your cocks." Energy courses through me like the start of a race. I love sex, I've decided. I like the thrill and adrenaline and speeding pulse. I like pushing myself out of my comfort zone to experience *more*. I squat down, about to drop to my knees.

Banks catches my elbow. "Not that."

"Although," Akara tells him. "Not a bad idea. Just not tonight."

"Not tonight," Banks agrees.

They just got me off, though. Can't I return the feeling? I remind them, "I'm not drunk. I won't bite your dicks off...if that's what you're worried about."

They laugh.

I flush and end up smiling. "What?"

"I'm not worried about your bite, mermaid," Banks says, and before I can process *those* words, he lifts me up and over his shoulder.

I have a nice view of his ass, and a nice view of Akara as Banks strides towards the bed. He plops me down on the mattress like I weigh nothing.

I bounce a little, my clit skimming the softness of the turquoise, velvet quilt, a quilt that reminds me of the sea. And the friction against my heat makes me shudder.

Neither of them follows me onto the bed.

Akara and Banks stand at the edge of the iron frame, hungered eyes grazing me in contemplative study.

A headiness descends in Akara's gaze that lights my core. "You trust us, Sulli?"

40

Sullivan Meadows

"YEAH," I SAY, not even hesitating. "A hundred and ten percent, yes."

Banks looks to Akara. "Which one of us do you think got that extra ten percent?"

Akara smiles, humor pooling between them. "Definitely me."

"Well, hell, I was going to say *me*."

The comedy show is entertaining, but I'd rather them be on the bed with me. "Both of you get the extra ten percent," I cut in.

They turn their attention back on me in a heated tidal wave. My bare skin pricks from the slight chill in the air, so I slip on a baggy see-through shirt.

They stare at my nipples.

Seeing and feeling their hot desire is a drug. Something I want to consume nightly. I've never felt this beautiful and wanted and adored than when Akara and Banks just *look* at me like I'm theirs, like I'm something to protect and cherish and make love to.

Fuck, how good and *gorgeous* they make me feel.

I've always wanted to be seen like this, but I know it always had to be the right people seeing me.

Akara leans into Banks' ear and whispers something that I can't hear.

Part of me is tempted to ask, but I like the mystery and the adrenaline rush when I finally feel and see.

Akara breaks away from Banks. They unbutton their shirts at the same time. Fabric hitting the floor, their bodies are stuff of legends to me. Sculpted muscles. Banks with his natural hair against his chest and those dog tags, and Akara with his beautiful tattoo, placed like a piece of armor on his shoulder.

My friends.

My protectors.

My lovers.

My spirit and my soul.

They shed their black pants. Leaving Akara in black boxer-briefs and Banks in deep blue ones, perfectly molding their packages.

My breathing deepens, and with my legs hanging off the bed, I break apart my knees. Spreading them open wider and wider. Still not wearing panties.

Akara and Banks are drooling over my pussy.

I ache for *touch*, and I go to slip my fingers along my heat.

Akara advances in a flash, and his hands are on my chin, lifting my face up to his. "Put your hands on your head," Akara says in a husky whisper. His voice commands obedience.

This is a side of Akara I enjoy a fuck ton.

I rest my palms on my wild hair, and Akara lifts me up and tosses me further on the bed. *Holy fuck*. I'm smiling and overcome.

Banks climbs onto the mattress next to me. "You like when Akara tells you what to do?"

I nod into a breathless word. "Yeah."

"Me too," Banks says. He draws me onto his lap so that I'm straddling him. I face the headboard, no longer in eyesight of Akara. "You know what he told me to do?"

Oh fuck. "What?"

Banks grips the hem of my cotton tee. "Rip this." He tears my white shirt in his hands and exposes my bare breasts. Out of natural instinct, I sink down on his hardness that pushes against his boxer-briefs. Grinding against him, Banks lets out a throaty grunt. "*Sulli*."

I love how he says my name in arousal.

Behind me, Akara kneels, and his chest pushes strongly up against my back, just like earlier in the maze. His skin against my skin is stimulation I didn't know just how badly I needed, and I quiver. "Kits."

Take me.

Take me.

Both of you fucking take me.

"Lay down," Akara says, and I realize he's talking to Banks. Telling him to *lay me down.*

Banks wraps his hands around my hips and draws me to his chest. His shoulders rest low on the iron headboard, a little propped, and with his height, my head reaches his heart, lips skimming the coldness of his dog tags.

Air divides me and Akara as I sink onto Banks.

I glance backwards, watching Akara collect a condom from my dresser before returning to the bed.

"Are you going to tie me up?" I ask him.

His smiling eyes flit to me, amused. "Would you like that?"

"Yeah," I smile back. "I think I'd at least like to try."

"Not tonight," Akara says.

"But—"

"Not tonight," Banks repeats even more firmly.

I pout against Banks' chest. "You both are such fucking teases." I wonder if it's because I drank tonight? Or because I need to level-up from beginner sex to kinkier sex?

Banks runs his hands down the slope of my back to my bare ass. "You're still gonna enjoy tonight, mermaid. Just hold on."

Akara steps out of his boxer-briefs, his erection standing at mouthwatering attention. *I want you inside me, Kits.*

Climbing on the bed, he kneels behind me again. This time, I don't peek over my shoulder. I see him in the mirror above and a little behind my iron-rung headboard. Akara asked me if he could place a mirror there a couple weeks ago.

I said *yeah, sure.*

Now I'm overcome with the fact that he imagined us having sex. And how much better it'd be if I could see both of them.

Just because I haven't had loads of sex doesn't mean I'm unknowledgeable *about* sex—I totally understand that Akara is about to take me from behind. I just…don't know if Banks is going to be inside me *with* him.

Palms flat on Banks' chest, I ask him, "Are you both going inside me?"

"No, not at the same time."

I wonder if they'll ever try or if that's in the "never" category.

It's hard to say, and my mind drifts away from that question just as Akara kisses the back of my neck and rips off the rest of my shirt while I sit up.

I'm bare on top of Banks.

My skin prickles more against the air. "It's cold," I whisper.

"You won't be cold much longer, Sul," Akara whispers against my neck, and our eyes flit to the mirror. His chest is against my back, and my head is titled as his lips suck against my nape. Desire pooling like a sauna, Akara has two handfuls of my breasts, and I reach back and slip my fingers through his black hair.

Feeling Banks' hardness press against my heat, I look down and fall forward, slowly lowering my chest onto him, and his lips find my mouth with ease. I sink into the kiss like I'm letting the ocean take me.

Akara skates his fingertips along my back until he has my hips in his possession. "I'm pulling her back."

Banks breaks the kiss while Akara tugs me. My cheek touches Banks' heart. I'm in both their grips, and it's utterly fucking intoxicating. I don't know where to put my hands. What to do. I'm swept up in these feelings and I let the waves crash into me.

Banks grows under my heat. His erection is vibrating my clit. I wiggle with need for the hard pressure inside me.

"*Sulli,*" Banks groans. "Christ."

"Fuck," I moan. "I just need…" I can't get the words out.

"What do you need?" Akara asks me, pushing me forward and rocking me against Banks. He's building the friction like the biggest tease-builder in the fucking history of teases. Only the cotton layer of Banks' boxer-briefs is between us.

"I need..." The words are lost under desire.

Akara stops moving me. "Breathe, Sullivan. Then speak."

I take a deep breath through my nose. "I need to be filled."

"By what?" Banks asks me, his fingers lost in my messy hair.

"Your cock." I meet Akara's sensual gaze in the mirror. "And your cock."

"I'll take that under consideration," Akara says with a wicked smile. How I fucking love that smile. It sets my blood ablaze.

And so does that phrase he's said twice now.

Akara keeps moving my hips. Friction, friction, more friction right against Banks' cock. I buck against his hard dick. Needing *more*.

Banks grunts, then looks over my shoulder. "Akara," he groans.

What does that mean?

Akara plants a hand on the small of my back, keeping me more still. Then he pulls me back onto my knees. Banks rests my hands on either side of him on the bed. I'm on all-fours, and my ass is up against Akara.

Akara watches me in the mirror and I watch him too, while his hand expertly sheathes himself with the condom. His long, hard length is going to be inside me—holy fucking hell.

I focus in on Banks as he sits forward, and his lips touch my lips. His hand slips down my body and finds my swollen clit. Our eyes devour, and I look into Banks as Akara knocks my knees open wider.

"Kits," I breathe and try to glance over my shoulder. *There's a mirror, dummy.*

Akara puts a hand to my head so I kiss Banks again.

Oh my *fuck*. Everything he does turns me on, lights me up.

Fingers caress my entrance. "She's soaked," Banks informs him.

"Pump inside her a couple times," Akara says.

I shouldn't love so much how they talk about me *in front* of me. But I do. I love that a lot. They both care enough about me to communicate with each other. And fuck, it's *hot*.

Banks slips his fingers into me. *Oh my God. Oh my God.* The fullness and pressure are fucking divine, and we lock eyes with heavy breaths. But it's over too quick. When he pulls out, I give him a starved look.

"Sulli," Banks laughs. "You're gonna get his cock in a second."

I'm about to challenge that statement, thinking the second has already passed, but with Akara gripping my hips, his length slides into me with one slow, spellbinding movement. I meet his eyes in the mirror.

"You okay?" he asks before moving.

I'm lost for words. Akara is inside me from behind while I'm on top of Banks. I'm literally etching this image in my head for fucking *ever*.

He smiles. "Sullivan."

"Akara."

"Are you okay?"

"I'm very fucking okay."

"I'm going to take you lower, okay?"

Take me however you want to, I almost say, but again, words are so fucking lost to the moment. He rocks slowly against my ass, and gently as he moves, he guides my knees out from under me. I'm lying down on Banks' chest like before, but Akara stays inside me and keeps my hips at a perfect angle.

At this position, Akara is more aggressive. He thrusts deeper, and my whole body rocks against Banks like a carnival ride.

"*Ahh...fuckfuck,*" I cry, and he slows, checking on me.

"She's alright," Banks asserts since he has a better view of my face. "Just overwhelmed."

Yeah, pretty fucking much.

I can't even catch my breath.

Akara thrusts again, then lets out a deep noise of pleasure. "*Fuck—* no one try to punch me." We don't. We even laugh, and then headiness, arousal takes over. Sweat glistens our bodies. Feeling Akara inside me and Banks up against me is doing a number on my senses.

I feel so close to them.

So connected to them. Their hands touch me in such fucking care and desire.

Akara pulls my legs so I'm back on my knees, but I stay sunk down with my back arched. He places a hand between my shoulder blades, keeping my breasts pressed to Banks' chest.

Akara thrusts quickly, surging pressure through the aching spot that craves depth and friction. His other hand clutches my hips again as he rocks into me from behind with a skilled, melodic pace.

Dizzying me.

Banks curves his arms around my shoulders, pinned tight to his chest. Our eyes crash together. He's feeling my body move against him while Akara fucks me. I look into the mirror. Akara is watching me unravel.

Moans roll out of me, no ability to stop them as I'm under their spell.

Akara mutters another aroused curse. And he fists the quilt while he pumps.

He slows down all of a sudden and my head spins. "How are you doing, Sul?" he asks in a heavy breath.

I mumble something. I don't know what. I'm lost in the wonderful fucking feeling of him inside me.

Akara stops suddenly, pulling out.

"No," I breathe. "Please don't go. Fuck, come back."

He slams harder into me, and I gasp, head almost colliding with Banks. But Banks holds me tighter to stop me from sliding up his body.

I whimper as Akara slows and the need to feel that force intensifies.

"I need you to come, Sulli," Akara tells me. "Can you do that?" He says it like a challenge. *Fuck yeah.* I press my ear to Banks' heart, his pulse quickened like mine.

"I can come," I tell Akara.

"Can you come with Banks' thumb in your mouth?" Akara challenges.

Oh fuck.

Banks cups my jaw with his wide hand and his thumb slips between my lips. "Suck on this for me, mermaid," Banks whispers.

I do as I'm told, my head alight with feelings. I pretend I'm taking his cock in my mouth like I've wanted. And as my lips wrap around him, Akara starts driving a little harder, a little deeper, a lot faster. He changes the tempo, and the sensations overwhelm me for a second.

They're both technically inside me. It's what I wanted. Maybe they knew that all along. Ecstasy mounts and mounts until Akara slides in and out, in and out, in and out—and he hits a pleasure point that sends me over the edge. I cry out, body shaking, and Banks pulls his thumb out of my mouth as the orgasm ripples through me.

Akara murmurs, "Sulli," as he releases, his cock twitching in me. He milks the climax with slow, languid thrusts and then carefully pulls out.

Before I can catch my breath, both men switch places. Akara is beneath me now.

Banks is behind.

"Breathe," Akara coaches as Banks lines up behind me like Akara had done earlier. I'm much more used to Akara being behind and Banks in front since we most often cuddle in that position. I like digging my butt into Akara and burying my head into Banks when we sleep.

But I love the switch-up too. It excites my pulse, which is why I'm having trouble breathing. I place my head gently against Akara's chest, and he caresses the top of my head.

I look up into the mirror. "Banks?"

He's hesitating. "You sure you want to go again?"

I lean back onto my knees, palms on either side of Akara. "Please." I glance over my shoulder as Banks slips on a condom. He's so big, and I pulse again, imagining him in me. "I want you inside me like Akara."

With Akara almost comes out of my mouth, but if I haven't leveled-up to being tied with rope, I doubt they'll want to both be in me at the same time.

If they're even *willing*, that is.

Bolder, I say, "Get the fuck inside me."

They both laugh, and their laughter makes me feel cute. Special, even.

Banks is much slower than Akara, taking his time. He's worried he'll accidentally hurt me. But I can take all of him. I know I fucking can.

I stay on all-fours over Akara. His hands push hair out of my face, and I smile. He smiles back, and I look up at the mirror.

Banks has my hip and a hand around his length. He eases slowly, *slowly* into me. I tremble. *Oh my fucking God.* At this speed, the pressure and fullness are even more noticeable.

Akara makes a hot sound, and I steal a glance at Kits. His nose is flared, pleasure in his eyes as he watches Banks enter me and sees my expression that's full of rapt attraction. Banks lowers my body further onto Akara's chest.

When Banks starts thrusting, I clutch onto Akara's biceps for support. *Fuck.* My toes curl. After climaxing two times already, I'm set so close to an edge, it's not taking much to push me off. I see him in the mirror, thrusting against me. *I'm going to come. I'm going to come.*

I'm going to fucking come.

"Are you all the way in?" I rasp. He has to be.

"No," Banks says.

What?

"I can take all of you," I choke.

"Not tonight," Banks tells me.

Sweaty, on the rise to the apex, I mumble out, "I officially...fucking hate...those two words."

Akara rubs my bare shoulder in comfort. "It doesn't mean *never*. I know you hate that word more."

"Can you hand me that pillow?" Banks asks Akara.

Akara reaches over for the avocado-shaped pillow and tosses it to Banks. It goes underneath me, arching my hips higher.

The angle feels better. Deeper, even.

"Whoa," I breathe out. "*Whoa.*"

"Is that a bad whoa," Banks asks.

I shake my head, in another blissful fucking world.

Akara smiles. "Definitely a good *whoa*."

Banks pulls out and pushes back in gently. I can tell he's going a little further in this time. Cheek on Akara's chest, I hold onto him and bask in how Banks takes my body.

Trust.

I feel it completely with both of them. As Banks thrusts, my pulse races and adrenaline spikes. *I'm going to come. I'm going to come.* I mutter the words against Akara's heart.

Akara holds me tighter against him. I'm on the same ascent, this time at a slower pace. *I'm going to*—I come. *"Banks. Kits."* I reach a beautiful peak.

A beautiful high.

Banks swears, then groans out, "Sulli…" He breathes hard and gently, gently slides out of me. Banks collapses next to us, tossing the filled condom, and I roll onto my side, cocooned between them. Like it's so natural and second nature, their arms drape over me.

"That was…" *Everything.*

I know they're smiling. Akara asks, "Better two than one?"

"It's more intense…so yeah, I think so. Do you guys like sex better when we're all together?"

Akara and Banks share a look, then Akara nods. "Yeah."

Banks says, "Yeah, same. It keeps me on my toes."

"Not literally," Akara smiles. "You're already too fudging tall."

"Hey, I like his height."

"She likes my height."

"I like Akara's height, too."

They're both laughing.

I want to laugh with them, but sleep tugs at me. I'm just about to shut my eyes when Akara's phone buzzes loudly.

Banks asks him, "Do you even know how to put that thing on silent?"

Akara grabs his cell off the nightstand. "I do, but it's never going to happen." He glances at the screen. "Shit."

I lazily tap his arm with my knuckles, too spent to do a real friendly slug.

He smiles down at me for just a split-second.

"Who is it?" Banks asks.

"Connor Cobalt."

41

Akara Kitsuwon

BUSINESS CALLS. Which I know I can't avoid.

I wouldn't.

I take care of Sulli and Banks and the rest of my men, and I'm trying not to drop a single ball because dropping one means hurting them. And everything I've ever done in security has been to safeguard these people who I love most.

I already dropped something.

For a hot, brief second, my fight with Banks roars back to life in my head. The crappy thing, I don't regret fighting him at all. But I do regret throwing blows *at* the Winter Festival. I bruised my company's reputation and almost lost the respect of my men.

Can't believe I did that.

And then, I can.

Because he's at the top of my list of who I'd do senseless things for. Right next to Sullivan Meadows.

Now we're in bed together, and I thought we screwed the tense parts of the night away. Sulli is sleepy and bare and totally gorgeous as she battles exhaustion, not wanting to miss a thing because of sleep.

I prop myself further up the iron headboard. "I'll put it on speaker if you two agree to stay quiet." I have no interest in relaying this conversation again.

Mainly, I have about negative-infinity desire to leave this bed for a phone call. *Not again.* We're all naked, sweaty, warm, and content. Leaving this peace and refuge is being erased off my to-do list tonight.

Sulli rolls over to face me. "My lips are sealed, Kits."

Banks mimes zipping his lips and chucking the key, then he sits up behind Sulli and focuses on the phone that I answer.

"Connor," I speak first.

"Akara," Connor says, his voice smooth and even-keeled almost always. "Have you seen the news?"

I briefly glanced at tabloids on our ride home. No articles ran with the headline *Bodyguards Fighting at Maximoff Hale's Charity Event*, but more time has passed. Is it out there now?

I push my hair back. "I'd like to apologize about the fight—"

"Not entertainment news. Financial news."

My face scrunches in a frown. *No*, I can't say I've been browsing MarketWatch or Bloomberg recently. Not my go-to channels, but I'm not a novice to those sources.

My dad worked in *stocks*. He used to have Bloomberg on the TV practically all the time. Even during dinner, he'd play the channel on mute in the background.

I motion to Banks.

He's already grabbing his cell from the nightstand nearest him. He hands it over.

"I'm checking it now," I tell Connor. On Banks' phone, I pull up the financial site.

No.

Dismay constricts my face, and I zero in on the first headline.

Cobalt Inc., Fizzle, & Hale Co. Stocks Down in Wake of Familial Leaks

I reread it *twice* just to make sure I'm not seeing things.

"Akara," Connor says.

"I see it," I breathe out. "The Royal Leaks are impacting the stock market now." Their companies are being adversely affected, and if my dad were alive, he would've seen this coming. He would've cautioned me about this *screwed* outcome.

Beyond my position as a bodyguard, my girlfriend is a shareholder of Hale Co. *and* Fizzle.

"It might blow over," Connor says diplomatically. "The public is latching onto the website now, and we have the ability to make this go away. But time is running out. I need you to find the source in any viable way and shut it down as soon as possible—primarily for our children's sake, secondarily for our companies."

"Understood."

"Daisy talked to Price Kepler tonight. Triple Shield will be trying to do the same thing."

I slip my tensed fingers through my hair.

Wonderful.

So very wonderful.

I'm in a race with Triple *fudging* Shield.

"I'll be upfront with you, Akara," Connor says. "I don't care who stops these leaks as long as they're stopped, but I'd rather it be you."

I hang onto his words in shock. I just showed my ass at the Winter Festival, and Connor Cobalt hears *all*. I'm certain he knows I punched one of my men. It looks...worse than bad.

Professionally, I might as well be writing with crayons. And guess what—you can't cash a check written in Crayola. *Childish*, sure.

Enough to write me off, maybe.

But Connor didn't.

He still believes in me. And he's still rooting for me in this quasi-competition between two security firms.

I could say, *it doesn't matter who finds the mole as long as they're found.*

But I want to prove my men are the best. *They* deserve that recognition for all the sleepless nights, heartbreak, and sweat they've put into protecting these families. And I won't screw up again.

"I'll get it under control," I promise.

"If you need any of my resources, I'm a call away," Connor tells me. "Stay in touch." We say a quick goodbye and hang up.

Sulli wraps the white sheet around her chest, sitting up. "I can't believe my families' stocks are taking a hit because of some dirty fucking mole." She yawns into her fist but keeps talking. "And…I can't believe my uncle is on your side of things. I thought he liked Price."

I pass my phone from hand to hand. "I guess he likes me more." I'm still stunned that he'd pick me over a bodyguard he's known for literally decades. I think back to when I started security. And I say aloud, "Connor gave me a lot of advice when I was his bodyguard. Advice for Studio 9. My company…*companies*." I tap my phone to my knee, remembering how I called him when I started up Kitsuwon Securities.

Having Connor Cobalt in my corner is like having a titan behind the ropes. Makes everything a little easier. Yet, I'm warring with his biggest advice to me.

The one where he told me to choose. Between being a bodyguard and a businessman. Price is a bodyguard and owns Triple Shield—he does both—but I know Connor is referring to me running an MMA gym on top of security.

Protecting Sulli comes before *anything*. That is written in stone. And I didn't create Kitsuwon Securities Inc. for accolades or pride. I did it for SFO. For men who needed out from under Triple Shield, and everything we do is to keep these families safe. They'd say they don't want the praises either.

They don't need to be told they're the best.

But it's nice when that hard work is appreciated. None of them will turn down a pat on the back, and yeah, I want that for them.

I want a lot for the people I love.

My gym is a selfish pursuit.

It's the one thing that's for me. Connecting me to my father and my mother, and I should *hypothetically* let it go.

Pain slashes my lungs even imagining selling the gym. Or shutting it down.

I can't.

I'm torn up. And I barely hear Banks and Sulli talking about Connor and his status as "king" among the families. I do a quick social media sweep.

Twitter.

Great.

"Kits?" Sulli sees the tension all over my face.

"It's fine." I'm about to pocket my phone, thinking she doesn't want to see, but she reaches for my cell and I just show her.

She groans into a wince. "That means Bodyguard Brawl is trending in Philly, right?" She points at the hashtag.

"Yep."

Banks leans over and reads over her head. She scrolls down through the most liked tweets and retweets.

Banks Moretti must have made a move on Sulli! Look at how he's carrying her. #BodyguardBrawl

Akara Kitsuwon vs Banks Moretti. My money is on Akara. #KitsulliWins #BodyguardBrawl

OMG Sulli has 2 men fighting over her!! GOALS #Meadows4Life #BodyguardBrawl

Banks is just mad he lost his chance with Sulli. What a loser. #KitsulliWins #BodyguardBrawl

Look, this #BodyguardBrawl proves one thing. Banks and Sulli are OTP. #SullettiWins

"Ship wars," Sulli murmurs. "Fuck me." She looks *crushed.* Sulli falls face-first onto the mattress and yells into a pillow, voice muffled.

Banks rests a comforting hand on her back. "You okay, Sulli?"

"Sul?" I whisper, my chest constricted. Banks and I exchange a concerned look. She's not unburying herself.

I fling off the white sheet. Dang. She has such a cute ass, and I have a flash of being inside her from behind. Sex with Sulli so far has been in its own league, probably because I have the deepest friendship with her, and even now, looking at her naked makes me want to scoop her in my arms and shelter her from storms and fuck her madly, wildly, until she's spent and happy.

But instead of scooping her up, I reach down and grab her *foot*. I blow a raspberry on her sole.

She jerks into a laugh, "*Kits!*" She's smiling for a brief second before the weight of the news descends. "Kitsulli fans were one thing. Having Sulletti shippers enter the chat is going to fuel the rumors about my love life. And I don't want the fucking *world* to pit you two against each other."

"Hey," I coo, "that's online bullcrap. It'll stay inside the internet."

"And even if they try us, we're not giving in," Banks adds. "The three of us here know there aren't any sides. We're all in this together."

Sulli breathes in our assurances. "Okay...okay." With a flop onto her back, she shivers, and Banks draws the white sheets up to her collarbones.

We all lie back down.

I collapse my head back against the pillow. Sulli rolls on top of me for a change, her cheek against my inked chest. Banks drapes an arm over her waist, and his hand brushes my bicep. Tension ekes from my muscles. The rise and fall of our breaths sync together.

Even with the ease of the air, the ease of my body, my mind is still wide-awake and racing.

Sulli lets out soft noises in her sleep, and Banks turns his head, meeting my eyes. He whispers, "What are we doin' about the leaks?"

"The only plan is the same one," I whisper back. "We dissect the next leaks that are dropped." I think for a second. "Christmas is coming up. We're all going to the lake house, so if the penthouse *is* bugged, then the leaks could stop over the holidays."

Unless they are hoarding them.

"Theoretically," Sulli mumbles, waking herself up.

I give her a look. "What happened to hating that word?"

"I still fucking hate it. Maybe even more." She yawns and tries to peel her eyes wide open.

"Sleep, Sul."

"I want to be awake with you two."

Banks murmurs against her ear, and his words ease her into deep, deep slumber. I watch her lashes flutter, then her eyelids close.

He kisses her head, and I press a featherlight kiss to her cheek.

Night, Sulli.

I nod to Banks.

He nods back, and I try to relax so that sleep can take me.

42

Sullivan Meadows

MY COACH WHISTLE THUMPS against my chest as I hop out of Booger. Cold wind whips across the snowy fields, and skeletal trees sway in the breeze. I'm still in Pennsylvania. *Tomorrow*, we leave for the Smoky Mountain lake house, burrowed in privacy and tranquility, and usually, the trip would be the chocolate sprinkles on the end of the year.

But my dad is still Team *Choose One Boyfriend*.

At least Moffy is being supportive. He said he'd have my back at the lake house. All my roommates did. (Minus Thatcher, who I don't talk to that fucking much.)

FaceTime on, I hold the phone screen up to my cold, reddened cheeks, and while I linger at the Jeep, I explain all of this to my best friend.

"I would've had your back too," Beckett smiles sadly. "If I could be there."

I wish he could join everyone for Christmas, but the Nutcracker is in full swing during the holidays, so he'll be working in New York.

"You've had my back the very moment I told you I fell for two guys. That's meant everything to me." I share his burgeoning smile. "And hey, the Nutcracker would be totally lackluster without you. They *need* your talent and not Leo-what's-his-fucking-face."

Beckett dunks his spoon into a bowl. He's eating cereal for lunch at his Hell's Kitchen apartment on his day off. "I was hoping the company thought the same thing and they wouldn't renew his contract."

"Did they?"

"He signed on to another year like me." Beckett looks peeved. "According to the company, we can't exist without the other."

"Really?"

"Our rivalry boosts ticket sales."

Beckett dances for the art, but of course, the ballet needs to make money, so I'm sure ballet politics play a part in everything.

He scoops a spoonful of Cheerios. "Did you talk to Moffy after the leak yesterday?" With the little time Beckett has to talk, he's more interested in hearing about our families.

Whenever we chat, I try to catch him up as much as I can. And yesterday's Winter Festival is still fresh on the brain.

"Yeah, we talked a bit this morning. He said he's okay and that he'll get through it. You know Moffy—he can handle any fucking thing." I usually smile with pride for Maximoff, but jealousy twitches my lips.

I want that *I can handle whatever you throw at me* kind of strength, especially in the face of the media. For so long, I just let Maximoff handle what I couldn't. Just like I let my dad.

"I was thinking of calling him," Beckett says. "But if you think he's okay—"

"No, you should call him," I encourage. "You know what it's like to have pieces of your sex life exposed." When Beckett's hookup broke her NDA and exposed their private text convo, he was angry and devastated, way more than Maximoff is outwardly showing me. "It feels good knowing you're not alone in something."

The Royal Leaks have even banded me and my roommates together, lessening the strain that existed between us. When the world is trying to tear us apart, our instinct is turn to the ones we trust the most, the ones who *understand* the most.

I want to say everything is cool on the roommate front, but…this morning was fucking awkward.

And not with Moffy.

"Speaking of sex lives…" I go into a whole rant about Thatcher's Penthouse Rules. Beckett's eyes widen midway through, and I say, "I'm serious, Beckett, Thatcher not only emailed me the Penthouse Rules but he stuck the list to the fridge. Rule #2: *don't have sex in communal areas.*"

Beckett makes a *what the fuck* face. Dipping his spoon in milk, he says, "You know what I said about Thatcher being someone I'd want to live with?"

"Yeah?"

"I take it back. That rule is bullshit."

"I know, right?" I smile, sort of fucking giddy over the fact that I can confide in my best friend over something new.

Sex.

I'm having it. I'm doing it.

With two guys.

And I always thought I'd be gushing to Luna and Jane first, but Beckett understands poly relationships more. He's not critical or worried about heartache and pain and potential break-ups.

In the next quiet beat, embarrassment returns and swaths me in uncomfortable heat. "I just broke that second rule last night, and I'm telling you, Beckett, somehow Thatcher knows I did it with his *twin brother* and his *best friend* in the kitchen. The timing of the Penthouse Rules is fucking suspect."

"Did you leave behind clothes or condoms?"

"No. Akara grabbed my clothes."

Beckett thinks while he eats. "What'd Banks and Akara say?"

I snort, "That Thatcher is just being Thatcher and not to worry."

"Did you ask Thatcher about it?"

"No, I couldn't even *look* at Thatcher this morning. I passed him in the kitchen and fled like I saw a fucking ghost." I groan at myself, my face hot. "I hate feeling this embarrassed over something that I actually loved." I sigh out, "And I'm not a good roommate."

"You shouldn't be embarrassed." Beckett swallows a bite of Cheerios. "Remember the FanCon Tour? I had sex in a communal part of the tour bus."

"Brother, you fornicated where?" Eliot overhears from behind him. A grin in his voice. "Do tell."

I smile at Beckett as he says to his younger brother, "I don't fuck and tell."

"But what about *fornicate*?"

Beckett smiles into a spoonful, almost spitting out the milk in a laugh. I'm about to let him go spend time with his brothers, but he tells me quietly, "As long as you cleaned the kitchen after, I don't see a problem."

Did I clean the kitchen?

Fuck.

"What if I didn't clean the kitchen?" My face is on fire, and I'm glad Banks and Akara are farther along the snowy farmland, outpacing me while I'm still near Bogger. The Jeep is parked up against the wooden fence.

Beckett eats slower. "How messy were you?"

I shrug, "I just…felt the moment. We always just feel the moment…" I think more. "Banks only went down on me in the kitchen, so it's not like we were throwing used condoms everywhere." Ugh, fuck, I'm still *burning* up from Thatcher possibly knowing his brother gave me head on the kitchen island.

He can't have all those details.

I try to hold on to logic and not anxieties.

"Sounds fine to me, Sulli," Beckett reassures. "They've been good to you? Banks and Akara?"

I instantly smile. "Yeah, they really care about me." *Which is kind of why we're in the middle of nowhere.* I stare around at my new surroundings. "I'm actually at a farm right now. Still in Pennsylvania."

A lone red barn lies in the far, far distance, and a horse freely moseys around the snowy farmland. Haybales kind of look like frosted cake logs.

"What are you doing there?"

"It's a date. They're helping me shoot a gun. I've been nervous to do it after the cougar attack." I undersell my fear. Maybe because I want to be like Moffy. Maybe because I'm hoping it'll be easy to hurdle if I act like it's a piece of cake.

"I hate guns," he says casually, then glances somewhere. "Who is it?" I can't hear the answer, but Beckett looks more interested. "Sorry, I have to go, Sulli." He gracefully stands. "Oscar's little sister is at the door."

"Joana?"

"Yeah."

She's a badass and a pro-boxer, but back in Scotland, I remember Joana being super quick-witted and taking plenty of shots at Beckett. And he fired back.

Beckett is sweet, but he's still a Cobalt, born with a library on his tongue.

"Have fun on your day off," I tell him.

"Have fun on your date."

We're smiling before we hang up. Breathing in the cold air, I see Akara and Banks waiting for me on the snowy field. Banks has an old friend from the Marines who lives alone out here, and he's letting us shoot some guns on his property.

No one is around but us for what feels like miles and miles, so they're not hovering like bodyguards. I'm just a normal girl out on a winter date with *both* of my boyfriends. Which, yeah, having two boyfriends is not that fucking typical, but I don't care.

I'm trying to take my own adventure, my own path. Not journey through someone else's.

I hike my leg over the wooden fence, following the snowy footsteps they made. I tug a beanie over my damp hair, not dry yet from swim practice this morning. I had to jump in and demonstrate the technique for the fly.

Or as I used to call it, the butter*die*.

Maximoff's favorite is the butterfly, and I dreaded having to swim it. Frankie is best at freestyle, like me. She struggled to pick up the stroke rhythm for the fly today and asked for a visual. So I went in.

Being in a pool the size of Warwick's transported me to a feeling I'd forgotten.

Like I was meeting up with my greatest friend again. Water kissed my skin, and I never wanted to leave. When I finished, I glanced up at the electronic board, almost expecting to see my time.

Expecting to hear the crowds.

Expecting to feel that big, glorious burst of pride in myself.

When none of those things reached me, I climbed out and watched Frankie go in. And a horrible thought crashed down. *I hope she fails.*

That thought has stayed with me the whole car ride here.

Akara zips up his red Columbia jacket and calls out, "Hey, slow poke! When'd you turn into a turtle?" He jokes, but his smile starts to fade in real concern. "Are you dragging your feet?"

"Hardy har," I say weakly. I am sort of shuffling.

Banks frowns. "You okay?"

I zone in on the guns in their hands, apprehension building. "Sort of..."

My spirits should be high, but after the cougar attack a couple months ago, I'm dreading holding a gun again. Fuck, I'm dreading *hearing* a gun again. On top of that, I'm sinking into a wave of guilt for wishing Frankie ill.

Positive thinking, Sulli

Okay...a major upside to swim practices: Coach Reed never asked me out again. He's been chill ever since the pizzeria, and I'm guessing it was Akara's threat that really drilled it in.

Despite that plus, anxiety swells a lump in my throat, and I realize I'm gazing haunted at their guns. They're staring down at me with a warm blanket of concern. One I kind of just want to wrap up into and forget what I need to do.

What I should do.

"We don't have to shoot today, Sul," Akara breathes. "Or ever."

I hug my Patagonia jacket tighter around my body. "I want to." Five glass bottles of various sizes are lined up on a haybale in the distance. To our right, a picnic blanket and portable heater are set aside near an oak tree.

I helped pack the picnic basket this morning.

Romance and a dash of fucking fear. It's a total Meadows kind of date. With my family, I've swam with sharks. Bungee jumped. Sky-dived. Adrenaline junkie activities, adventure sports—I know them well.

Yet, I've run when things get uncomfy, and I'm afraid I'm going to shoot once and bolt like a coward.

"I don't want to mess this up." I motion to everything—our date, the bottles on the haybale, the *guns.*

"You're not messing it up," Akara says like that's impossible.

Banks catches my gaze beneath his lashes. "We can skip the shooting part and go straight to the picnic, but I think it'd be good to at least try." He picks up the extra handgun, *his* gun, the same type I'm interested in purchasing. "I don't want to push you too far—but I'm gonna push you a little bit."

I start to smile. Pushing myself is easy when fear isn't attached. I've never been scared to stay late at swim practice or sacrifice family outings for extra Olympic training sessions. Kicking myself is second-nature, and so is disappointment when I don't achieve *enough.*

But I need help going forward now. "Yeah?"

"Yeah." His mouth curves up. "I have plenty of experience living outside a comfort zone, and I'll take you there when you wanna go."

I want to go. He knows I do.

But I tell him out loud anyway, "I want to go there." I glance between them.

Akara has a smile in his eyes. "I'll be there to protect you. Like I've always done." His fingers loop in the rope of my whistle. "Like I'll always do." Just when I think he's drawing me closer, he flings the rope off my head and *steals* my whistle. Too fast for my reflexes.

But I slug his side. He makes a grunting noise that boosts my confidence.

Akara blows the whistle, straightening up. "Unsportsmanlike conduct from Player Three."

"You want unsportsmanlike, I can show you un-fucking-sports-manlike—" I'm grinning, about to chase Akara around the field, but he holsters his gun to protect me before I try to tackle. And my smile fades into the reality of what we're doing.

I'm not here to pounce on Akara Kitsuwon like a snow leopard.

With a deeper breath, I keep teetering between a smile and a frown. *Fuck these fucking nerves.* I don't want to be scared forever. If I'd been afraid of a gun during the cougar attack, Akara might not even be alive.

And I think my dad always intended for me to own my own handgun, but the minimum age in Pennsylvania is twenty-one. The opportunity only arose this year.

Both guys study me as I go quiet again.

"If I seem down," I say softly, "it's because I'm a horrible fucking person and I had a horrible thought at practice." Before Akara contests how I'm not horrible at all, I just tell them, "I wished Frankie would fail." I expel a pained breath. "And it doesn't even make much sense. I'm coaching her. Her success is my success in a way."

Neither Banks nor Akara seem shocked. I might as well have just said my hair is brown and snow is beneath our feet.

"Okay, something is seriously wrong with both of you." I reach up and touch their foreheads. "You must be running a fever because you should be looking at me like I'm Satan incarnate, or at least, I traveled close to Satan's butthole."

Banks lets out the loudest laugh.

Akara smiles. "Sulli. You can't be riding up against other people's buttholes, devil or not."

Humor makes me feel better. "Seriously, though. I wished failure on the girl I'm coaching."

"You're competitive," Akara says like he understands the feeling. "It happens."

"It shouldn't just *happen.*" I wince. "I retired from competitive swimming. I'm not going back." Those last four words plunge a knife in my ribs. Breathing in the sharp, cold air, I wince more. I was *fine* with retiring at eighteen. Why have my feelings changed?

I shake my head a few times. "I don't want to talk about it anymore. Let's just shoot."

Banks passes me earmuffs, and I fit the ear protection over my beanie. Sounds immediately soften. Akara goes first. We stand back while he positions himself behind a low haybale.

Akara is quick to check the magazine, rack the Glock, and then squeeze the safety. Like ripping off a Band-Aid, he just fires.

Pop. Pop. Pop.

I flinch each time. Unblinking, I hear the hellacious *growl* and feel a heavy, cumbersome weight on top of my body. The warmth of blood soaking against my skin.

And then silence.

Pure fucking *unbearable* silence.

Agony and panic roars into me, the same feeling that slammed against me when I thought I lost Akara and Banks. When I thought they died.

I blink into focus.

Banks has an arm wrapped around my waist, and he's slid one earmuff back. So I can hear him say, "Sulli?"

I'm alright. I can't produce the words.

"Take a big breath."

I inhale a lungful. Adrenaline still surges and courses through my veins. Heat bathes me under my winter jacket.

Akara comes over, seeing my state of unease. "You don't have to go any further."

On instinct, I shake my head. "...I need to shoot at least once." I take another breath. Quitting isn't in me today. I don't want to have fear in me either.

Banks holds out the gun.

My fingers slip around the grip. When he lets go, it feels heavy in my hand. *I can do this.*

I can fucking do this.

I line up, facing the haybales and bottles. Glass and half-cracked bottles already scatter the snow. Akara broke 2 out of his 3 shots. Eight bottles are still whole.

Beside me, Banks says, "Beat Akara."

My lips rise. *Goals.* I love making them. I fucking love *completing* them. "You ready to go down, Kits?" I talk some trash.

He smiles near Banks. "I'm not worried."

Game on. I concentrate. After fitting my earmuffs back on, I check the magazine and rack the Glock so a bullet enters the chamber. My mouth dries as I raise the gun.

Beat Akara.

Weight on my body.

Warm blood.

Pain.

Beat Akara.

The gun trembles in my grip. "Fuck," I curse.

Banks' body melds behind me, arms stretched against my arms, and his hands fit over my hands. "Just breathe, Sulli," he says, loudly enough to hear through the earmuffs.

I relax against his strength. Inhaling through my nose, I squeeze the safety that lies against the trigger. My stomach cramps.

More weight starts bearing on my breastbone. Everything seems to spin. Why is this so fucking hard?! *Just shoot!*

I shift my stance, feeling Banks.

His body against my body brings me back to the present.

Focus.

Concentrate.

I don't want this fear.

Like Banks says, *pack it up and ship it away.*

Please.

Please.

I pull the trigger.

A shell flies from the chamber, and the force against my hand is an electric shock. I'm quaking, and Banks wiggles the gun out of my grip. Away from me.

I press a fist to my forehead. "Fuck."

I struggle to breathe a full breath.

Akara comes over quickly. "Sul?"

Banks slides my earmuffs to my neck. "Talk to us…" He cups my cheek.

"I…that…" I inhale sharply. "That did not feel good."

Banks unloads the magazine. "Baby steps, mermaid. You're still getting the hang of your feet on land again."

I wince. "I want this feeling fucking *gone*. Like today."

Akara pulls me into a hug. I hang on tight as he says, "You can't jump into the deep-end on this one, Sul."

Banks lightly taps my temple. "You have some post-trauma. It's not gonna resolve itself in a day."

I swallow, contemplating their words. Pulling out of the hug, I inhale one more breath. "Practice makes perfect, right?" I'm great at training towards hard goals, but *fuck*, even picturing shooting another bullet sends panic. "I think…I think baby steps are good." Fifteen-year-old Sulli would choke at that statement and say, *who fucking are you? Kick your ass into high-gear—get it done.*

I can't.

Banks nods strongly to me. He was true to his promise of pushing me a little but not too much. "You did a lot, Sulli."

I did?

"You're not failing," Akara says too. "Sometimes *slow* is good."

I smile. "Like how slow you were to admit you want your P in my V?"

Banks laughs. "I'm gonna remember this."

Akara nods, smiling, then blows the whistle. "Foul play."

"Hey, I spoke the fucking truth!"

We're all grinning.

And I totally forgot about whether I broke a bottle with my one shot. As I glance to the haybale, seeing only *two* bottles broken (both from Akara), I mutter, "Cumfuck."

Akara suddenly steals my beanie and messes my hair.

"Kits!" I roar into a smile, and I attempt to retrieve my beanie. He holds the hat up over my head. "Banks," I call out. My boyfriend lifts me up by the waist, giving me a boost. I'm able to snatch my beanie back in no time.

Akara blows his whistle. "Interference from Player Two."

I extend my arms. "We're just taking a page from Player One and playing dirty."

We joke and laugh on our way to the blanket and heaters near the oak tree. Curled under a quilt between Akara and Banks, I flip open the picnic basket.

Knock knock.

Knock knock.

The sound steals happiness and smiles.

They pull out their cellphones with vigilant gazes. I hold my knees to my chest, wishing we could just ignore the leaks and eat lunch, but the uncertainty of "what leaked?" would hang uncomfortably.

And they can't ignore security threats.

Their whole duty is to keep me safe.

I peer around Akara's shoulder to read.

THE ROYAL LEAKS

We reveal all the truths about the American Royals. These are verified and come directly from the source.

ROYAL LEAK #1: Sullivan Meadows ate a chocolate donut made with milk and eggs.

ROYAL LEAK #2: Thatcher Moretti cheated on his wife with another woman.

#TodaysLeaks #VeganNoMore #cheaters
#SisterBetrayal #HusbandBetrayal

The second leak slams me backwards. "Thatcher *what?*" I dig for my phone in my jacket. My pulse is racing. I need to call Jane and see if she's okay. Fuck the bit about me.

Yeah, I ate a chocolate donut right before we left the penthouse. Akara and Banks saw me on the scale this morning and how much weight I've dropped in *one week*.

Being such a picky eater, I haven't been eating enough. All the vegan alternatives to my favorite foods hardly compare to what I'm used to.

My boyfriends' concern overpowered the sisterly happiness I feel whenever Winona illuminates at me being vegan. So I scarfed down something I knew I'd enjoy, and I ate the donut with guilt. Now my sister will know before I even have the chance to tell her. Which I hate.

But the bigger news, the bigger *what the fuck*, is the second leak.

Banks shakes his head roughly. "No, he couldn't have. My brother *wouldn't*. Jane is the world to him. And he's been cheated on in the past—he knows what that's like."

"Call him," Akara says, but as soon as we start dialing Jane and Thatcher, they text us.

Thatcher didn't cheat. We made up a fake fight in the library to bait the mole. We both claimed to be cheating on each other, but the mole only ran with half the lie. The library must be bugged. All is fine. — Jane

"All is not fucking fine!" I shout at my phone. "*Jane.*" I groan out, wishing she didn't do this. Their relationship is going to implode online.

Maybe they think they're strong enough to handle the fallout.

Stronger than me.

I think you're too weak for it. Charlie's opinion from last month is haunting me. Like he's my Ghost of One Month's Past.

"My brother is a fuckin'…" Banks swears into a growl under his breath, typing a message to Thatcher fast.

Akara is on the phone with a surveillance team. The library is now off-limits until the all-clear. Everyone is leaving for the lake house tomorrow anyway, so I'm guessing there'll be another big sweep of the whole penthouse.

Tightness hangs on my chest, and I lean over and grab the bottle of wine from the basket.

Jane will be fine.

She's strong.

I'll be fine.

I can be strong too.

I repeat the mantra as I untwist the cap and drink from the bottle.

43

Banks Moretti

"MOTHER OF DRAGONS," I curse. My big toe throbs from the edge of a picnic table. A lot of obstacles lie from the graveled driveway to the lake house. Icy paths, tree stumps covered in snow, this fuckin' picnic table, and a bunch of other bodies weaving in and out carrying luggage and groceries.

Two duffel bags hang from my shoulders, and I cradle the most precious thing in my hands. A custom birthday cake in the shape of Bilbo's home in the Shire. Xander's birthday might be five days away, but there aren't any bakeries close to the lake house. Especially not ones that'd master this *Lord of the Rings* setting.

Don't drop the cake.

It's my one job.

The front door is too heavily trafficked, so I take the steps up the back deck slowly. I have the best view of the frozen lake, and off in the distance, smoke plumes from the chimney of security's cabin. One that Triple Shield shares with Kitsuwon Securities.

I stop for a second, letting this moment settle in.

Being *here* with Sulli's family for the holidays is new. It's different. Don't know if I need someone to pinch me to make it feel more real. But I'm not sure it feels *wrong*. Anywhere Sulli goes, feels right to be alongside her. Not just because I'm her bodyguard.

Ingesting a deep breath of fresh air, I land at the backdoor, and I slide it open with my elbow. Carefully balancing the cake, I slip inside and shift some groceries on the counter. Finding room to place Bilbo's home.

"Oh hey," Sulli says, dumping a case of water in front of the fridge. "You made it?" She sees the cake in one piece.

"Just barely. I almost broke a sweat."

She gathers her hair in a messy bun. "Now I know your weakness. Carrying cake."

I scratch the back of my head, then stuff my hands in my pockets. "I have plenty of weaknesses." My mouth curves up seeing Sulli drift closer to me.

I near her.

"Like cigarettes?" she asks.

I smile a little more. "Yeah. Plus, a medium-rare ribeye, a good porter—"

"Friday Night Fight," she interjects with an elbow nudge to my waist. "You always watch wrestling. I bet that one's your favorite."

"Yeah, it is." My smile keeps spreading. "I'm also weak for late-night card games."

"Gin rummy."

I've been teaching her how to play.

I nod, "Gin rummy."

And she steps forward. Like that correct answer earns a foot closer to me. She's one competitive beauty.

I watch as Sulli places her soles on the outside of my feet. With no more room to go forward, her body knocks against my chest, and I press a hand to her lower back. Stabilizing Sulli, I keep her up against my muscular build.

Her fingers curl around my shirt. "What else are you weak for?"

"Water ice," I breathe. "Pizzelles during Christmastime." I dip my head to whisper huskily, deeply, "And the smokeshow right in front of me."

She drinks me in. "I'm a weakness?"

"You make me weak at the knees, strong at the heart."

Sulli chews on the corner of her lip that grows in a giddy smile. "Fuck, you…you do this thing where you look at me like I'm…" She expels a shortened breath. "Banks."

"You are fucking gorgeous, Sulli." I skim her strong features. "And if you haven't figured it out by now, I'm the poor bastard you've devoured whole."

Her eyes build with emotion. "I'm *really* glad you came here. I know you could've spent Christmas with your mom and grandma—who wouldn't rag on you like my dad might—and I just…I'm just really fucking happy to have you here. With me."

I slide my hand against her cheek, holding her face in a sturdy grip. Her breath hitches, and it takes everything in my unholy soul not to pin her against the fridge and lift her leg around my waist.

Don't let this end. Don't let her go.

I know Ryke Meadows wishes I'd just fuck off already, and that constant reminder is gonna be up-close-and-personal this holiday season.

But I'm not a coward. I wasn't going to bail out of fear, and Sulli wants me here. She wants *both* of her boyfriends here.

"I wouldn't want to be anywhere else." I cock my head to Bilbo's home. "And from now on, I'll give you the cakes to carry."

Her chin raises to meet my eyes better. "You really trust me with cake?"

I almost laugh. "No. I know you'll either eat it or throw it."

She matches my smile. "Then why give it to me?"

"Because you love cake," I breathe, my hand still encasing her cheek. "And I want to give you everything you love. Even if you devour it all in the end."

Her green, green eyes drop to my lips.

I lower my head more, so close to kissing Sulli. And then a shape enters my peripheral. *Someone's here.*

They clear their throat.

Sulli jumps. "Fuck." She holds her heart, stepping out of my embrace. "*Fuck*, Moffy. I thought you were my dad."

Maximoff places a plastic tub on the floor. Sharpie on the side reads *Christmas Garland.* "Last I checked, I haven't been body-snatched." He straightens up. "So nope, not Ryke." He nods to me in greeting, but a slight toughness lingers behind his green eyes that says, *don't break my cousin's heart or I'll fucking destroy you.*

I remember Thatcher being gifted that treasure of a glare, and Maximoff Hale thinks he's being all tough with me. Little does he know, I'm *honored* to be on the receiving end of his protective threats.

Means I'm with Sulli.

So I slip a toothpick between my lips and bite down, trying not to smile.

"This is all the garland I could find in the attic," Maximoff tells her.

Sulli explains to me, "We all pitch-in and decorate the house on the first day. I always do the garland and wreaths. Which is a good thing you're here—because last time I tried to hang a wreath on the highest window, I had *Tom* hold my ankles while I was halfway out of a windowsill. Let's just say I dropped the fucking wreath and Tom almost dropped me."

Jesus.

"Rest assured, I'm not dropping you out of a fuckin' window."

"Totally fucking assured." She grins.

Maximoff moves to leave and tells Sulli, "Fair warning—if you want *zero* conflict this week, then you probably need to keep the PDA on the negative-hundred level when my dad shows up. He's still not really cool with you three dating each other."

No surprise there. Loren Hale is the most overprotective of all the dads. And he's Ryke's half-brother, so I'm sure he's waiting to boot-kick my ass out of the lake house.

Sulli nods stiffly, smile gone. "Thanks for the heads up, Moffy."

We wait until he leaves, and then Sulli pulls back into me. "Where were we before...you know?" She motions to where her cousin left, her yearning eyes never leaving mine. Never wanting this to end.

"Right about here." I discard my toothpick. And I lean down. Clutching her cheek in a strong hand, I close the distance like I'm crashing through a door.

I kiss Sulli with all the desire erupting inside me. Our lips meld, and she melts and arches and I hold her closer. Feeling her eagerness to journey fast and far up against my tongue, I urge deeper. Soulful force bridges us together.

Her hands don't stay still. Can't stay still. They roam all over me like they never want to land, and my pulse beats in a rushed, heavy fucking rhythm.

I take her ass in my palm.

She gasps in a breathy, raspy *wanting* sound, pummeling me.

Our eyes cling tighter than our hands, and Sullivan Meadows is eating me alive. We crash into another mind-blowing kiss that screams and claws. Her fingers clench around my shirt, and my hands are snared in her wild hair.

We're at her dad's lake house. Before I'm tempted to walk her into the fridge, I break the sweltering kiss. Leaving us breathless.

"Fucking whoa." She grips the counter, dizzy. "That was…not negative-hundred."

I rub my lips that start to upturn. Lord knows I want to kiss Sulli without cracking a crater into hell, but if hell is where I need to go, I'm going. "You wanna dial it back?" Even as I ask, I can see the answer on her face.

"Fuck, *no*." She touches her reddened lips. "I guess that was what…a level-seventy?"

"Yeah, about there."

"Let's just keep PDA at that level then. Respectful but not fucking hiding."

"Amen," I nod with a growing smile. "I'll let Akara know." He's at security's cabin right now having a meeting with Oscar, Quinn, Gabe, and Donnelly. The guys who aren't dating a famous one.

When I bend down to unload the water bottles, Winona slips into the kitchen with three canvas tote bags of groceries.

"Hey, Nona, I've got that…" Sulli trails off because I already take her sister's bags.

"Thanks, Banks," Winona says, a little cautious around me. Like she's still determining my intentions with her older sister. Sulli told me Winona is Team Triad, but Akara and I think that's what Winona *hopes* to be.

She doesn't really know me. I've never been a Meadows bodyguard until recently. She hasn't really *seen* me with her sister like she's seen Akara.

It's alright.

I'm used to being seen but not seen. *The twin.* It always takes extra effort for people to get to know me.

I nod to Winona. "No problem." I place the groceries next to the Bilbo cake.

She ties the bottom of her cargo shirt that came undone. "Sulli, I, uh, have some bad news." She winces and tucks a strand of dishwater-blonde hair behind her ear.

Sulli frowns. "What is it, squirt?"

I kick the fridge open, listening as I shove a few water bottles onto the shelf.

"My Christmas present for you." Winona is still wincing. "I have to tell you what it is. I don't think you'll want it anymore, and I don't want you to be bummed out when you open it."

"There's no way I'd—"

"It's a *Vegan Lover* shirt and a mug," Winona cuts her off nervously. "And a vegan restaurant guide. I should've realized you weren't that into it. I just—"

"Oh no, those are fucking awesome presents. I still want them."

"Are you sure?"

"Positive." Sulli smiles off her sister's smile. "And hey, I might not be vegan, but you all are fucking rock stars to me. Even more than before."

Winona bounces towards her sister like a kangaroo, and they do a long, secret handshake that includes howling.

My mouth curves up again.

Meadows girls.

I watch Sulli for an extra beat, her brown hair spilling madly around her squared jaw and lively green eyes. *You fucking fool, Banks Roscoe Moretti, you fell in love with a Meadows girl.*

How this all plays out with her family and the world is yet to be seen. All I know is I'm not leaving willingly. Who's gonna drag my ass away?

Her dad?

Paparazzi?

Internet trolls?

Come at me.

"NONA! WHERE YOU AT?!" Vada Abbey's voice sounds off from the front door.

Winona's face brightens. Her friends are here.

"WINNY WINNY NONA!"

The Meadows sisters squeeze each other in one last tight hug before Winona races off. She peeks back at me, and I just wave goodbye.

I'd like to think she's smiling, but the wall out in front of her knows better than me.

Sulli comes closer. "I know Winona doesn't care, but I still wish I could've lasted longer."

"You couldn't be vegan forever. It's hard for people who aren't picky eaters, and no offense, you're probably the pickiest of 'em all."

She mock huffs. "I am thoroughly fucking offended."

"That so?" I abandon a water bottle to edge nearer.

My hands fall to her hips.

"No, I haven't fucking told her," Ryke says. His gruff voice sounds close, and Sulli and I share a frown before we split apart.

Her parents aren't supposed to be here until tonight. After clutching her hand, I follow the sound a quarter down the hallway.

Maximoff's broad shoulder peeks from the study, and I pull Sulli against the wall before we reach that room.

I press my finger to her lips. Her heart thumps hard against my chest.

"Are you planning on it?" Maximoff asks on *speaker phone*. With Ryke.

"I don't fucking know," Ryke curses into a groan. "She's going to be so upset with me. I'm fucking everything up these days."

Someone else laughs dryly over the phone. "Christ, it's about time. For a minute there, I thought I was the only screw up." Loren Hale. *Maximoff's dad.*

Maximoff must be on a three-way call with his dad and uncle.

Sulli's shoulders drop, and as quietly as she can, she whispers to me, "You think he regrets trying to make me choose one of you?"

Could be. I shrug while we listen more.

"Gloat all you want, Lo," Ryke says. "I'm still fucked."

"You ate a burger; you didn't commit a mortal sin," Loren retorts.

Sulli looks crushed. His whole regret was about Winona, not her. Ryke was supposed to be vegan. Her face contorts in a series of emotions, some I can't pull apart.

I step even closer, my body welding with hers and she wraps her arms around my waist. Burying her head in my chest.

It's alright, mermaid.

After a few minutes, we return to the kitchen and unload some groceries. Sulli is quiet, putting away some squash and zucchini. And then she grabs a Yuengling from the fridge and kicks the door closed.

Before I say a thing, she pops the cap and takes the biggest swig.

My family are drinkers. Whiskey with coffee. Wine with dinner. Beer just because. But I've never told anyone to *stop* because I feared they were abusing alcohol.

I have my own vices that I've been trying to kick.

And seeing Sulli turn to alcohol during rough times reminds me of *me* and my toxic relationship with cigarettes.

I rake a hand over my mouth two times, then drop my palm. "We sharing that?" Not waiting for an answer, I grab the bottle and take a very generous swig.

"We are now." She wipes her lips with her bicep, then snatches the beer back.

Backdoor suddenly opens.

Perfect fucking timing. I'm not the only one who's noticed Sulli reaching for alcohol when she's feeling down.

Akara struts inside and brushes snow off his black hair. He sees me first. "As a parting gift at the security cabin, Donnelly and Quinn pelted me with snowballs."

I crack a smile. "Sounds about right."

He sees the beer in Sulli's hand. "What's going on?" This isn't good. Alcohol should not be an indication of *what's wrong with Sulli?*

Akara's head swings to me.

"We should talk upstairs," I suggest.

He nods, and I take Sulli's hand in mine.

When we exit the kitchen into the humongous living room, the fake Christmas tree is halfway erected, and I see plastic tubs of holiday décor on the second and third balcony level. Ben and Xander are arguing quietly while they unravel multi-colored lights on the couch.

They go quiet as we pass. I feel their curiosity on us. They know about our triad, but it's not often Sulli's younger cousins see us together.

Sulli swings back around to face her teenage cousins. "Yes, these are my *boyfriends*."

Xander looks at me like I'm nuts. "You're also dating Akara?"

"Not exactly, kid."

Confusion scrunches his face. "I don't get it."

"You don't have to get it," Sulli interjects. Her hostility originates from what she overheard with her dad, but it unleashes on these two. "It's *my* fucking life."

"Whoa, okay, Jesus." Xander shrinks back.

Ben frowns. "Why are you so angry?"

"I'm not angry!" she shouts, clearly angry.

Akara tells them quickly, "Okay, hello, goodbye." He ushers Sulli forward, his arm around her broad shoulders.

My hand is still in hers, and she's squeezing harder. Her face is bright red. And I want to take away the pain she's been feeling. Her hurt and frustration and everything else bearing on her body, but it's not as easy as counting *one, two, three.*

We climb the staircase to the second floor. Stepping over a box of ornaments and moving around a four-foot Santa, Sulli swigs more beer.

Akara steals the bottle this time, finishing off the last drop as we all slip into a guest room.

Our room for the holiday.

It's a fuckin' miracle her dad is even allowing me and Akara to sleep at his lake house, let alone in the *same* room as her. But Sulli threatened to spend Christmas in Costa Rica if they didn't let us come along.

Ryke caved.

Sulli plops onto the green reindeer quilt, bedding already switched for the holidays. "I fucking hate this."

I lean on the dresser. "Which part?"

Akara gives me a look. "How about we start from the jump?"

"We overheard Maximoff talking to Loren and Ryke." I explain the rest in a couple seconds.

Sulli holds her bent legs. "He regrets breaking a promise to Winona more than he regrets trying to kick one of my boyfriends to the curb." Her face twists. "It's fucked up. And…this whole time, we could've commiserated about how hard being vegan was. He could've confided in me. Instead, I had to *eavesdrop* to fucking know anything."

"You'll get back there," I tell her.

"No we *won't*, Banks," she says with reddened eyes. "I'm *never* going to get back there if he doesn't accept that I'm with you and Akara."

I shake my head. "I have to believe he'll come around." If she's losing hope, then the best I can do is keep hope alive for us.

She stares at the floor.

Akara grips the waist-high, wooden bedpost. "Is that why you're drinking, Sul?"

Sulli bristles. "I just like it…and yeah, I guess it makes me feel better." Her eyes flit from him to me. "Lots of people drink to calm their nerves."

She's not wrong.

"Kits, I've seen you grab a beer after a long, hard fucking day a ton of times."

Akara touches his chest. "Maybe I shouldn't have."

She gapes. "Seriously? You're just saying that because you're worried about me?"

Akara pushes his hair back, then glances at me like, *you should take this one, Banks.*

I step away from the dresser. "When I'm in my fucking feelings and need something to soften the edge of the day or night, I call on the worst friend I've ever made."

Sulli processes, and I shrug to her. "I smoke. Cigarettes are my no-good, very bad fucking friend, and you don't want a friend like that."

She presses a hand to her flushed cheek. "It was *one* beer. Look, I *know* alcoholism runs in my family. I've been careful. I'm still careful."

Is she?

Doubt touches her eyes as she stares from me to Akara, back to me. "Don't look at me like that. *Please.*" Her voice cracks. "I'm *fine.*"

"It wasn't just one spiked hot chocolate," Akara refutes.

"I'm paying attention to what I'm drinking, I promise. *I fucking promise.*" She's almost in tears. "Fuck." She buries her face in her palms.

"Hey, hey, hey, mermaid." I cross the room the same time as Akara. Our urgency and concern speed us towards Sulli like a bullet, and I sit on her left. Akara on her right.

He breathes against her ear, "We're not trying to gang up on you, Sul."

"I just need you both to trust me. I can't have you against me...I don't want to be all alone."

I touch her head. "You're not alone. We're not going anywhere."

"We have to be honest with you, okay?" Akara tells her. "We care too much about you."

"We don't want anything to happen to you," I add.

Sulli peels her hands off her face. She swallows hard, unable to lift her gaze.

Akara is tensed. My muscles are flexed. We're walking a thin rope between comforting her and making sure we don't enable something that could go south fast. But so much shit has hit the fan recently. Christ, all I want to do is hold Sulli.

Akara ends up continuing, "All we're saying is that you're strong enough to deal with this *crap* without needing alcohol to calm your nerves."

She frowns deeper. "So what…I'm not allowed to drink now?"

"That's up to you, Sul." He wraps an arm around her waist. "We're not giving you rules. We're just trying to look out for you."

"I can handle it," Sulli says under her breath. "I know my limits. I promise, I do."

She's been trying to prove to her family that she's a responsible, capable adult.

But she doesn't need to prove that to me.

"You're always gonna be a strong woman in my eyes, Sullivan Meadows," I profess, and her green eyes lift up to me. "Even when you're crying, even when you're struggling—I see your iron-will. You don't ever need to be tough for me."

Sulli wipes at her wet cheeks, intaking a deeper breath. She looks to Akara.

"Or for me," Akara says, "though, you're more like a little playful racoon around me—the donut bandit."

She almost smiles, then lightly elbows him. Her glassy eyes drift between me and Akara. "I know…I know you both might disagree, but…I think I can figure out moderation. It's in me." She swallows harder. "I'll try to be more aware of *when* I grab a drink so it's not my no-good, very bad fucking friend. But I'm not spiraling or anything."

It's good that she's aware. Right now, that's all we're hoping.

"Okay," Akara says with a strong nod.

"Sounds good to me," I chime in.

Sulli holds out her two fists for us to bump, a sad smile on her face. Like she thinks we're gonna reject her.

No way in hell.

I touch knuckle-to-knuckle.

Akara fist-bumps her other hand.

And then Akara and I exchange a look, and we start to smile. In unison, with our arms around Sulli, we pull our girlfriend down to the bed as we go down with her.

She laughs, and the sound floods my body. *Christmas at the lake house.* It won't work unless the three of us are a united front. We're not splintering.

Sorry, Ryke Meadows, you'll have to wish upon a different fucking star. Mine's shooting right past you.

44

Sullivan Meadows

THE LAKE HOUSE IS A CHRISTMAS safe haven. Like we're somewhere far, far away on the North Pole hanging out near Kris Kringle. Two years ago, I spent December 25th on a tour bus and then last year, I was stuck in Scotland, and this year, I'm finally able to do what I always used to do.

I wake early, *early* on Christmas morning. Before the sun is able to crest the Smoky Mountains, I'm out of bed.

"It's my lake house Christmas tradition with Luna," I whisper to my boyfriends while I jump into pants. They're very much *naked* in bed.

We didn't have sex. I've been nervous about being too loud since I'm staying on the same floor as my parents. So we just ended up cuddling.

Last night, we naked-cuddled. Or what I'm calling *nuddling*.

Banks and Akara were dying laughing this morning when I woke up and said "I really like nuddling with you two."

And then Akara naked-grinded me with a playful, teasing smile and said, "How about naked-grinding?" He humped my leg, and *I* couldn't stop laughing, especially as Banks joined in.

They both showered me with neck kisses, and I had the hardest fucking time leaving the bed. I wanted to stay, but Christmas tradition calls.

I snap on a bra. I'm still hot from all the teasing last night.

How we survived without going all the way is a fucking accomplishment that makes me smile.

Banks called it a Christmas miracle and Akara said, "Santa Claus isn't the source of our willpower. Ryke hearing us fuck his daughter is."

He has a point.

But Kits can be a Scrooge around this time of year. He'll say bad things tend to fall during the winter months. I love how Akara steps one foot into logic and then one foot into something more instinctual and spiritual.

"Why's the tradition with Luna and not Winona?" Banks wonders, watching me pull an ugly Santa sweater over my head.

"When I was younger, I used to share a room with Luna, and I'd wake her up to go to the lake." I shrug. "We're closer in age, and I think our parents hoped we'd be best friends...but she always gravitated towards Tom and Eliot, and I ended up hanging out with Beckett." I find my jacket on the floor. "At the lake house, though, we'd share canoes and do things like that, but it really wasn't until we roomed together at the townhouse that we got a lot closer."

So this year, I'm pee-your-pants-on-Christmas-morning kind of *excited* to experience this with Luna again. We're closer than we've ever been, and that means something to me.

I tell them, "I'll be done before everyone wakes up for presents and home videos." We always rewatch old home videos that my mom captured.

"Text me if the ice looks like it's melting," Akara says.

"Will fucking do." Fully dressed in winter gear, I return to the bed. "See ya later." I kiss Akara lightly on the lips, then Banks—each kiss is a peck. To be frank, I can't stop smiling at the fact that this is real.

My boyfriends with me on Christmas morning.

I get to go outside in the privacy and peace of the lake house.

And they're checking me out like I'm still as beautiful fully clothed as I am naked.

"She's smitten," Akara tells Banks.

He wears a crooked smile. "Can't even look at us without blushing."

"*Goodbye*," I say, face burning. Fuck, they're way too hot, and I'm just trying to make a semi-graceful exit.

"Bye, string bean!" Akara calls after me.

I flip him off without looking back.

Their laughter stays with me all the way down the stairs. I grab my ice skates from the mud room, steal a pizzelle from the kitchen (Banks' grandma made batches of the Italian waffle-like cookie for her grandsons—and I'm fucking obsessed with them even more than Banks), and then I head to the back porch.

Last night, the lake was frozen over enough that my tradition with Luna should be a go.

Early morning ice skating, I'm coming for you.

Outside, snow-tipped wreaths, strung lights, and real icicles adorn the lake house. Festive and magical. The sky is a muddy shade of dark blue, and I decide to wait for Luna on the snowy deck.

A minute passes.

I watch the sky lighten.

Another five minutes. I check my phone. Maybe she forgot? Fuck, I should've reminded her last night. Or maybe she slept in on accident. Luna isn't exactly an early bird.

Or maybe this tradition just meant more to me and less to her. I'm the one who always woke up Luna. I'm the one who grabbed her ice skates and said, *let's go.*

Maybe she never really cared.

My stomach sinks lower and lower and lower.

Orange hues crest the mountains, and another two minutes tick by. I'm about to text her when the backdoor opens.

"Hey. Hi. Heidi. Ho. Howdy." Luna lifts up her ice skates, poorly painted neon-green years ago, and decorated with old Lisa Frank stickers.

I laugh into a smile. "You remembered?"

"I never forgot."

My heart swells.

"I'm not late, am I?" Luna asks, pulling on a multi-colored chunky sweater she knitted herself. "I set my alarm, but I slept through a few minutes."

"No, you're right on fucking time." I sling an arm around her shoulders, and she grins. We head down the slick, icy stairs. "Watch that one," I warn as I almost slide.

"Got it." Luna skips the stair and grabs the railing.

Reaching the bottom, we head down the snowy hill towards the lake. I make out an approaching figure. *We're not alone out here.* Like he took an early morning jog, Uncle Lo is decked out in running gear and hiking up the hill.

"Hey, Uncle Lo," I say in greeting as we pass. "Merry Christmas."

He nods stiffly, cheekbones sharpened. "Merry Christmas, Sulli." He tries to force a smile, but the entire act looks painful on his face. Once he sees his daughter, he softens a little. "Luna, you two be careful on the ice. We don't need any Christmas calamities, alright? The Avengers aren't phone-able out here."

Luna smiles. "Uh-huh, no accidents, Dad." Her breath smokes the air. "I'm not planning on ruining Xander's birthday."

Her younger brother turns *seventeen* today. All of our siblings are growing up so fucking fast.

We are too.

I chime in, "We're always careful Uncle Lo."

He cringes into a tiny wince like that's un-fucking-true. Like I'm bathing in pure, toxic *risk* these cold winter days. He opens his mouth to speak, but I guess he thinks better of responding. And Uncle Lo just leaves for the house.

It stings.

I try to fortify iron walls, but a pressure still weighs heavy on me.

Luna follows close behind me and gives me big wide eyes as soon as her dad is gone. "Jeez, I've never seen my dad that frosty." She fixes her beanie, which is actually a full-on face ski mask that resembles an alien head. Bright neon-green and all, but she folds the fabric up like a regular ole beanie.

"He's been the same way to Akara and Banks," I say with a lump in my throat. We reach the wooden dock, covered in soft white powder. "I thought he'd be a little warmer, but it's been five days."

And it's Christmas. If the holiday spirit couldn't warm Uncle Lo to my relationship, then nothing during this trip will.

Luna shrugs. "He's a Slytherin." She says his Hogwarts House like it explains everything.

Stop expecting everyone who disagrees to come around. Disappointment and hurt aren't feelings I wanted to attach to me this morning. I glance back at the lake house, remembering how happy Akara and Banks made me feel when I woke up in their arms.

I always thought the lake house is the refuge of my life, but I'm starting to feel like they're my greatest safe haven.

Fucking ironic, considering everyone else believes they're the biggest danger and the greatest threat to my life.

Luna and I sink down on the snow and start putting on our skates. I untie knotted laces. "At least my dad is talking to Banks and Akara now."

Albeit he's *not* very fucking nice. My dad curses out my boyfriends and tells one to go away if they're in the same room together. I swear my dad is trying to manifest a break-up.

I try not to picture losing Banks or Akara. A sharp pain stabs into me.

Luna kicks off her boot and fits her foot in a skate. "That's the important thing, for sure. My dad's opinion on your love life shouldn't matter at all."

I tie the laces on my skate and glance at Luna. "His opinion shouldn't matter for your love life either."

She frowns more. "I just don't like being the fuck-up in my family… getting their praise just feels better."

"I get that," I mutter, knowing I've been hoping for my dad's approval when I shouldn't *need* validation from anyone. "And just so you know, you're not a fuck-up, Luna."

She shrugs. "I don't always make the best choices."

I think about me and the spiked hot cocoas at the Winter Fest, plus my talk with Banks and Akara about alcohol. "Me either," I say softly and mull this over. "I have a theory," I tell Luna, "that maybe this is just part of getting older. We're not supposed to always make the *best* choices, but we're doing the best we can."

"If getting older means making a few bad choices, then I'm good with that." Luna laces her second skate. "Aunt Rose and Uncle Connor didn't seem to be any different around you."

"They weren't," I say into a smile. "Jane said her parents were cool with me having two boyfriends. They're more worried about the leaks."

The gossip site has been inactive since we left for the lake house. Which has raised some suspicions, but Akara said the surveillance team found *zero* bugs again.

Not even in the library.

If the mole thinks my roommates and I will start cannibalizing each other with accusations and distrust, they've miscalculated our allegiance to each other. None of us are pointing fingers.

Luna knots her laces. "My mom is also *very* much on your side. Her Christmas present to you is kinda like…" her face lights up. "Well, I can't say exactly, but it's definitely *pro*-Kitsulletti."

Kitsulletti.

I breathe in the sound. That's the first time I've heard that ship name out loud. My spirits lift, floating on the clouds. The sun begins to peek over the rolling hills of the Smoky Mountains. My face hurts from smiling. "Your mom is a fucking goddess."

"So is yours," Luna sing-songs cutely, her cheeks rosy from the cold.

Skates on, we walk out onto the ice. Early, early morning with Luna, the world is calm and peaceful, and we twirl around each other with good balance from years of practice and falling on our butts.

We skate in zig-zags, clasp hands, let go and laugh. We try funny maneuvers like we're pro ice skaters. One corkscrew has Luna tumbling down, and I zip by and help her up.

Her palms are red from the ice, but she barely glances at them. "You know how I've been taking online college courses?"

At the University of Pennsylvania. I nod, "Yeah."

We've gone still, and she tucks a strand of light brown hair behind her ear. "I'm going to take more next year." She pulls the beanie down her face. Her entire head looks like a green alien. "But the class I want to take isn't offered online, so I'm going to have to actually *go* in." Her words come out muffled but clear enough.

Back when we were living at the townhouse, we used to hang out at the bars together near Penn, and now she's actually going to *go* to Penn in the flesh.

"Are you nervous?" I ask since she's told me she's "resisted" doing the college lecture hall setting. Afraid it'd be too much like high school catty drama.

"Kinda. But I want to take these courses. In a way, you've given me the push to try."

Something wells up in me. "Really? Me? Not Moffy or Jane?"

Luna shakes her alien head. "No. *You*. I know how cautious you are around the media. And despite that, you're still holding onto the guys you love. I don't want to be afraid of a repeat of high school. So I'm going."

My lips part in surprise. To think that I could be a leader—that someone in the family could be inspired by *me*, and not for my goal-oriented, Olympic-driven spirit but something else that might define me—I go utterly fucking speechless.

Before I can say *thanks* or find some sort of vowels, Luna's phone buzzes.

Pulling up her beanie, she uses face-recognition to unlock her phone.

"Orion," Luna says in longing. "I miss his wet nose."

I skate around Luna and peer over her shoulder. Uncle Stokes texted a pic of Luna's 8-month-old puppy chewing a bone in his kitchen. "That was rad of Uncle Stokes to dog-sit," I say.

Uncle Stokes is my mom's brother-in-law. His full name is Samuel Stokes. Him and his wife, my Aunt Poppy, have stayed out of the limelight. Most fans and public don't realize there's actually a *fourth* Calloway sister and that my Aunt Rose isn't actually the oldest.

Poppy Calloway is like the lost Jonas brother or the least recognizable Hemsworth brother. She purposefully avoids big family functions and media attention. To the point where everyone forgets she even exists, outside of a Wiki search.

But Aunt Poppy and Uncle Stokes are close enough to the fam that I could call either of them and they'd do just about anything for me.

So when Orion and Arkham got fleas the day before the lake house trip, me and my roommates decided to flea-bomb the penthouse and leave the puppies home for the holidays. Uncle Stokes planned to cat-sit for Jane anyway. After the leaks, we've been hesitant to let *any* strangers into the penthouse, including the cat sitter Jane hired.

Luna pockets her phone. "Yeah, Uncle Stokes is pretty nice. I kinda feel bad that he's not here for Christmas."

From what my mom told me, Uncle Stokes been in a pressure-cooker to fix things after Fizzle's stocks plunged. So he stayed back in Philly.

"Yeah, me…" *Too.* The last word sits on my tongue as voices pitch into the quiet of the morning. Luna and I spin on our skates and peer out at the lake house.

People start crowding the upper deck. I spot Moffy and Jane, then Farrow, *Thatcher.*

"The Seasons?" Luna says to me. "Do they look…?"

"Uneasy, *yeah.*"

Jane is pacing.

Luna tilts her head. "Maybe it's the fake cheating scandal. I don't think Jane's public statement about the leak being false helped all too much. Thatcher is still being dragged on Twitter."

I wince. "Fucking ugh. People need to stop attacking *love.* Seriously…" I plant my hands on my hips, then cross my arms. "Wait, is that Uncle Lo? And Aunt Lily…"

"And the girl squad," Luna adds, both of us frozen on our skates. She holds up a hand to block a ray of sunshine over the mountain. "What in the *Thebula* is going on?"

"No fucking clue."

We watch as more and more people pile out until the deck is packed to the very brim. Their voices are too far and too muddled together to distinguish actual syllables and words.

My heart thumps harder. "What if it's another leak?"

Luna shakes her head. "Uh-uh. There hasn't been a single one since we've been here."

She's right, but it's *Christmas*. An important day where the mole could've dropped a stink bomb onto someone's life.

My mouth dries.

"Best way to find out." I'm going to go to the source and ask my family what the fuck is up. With power, I skate towards the edge of the lake.

The closer I am to the snowy bank, the more heads turn. The more eyes cast down on me. My pulse ascends to my throat, but I don't stop.

I skate and skate, cold pricking my cheeks, and then I see them.

Akara and Banks push out from the crowded deck. From my family. They sprint down the icy stairs, they rush down the hill, and I swear as soon as my skates hit *land*, everyone on the deck goes silent.

Hushed.

Like the calm before a tidal wave.

My head spins.

I cage breath, and it feels like I'm a part of that nursery rhyme *The Three Little Pigs*, and I'm standing inside the straw house. Only *I'm* the wolf. And I'm terrified of blowing it all down.

My boyfriends are only feet away.

"Sulli," Akara says my name *tenderly*. Too tenderly.

Banks holds my gaze with concern in his brown eyes. "It leaked, Sulli."

I shake my head tensely.

No.

We were supposed to have until my birthday. February 4th. Our relationship couldn't have leaked today—it's too early.

No.

No.

The pain that cracks their faces says, *yes*.

"Sulli," Akara breathes.

Pressure hammers my lungs, and I just need to go. Go. *Go.* I tear off one skate, and I pull off the next. My socks tug off with them. To my boyfriends, I choke out what I need, "Chase me."

And I run. Feeling the eyes of my family on my back, I push harder. Banks and Akara's urgent footsteps charge after me. Barefoot, I bolt to the east and race straight into the dense woods. Woods that I've jogged and sprinted more times than I can count.

Twigs whip at my hair and brush against my face. Snow numbs the soles of my feet. My muscles scream, but something in me is screaming louder and rattling to break free.

I outrun my boyfriends.

But I can hear the branches they slam aside and the rumble of earth beneath their heavy, unwavering feet. *I'm not alone.*

I'm not alone.

We're together.

Fuck everyone else.

Everything is going to change.

Everything is going to *fucking* change.

I'm prepared.

No.

I'm not ready.

I was never going to be ready.

I swerve through two trees, ducking, and blood rings in my ears. I can't feel my feet. Warring emotion clashes inside me like a free-for-all showdown. Confidence and doubt, positivity and fucking insecurities. All the peace I've felt with Akara and Banks is slipping out of my fingertips. Once I leave the lake house, *everything is going to change.*

Hot tears prick and fly out of the corners of my eyes, legs pumping viciously beneath me. I grit my teeth and push and push.

Ice pulls my foot out from under me—I slip and trip and land on my hands and knees. And as I shake with adrenaline, arms scoop around my frame and lift up. Banks cradles me, and I curl into his chest.

"Let it out," Akara breathes.

I scream out the emotion that thrashes, that crashes, that grips and pulls and weighs. The noise fades into Banks' body. I fist his jacket and reach out to find Akara, but he finds me. He puts my palm on his heart that thumps, thumps, thumps at a calmer pace.

I breathe and breathe.

Pulse slowing, throat raw.

Tears still build. "I'm so angry," I choke out and wipe at my cheeks. "I have no control over my own fucking life, and this is about to hurt both of you. Your lives are...your privacy..." *Everything is going to change.*

"We're gonna get through it," Banks murmurs in a husky breath, keeping me in his arms.

I peel my face out of his chest.

Their eyes are reddened, despite the confidence in Banks' voice. Akara nods a few times to me, "I wish we had more time, Sulli..."

My chin quakes. "Me too, Kits."

We were supposed to have more time.

Cold wind whistles through the fir trees. Banks doesn't struggle holding me, and I realize he's not setting me down while I'm barefoot and my feet are stinging.

"They're bleeding," Akara says, watching me stare at my toes.

He clasps a hand around my ankle and inspects my foot in concern. "You have many splinters, Lady Meadows."

I let out a weak laugh. "I feel like one giant splinter..." I'm splintering inside, and my face breaks.

Banks holds me tighter while I silently cry. I don't want to cry, but it's leaking and I can't stop the fucking waterworks. I'm angry. Sad. Frustrated. Every emotion under the sun. Banks cups the back of my head with such comfort, and Akara says magic words, "Let's just stay here for a second."

Banks nods in agreement, and we all drop to the ground. I lean against Banks and then Akara, their arms around me while we rest against a tree.

I'm spent, but they look equally destroyed by the news. Akara lifts up his leg and rests his forearm on his knee, staring out.

He keeps muttering, "I just wish we had longer…"

Banks places a palm on Akara's head, consoling him.

I encase both of my hands around Akara's hand. After I ask, he ends up showing me the gossip site on his phone.

THE ROYAL LEAKS

We reveal all the truths about the American Royals. These are verified and come directly from the source.

ROYAL LEAK #1: Sullivan Meadows is dating Banks Moretti & Akara Kitsuwon at the same time.

#TodaysLeaks #didnotseethatcoming #polyamory #StillAVirgin? #DoubleStuffed

That last hashtag makes me see red, but I calm down when Akara places a hand on the small of my back and Banks weaves an arm around my shoulders.

"Happy Holidays to us, right?" I mutter, more hot, angry tears brimming. "This mole is the fucking cummiest cumwad."

Banks almost smiles.

Akara leans his head back, eyes ablaze.

"How are you two handling this?" I whisper.

"Livid," Akara says.

"Annoyed," Banks answers.

I swallow a knot. "What if it won't be as big of a change as we think?" I wonder. "What if no one cares? What if paparazzi just shrug?"

"The world will care," Akara says certainly. "They care about you."

"Not like Jane and Moffy."

"They will now," Akara whispers. "I'm sorry, Sul, I can't let you think it's going to be the same when we leave here. Your safety is the most important thing to me. I can't let anything happen to you." His voice almost cracks. He stares off into the thicket of snowcapped trees. "You're my heart."

I lean up and touch his face.

Akara clasps my hand against his jaw. "I love you, Sulli."

"I love you too, Kits." I nod a few, pained times. "I don't want to be naïve about what we're facing either…" *I have to be prepared.* "But the media hasn't fucking won yet."

They haven't.

They haven't.

Akara nods with me. He takes my hand and kisses my knuckles.

Banks digs in his pocket, taking out a pack of cigarettes. He toys with opening the carton, but when I lean my head on his shoulder, he closes them. "Come hell or high water, the three of us are surviving together. I don't care what anyone throws at me."

"They're going to throw shit at her, Banks," Akara reminds him.

"We're protecting her," Banks shoots back. "There is no path where we don't."

He's keeping the hope alive, and I breathe every ounce into my bloodstream. I look up at Akara, and his confidence bears back down on me.

"Banks is right," he tells me. "There is no path where we don't protect you."

We're surviving together. And we listen to the wind whistling, the shake of the fir trees, and our breaths that try to calm. I don't want to go backwards. I can't lose their companionship, their love, everything they mean to me.

The woods are where we started, but I don't want this to be where we end.

45

Banks Moretti

SUITCASES LIE OPEN on the ground in our room. Clothes stuffed and half-folded inside. Tomorrow, we leave the sanctuary of the lake house, and the three of us are dragging our feet. No real motivation to pack up and head back to Philly in the morning. It's been four days since the leak, and social media has gone wild with theories.

While I try to fix an extra radio, Sulli lies sideways on the bed with her head in my lap. She holds a cellphone above her maddened eyes and scrolls through comments under a news article. The title:

Olympic Gold Medalist Is Dating Two Bodyguards!

Other headlines are variations of that one:

Heiress of Fizzle & Hale Co. Fortunes Reportedly in A Polyamorous Relationship

Shocker! Is Sullivan Meadows Banging Two Bodyguards at Once?

American Royals are Scandalous Like Us

The articles about Sulli dating the twin brother of Thatcher Moretti are buried beneath the triad explosion. A saving grace, really. I'm not jumping for joy knowing Jane and my brother might be pulled into this mess just because I happen to look like Thatcher *Alessio* Moretti.

Plus, *I* hate those types of comments. It's like shrapnel in my eardrums. Infuriating as hell. I saw one buried comment about "it's weird" that Jane & Sullivan are dating two brothers who have the same face, and steam shot out of my fucking ears.

Christ, I'm *not* my brother.

Sulli takes a tight breath, and I angle my head to see her phone screen. Reading the comments with her.

It has to be true. The families have only denied 1 leak out of how many??

No way is Sullivan Meadows in a poly relationship! It's not in her character.

WOW. Can you imagine what Ryke & Daisy are thinking? Maybe Sulli is the sex addict of the second gen *eyeball emojis*

She's such a slut. Two guys at once? Come on.

This is so juicy! Does anyone have more details?

I've been trying to find more pics of these three online. Not a lot to go on yet. Definitely sus.

Sulli clicks her phone, and the screen goes black.

"You alright?" I ask as she tosses her phone and looks up at me from my lap.

"I'm used to being Sulli the hairy ogre. Sulli the *Sasquatch*. I didn't think I'd ever be Sulli the Slut, and it's fucking *trending*, Banks."

I stop tinkering with the radio, pain in my chest. The need to go apeshit on the internet has never fully crashed into me until now.

"People who want to fling around *slut* and *whore* as insults are just shitbags. Useless, wasteless, not worth your time or a fucking dime."

She presses her fingers to her eyes. "Fuck, I know. I shouldn't care what the public thinks. I want to *not* care."

I'm right there with her. "For what it's worth, it enrages the hell out of me too."

Sulli pulls back her hands. "Really?" She searches my cold gaze. The frost isn't directed at her.

"A bunch of trolls are calling my girlfriend a slut—*yeah*, I want to crawl through the phone screen and have more than *words* with them."

She sits up a little to better look at me. "It feels good knowing I'm not the only angry one."

"You're not alone," I breathe. "I think we all have some kind of fire in us."

Sulli stares off in contemplation. "Strong for loving *and* strong when ticked off?"

I bob my head. For a moment, I consider popping open my Twitter account. Mainly inactive. But the desire to defend Sulli is at an all-time fucking high.

"Kits has been pretty composed, though."

I widen my eyes at Sulli like that couldn't be further from the fucking truth. "He threw a pillow at the wall last night when you were taking a shower."

Sulli snorts into a smile. "For real?"

"Yeah, and he made a 'growly' noise and screamed into said pillow."

Her smile fades. "He's upset that paparazzi will be more intense."

"He's upset that his girlfriend is the target," I tell her. "I think like you, he's more used to the Sasquatch comments and virginity speculation than the shit you're receiving now."

Sulli shifts to face me more. Knees bent, she picks at her frayed ankle bracelet. "I hate that the world is debating my love life like I'm some character in a mystery movie and they're trying to solve the fucking case."

She shouldn't go on Reddit then. The "Calloway Sisters" subreddit is alive with fervor right now over the leak. Akara told me to do a deep dive to flag any threatening posts.

Nothing too dangerous so far. Just...overwhelming curiosity.

"People always want more than you'll ever give them." I hold her gaze. "It's a true cost of fame."

Over the years, I've seen how Xander would close off and shut down, and no matter how much he retreated, fans who love him still grasp at *anything* they can see, anything he can give.

A new haircut.

A growth spurt.

How he spreads cream cheese on a bagel.

It's hard to picture myself walking into a similar showdown. I can't imagine a world where people would fawn or obsess over *me* the way they've done Xander. Which is why I believe there's still hope the three of us come out of this unscathed.

Sulli scoots closer, until she's up next to me, relaxed against the wooden headboard. "This is a new phase of my life...and I wouldn't want to experience it without you or Akara. It hurts even picturing being in this room alone. Going through this alone." She slips me a small smile. "I guess I just want to be in the company of a bunch of knucklefucks like me." She uses my words from the Carnival Fundraiser.

I curve my arm around her shoulders, lips lifting. "You've come to the right place. I'm definitely of knucklefuck stock."

She takes my hand that hangs over her chest and presses a kiss to my knuckles.

Warmth bathes me, and the brewing ire towards online pests is drowned out for a moment.

The bedroom door slowly opens.

Akara has been showering down the hall, so I'm not surprised to see him. Towel around his waist, he shuts and locks the door.

Sulli lets out a wolf whistle.

Akara mockingly bows. "My lady." He makes a face at me. "What's with the old radio?"

"I misplaced my good one."

His face flatlines. "You mean you *lost* your good one."

"Still haven't lost my mind." I open up Twitter.

"*Frack*, Banks, that's not reassuring..." He trails off. "Don't post on Twitter." He must see the screen from afar. That Cellphone Whisperer.

Sulli peers over at my social media. "You were going to post?"

"Maybe." I have a staring contest with my boss. "Come on, just *one* tweet."

"What are you going to stay? Eat dung and die?"

"No, that's what *you* want to say."

Akara rolls his eyes and lets out a heavy breath. I'm not wrong here. He pushes back his wet hair. "Remember, I told *Donnelly* to suspend his own Twitter account after he kept getting into fights with Farrow-haters. Even if I want to, I personally can't do what I reprimanded one of my men for, and I can't play favorites with you, Banks."

"But I am your favorite," I mention.

He gives me a look like I'm being ridiculous.

"Just say it."

"You're my *metamour*. Of course you're my favorite in Omega. *They* don't need to see that, man."

Sulli bites her thumbnail. She's smiling while listening to us innocently bicker.

"I'm not looking to get in Twitter battles. I'll just tweet one hashtag," I tell him. "*Sulli the Sea Goddess.*"

Sulli's lips keep rising.

Akara sees her reaction. "Okay."

"Okay?" I'm shocked, then I nod to him. "You tweet something too."

"No."

I frown. "They might speculate that I'm only with Sulli if you don't defend her with me."

"That's fine." His voice is cut and dry but pained.

Sulli cuts in, "No it's fucking not."

Akara looks between us. "We're not confirming our relationship yet. We all agreed on that. If there's a way to let this blow over, we're going to try."

Sulli steals my phone out of my hand. "Don't tweet anything then, Banks. Let's just wait."

I nod in agreement. If I can't make it better, then I'm not going to make it worse.

Akara places his phone on the dresser. Still in a towel, he rotates back to us. "More like Sulli the Shrimp."

Sulli wrestles up to her knees. "Shrimp?"

I boo him.

Sulli grins more. "I'm *six* glorious fucking feet tall, and you like it, Kits."

"I do," Akara smiles with a laugh. "I really do."

Sulli breathes in the compliment and studies his body, eyeing his crotch a ton. "I show you mine, you show me yours." Sulli grips the hem of her striped long-sleeve tee and pulls up the fabric. Braless. She flashes Akara her perky boobs.

In a quick second, she yanks the fabric back down.

Heat pools down south.

Akara keeps a hand on the knot of his towel, his playful smile turning lustful. "String bean, you got that backwards. You're supposed to ask me to show mine *first*."

She flushes into a smile. "I did it how I fucking wanted to."

My mouth curves. "The mermaid makes her own rules."

Akara stops at the edge of the bed. Chest damp from the shower, his snake tattoo clear as day on his shoulder and upper chest. He's got some well-defined abs. We're equal on that front.

Am I attracted to Akara?

The question has struck me more than once since my talk with Thatcher. Like my brain is searching for evidence to my response to him.

Threesomes are something I've found I enjoy with them. But I haven't found myself reaching over to please Akara. I just want to please her.

Still, the question stays. Unanswered for now.

"I thought we established that I'm the one who makes the rules," Akara says to me and Sulli.

My fingers slide down to Sulli's wrist, and I can feel her pulse quicken. To Akara, I say, "If you give them, I'll follow them."

"Same," Sulli says.

"Same?" Akara questions her. "Is that so?"

She nods strongly. "You give me rules, Kits. I'll follow them."

My lips quirk. She's setting herself up for a ride, and I think she knows the danger on the other side.

"Just to be crystal," Sulli breathes, "I want your cock and his cock inside me while we're still here…while things are still calm…and we haven't confronted the whole world yet…"

That need grips hold of me. Whatever hellfire we're headed for, we have this moment of peace together, right now.

"So I'm not weirded out about having sex in the same house as my parents anymore, but I'd rather them *not* hear us, if that's fucking possible. I know I can be loud…"

"It's possible, Sul," Akara whispers.

"Okay, good." She relaxes.

"The two of us are gonna have to be quiet too," I tell Akara. "Everyone's packing up today." That means bodies will be shuffling around outside these doors.

Akara nods strongly. "First rule." He eyes Sulli. "No talking. Unless something's wrong, then you need to tell us."

She tilts her head backwards to me.

"Oh no, mermaid, that rule is just for you."

Her brows scrunch. "Really—?"

Akara grabs her ankle and tugs her all the way down. Her ass reaches the edge of the bed. Her breath deepens, and I climb off the mattress. When I pass Akara, he whispers to me, "Grab my rope."

I smile.

So we're doing this.

"You okay?" Akara asks her.

Brown hair unkempt and wild, Sulli nods, remembering not to talk. *God,* I want to run my hands all over Sulli and hear her whimper against my lips.

The overcome sounds she makes is an immediate fist around me. Akara agrees, and it's one of the things we both seek. Make her writhe. Make her cry out.

Quietly, today.

Akara keeps one hand on his towel, the other on her ankle. I'm quick, knowing where he's kept his rope. I slip the spool of black, synthetic rope from the side pocket of his duffel.

Slicker, faster-moving rope than cotton. I'm not a fucking bondage connoisseur—everything I know is from Akara. He has plenty of experience with knots and restraints.

I hand the rope over.

"Undress her."

I smile. He's always good to me.

Her attention veers between Akara and me, like she can't devour us fast enough. Her chest rises and falls in heavy rhythms, and I rest a knee on the bed while I slip my hands under her striped, long-sleeve tee.

I run my fingers over the curve of her beautiful fucking body, feeling the lines of her abs, and I smile as I pull up her top.

"Arms up, Sulli." She's in a daze, keeping her arms locked down, and quickly, she wakes up and stretches her arms above her head.

Top off, I expose her perked nipples. "Someone's aroused," I whisper to Akara.

He's slipping a fast knot around the post of the bed. He glances over, and his lips lift when he sees her breasts.

Sulli squirms, arching her hips.

Arousal pummels me, flaring my nose. Hardening me.

Lord have mercy on my soul.

I want deep inside Sullivan Meadows. She lets out a breathy, raspy sound, and Akara immediately covers her mouth with his hand. We're both hovered over her, and her desirous eyes ping from him to me.

Akara whispers back to me, "She's not undressed." His voice is stern.

Sulli snorts. At me. Like I'm falling behind on the *do what Kitsuwon says* game.

"You enjoy when he bosses me around?" I ask her.

Flush ascends her neck. Akara uncovers her mouth, straightening back up, and I grip the waistband of her sweatpants. She nods strongly to me.

I lean down, lips brushing her ear. "Me too." I slowly roll her pants down. "You know why?"

She shakes her head.

"Because it turns you on," I tell her, and then I tug her bottoms all the way to her calves. She keeps nodding—*please, fucking please, don't stop* all over her green eyes.

Akara lets go of her ankle as I slip off her sweatpants completely. I loop my fingers in her panties, brushing my knuckle against her heat.

She quivers and gasps, fisting the reindeer quilt underneath her.

I slowly draw the cotton fabric down her long, long legs. Tossing her panties aside, Sulli is left bare on the bed. Waiting.

Fuck. She's the stunner, the gorgeous girl I want to spread open and thrust inside. Instinct says, *need in her.* Only her.

Sulli locks eyes with me, staring deep like I'm not just a carnal body. I'm not just anyone to this girl, and the feeling of being *seen* pumps my blood with five-million-degrees of yearning and heat.

My cock throbs.

I wave a hand towards her. "Satisfied?" I ask Akara but stay latched to Sulli's gaze.

She takes a deeper inhale like I've just stroked her clit. Understanding what arouses Sulli has become easier and easier the longer we're together.

"Almost." Akara pulls at the rope, tight on the wooden bedpost, and then he takes her foot and whips the rope around her ankle into a specific tie within two seconds. He knots and tells me, "Single-column tie."

Yeah, I fucked that one up on a shoelace practice.

With one of her ankles restrained to the bed, the heat ratchets up. *Christ.* I grip the back of my shirt and pull the fabric off my head. Next, I step out of my pants. Sulli watches me, propped up on her elbows. Swiftly, Akara sheds his clothes, until all three of us are naked in the room.

He edges near me, leaving her side. She shivers on the bed.

"Kits? Banks?"

Akara glances back at her. "Are you okay?"

"Yeah."

"Then don't talk, Sullivan," Akara says firmly.

She exhales a breathy *fuck* before collapsing back on the bed. Sulli knocks her knees together and then swings them open. She does that on repeat. Open and closed, open and closed, toying with us, and the glimpse of her pussy is fucking killing me.

Akara catches her knee. "You're begging for your other leg to be tied up, *Lady* Meadows."

Her eyes glitter and say, *I dare you.*

"One ankle at a time. *Baby steps.*"

She huffs with a peeking smile.

Akara turns back to face me, smiling too. She can't see him, but he's enjoying this just as much as her. Just as much as me.

"You first," Akara whispers.

My brows shoot up. I haven't gone first yet.

"You'll be fine," Akara tells me. "Just go slow, Banks. We'll switch on and off. She'll like that." *Yeah, she will.* And what she enjoys, I really fucking enjoy.

"Without coming?" I whisper back.

"Yeah, as long as you can hold out." He squeezes my shoulder. "I'll get the condoms." He leaves for my duffel this time.

When I focus back on Sulli, she's tugging against the restraint on her right ankle, testing the knot.

I smile. "You wish you had a mermaid tail right now?"

She nods, eyes lighting up.

"Wouldn't do you any good," I say as Akara passes me the condom. "Akara would just tie up your wrists."

Sulli lets out a soft, aching whimper—*that noise*. I bend down and kiss the sound. Her lips urge mine open, but I drive my tongue deeper, and her body pulls up against me.

Fuck. I pry away from her mouth to rip open the packet. Sulli is hawk-eyeing my rock-hard cock. Partially salivating, partially studying how big I am—like she's imagining every inch filling her pussy.

I sheathe myself, and her lips part in breathy want.

Akara moves to the right side of the bed where her left ankle is unrestrained. He takes her calf in a firm hand and pulls her legs *wide* open for me.

Her lips stay parted, panting.

I slip my hand along the inside of her thigh. She shudders. Breath heavying. *Fuck.* My muscles tighten. Clench. Searing need and want rupture through my core.

My fingers slide against her heat, the slickness stirring more cravings through me. "You want to feel how wet she is?" I ask Akara.

"She can't be that wet," Akara teases as he steps over.

Sulli gives him her classic competitive stare.

I smile and slide my hand to her soft thigh, keeping my palm planted on her warm skin. Akara is close enough that his waist brushes against me. He slips one finger inside of Sullivan. With her legs spread, I have the best fuckin' view.

Her hips buck, a softer noise escaping her parted lips. "And…?" she asks Akara.

"*And…*" Akara whispers. "I told you not to talk."

"But are you surprised that I'm wet?" She tries to whisper.

Jesus, she's fucking adorable. "She wants a win," I tell Akara.

"She wants to best me," Akara nods in agreement. His eyes flit to her. "You're very wet…"

She smiles.

"String Bean."

Her eyes flame again.

He's smiling. "How about you take another finger?"

Her breath hitches.

Akara nudges me with his foot. She can't see. He means *my* finger. With his. Blood pumps harder to my dick, and not breaking my gaze with Sulli, I slip my finger inside her warmth. I can feel Akara's finger. I can feel her pulsing around me.

She writhes again, her legs twitching in apparent need.

"Settle," Akara breathes. "We're not even moving in you, Sul."

She circles her hips to try to feel *more* and *deeper.* Wanting that friction.

Akara pumps his finger inside of her, along my finger. I'm too focused on her eyes, the way she's drinking in this whole scene. Something else courses through the room. An understanding, a desperation, a rage and passion and peace that feeds us, drives us and overwhelms us—and this isn't the end.

What I have with them isn't for a short time.

It has to be for a long time.

Akara removes his finger. Swallowing an emotional, aroused knot, his Adam's apple bobs. He touches my bicep. "Fuck her," he tells me.

Sulli hears and lets out a noise I've never heard her make. She sounds like an animal in heat.

Akara solidifies next to me, and he lets out a whispered, *fuck.*

Christ. I'm dying to fill Sulli.

And I'm first.

No hesitation in me now.

He keeps her leg spread, the other attached to the bed post. Resting a knee on the bed, I'm at a better height, and I grip my erection and carefully ease into Sulli. *Holy shit.* Her tightness and warmth send shockwaves down my body.

Her thighs tremble.

Fuck.

She mouths my name, eyes almost rolling.

I rock once, twice, and she grips the quilt, quivering. Fuck, the friction throttles my senses, and our eyes latch again. I arch into Sulli, but I make sure not to let her take me completely.

Even as she bucks up and tries. Akara keeps her as still as he can, while stroking himself with his free hand.

After a couple more thrusts, sweat built on our skin, I leave her warmth. My cock hates me.

She looks crestfallen for a moment, but her arousal returns as Akara takes my spot. I hold on to her ankle now. Like Akara, I can't keep my other hand still. I rub myself as I watch him edge up to Sulli's heat.

"I'm going to plow you until you can't take it anymore," Akara whispers deeply, "and then Banks is going to pump inside of you until you struggle to breathe. And then we're going to trade off and on, off and on, until you *crash* into a peak." He kisses her aching lips. "How does that sound?"

I swear she whispers, *ravage me.*

Akara and I are smiling.

He slowly enters Sulli, his erection slipping inside her pussy. She instantly gasps. His pace starts steady and then quickens in deep, long, fast *thrusts.* Faster than I'd been. And I have to keep her leg in a firmer grip.

Her hips arc, toes curling, and a cry nearly breaches her lips. She's on the verge of an orgasm, and Akara pulls out.

She grips the quilt, burying her face in the reindeer fabric for a second.

We switch places.

And we carry on like that.

Back and forth.

Back and forth.

Sweat builds, her high-pitched noises—we try to catch with our palms. But soon, we're all heavy fucking breath, raw emotion, and something more. Our gazes cling. Our bodies weld. We're fastening onto each other, connected deeper, deeper, and *deeper.* Trying not to let anything outside this room sever the feeling we've felt—the feelings we feel. We're riding and cradling and gripping onto our love.

Emotion stronger than arousal clouds the air, pierces my lungs, and sends me.

Back and forth.

Back and forth.

"*Banks*," she breaths. "*Kits*." We let her say our names.

I can only handle entering Sulli for one quick pump. Akara does the same. Muscles flexed, I'm burning with emotion and need.

Standing so close to Akara, our bodies brush and touch and I don't fuckin' care. Sweat is slick. Heat engulfs. Feelings surge.

One solid thrust and then his turn.

One more for him and then it's mine.

She's shaking.

Quivering.

Trembling.

Sulli is overcome in this moment, and I'm way too close to the edge.

"I'm gonna come," I whisper to Akara as he passes me on our switch.

He nods. "Me too."

I take a deep breath and fill her again. Not all the way. But enough. With a few more thrusts, Sulli twitches, and her body arches up. She contracts, and light reaches my eyes. *Fucking...* The crescendo to her pleasure wraps tightly around my length, pulsing against me. *Fuck. Fuck.*

Fuck.

Christ.

Breathing hard, I leave Sulli so Akara can release.

She's coming down from her orgasm, sensitive as hell, and he's tender with her as he takes his moment to reach a climax inside her.

She shudders, twitching again like she's reaching another orgasm with him.

Goddamn.

I slip my boxer-briefs on, and after they're done, I help Akara with the rope. When she's untied, she lets out a deeper breath. "Fucking whoa," she tells us. "That was…fuck."

I smile.

Akara smiles.

"You enjoy that?" I crawl onto the bed next to her and plant a couple light kisses at her neck. She snuggles into me.

Akara kisses her ankle.

"Yeah, I really fucking did." Her eyes flutter a little. Spent.

Akara climbs into the bed on the other side of her, his arm draped around her waist. She grinds back into him until he shifts even closer.

She mutters, "I never wanted it to end."

Akara and I share a soft look. *Neither did we.* Outside of this room, back in Philly, we're gonna meet some type of hell.

We all know it.

"Sleep," he urges.

She lightly strokes our legs with her ankles. "But I want to…stay awake…and hear you guys…talk…about me." She yawns.

We laugh.

"FOMEFT hitting you?" I ask her.

"*Hard.*" She tries to open one eye. Maybe because the one thing we're holding fiercer to right now is our bond together. The three of us.

"Then we won't talk about you," I tell her. "We'll save that for when you're awake."

"Just this once," Akara adds, giving me a look. Yeah, we're not going to be able to keep that up for forever.

"Deal." Even as she starts to drift off, even with this deal, she fights sleep. Like she's immortalizing us, these feelings, so no one will rip away what we found. What I feel for Sulli is cemented so deep inside my unholy soul.

The world will have to bring me to my knees to take her away from me.

46

Sullivan Meadows

NEW YEAR'S EVE.

We've neither confirmed nor denied the leak, which has only fueled the speculation and attention that rages down on us. Fucking chaos. It reigns supreme outside the penthouse. Ever since we returned from the lake house yesterday, news vans and paparazzi have been camping outside the high-rise. With telephoto lenses, cameras upon cameras, and feverish eyes, like vultures waiting to dig into a carcass.

While I watch, I'm dreaming they're not here for me. They're staked outside to catch a glimpse of Moffy and Farrow and their squishy-cheeked, blue-eyed baby.

But I can only fool myself for so long.

All my roommates have already left for New York, where Aunt Rose and Uncle Connor are throwing a gala for friends & family. Akara enforced a "staggered" departure.

And I watch each of my cousins leave.

I watch the paparazzi stay put.

Waiting.

For us.

Scuffling back from the expansive window and Philly skyline views, I grab my footwear and go to the velvet couch. While I'm sitting, I stick my feet in sneakers, and I reach down. My hands tremble as I tie the laces. I swallow my anxiety, and I hike up my dress a little more.

The emerald-green razorback dress hugs my athletic frame, and I figure I need proper *runaway* shoes in case shit hits the fan. Shit meaning the hot steaming spotlight on me. I'd like to fucking bust the bulb to that thing.

But I don't know how.

My fingers slip off the lace.

Banks squats down. "I've got you," he says with deep confidence.

My heart soars out of my chest as he ties my sneaker. "I'm not used to being the one that needs all the strategies just to walk out the door." Sure, we had to have *plenty* of strategical entrances and exits during the FanCon Tour. But that was different.

This is my normal life.

It's supposed to be at least.

Akara touches the mic at his ear, and then his eyes dance over to me. "It should be better once we're at the venue, Sul."

"Why is that?"

"Because your parents, aunts, and uncles agreed to arrive at the same time as you. The media and fans should latch onto them and let up on you for a second."

My parents, aunts, and uncles are way more fucking famous than me and my cousins. It's just how it is and how it's *always* been.

The fact that they'd create that diversion for me…

I breathe easier.

"They're kind of fucking awesome," I say out loud.

"Yeah, they are," Banks nods with that shadow of a smile. He finishes knotting my other shoelace, and we stand up together.

Akara nods to us. "Our turn."

On our way out, I grab my apple-red trench coat, and as I start to slip my arm in a sleeve, Akara catches my wrist. "You can't wear that, Sulli." He hardly blinks.

"I can't wear a coat?" I frown, confused. "It's *cold* out tonight, Kits. This is a sleeveless dre—"

"It's red," Akara cuts me off. For a second I expect him to make a Red Riding Hood reference, but he explains, "You'll stand out in a crowd like a neon light, which is not how you slip past paparazzi."

I never really considered that before.

I never really needed to. I haven't been "of interest" enough to paparazzi to be a focal point that needs shading. Until now.

The trench coat is the nicest I own. "I think I might have a different jacket." Minutes later, I return with an old parka, sportier and *blue*. "Is this okay, Kits?"

"Better."

Banks has two fingers to his earpiece, listening to comms. Seeing them so vigilant and single-focused on security is ramping up my adrenaline but also reminding me that they'll keep me safe. They're keeping me safe.

Everything is fine.

Everything is okay.

I try to calm my fucking nerves as we ride the elevator down and then leave through the high-rise's private parking deck. Secured.

Banks buckles into the driver's seat of a black Range Rover. A security vehicle. I snap my seatbelt into the backseat, and Akara adjusts the passenger seat. He fits dark Clubmaster's over his eyes and passes Banks a pair of darker Wayfarer's.

It's nighttime.

But I've seen bodyguards slip on sunglasses to block camera flashes at night before. Just…rarely, and not solely because of my fame.

"You okay?" Akara keeps asking me.

I nod, feeling alright. "Just a tad nervous."

"This initial part might be intense," Akara warns. "But it'll be way better after, I promise." His assured voice soothes me.

I try to nod back again, but my head feels heavy. I zip up my jacket. "Let's go."

Banks turns the ignition. Driving down to the ground level of the parking deck, anticipation surges in my body, and we wait for a second as the gate lifts. City lights and the night should be on the other side, but as the gate disappears, all I see are bright, piercing flashes.

I sink lower in my seat.

Cameras go off more as Banks tries to pull onto the Philly street.

"Speed up," Akara says.

Banks jerks to a stop, gripping the steering wheel tight. "Can't. There's a shitbag standing in the middle of the street." *How can he even see that?*

Akara begins to roll down the window.

"No, Kits!" I yell at him, crashing forward to grab his suit jacket, but the seatbelt locks and jerks me backwards. *Fuck.* I don't want anyone to hurt him.

His deep brown eyes hit mine. "I'll be fine, Sul."

"SULLIVAN! LOOK HERE, SULLIVAN!"

My pulse hammers in my ears against the caustic screams and shouts of paparazzi. With the window an inch down, I hear them even clearer.

"SULLIVAN! IS IT TRUE?! SULLIVAN!"

"ARE YOUR BODYGUARDS YOUR BOYFRIENDS?!"

"LOOK HERE! LOOK HERE! LOOK HERE!"

"Sulli, *Sulli,*" Akara calls, his sunglasses off.

I'm panicked, staring at the flashes and screams, but I return to his reassuring eyes.

"I'm your friend. I'm your *boyfriend.* But before those two things came true, I've been your bodyguard, and I have to protect you." He unsnaps his seatbelt. "They're not going to hurt me."

The SUV hasn't budged, and I trust him. In all the fucking times he's kept me safe. In all the ways that I know he will.

"Come back to me, Kits."

He offers a classic Kits smile, sparkling his eyes. "I wouldn't dream of anything else." And then he exits.

"BACK UP! BACK THE FUCK UP!" Akara sneers. "We're leaving, and *you can't* stand in the way of the fucking car."

"ARE YOU DATING SULLIVAN MEADOWS?!"

Please don't hurt him.

Don't hurt him.

A thousand dangers stand outside. I'm not the only one they want.

"KITSULLI!" I hear with a shrill shriek.

"WHERE'S BANKS?!" someone else screams.

"NOW!" Akara shouts, then the door opens. With fucking haste, he slips back into the passenger seat and smashes the door shut, sunglasses back on. "Go with instinct."

Banks slams on the horn.

People scatter, but the cameras flash feverishly, more incessantly. I shield my eyes with my hand. Spots dance in my vision. And then Banks floors it.

My stomach rolls when I feel a *thud.* "Oh fuck, did you run someone over?"

"That was a purse," Banks says calmly, speeding beyond the madness.

Relief barely touches me. I don't breathe again until Kits fully rolls up the window and clips in his seatbelt. They both remove their sunglasses.

"I fucking hated that," I choke out.

He rotates in his seat to face me better, looking me over in a quick sweep. "You need a water?"

"I could use a fucking hug. Unless you can't..." I trail off. He's already unbuckling again.

Akara crawls into the back and wraps his arms around me in a warm, safe embrace. I burrow against him, and he kisses my cheek. "We should be good until we get to the venue." As he says those words, a couple paparazzi vans pull up to our left and snap photos while we're driving.

He has to return to the passenger seat. Security comes first. I hug my legs to my chest. *I'm cool. Totally fucking cool.*

Banks checks on me through the rearview mirror, and I hold onto his strong gaze. Akara adjusts his mic and speaks to the team, and to Banks, he says, "Take the left up here."

Nerves at an all-time fucking high, I watch them navigate the roads to New York. Time passes anxiously. It feels like *forever* until we reach the glittering high-rises of Manhattan.

More than anything, I despise all the paparazzi who think it's cool to snap photos while we're *driving.* It's the perfect recipe for an accident.

Banks pulls up to the curb and slows down. A lighted awning leads into the theatre. Large crowds—of what appears to be a mixture of paparazzi and fans—already gather overzealously outside, pushing at the venue's security.

Olympic buzz and craze was a different sports beast and not as in-your-face as this kind of celebrity paparazzi.

Right now, they're being held back enough. And I spot a clear *open* pathway from the street to the door.

"The backdoor is just as crowded," Akara tells me. I'm sure SFO and bodyguards on Triple Shield are giving updates through their mics. This must be the best path of entry.

Banks shuts off the car. "We're just waiting for your parents now."

I exhale. No one in the pushy, excitable masses has realized this car belongs to us yet. Thank fuck.

I try to let go of my legs and drop my feet off the seat. "I haven't been this nervous since the FanCon," I admit. Back then, the feverish attention was newer to me. I thought, afterwards, I'd grown more comfortable with the spotlight.

Maybe not to this extreme level.

Banks turns to me. "Just take a breath."

I inhale deeply, exhale deeply. Feeling a bit better. "What if we make a run for it?" I ask, eyeing the door. "I think I could sprint that, no problem."

"Too many people are near the door," Akara says.

"And we wouldn't be able to keep up with you," Banks reminds me.

Akara tips his head to me. "No one would."

"Right," I nod. "Forgot how slow you two are."

Banks smiles. "She makes jokes."

Akara meets his eyes. "Not funny ones."

"I think I'm fucking funny," I say into a smile that vanishes quickly. Hordes of people start *screaming* like the most popular boy band of the century has arrived.

"Lily and Loren are here," Akara says.

Banks nods. "Showtime."

They both jump out of the car.

Wait for Banks to open the door. Akara's instructions enter my head.

My side door opens abruptly—Banks barely gives me a glance before taking my hand swiftly. I'm pulled underneath his arm in a second flat with such haste and acceleration that my breath struggles to catch up to my feet.

But we're walking. We're moving.

Street pavement underneath my sneakers. *I can do this.*

"Curb," Banks says, out in front of me.

I step over the curb.

Akara's body pushes up behind me. Protected front and back. Ass and boob coverage. Though I can't let the joke fly free now. They can't joke either.

Their warmth.

Their warmth, I hang onto like water wings that I've never needed. Not in a pool or an ocean. I'm flung out to sea tonight, and I want to be Sulli the Sea Goddess.

Their warmth up against me. In the cold. Among the shrill screeching of paparazzi's rapid-fire questions and fan's intensity.

Their warmth. It keeps me upright. Keeps me moving.

They're here.

I'm between them.

They're here.

A couple feet away, I distinguish my mom and dad, their own bodyguards flocking closely around them. Fans push towards my parents and ask for selfies. Some hold out old *Princesses of Philly* posters for my mom to sign.

Paparazzi snap photos and yell questions over the screaming of fans. I can't see Aunt Lily or Uncle Lo, and I figure the crowds must be too congested around them.

Uncle Connor and Aunt Rose walk slowly behind my parents, stopping to even sign things like phone cases and purses. Their interaction stirs more attention, and fans push towards them, wanting selfies that my aunts are agreeing to take.

I almost smile.

My family did that.

For me.

"SULLIVAN MEADOWS!" My name ricochets off Manhattan buildings like a gunshot in the air. Ear-splitting shrieks pierce the night, pierces right through me.

And the last thing I see is my mom.

My mom in her golden dress that reflects the golden honey of her hair. But her eyes are what grip me.

Her beautiful green eyes.

And the sheer *terror* in them.

Like a flip of a switch, all the crowds congregated around my parents and my aunts and uncles suddenly converge on me. Onto us.

It's a slingshot.

A snap of time.

Banks grabs my hand, but he's being physically pulled forwards.

Akara has my other hand. And he's being ripped backwards.

I'm in between like the center of a wishbone.

"SULLI!" Banks screams.

"SUL!" Akara yells.

Pain surges in my limbs, but I want to hang on forever. *I don't want to let go.* Camera flashes are blinding, and the light goes in and out on the two men I love.

One second I can see their lips moving, screaming my name. The next split-second, they're gone into darkness. Then they're lit up again with urgency and viciousness in their gazes. Fighting towards me as they're being wrenched back.

Flashes, screams, hands. I can't see.

I can't see!

Other hands start to latch onto my body as Akara and Banks are forced further away. Fingers yank at my hair.

I'm not letting go.

Take my fucking hair. I'm not letting go of them!

I try and force them back towards me. Hands still in their hands, my muscles sear as I pull and pull and use all my strength to bring them back.

Please.

Fucking please.

"SULLI!" My dad's voice breaks me. The fear and pain.

I won't…let go.

Lights and flashes. Shrieking. Hands. *Hands.* Their hands are still in mine. "Sulli, look here!"

"Sulli, sign this!"

"Sulli, you're dating both guys?!"

"Sulli, who do you love more?!"

"Sulli, are you a virgin?"

"SULLI!" Akara slingshots back into me. My arm aches, and he pushes me ahead. Banks closes the distance. Somehow.

How?

I'm in a daze as they battle to get me through the door, and as soon as I step into the theatre, the venue's security blocks the entrance. Paparazzi pile up and push against the glass doors to snap photos.

I can't stop staring at the hysteria that builds.

"She's in shock…" I hear someone say.

I blink. "What?"

"Sulli." Banks has his hands cupped around my cheeks.

I blink harder. "How did we get in here?"

I don't understand.

And then I look up and realize who's standing around me. *Farrow, Thatcher, Oscar, Quinn, Donnelly, Gabe.* The six of them have made this little circle around Akara, Banks, and me. And we're *in* the venue.

Akara explains, "They came outside to help."

The magnitude of what we just went through is slowly catching up with me. "That should have worked, right?" I ask all of Omega. "The core six creating a diversion." I use their fandom name because it reminds me how famous they are. Reinforces what I know to be fucking true. They're more famous than me.

"It should have," Farrow says into a nod.

Oscar and Donnelly share a wary look.

Thatcher's concern drills into his brother. The sleeve on Banks' suit is ripped at his shoulder. Akara's tie is gone. *No.* My mind paints graphic details of what they just experienced, and sickness burns my throat. I know it's their job to take that *for* me, but it doesn't make it any less agonizing to see.

They keep sweeping my body, assessing for signs of hurt.

My dress is in one piece. Jacket is fine. Scalp kinda hurts.

And my arms are fucked.

I shake them out, muscles searing.

"You alright?" Banks asks, watching me.

"A little sore," I say. "It's okay."

"It's not okay," Akara refutes.

I'm about to reply when I hear my mom's voice. "Where is she?"

"I'm over here?!" I wave my hand. Quinn backs up a little, and my mom and dad push their own security into my cluster. They sprint to me.

Immediately, they pull me into a hug. "Sulli," my mom says like she almost lost me.

"It's okay," I tell her.

"But are *you* fucking okay?" my dad asks.

That breaks me completely. Like a hammer to glass, I shatter. My sob chokes me for a second, and my mom hugs me even tighter.

I don't want to be more famous than them.

I don't want it.

I don't.

I'm not fucking ready.

Please.

I'm not fucking ready.

I was never going to be ready.

47

Akara Kitsuwon

IF YOU LOVED HER AT ALL, you wouldn't do this to her.

Ryke's words rage and rage and rage inside my head. When I'm on-duty, I stay *focused*. No drifting, but shit, it's hard to concentrate on the New Year's Eve party around me. And I've cursed so many times in my *fucking* head, I'm surprised I haven't launched into a string of profanities out loud and just welched on the bet that I lost back in November.

She's safe from any hands now.

I hang onto that fact.

Sulli, Banks, and I have taken box seats in a theatre. No fancy opera or ballet are performing on stage.

Tom Cobalt's band, The Carraways, in all their emo-punk glory belt out head-bangers to a crowd of old and young. Of course, Rose and Connor Cobalt would want their son to take center stage at their party. And Tom looks completely in his element. With heavy eyeliner and emotive baby blues, he sings passionately into the mic like his life is on the line. Captivating almost the entire audience.

I'm barely engaged. Not a knock on the music, just a knock on a terrible damn night.

Younger crowds gather near the stage to dance, friends of the families. Some *are* family, like the girl squad, Luna, and some of Tom's brothers. Others, like us, retire to seats to munch on hors d'oeuvres.

My mini smoked salmon tart remains untouched on the table next to me.

"Go Fish," Sulli says softly and sips on champagne.

Banks and Sulli play cards in the seats beside mine.

I decline for security reasons. I'm eyeing every entrance and exit like her life depends on my vigilance. Because it does. I don't trust anyone.

They all want a piece of her.

They can't have her.

I spot someone snapping photos towards us from the second row below. I click my mic. "Akara to Thatcher, second row. Camera."

"I'm on it."

After the entrance from hell, SFO agreed to look out for Sulli tonight. They'll put temps on their clients if they need to be pulled away.

I appreciate that.

More than they can possibly know.

But still…

If you loved her at all, you wouldn't do this to her.

I did this to her.

"Go fish for a card there, mermaid," Banks says.

Sulli's hand trembles on her way to pick up a card. "Fuck. Sorry."

"No apologies necessary," he says tenderly. "Here." He picks up the card for her.

"Thanks." They tried playing gin rummy and she couldn't grasp the game right now. Banks has been comforting her and briefly surveying the concert.

I asked Sulli if she'd rather just ditch the party and go back to the hotel, but she said she wanted to brave this out. No quitting, no bailing. *It's what Jane and Moffy would do*, she said.

The more she shakes, the more a knife is plunged in my gut. She shouldn't have to brave this out. Hiding in this box seat isn't a part of the plan. Normally, she'd be on the floor with Luna and banging her head unrhythmically to punk music.

I think about her life, and how we all know it's going to change now that she's dating me and Banks in public. I don't want Sulli to miss out on anything.

I feel like I've stolen something from my girlfriend. Her life. Her ability to experience *everything* and miss out on nothing, with no one impeding her fast, vigorous stride.

I've thrown her to the wolves.

I'm letting her be eaten alive.

Shit.

I run a hand through my hair and try to shift my mind. I listen to the music more as Tom's band switches to a drums-heavy song. The drummer bangs his sticks slow, off beat. I cringe. Before Sulli, I was Tom's bodyguard for a little over a year, and there's one thing I know about him.

He's a perfectionist.

So I'm unsurprised when he shoots a look back to the shaggy-haired blond.

The upside—I doubt anyone else notices the drums. Maybe I'm only picking up the bad tempo because I used to play them.

"Price to Alpha, Epsilon, Omega." The owner of Triple Shield is on comms. "The venue's security is having trouble with the front door. I need three men from each team."

I roll my eyes, a little annoyed that he's referring to Omega like my men are still under his flagship. I click my mic. "Copy. I'll send you three guys from Kitsuwon Securities."

Banks glances at me. "You need me?"

She needs you.

I shake my head. "I'm sending the Yale boys." I radio it in. I trust them to show Triple Shield that we're more than capable of handling front-door security.

Sulli lays down a pair on the little café table. "Everything okay?"

I don't want to lie, but I'm trying not to freak her out. "They just needed more security at the front door."

She nods. "My mom says it'll blow over once people start forgetting about us." She tries to shrug, but the motion is weak. "I know that won't be tonight. But maybe it'll be sooner than we think."

It could be never.

The thought is another blade in my chest. Stabbing. Cutting. Slashing. I don't want to think the worst, but I'm trained to look out for the worst. I'm trained to stop the crash before the damage is done.

You can't stop this crash, Nine.

I have to.

Preserve her happiness. Preserve her life. What's left if the world rips her to shreds?

The Carraways stop playing suddenly and Tom grabs the mic. "Okay, lovely people, it's that time. Grab the person you love. We're counting down to the new year!" Cheers erupt.

"TEN!" The shouting begins.

This past year flashes through me, all the ups and downs. Peaks, valleys, *tears* and laughter. Beginning in Scotland. Snowed-in. Coming back to a fire. Watching Sulli's home burn down. I created Kitsuwon Securities. We went to Anacapri.

Three weddings this year.

No funerals.

One baby.

We drove to Montana.

Sulli climbed mountains.

We cheered her on.

We were happy in the woods. Happy in the penthouse.

This long, eventful year is ending, and maybe this is where it's supposed to close. This is where everything reverses. Back to normalcy for Sulli.

Back to a life she can live without being suffocated by the world around her.

"SIX!" Tom and the crowd shout.

"Should we kiss?" Sulli asks us over the countdown.

Before tonight, I would've said *no*. We weren't public. This is a public event. But our relationship is now technically out in the open.

Yet, we still haven't confirmed anything.

"FIVE!"

Banks is looking for me to make the call. At the end of the night, this is a security decision.

"FOUR, THREE—"

I shake my head. "I don't know." *That's a lie.* In my gut, I know what *should* happen.

We shouldn't kiss.

"TWO, ONE."

They don't.

We don't.

Right now, we have a chance to resolve this. I'm already coming up with a plan in my head. I'm already starting to realize there's a way out.

There always is.

"HAPPY NEW YEAR!"

LEAVING THE THEATRE PROVES AS DIFFICULT AS entering, but this time we're more prepared. All of SFO help us reach the car. The parking garage for the five-star hotel is already secured.

We ride up the elevator. Slip into the empty hallway. I look left and right. *She's safe here.* Exhaustion wears all of us down as Banks swipes the keycard, and the three of us enter the hotel room. It takes me and Banks a couple more minutes to search the room.

No strangers.

No hotel staff.

No bugs.

All clear.

Banks kicks off his shoes, and Sulli immediately heads to the minifridge. I stay beside the door, leaning against the wood. Outside the hotel windows, snow drifts in the night sky. With tightness in my ribs, I watch the soft flurries float sideways, downward.

Nearly every shitty day of my life, it's been snowing.

Banks rakes a hand across the back of his neck. His concern flits from Sulli to me. "You don't need to watch the door all night, Akara."

"I know," I breathe out. Am I really breathing though?

He shakes his head, brows knitting like he's stumped on why I haven't moved my ass. The door is locked. *She's safe.*

But what about tomorrow? What about years from now?

Sulli picks through the snacks in the fridge, choosing Reese's Peanut Butter Cups. "What's going on?" She stands up with unease.

Banks threads his arms, eyes on me. "I'm trying to figure that one out."

I take a breath. "I've been thinking about how to fix this."

Sulli sighs out in relief. "Thank fucking God. You have a plan." She plops on the edge of the bed.

Banks looks more skeptical. "Akara—"

Pressure slams on my chest. I'm already in pain as I open my mouth to speak. *Say the words. Say the words.* I look from him to her. "I'm breaking up with both of you." My voice sounds raw and constricted.

Wind rushes out of our hotel room.

Sulli loses grip of her chocolate and the package *thumps* to the floor at her feet.

Banks pushes forward. "Say again?"

I grind my teeth, nose flaring. "I'm breaking up with you. *Both* of you. It's over. This is over."

Her eyes glass. Mine are burning. "As a media stunt, right?" Sulli asks. "It won't be for real."

I shake my head, neck tight. "No, it's for real, Sul." *She's not living a lie for the rest of her life.* "It needs to be real. This is a clean break. It'll be like you only chose Banks all along."

"But I didn't *just* choose Banks," Sulli chokes out, hurt and confusion coursing through her green eyes.

Banks glares at me. "You're not even gonna ask for my advice? You *always* ask for my fucking advice." He pushes closer, arms outstretched like *come at me.*

I'm not fighting him on this. "I know what you'll say, Banks." I grimace into a wince. "You'll tell me I'm a fucking idiot, a *stunad.*"

"You don't think you're being one?" Banks questions coldly, his eyes reddening as he sees how staunch in this decision I am. "You don't want to fucking do this—I know you don't."

"I have to!" I yell from my core.

"I'm telling you, *you don't*," Banks growls out. "Don't fucking do this, man. This won't change anything—"

"It'll change *everything*. And you know it, too. We have time. We *still* have time. We haven't confirmed anything or been caught as a triad. Once the world knows it's just you two together, they'll back off Sulli." I shift my weight and point at the ground. "And this is how it *should* be, Banks. You deserve to be number one in her life—"

"We're *both* number one, you dumbass," Banks says with hurt. "Whoever's in your head telling you I'm second, cut 'em out."

I hear him, but all I see is a path where Sulli is free of pain and misery. That path doesn't include me. Maybe it never did, and to even go for her was selfish. "Things will be back to normal once I'm out of the picture."

"No," Sulli snaps, jumping off the bed and coming forward beside Banks. "I don't want that. I want *you*." She keeps her distance, like she's scared I'll physically push her away too.

I run my tongue over my teeth, my face cinching in pain. "I'm not putting you through what just happened again, Sul." I strengthen my voice, my decision. "I won't. I *can't*."

Banks is shaking his head vigorously, glaring murderously.

Sulli is frozen in a state of shock.

I take a bigger breath. "I'll remove myself from your detail so it won't be hard. I'll grab my stuff out of your room tomorrow—"

"STOP!" Sulli yells at me, tears surging and slipping down her face. "Fucking stop!" Her voice cracks.

My gaze scalds, fighting back my own tears.

"Stay tonight," Banks forces out. "Let's talk about this. Don't just fucking run away!"

"I'm not running. I'm protecting *us*. I've been protecting you two this entire time, and somewhere, deep down, I knew..." I push back my hair, breath shortened. "I fucking knew *this* is what it'd have to come to. You don't know, but I told Ryan Reed you two are secretly dating."

"You did what?" Banks almost yells.

Sulli has her hands on her head. "Fuck, *fuck*."

"I hoped he'd go spill it," I admit, rubbing my nose that runs. "I wanted *that* out in the world—the relationship that has the *least* pain, the *least* heartache, the *most* strength. It's you two. It was always supposed to be you two. I cut in—"

"I cut in," Banks refutes.

"You kissed her first."

"She's always loved you."

Sulli's face contorts. "It's the three of us. It was always supposed to be the three of us." She turns to me. "How is this protecting us, Kits? This media craze could be over in a couple weeks. We just need to wait it out like my mom said."

"Like your mom said," I repeat those words. Distress cramps my chest as I picture where Sulli is headed. "She's wrong, Sul."

"No, she's right."

I shake my head. "Lily Calloway and Loren Hale never shed their fame."

"I'm not my aunt and uncle."

"You're not," I agree. "But think about it, Sulli. Everything they did kept bringing more attention and more eyes and more curiosity and more click-bait. The headlines sucked people in. *The sex addict living with her sisters. The sex addict and alcoholic getting married. The sex addict and alcoholic having kids.*"

Banks has his arms around Sulli as she wipes at her eyes. He asks me, "What does that prove?"

"How do we know this is any different?" I wave a finger around the room. "The headlines are right here. *The Meadows Olympian dating two men. The Meadows Olympian fucking two men. The Meadows Olympian having babies with two men.*"

Sulli blinks and more tears fall.

I take a breath. "Just living your life, Sulli, is going to be a spectacle." I touch my chest. "I love you both too much to put you through that." Pain lances everywhere. "I have to end this."

Leave.

Never look back.

She has Banks. She'll be okay.

Turning around, I grab the doorknob.

Sulli lets out a sob that rips me apart.

Banks grabs at my shoulder. "Don't fucking leave." He's choked.

I spin around, the pain in his eyes reflecting the pain in mine. "She loves you, Banks. She'll be happy with you. She'll be safe with you."

"Even if that were true, what about *you*?"

"What about me?"

"Don't do this to yourself. I've seen my brother sacrifice what makes him happy for what he feels is right and just, and you can't do this. Don't fucking do this." He fists my shirt. "*Be happy*."

I'd rather leave them knowing they're happy. I can suffer alone. "Unlike the two of you, I grew up as an only child. I've lived with no family in Philly. I'm used to being alone."

"And you hate it," Banks says coldly. "I need you. She needs you. *We* need you."

Sulli rubs at her face and comes closer, her hand brushing against my hand. "This won't fucking work without both of you. *Kits*."

I meet her eyes. "I don't know if I ever believed that."

Like I detonated a bomb at our feet, Sulli stumbles back. "What?"

Banks catches her from falling onto the floor.

"In my heart," I say tightly, "I think if I didn't exist, you two would still be perfect together. But for me to be with Sulli, I'll always need Banks."

Banks groans out with the shake of his head. "That's horseshit and you know it."

"I don't," I say, swallowing a lump in my throat. I need to go. Just standing here is killing me. "I guess we'll find out."

"KITS!" Sulli screams.

But I'm faster than the Olympian this one time, and I've exited the door before she reaches me. For security reasons, I'm positive Banks won't let Sulli leave the room.

Even on the other side of the door, I hear her sobs.

I was happy, wasn't I?

You were, Nine.

But this pain will end eventually. It has to.

One day, I'll wake up and I'll see Banks and Sulli happy. Married. With babies. Living a conventional life. And I will know I gave them that.

As I take every weighted, horrible step away from them, I try to believe this won't kill me.

48

Sullivan Meadows

I THOUGHT THE PAPARAZZI outside the theatre would be the worst part of the night.

Wrong.

Totally fucking wrong.

This took the cake. I'm on my knees in the hotel room, and Banks is kneeling in front of me while I'm buckled over in his arms.

"It hurts…" I choke out, silent tears streaming. My agonized gaze hasn't shifted off the ground.

Banks cups my wet cheek, lifting my face to his bloodshot eyes. "It's gonna be okay." Banks is good at holding on to hope, and I see him scavenging for those obliterated pieces.

I nod with him, but my throat swells. Pain surges back inside. "We should run after him," I rasp. "Let's go."

Neither of us move.

Because we know.

We know.

Banks says the words aloud. "He doesn't want us to."

He'll push us away. He'll keep pushing us. He's made up his mind, and until he sees this through, there is no stop in Akara.

I squeeze my eyes closed, then open them onto Banks. He's distraught. Akara used his words carefully. He broke up with Banks too, not just with me.

Their friendship is done.

Weight crushes me. It's crushing him. He could so easily follow Akara, repair their friendship. Abandon me.

I grab his bicep. His hand strengthens on my cheek, and between shortened breath and glassy eyes, I choke, "Don't leave me."

"I'm not. I'd *never*." Banks holds up my head that heavies. My tears drip down his fingers, and he tells me powerfully, "*I love you. Akara loves you, and it's why he's being a selfless dumbass.*" His voice breaks.

I try to laugh, but I just cry against his hand. *Fuck.*

He brushes away my tears, our eyes diving to the raw center of each other. "I'm never leaving your side, as long as you'll have me, and I'm not giving up on him—he'll wake up eventually."

His confidence and love for me and hope for Akara soothes the broken pieces inside me. He brings me closer to his chest. Holding me while I cry. After a few minutes, he picks me up and carries me to bed.

Eyes swollen, head spinning, I slip beneath the covers with Banks. Still in our clothes, he pulls me firmer to his chest, and I burrow my head into his warmth.

"It's gonna be okay," he whispers, his hope like a drug.

I take calmer breaths.

Akara was so resolute.

So sure.

That hurts more and more. That he believes this is going to salvage everything, when it feels like he's burning it all to the ground.

"He broke up with us," I mutter the words, thinking the truth might lessen the pain. But my heart clenches. Everything hurts like someone shoved me into concrete and I'm just sinking...sinking...sinking.

"Jokes on him," Banks whispers. "He's still my boss, so he's gonna have to hear me tell him he's wrong every fuckin' day."

I sniff hard. "I don't know how you'll be able to look at him and not cry."

My eyes feel raw.

Banks squeezes me harder. "I'm not much of a crier. I shed most of my tears when I was kid." He looks down at me as I pull back to see his dry, still bloodshot eyes.

I don't think Banks needs to cry to have the face of someone who feels like sobbing. "I hate knowing he's going to be miserable so we can try to be happy." A piece is always going to be empty without Kits. How can we *truly* be happy without him?

"He's just doing what he always does. Taking the fall for the people he loves."

"I should've walked away first," I mutter.

"I wouldn't have. That was never gonna be me," Banks admits, and I understand why. They're two totally different guys, and they were never going to choose the same path in this scenario. In a lot of ways, I think the only reason Akara left is because he knows I have Banks.

But if the roles were reversed and Banks was gone, I'd be just as devastated. If I left them, I'd be just as heartbroken. Like I've known—like I told Akara—the only way this works is for the three of us to stay together.

That's it.

He's doing this for me.

For us.

He's trying to protect my life from impending doom. He's trying to protect me from experiencing events that could scar me and irreparably change me.

It's a selfless, loving act.

More tears cascade.

Kits.

He didn't have to do this, but I know why he did. Just like Banks promised to never leave me, Akara promised to always protect me.

With a hoarse voice, I ask Banks, "What if I text him that he's putting my safety above my happiness and that's not a good idea?"

He nods. "Yeah, you should try."

I do try with quaking hands. I send a text.

We wait a full hour.

Akara never responds. He leaves me on *read*.

"Fuck," I mutter. "I guess…I guess he thinks I'll forget about him." I rub at my eyes. Akara knows the truth. I am happy with Banks, but he doesn't realize I'm *happiest* with him and Banks.

"He won't forget about us," Banks tells me. "He'll come around."

"He's not my bodyguard anymore," I realize with a sharp inhale. "What about my friend? Did I lose that tonight too?"

"In his eyes, I think so. He wants a clean cut," Banks says under his breath, and I hug him more. Before my brain can drive down a tormented rabbit hole of *holy fucking shit, Kits is no longer in my life* realizations, Banks adds, "He's gonna come to his fuckin' senses."

Tears well up as I struggle to keep hope alive like Banks.

I want that torch to stay lit, and I know it always will. But there's a part of me that wonders if this is it.

If Kits is just *done*.

And there will be no returning to what we once had. The sadness in that thought bowls me over again. And again.

And again.

MORNING COMES, AND AFTER ANOTHER LONG-winded, anxiety-fueled ride avoiding paparazzi and camera flashes, Banks drops me off at the gated neighborhood in Philly.

My childhood home.

I can't keep the break-up a secret. I could go back to the penthouse and field concerned questions from Moffy and Jane. Maybe they'd sigh in relief. Maybe they'd think, *I told you so, Sulli. This triad was never going to last long.*

I'm not afraid to confront them, but I've decided I'd rather be with my mom and dad first. They're the ones I used to always retreat to when the rug was swept out from under me.

Banks assured me he's fine, and he needs to check in with his mom and grandma anyway.

I text Kits again. Hey, hope you're doing well. Maybe we could talk again?

No response.

Banks is right. Akara is just looking for a clean cut. A breakaway. But he can't sever our relationship *and* our years-long friendship with one single slice. Jagged edges and debris lie in the wake of his painful departure—there's *nothing* clean about this.

I stare solemnly at the marshmallows floating in my hot chocolate. Goldilocks rubs up against my ankles while I sit at the window nook. Snow blankets the yard and cul-de-sac outside, and every now and then, I catch brief glimpses of my dad shifting a ladder against the roof. He's been removing Christmas lights.

My mom left to grab something upstairs. She didn't say what, but after she added extra marshmallows to my hot chocolate, I can tell she's pulling out the best for me. I know it's because she thinks I'm shaken from last night's theatre chaos.

The sheer dread and terror in her eyes still haunts me.

"I'm okay, Goldi," I breathe, stroking her soft, golden fur.

She sits politely, tail swishing back and forth.

"She misses you," my mom says, returning to me with an assortment of chocolates, a little doll, and a wrapped package. A flower crown of dried daisies is nestled on her blonde hair.

"I try not to miss her," I admit. "It makes me miss Coconut." The white Husky I grew up around, and I almost wince at Goldi. "Fuck, I'm sorry, girl. You know I love you." I kiss the top of her head. She nuzzles against my cheek.

Sadness lets up for a single second.

My mom slides into the window nook beside me. "I miss Coconut too." She scratches Goldi's ears with a softer smile. "But I think she'd be happy we have Goldi now."

Yeah.

I sip hot chocolate, trying to unknot the pretzel in my stomach. And then I immediately reach for the little Peruvian doll in surprise. "Rue? Where'd you find her?"

"The back of your closet." Mom peels the foil off a chocolate.

I touch the doll's soft red dress, faded from the sun and all the picnics we had in the backyard together. I haven't seen Rue since I was eleven or twelve.

"Do you want her back?" Mom wonders.

My eyes still feel swollen from crying last night. They hurt with each blink. "I shouldn't…I guess I'm too old for dolls…"

"Who said that?" She crinkles her nose, then puts a hand to her heart as her feet rise and legs cross like mine. "In this glorious world, I decree *young* and *old* shall carry dolls if they want to." She gasps. "And the *immortal*. We can't forget about your Uncle Connor."

I want to smile. Her humor usually cheers me up fast, but I'm sinking under heavier emotions. "I can't take Rue back." I place the doll on the windowsill. "I want to be taken seriously and treated like an adult, Mom. Like I'm capable of making my own decisions about my own life, even if I'm headed for heartbreak." I hear my voice crack.

"Sulli," she interjects with such empathy that I go quiet. She's set aside the chocolate and her hands touch her chest. "I understand what that's like, more than you realize. People thought I couldn't make good choices for myself because they saw me as naïve and reckless. But I knew what I was doing. And as I grew up, I knew what I wanted for my life. And then people thought I shouldn't be with your dad. People thought I was too young to try and have a baby. People thought I wasn't responsible enough to build a summer camp."

But she married Dad.

She had me at 21: her firstborn, baby girl.

And she built the summer camp. Despite all the cynics.

"You proved everyone wrong," I say softly.

"I just did what I wanted." She has a gentle smile that eases me. "So hey, all you need to do is *live*, Sulli. Live your life as awfully *wonderful, beautiful,* and *dangerous* as you want."

She's saying this after watching paparazzi descend violently on me. Her eyes are glassed, and I can see, even through her fear, she still wants me to have the life *I* want. Not the life she wants for me, or the life my dad wants for me.

My heart tries to fill. I don't know what I'd do without my mom. "I wanted to be fearless with my life like you were with yours."

She searches my eyes like I can't see what's in front of me. "You already have been."

Have I?

He broke up with me, Mom. The truth is a knife I can't remove without bleeding out. Not yet. And I'm quiet as she places the wrapped package on my lap.

"I know your birthday is still about a month away, but I think you should have this now."

My birthday present?

"Open it," she urges with a smile.

I unfurl the donut-print paper, and I take a breath, my fingers moving over red winterberries, pieces of a fern, and blue flowers, twisted into a winter crown.

"Those are Forget-Me-Nots and Winterberry Holly. I know I've made you plenty of flower crowns when you were younger, but this one is different."

"How?"

"It represents more than just your childhood. You're a loving, courageous, *spirited* woman, and you don't have to let go of Rue and the things of your past to embrace the things of your present and your future." She settles the winter crown into my hair while I lower my head.

I look back up.

"So this crown, I made with you in mind and with your love of Akara and Banks in mind."

I try to fight tears. Green fern. Red winterberries. Blue Forget-Me-Nots. "You knew their favorite colors?"

"I may've asked around town and some little birdie told me."

"Who?" I wonder.

"Beckett."

I blink back more waterworks. *Akara broke up with me.* Whatever present and future existed with us, it's been ripped away for the moment, maybe…forever.

"Thanks, Mom. I love it," I say with a constricted throat. *I love it too fucking much.* The flower crown of my dreams is not the one of my reality, like she thinks.

I'm the princess of nothing.

"Do you want to talk about yesterday?" she asks, seeing my sorrow and faraway gaze.

I place my hot chocolate down, knowing she means the theatre. "There's not much to talk about. I don't remember everything…it all happened so fast; it's like a fucking blur."

She nods, understanding.

I think she understands more than anyone can know. My eyes graze the long scar across her cheek. Once upon a time, she was a bystander in a riot. Swept up in chaos and struck by a two-by-four—a nail was jutted out of the wood.

"Blurry moments still have an impact," she tells me softly. "If not me, you should talk to someone. Banks or Akara, maybe? Or a therapist?"

Hearing Akara's name again nearly breaks me.

She frowns more, sensing something's wrong.

"Mom," I start, about to tell her the truth—and then the backdoor opens. Our heads turn as my dad stands in the kitchen.

"Sul?" He's already outfitted in a warm winter coat and a beanie. He holds up my old jacket in his hand. "Can we talk?"

I glance to Mom.

"Go. Maybe you'll spot a Big Foot." She wags her brows with a playful smile.

I smile back this time and hug her for longer than just a second. *Thank you for everything.* And then I spring off the window nook.

After taking the jacket from my dad and slipping on boots, we leave through the backdoor. We're quiet as we walk toward the woods, and I pick the winter crown off my head.

Berries and flowers are striking against the stark white snow around us. Do I even deserve to wear something this pretty? Am I even the woman my mom thinks I am—or am I still wishing and hoping to be that courageous, that spirited and loving?

With a single breath, I hook the crown to a rung of the treehouse ladder.

My dad watches with hardened eyes and furrowed brows.

I leave the crown behind on our trek, and we keep moving. Snow crunches underneath our soles as we pass the tire swing.

We stay silent. My dad and I aren't on the best terms still. No resolutions made at the lake house, and I don't expect any today.

When I tell him Akara broke up with me, I know he'll be *happy*. And his happiness will be an arrow through my chest. Another kick into the ground.

Venturing further and further into the woods, we stop at a clearing with makeshift rope bridges strung between the trees. Ropes hang down from skeletal limbs. Wooden planks are nailed into the largest trunks, easy to climb. Growing up, Winona and I loved having our very own ropes course. For me, especially, I enjoyed working out on the ropes. Scaling up and down them.

Snow cloaks the wooden bridges, and I wipe some ice off a hanging rope with my ungloved hand.

My dad watches me for another second. "Last night was one of the worst nights of my fucking life."

His words are like a boomerang, flinging from me and back to him. *It was mine too, Dad*, I want to say, but my tongue feels thick in my mouth.

Our eyes meet.

His scruff is scruffier, but he's the same dad, stone-faced with a mushy heart. The one who dressed in a tutu for me, the one who rallied at my swim meets, the one who showered me with chocolate, the one who said *yes* more than he ever said *no*—the dad who I'll always fucking love and never want to hate.

"I couldn't see you," he says, muscles constricted. "And in that fucking moment, I just saw what happened to your mom..." He hangs his head. "The riot." He takes off his beanie and runs a hand through his disheveled hair. "I didn't ever want you to have to go through this."

My eyes burn. "I know you tried to protect me."

He nods strongly several times. "That's all I've ever fucking wanted to do." We just look at each other for a long moment, his gaze reddening with raw emotion that we've felt since the initial blow-up, since the origin of the strain. Quietly, he breathes, "I know I've made mistakes, and making you choose between Akara and Banks is a big one."

"What?" I rock back.

His face contorts in a series of sentiments, but I see his remorse most clearly. "You love them both, don't you?"

"Yeah. I told you I did months ago."

He falters for a moment, his eyes flitting from the ground to the sky and then back to me. "I could see it back then, how much you love them, but I cared more about protecting you—and that was wrong. I was fucking wrong."

I hug my arms to my chest. Confusion compounding. "Why now? What's changed that you suddenly regret being the Choose One Ambassador."

His brows rise. "The *Choose One Ambassador*?"

"No one else was making me choose," I shoot back. "So yeah, you were the fucking ambassador."

He grimaces. "I guess that's fucking fair." He fits his beanie back on his head, tugging the fabric down over his ears that are pink from the wind. "Your relationship is leaked to the public. It's out in the world. I wanted to believe it wasn't fucking inevitable, but I see now it was."

Inevitable.

Because Akara and Banks and I wouldn't break up. Because there would be no universe where it could be *two* instead of *three*.

I choke on brittle air. Water sears in my eyes from the cold. "Before you start down this apology tour," I tell him. "You should know that Akara broke up with me last night."

My dad physically sways like I pushed him. Confused lines form between his eyebrows. "*What?*"

I don't repeat it. I know he heard. Riled, hot tears form. "It's what you wanted, right?" I snap. "For one of them to leave. Well, congratulations—"

"Sulli, what the fuck happened?" he interrupts, concern outplaying his confusion.

My chin trembles. "He thinks since we haven't *confirmed* our relationship, he can…make a clean break and save me from the media attention."

My dad's hands fly to the top of his head like he's winded. "Fuckfuck*fuck*," he curses out and starts to pace.

I frown. "I…I thought you'd be happy."

He stops pacing to pinch the bridge of his nose, holding something back.

Pain latches onto me. "You basically told him to leave to prove his love for me!" I yell.

"I know!" my dad screams back. Birds flap away from the trees and he glares up at the sky. "I'm fucking sorry, Sul." He takes a deep breath through his nose.

"Sorry for which part?"

"Raising my voice at you," he says, his reddened eyes meeting mine. "And for saying that to Akara. I didn't want him to leave you after… *fuck*."

"After what?" I take a heated step forward. "After my relationship leaked? Because Akara might be right, Dad. This might all return to normal once the world thinks the triad was a lie and that I'm just with Banks. Then will you go back to being happy again that Akara left me? That your grand idea of *Choose One* worked? Or were you just hoping that Banks was the one to self-sacrifice?"

"No." He shakes his head a few times, gaze dragging across the snow until he looks to me again. "I'm so fucking *sorry*, Sulli. Leak or no leak, private or public—it doesn't fucking matter because it doesn't change something."

"What?" I cage my breath.

"You'll never be completely happy if you lose one of them. And I know…" He chokes on emotion and pinches his eyes. "I know what it's fucking like to drag yourself down—and I'm angry at myself for asking Akara and Banks to shackle themselves with that weight. I asked them to step back from what makes you all fucking happy, when life's *too* fucking short." He almost starts crying. He blinks back tears, staring up at the sky. "I just thought you'd be alright with one—you'd still be happy with one—and then I saw you three at the lake house. I saw them run after you into the woods."

Pain passes between us. I'm barely breathing.

"And I realized I've been trying to take away the people you need and love in this world, and that's not fucking right. It's not okay—you won't be okay, and I can't lose you to *that* or to silence or anger or resentment. I want you to be able to live your life one-hundred-fifty miles per hour. No brakes. And I'm so fucking sorry I tried to slow you down."

My cheeks are wet. Heart pounding with a ragged tempo. I've waited *so long* to hear those words. Fuck, I thought they might never come. He apologized three separate times, and hearing everything he said should bring relief and happiness, but I'm weighed down in unbearable grief.

"Your approval is too fucking late," I tell him, holding back more tears.

He wipes at his own eyes. "I fucking know that, Sul." He drops his hand. "I fucking know."

I take a short breath. I think about *forgiveness*. How I suck at it. How in times like this, I wish to be better than my past. How I'm in so much pain. And right now, I just really need my dad.

I rub my fist over my tear-streaked cheeks. "But I'm not going to hold it against you."

His eyes rest against mine in confusion. "I'd understand if you fucking did."

Tears build and more squeeze out of my eyes. "No, I need you too much to be mad at you."

His face breaks. "Sulli—"

I clutch at my jacket. "It hurts really bad. And I don't know how to get it to stop."

My dad bridges the final distance, and he wraps his arms around me in a hug. He's the sturdy foundation that I'm built from. The mountains. The air. The ocean. "It'll fucking be okay."

"But I love him. I *still* love him." I don't see how that's going to change.

Akara is already gone.

49

Akara Kitsuwon

I STAND AT THE TOP of a mountain, water in every direction. A breathtaking island. Palm trees sway on sandy beaches. Waves crash into jagged rocks, and snow…snow falls from the sky and kisses my skin. It builds on the island mountaintop.

My breath smokes the air as I see *her* standing at the edge of the cliff. Sulli stares off at the horizon, back turned to me. Her wild, brown hair blows in the cold breeze.

"Akara!" Banks screams. He's standing close but out of reach from me. Feet chained to the ground.

I try to move to him, but my body jerks back. *Shit.* Chains wrap around my own ankles.

Snow falls harder, and I glance up to the cliff. Sulli whips around, green eyes on both of us. She scoots backwards towards the edge. "SULLI!" I yell, pure terror shooting through me.

"NO!" Banks screams.

I yank at the chain.

He grapples with his restraints.

She keeps stepping backwards. Her eyes numb to the world. "SULLI! STOP!" Panic rips through me as I claw at the lock on the chain. Fingernails bleeding. "STOP! *STOP!*"

"SULLI!" Banks screams louder, his veins protruding from his neck, face reddened.

"STOP! *SULLI!*" Spit flies from my mouth as I yell with raging desperation, and I start tugging with my ankle. I can break it. *I can break my foot.*

I have to break my foot. I have to reach her. *I have to reach her.*

All the while, my eyes stay fixed on *my heart* who's faltering at the edge of a cliff. "SULLI!" My voice dies in the wind as she goes over.

Her brown hair billows around her body.

I jolt awake, choking for breath.

Sweat built up, I grip at my damp T-shirt, feeling my speeding pulse. I rub at my eyes and roll over to my alarm clock. *Three in the fudging morning.* Great.

Awesome—so awesome.

I sit up and hug my knees to my chest. My nose flares as I recount the dream again and try to level my breathing.

Third consecutive one this week.

All three have been the same. The island. The cliff. The chains.

First one, I was at the cliff. Sulli and Banks were chained.

Second one, Banks fell over while Sulli and I screamed for him.

Now this.

I dig the heel of my palm in my eyes as emotion begins to build. "I know, Dad, I know," I whisper to myself. He'd be dishing out so much advice if he were here right now. Telling me to *listen* to these nightmares. They haunt me like they did before the three of us got together. Somewhere, deep down, I'm aware how much I need them. Love them.

I can't shake it.

It's in me deep, and maybe one day these will just *stop.* Right now, that seems unlikely.

I reach over and snatch a bottle of sleeping pills from my nightstand. My eyes graze the bed on the other side of the room. Empty. Banks still stays over in Sulli's room, and I'm glad about that. I don't want them to break-up.

I don't want her to be alone.

I don't want him to lose her.

YAWNING INTO MY ARM, WIND WHIPS AROUND ME.

This time, I'm not asleep in a screwed-up nightmare.

I'm on the ski slopes.

Seven days have passed since I broke up with Sulli and Banks, and in that time, I've coped with sleeping pills and burying my head into work.

No new leads on the mole. Which means I'm not any closer to stopping another leak from hitting the internet. Plus side: I was able to open my gym for a couple days this week. Since I'm no longer Sulli's bodyguard, I've had time to manage Studio 9 myself.

But sitting behind a desk all day, answering phone calls and welcoming potential new members with their "first day free" promos has been less than stellar.

It gives me way too much time to think about them.

So when Donnelly and Quinn pulled me out of bed this morning and said *we're going snowboarding*, I didn't combat them. Didn't tell them not to take the day off for me.

They're my roommates, my employees, but I also know they're my friends.

Donnelly is snowboarding on an easier hill, off on his own, and I'm at the top of a Black Diamond with Quinn. Already unmounted from the ski lift, Quinn buckles his foot to the board.

Snowboard goggles on the front of my helmet, I bring them down as the sun casts a glare on the bright white slope. "You sure you can handle this one?" I ask him.

I've seen him on some decently difficult runs in the past, so I'm not too worried. But he's never been on a Black Diamond with me.

"One-hundred percent. Outside of the gym, my sister and I would spend all day on the slopes. We're big snow bunnies."

I give him a sideways look with a near-smile. "Back in my day, we called snow bunnies hot chicks who hang out at the lodge. Not six-foot-three *Quinn Oliveiras*."

"Back in your day," Quinn laughs. "Come on, Akara, you're only like two years older than me—hardly a senior citizen."

"I'm six years older," I correct. "And your rabbity-ass is going down." I wish I could compete with Sulli on the slopes, but at least Quinn is game for a good old-fashioned race.

Quinn is smiling as he puts on his goggles. "Catch me if you can, bro." He'll definitely be easy to spot. His helmet is a bright neon orange that matches his jacket and pants.

Oscar gave him shit for resembling a traffic cone, and Quinn just laughed it off. It reminded me about *therapy*. The scheduled therapy I have with Banks starts in a couple weeks, and I'm thinking about canceling it or…in the very least, move the start date.

Everything is too raw to hash out right now.

Quinn gives me a quick fist-bump before taking off with a laugh and exclamation of joy. He's in high spirits after I let him know the good news on our drive here.

He's going to be transferred to Baby Ripley's detail.

Maximoff agreed to my proposal.

At least something is going right.

I hang on to that win. And I should follow Quinn fast—obviously, I'm *racing*—but something roots me here.

Them.

I balance on my snowboard and take out my phone. Check the news outlets. *Nothing.* I expel an agitated breath.

Over the past few days, I've texted Sulli and Banks reminding them to *announce* their relationship online. None of this works if the public still believes the leak.

I'm going to have to call them. *Shit.*

With a glove wedged under my armpit, I dial a number and press the cell to my ear.

Once the phone rings, panic escalates in me. I haven't spoken to her in a week. One whole week. Barely even talked to Banks on comms.

The line clicks on the second ring. "Kits?" Sulli's hopeful voice nearly tears me apart.

"Hold on a sec." I put her on hold and call Banks.

He picks up on the third ring. "Akara," he says, relieved.

I inhale a sharp breath and ignore skiers in pink vests who shuffle around me. "Wait for a second, Banks. I have Sulli on the other line." I merge the calls with one click. "Okay, can you both hear me?"

"Loud and clear," Banks says.

"Yeah," Sulli replies. "What's going on, Kits?"

"You've both been ignoring my texts."

Silence bleeds over the line, and for a moment, I think they've hung up on me.

Then I hear Sulli's strained breathing.

Don't do this, Nine.

I blink back pain. "Hey, this isn't up for negotiation," I say lightly like we're all still friends, even when I know we're not. "I need you to announce your relationship."

Banks lets out a rough noise. "You can shove that order up your ass. You're gonna have to fire me."

My hand clutches the cell tighter. Cold bites my exposed flesh. "Then you're fired."

"Kits!" Sulli yells. "You can't fucking do that."

I grind my teeth. "I know what you're both doing," I snap. They're stalling. Hoping. Waiting. For me to change my mind. I tell them bluntly, "I'm not changing my mind. Announce your relationship or I'm going to start shifting Banks off your detail."

Firing him is a crap bluff. It isn't in me.

Silence again.

Then Sulli breathes, "How do we confirm it?"

"However you would've announced all three of us."

"No, I won't fucking do that," she refutes.

"Then some way," I snap. "I don't care how as long as it gets done."

"Why the rush, man?" Banks asks.

Because it hurts.

Because I need the door shut.

Because if I have a chance, I might run back. And I can't. *I can't.* This is how it was always supposed to be. They need to be happy without me.

"Just do it today," I say coldly. Then I hang up.

I press the side of the phone to my forehead, gripping it tighter. *AHHHHHH!* I silently scream in my head. Nothing feels right. Even in my winter gear with my favorite snowboard beneath my boots, I feel sideways and bent.

I slip my phone back in my pocket, and with my glove back on, I take off—Quinn way ahead of me and out of sight. Wind whips against my face as I speed down the steep slope with precision and ease, shifting my body left and right.

For a mere second, troubles fall to the wayside and I just breathe.

And then I hear a guttural noise—a *scream* that pitches my mind back to the horrific sounds inside my dream. I'm dunked into dread. Until I realize the scream isn't mine and it's not in my head—it's coming from somewhere further down the Black Diamond.

Birds squawk and flap away from treetops. The scream morphs into a groan, and my dread becomes nothing but urgency. Someone's hurt.

Quinn.

It can't be him.

He's a *fudging* snow bunny.

It can't be him.

I accelerate as fast as I can go without losing control of my board.

Halfway down, I easily spot the bright *orange* blob lying against a tree on the right bank. No. *No.* "QUINN!" I yell, crouching expertly and gaining more speed.

When I reach the tree line off to the right, I apply pressure to the edge of my board, coming to a stop, and I snap off my buckles. "Quinn, talk to me." I whip off my goggles.

He groans, banging his head against the pile of snow. "I tried to... slow down, the tree."

"Okay, okay—what hurts?" I pull out my phone to call the ski patrol.

He winces through his teeth. "My leg. I think...I must've just sprained my ankle...a little. I'm okay. I can...I can walk it off." He's about to vomit.

I talk to ski patrol and call in the accident on the Black Diamond. While I do, I silently wish Farrow were here right now to assess his injury. *Fuck.*

Shit.

I swear up and down in my head. "Okay, thanks." I hang up. "Ski patrol is coming."

"Is he okay?!" A couple girls slow on their skis.

Quinn makes a woozy smile. "Yeah...just a scratch. I'll be...fine."

"Oh...you're Quinn Oliveira," the girl in a purple puffer jacket gasps. "Are you sure you're okay...?"

Great. Just great. The Casanova of SFO is attracting not two but suddenly *five* girls. They congregate around me and an immobile Quinn, but the purple-jacket girl is the only one who says her name: Nessa Nolan.

As the audience shouts over each other, I cut in, "Everyone *shush.*" Yeah, I just shushed them with zero bowls of Instant Regret. Quinn is my responsibility. He's only twenty-two, and I need them to back off.

Shit, he's been like a little brother to me. He's my roommate. He said he was a fucking snow bunny?! *How did he end up here?!*

FUCK!

I swallow the curses, and while the girls quiet, I shift his oversized ski jacket that blends into his pants. Getting a better visual of his leg, and I go cold.

"Oh my God, his leg!" Nessa gasps, dropping to her knees at his side. "It shouldn't be bent like that...is that his bone?" She turns to me, wide-eyed.

"I can't look," another girl says.

Yeah. His *bone* ripped through his pants.

"I can walk..." He blows out a measured breath. "Just...help me up, Akara."

"No, don't move. That's an order."

He pulls off his goggles, squeezes his eyes shut. "It's fine....I promise, I can walk. I can walk." He opens them on me, his desperation and pain clawing at me. "I'm going to work tomorrow...I'll be there, on the dot. You don't have to worry about me…" His nose flares, eyes welling up.

Mine burn. "It's okay, just breathe, Quinn."

"I'll *be there*…you can still count on me for Pirate Parrot." *Pirate Parrot* is the code name for Baby Ripley, which rarely ever needs to be used, but Quinn is smart enough not to mention him around these five girls. The more he sees my unease, the more he tries to stand up. "I can walk, Akara. I can—"

"*No.*" I put a hand on him.

"I can walk!" he screams, almost as excruciating as his first wail at the collision.

"Your leg is a *pretzel*," I force out. "I'd rather carry your ass down this hill than see you hobble and break your face, okay?" My pulse is pounding, and his features twist in anguish. He almost tries to sit up again, but Nessa holds his other shoulder.

"Just wait, okay?" she says. "You're really hurt, Quinn."

I send a quick text to the Yale boys about the accident. "Let's just get you to the ER."

Quinn tries to ease, but he can't. What this means for his job, his career, his *future* on SFO—only I have those answers. And my head is spinning, not even wanting to land on the dark reality.

"I see the ski patrol!" Nessa shouts. "Over here!"

"OVER HERE!" The girls wave.

"You're going to be okay, Quinn," Nessa says. "Just hold on." She clutches his hand tight.

He nods through a pained grimace, then asks me, "Can you call my brother?"

A PHONE CALL WITH OSCAR, A HOSPITAL RIDE, and an X-ray later, we all learn Quinn Oliveira broke his tibia in three pieces. Since it's an open fracture, his surgery is scheduled later today and will probably include metal pins. At least six months of recovery.

A half a year without Quinn able to go on-duty.

He's okay.

I try to hold on to the positive. Which is big. No head injury. No fatal wounds. Farrow already stopped by and examined the X-rays.

He left earlier, but I asked him if he thought the recovery time could be shaved. He told me under his breath, *it's a bad break. Six months is realistic.*

Six months.

He's okay.

Quinn lies on the hospital bed. Flowers overflow the room after his snowboard accident was leaked. This time *The Royal Leaks* wasn't culpable.

Nessa North, the purple-jacket skier, shared the news on her Twitter account. She currently hovers over Quinn with her friend. They followed us to the hospital and haven't left his side.

Oscar keeps grinning every time they flirt like his little brother is about to ascend the Olympic podium for *Hottest Person on Earth.*

Quinn's hotness is unquestionable at this point, but even if I'd prefer to kick the girls out, they're the only thing *slightly* taking his mind off his injury and bleak future on SFO. I think that's why Oscar is entertaining this whole sideshow.

"Does it hurt more?" Nessa asks for the umpteenth time.

"Not really," Quinn says.

"You must have superhuman pain tolerance."

Oscar pops a couple chips in his mouth, shaking a bag of Doritos. "Or he has super strong Vicodin running through his veins."

Quinn shoots him a look to shut up.

I just need to rip off this Band-Aid. Let the gavel fall. "Nessa, do you think you and your friend could grab Quinn a sports drink from the vending machine?"

"We can *definitely* do that." Nessa speeds out of the room in a hurry, her friend right behind.

Quinn watches Nessa longingly.

Crap, I hate being the bearer of *shit* news. But I clear my throat. "Quinn."

"Sorry," he says, sort of morosely. "She's cute, right?"

Oscar laughs. "Super cute, little bro."

I hear *super cute* and an image of Sulli flashes in my brain. My chest tightens, trying not to think about her.

Staying on track, I tell Quinn, "Nessa is also a fan."

"A fan of me, not of the families," Quinn says, like that makes a difference.

He shouldn't be dating or screwing *fans* of SFO. It's messy—so very messy—and a current rule that's spelled out in the Kitsuwon Securities *rulebook*. That I'm positive Quinn has ignored. I know he's fucked fans before. I live with him, and I let it slide.

My life is messier.

Yeah.

Obviously.

Oscar continues to munch on his Doritos.

I snap my fingers to my palm. "So you want the verdict?"

Quinn tries to sit up a little. "Yeah…let's hear it…"

Oscar crumples the snack bag, seriousness sobering his features. "Are you letting him go?"

Here's my dilemma:

Thatcher protects Jane.

Farrow protects Maximoff.

Banks protects Sulli.

Donnelly protects Xander.

Oscar protects Charlie.

Quinn protects Luna.

Gabe is the floater.

And no one protects Baby Ripley.

If Quinn is on crutches, he can't be transferred to Ripley's detail. My master plan for the baby to have a bodyguard has imploded.

Gone to smithereens.

I suddenly hate snowboarding.

And beyond that, he can't protect Luna. He can't protect anyone. So I tell him, "You can't be a bodyguard with a broken leg."

Oscar stiffens.

Quinn nods slowly. "So you're firing me."

"No, not exactly." I massage my knuckles. "If I have to sit behind that desk at Studio 9 for one more day, I might honestly lose my mind." I nod to him. "I need a manager for my gym. You want the job? It's yours."

Quinn mulls this over. "Will I be let back on the team?"

"When you pass physical exams, a spot will be waiting for you."

His lips lift, ever so slightly. "And you're giving me another job in the meantime?"

"It's a pay cut."

"I'll take it," he says instantly this time.

The Oliveira family saved Studio 9 from going under once. Maybe Quinn can help me save it again.

"You can still keep your room at the apartment," I tell him. "I'm not kicking you out." I feel responsible for his injury, and I can't toss Quinn out with no place to go, except maybe back to live with his parents.

He can stay.

Oscar motions to me. "Gabe's already complaining about his contract. This won't win you any friends with new hires."

Yeah, in the new Kitsuwon Securities contracts, I put in a *one-year probationary period* before housing is offered for new full-time bodyguards. Gabe signed anyway, but I see how this will ruffle a few feathers. Quinn won't be on SFO anymore, so he really shouldn't be getting a free room.

Still, he's one of my men.

"What about Luna and Baby Ripley?" Quinn asks. "Is Gabe going on her detail and you're protecting the baby?"

I'd make that transfer in a heartbeat if I thought Farrow would let *me* on Baby Ripley's detail. But I don't think he wants his boss hovering around him, which I get. And I don't necessarily want to be around Farrow 24/7.

Oscar's already shaking his head like he knows his brother is wrong.

"Gabe is staying as the floater. Ripley has no bodyguard yet." I take a breath. "And I'll be on Luna Hale's detail. Permanently."

Back to protecting a client.

This one just so happens to live with my exes.

50

Banks Moretti

TAKING A WEEKEND TRIP with Sulli to Atlantic City—I've been saving up my paychecks for this short getaway, and I thought of cancelling the date after the breakup. I didn't imagine sweeping my girlfriend off her feet while a fuckin' crater just slammed through us.

Hell, I didn't see a fallout with Akara coming at all. I thought he'd be here with us.

But Sulli still wanted to go. "No time like the fucking present," she said.

We agreed we're not here to forget about him. That's what Akara wants, and we're *not* giving him everything he wants.

Mini-Akara is in Sulli's macrame backpack. After printing out a picture of the Thai-American "boss" wearing a muscle shirt, a backwards baseball cap, and smartassy smile, we hot-glued the photo to a popsicle stick. Sulli had to eat a dreamsicle to get the fucking stick, so a lot went into this Kindergarten creation.

She sent him a photo of Mini-Akara.

No direct reply.

He's really plunging that sword deeper and deeper into his body, and we're not making this easier on him.

He's also not making this easier on us.

While we ride a Ferris wheel on the pier, overlooking the murky ocean in January, Sulli and I share a bucket seat, my arm wrapped around her broad shoulders as she grips pink & blue cotton candy—*and* our phones go off.

"That's the *third* text from Kits in ten minutes," Sulli sighs out. It's not the sort of texts we want to read from him. He's still threatening to fire me if we don't confirm our relationship to the world.

"He won't do it," I assure Sulli. "He needs me." There's no way in any hell he'd put a *temp* on Sulli's 24/7 detail right now.

Paparazzi are gathered on the pier, flocking the base of the Ferris wheel, and I've had two other temp guards assist me since New Year's Eve ten days ago. Every time our bucket rotates to the bottom, our extra security restrains cameramen from bum-rushing the ticket-taker and reaching us.

Sulli picks at the cotton candy and stares off into the bright sun and the rolling foam tips of ocean. Despite being cold winter, it's a pretty day. She's wearing her jean jacket and leans her weight into my side.

Her green, green eyes lift to mine. "But he *could* fire you. We don't know what he's thinking while he's alone."

"He's probably thinking he misses us and he hates this and it's what he *has* to do."

"Like he might think he *has* to fire you—that we've given him no choice," Sulli says with a haunted look. "I don't want to take that fucking risk, Banks." The Ferris wheel swings to a pause midway to the top. We rock back and forth. "I can't lose you too."

I hold her broken gaze. "You're not gonna lose me. He wouldn't do that to you."

"But I know Kits—if he's set his mind to something, he'll see it through." She squints in the light. "We have to protect some *part* of what we created—we have to." Her chest rises and falls like we're on the brink of the end.

I picture being torn from her detail.

Abandoning Sulli.

Muscles flexed, I breathe through my nose, and I know that Akara is going to win this round. Gotta hand it to him, he came to play. Our Mini-Akara popsicle stick versus his job termination threat. Looks like we need to up our game.

"Okay," I nod strongly to Sulli. "Let's confirm *us* to the world."

We're doing this.

My pulse picks up vigor as Sulli digs for her phone. I take the cotton candy and hoist the big fluffy cloud of pink and blue to block sunlight from her eyes.

Under the sudden shade, Sulli smiles, but her lips falter fast. "So… should we just do an Instagram post like what Moffy did?"

"Probably."

"Help me find a pic of us." She scrolls through her camera roll, and I peer over her shoulder. Most pics are either selfies Sulli took or they're photos Akara snapped.

As the Ferris wheel moves again, we ascend to the very top. A drop of blue splats on Sulli's cheek. *Fuck.*

"What was that?" She looks up.

"The cotton candy is melting. Here." I brush my thumb over her cheek, her breath shortens—our eyes crashing together, and in a quiet moment, I show Sulli the melted blue sugar.

She takes my hand and tastes the blue sugar off my thumb. Her gaze still on mine, as though lassoing this sweet moment around us, knotting the thread, and I feel the emotion squeeze us together. I slide my hand beneath her unkempt hair, against the hardness of her jaw and softness of her cheek.

While I cup her face, she holds onto that hand, our eyes latching stronger. "Banks," she rasps. "We can kiss in public…"

The new realization settles between us with anticipation and grief. Our greedy asses want more. She wants more. I want more. And we're not ready to let go of Akara. I'm not picturing the life he's ready for us to live. The one without him, but I feel that future rolling into us like the ocean in the horizon.

Our bucket sways to a pause at the top.

Paparazzi can catch us making out. We're about to confirm we're together. Technically speaking, the only thing stopping us is fear.

Fear that we'll lose him forever if we go forward, but I can't stay stationary. I can't sink into quicksand and struggle to come out.

I clutch her cheek with a stronger hand. Her breastbone lifts with a bigger inhale, and I whisper huskily, "You want me to kiss you?"

Her eyes scream, *fuck yes*. Her lips say, "Every day…every fucking night."

I move in fast, and we slam into each other with a string of desperation and affection and something else, something we're hoping to heal and hang on to.

We kiss on a Ferris wheel. Sweet, *sweet* taste of cotton candy on our tongues, and we pull closer, kiss deeper, slower. My fingers lost in her hair, I feel her lips urge mine to keep going, don't stop. Never stop. And so we keep going 'round and 'round.

Ignoring the camera flashes as we reach the bottom.

Ignoring the gasps and questions.

Ignoring comms in my ear.

It's a perfect heart-aching moment, and after two full rotations, I press my forehead to hers, staring down into Sulli while she stares up into me. Guilt paddles inside our affection and love, and I hope that changes in time. And not because we left him behind.

"One pic just to solidify it?" Sulli asks.

"Yeah."

We choose one that Akara took in her bedroom.

I'm carrying Sulli upside-down. Her hair cascades over her face and smile, and I'm caught mid-laugh. The caption we agree on: When the boyfriend carries you to bed.

We both sorta hate that line.

So we type it out.

If Akara thinks we're taking this announcement with grace, he's fucking wrong. We're not happy-go-lucky, honeymooning over here. Hopefully he realizes he hasn't left *joy* in his wake.

ECLIPSE HOTEL & CASINO IN ATLANTIC CITY JUTS

out in a row of casinos that glitter and glow. Been here once upon a time for a cousin's bachelor party. Got shit-faced with Thatcher and we ended up passing out on the floor of the hotel room where eight other guys crashed.

Never thought I'd be back here with a girlfriend, but after the Ferris wheel, Sulli and I are on a new mission.

One that involves gambling *my* paycheck and a chunk of her monthly trust fund allowance. All in the name of my ex-metamour and her ex-boyfriend. For one, if we make some extra funds, we're gonna slip the cash into Akara's PO Box. Help out Studio 9.

For another, if we lose big, then we'll be texting Akara about our misadventures in gambling—and maybe he'll get his ass out to Atlantic City to stop us from making dumb choices.

He thinks I'm a cowboy. Well, giddyup, motherfucker. I bite down on a toothpick. "Three-hundred on red," I tell Sulli as I shift my stack of chips.

People crowd around the roulette table to watch, our extra security shielding Sulli's other side while my arm slips around her waist. I'm eyeing the hell out of anyone who edges near her.

"How much should I put on 4, 9, and 18?" Sulli asks, sifting through her chips.

"However much you feel."

She places a sizable stack on each number. A middle-aged man clicks his camera phone in front of us, a flash going off in both our eyes as the dealer calls for final bets.

Sulli sinks back on her chair next to me, then scrolls through her phone.

I glance over her shoulder, seeing our Instagram post popped up. "You still checking it?"

"Yeah," she winces. "The comments are fucking awful."

I spot the first few comments.

I knew Banks was the one!

Kitsulli was never real. OMG.

Let's go Sulletti. Sail that ship into the fucking horizon!!!!

My stomach churns.

This is what Thatcher and Akara wanted. For me to be loved and number one in the eyes of the public. I'm not happy about it.

I swipe a hand down my face as my eyes graze over the photo.

Sulli lets out a groan and pockets her phone. The dealer spins the white ball on the roulette wheel. I want to tell her it'll work itself out, but it's been ten days since Akara broke up with us. Each day has felt like another door closing in our faces, even when I keep trying to shove them back open.

"Sulletti wins!" someone yells across the room.

Casino's security descends on them in a blink.

My muscles tightening, I keep Sulli pinned closer to me. "Red. Red. Red," she chants under her breath. The ball spins and spins. "Four, nine, eighteen. Four, nine, eighteen. Come on."

I make the sign of the cross. I have three-hundred bucks on the table. After my two months' pay-cut from the Winter Festival fight, this is like tossing down gold for me. My fifteen-year-old self would be dragging me by the underwear out of this casino.

Dumb.

Stupid.

Foolish.

And I'm doing this dumb thing for Akara. *He might not even care.* I shake my head to myself and grind on the toothpick. He'll care.

He just might not show us.

That hurts too. Knowing he's probably somewhere alone, beating himself up. *Christ.*

"No whammies," I mumble on my toothpick. Trying not to shit myself.

One thing's for sure, I don't have the stomach for gambling like my dad. How he could continuously blow his earnings at places like this—I'll never understand.

As the ball slows down, I think about how I bailed on the Flyers game. I drove to the hockey arena, and I saw my dad outside with Thatcher, waiting for me.

Anger bubbled up. My whole body went taut. I could barely move. I sat there for what felt like eternity. I couldn't get my ass out of the car.

So I texted them I couldn't make it. And I left.

Cowardly.

Or maybe I just didn't want to make a scene in public. That's what I keep telling myself, anyway.

The white ball *ping ping pings* along the roulette wheel, and then comes to a dead stop.

"Black 13," the dealer calls out and scoops up Sulli's chips. My chips. All gone.

I glare. "Fuck-a-duck."

Sulli smiles at that phrase, then snaps a photo of our losses and texts Akara. "You think he'll take pity on us?"

"I hope so."

She angles the phone to me. "Make a sad fucking face like it hurts you're down a grand."

I immediately cringe in pain. A grand down the shitter—what I could've done with a grand…

"Oh hey, Banks." Sulli hugs my side, seeing that I'm actually torn up at the losses. "We can stop here. Fuck, I can pay you back—"

"No—this was my bad idea." I lift my arm to her shoulders, and the hand that hangs over her, she laces her fingers with mine. "The guy with the good ideas is supposed to come and rescue us."

"Hey, he doesn't always have good ideas," Sulli nudges me. "Case in point." *The break-up.*

"He thinks it's a good one," I tell Sulli. "At least I know they're *both* bad ideas."

"Which is why Kits needs you." Sulli counts her chips. "I can do another five grand."

"I can do a hundred." I only have six-hundred left on me, and I'm saving the cash for dinner and any problems we might meet. And last thing I want is to beg Thatcher for cash to get me by on groceries next week. "Beg" in quotations because my brother would toss money at my face without a second thought. Though, he'd give me a hell of an earful.

As we stand up and shift our chips on the table, my phone buzzes. Akara finally responds to our group chat.

Stop burning cash. I'm not coming. – Akara

Expected that.

I dig for my cigarettes. "Tell him we're not stopping."

She texts. "Done." And then Sulli shoves her chips on number 9. "For Kits."

For Akara, I think, shoving mine onto red.

Cigarette between my lips, I light the thing. Sulli watches me with worried green eyes.

"It's just *one*, mermaid," I remind her.

"Drinks?" A server leans in to ask.

"I'll take champagne," Sulli says, and I try not to overthink my bad influence. *She's only having one drink.* Like I'm only having one cigarette. She said she knows her limits, and I'm trusting that while I'm currently fingering my own vice.

The server glances to me, and I shake my head. Muscles stiff, I take a deeper drag from the cigarette. Sulli steps in front of me, fitting against my body like a glove. I wrap an arm around her collarbones.

"Red!" Sulli and I chant loudly. "Nine! Nine!"

The entire crowd around us joins in. "RED! NINE! RED! NINE!"

The ball stops.

A sea of groans crash into the room. *Black twenty-nine.*

"Fuuuuuck." Sulli leans back into me even more, and like a fucking lightning strike from Zeus, my temple starts *throbbing* something awful. I wince. Suddenly, the flashing lights from the slots are neon daggers to my skull.

Mother of Christ.

I breathe through my nose. I'm on-duty. I'm on motherfuckin' *duty*. I repeat the mantra to calm myself, to set my priorities straight. I can't go down while I'm supposed to be upright.

I can't.

I lick my dry lips. And a second dagger to my skull surges nausea. I snuff the cigarette on an ashtray.

Sulli leans her head back to glance up at me. Seeing my fucked expression, she spins around completely. "Banks?"

"Bathroom," I tell her.

I'm going to be sick.

51

Sullivan Meadows

KNELT BEHIND BANKS IN a bathroom stall, I rub his back up and down while he grips onto the toilet lid. Seeing my boyfriend fighting the urge to puke is tearing me apart inside. He didn't eat spoiled shellfish or drink too much whiskey. He's in so much fucking *pain* that he's a second away from barfing.

I want to rip that pain out of him. To jump inside his head and race against his migraine, until it's defeated and he's the sole fucking victor—but I can't battle the thing in his head.

Rubbing his shoulders, I lean closer. "I'm right here, Banks. I'm right here." I kiss the back of his neck.

I swear his mouth curves in those almost-smiles. He peeks over his shoulder, using a fuck ton of effort to rest his eyes against mine. He's exerting way too much energy.

I try to urge him back. "Don't look at me."

"I like looking at you, mermaid." He takes a measured breath. "You're the most stunning sight a guy like me could ever see." The way he's staring at me, like he's telling me *goodbye*, is killing every part of me.

"Stop," I force out, tears building. I wipe them fast. "Just hug the fucking toilet."

He curls his hair behind his left ear, then right. Not facing forward yet, he breathes, "You're the love of my life, Sullivan, and wherever I'm going in this world or after, I'll be waiting there for you—just don't meet me too soon. You better become an old woman—"

"*Stop.*" I try not to burst into tears. "I'm not letting you die. You're not allowed to fucking die, so you reach into your brain and tell your migraine to fuck off." I lift up higher on my knees and speak into his hair. "Fuck off, Migraine. We fucking hate you." My tears drip into his hair.

Banks holds my waist, and I feel a soft, low laugh tumble out of him. And then he lets go as he spins quickly back towards the toilet.

And he pukes.

I circle my palm along his deltoids, and with my other hand, I fumble in my macrame backpack for my phone. Temp bodyguards are posted outside the small bathroom. We're in the VIP section of the casino, so less foot traffic, and I'm not worried about a pervert or heckler trying to mess with us in here.

Even while enduring this migraine, Banks ensured the bathroom was secure. He shouldn't have had to do that for me.

He spits into the toilet.

"Can I call Thatcher?" I ask before I dial the number. Even though I don't have a great relationship with his twin brother right now, Thatcher should know what's going on.

Banks groans, "No." He vomits again.

Fucking God. I can't just watch my boyfriend suffer in pain?! "I'm calling an ambulance."

"*No.*" That was a much *harsher* no. He spits again. "It's passing..." He takes another deep breath. "I promise it's passing, Sulli."

"Like you promised you'd go to the doctor? Like that kind of fucking promise?" I grip the phone tighter. *I can't lose Banks.*

"I'll keep my word. I'll go. Just give me a sec." He hangs his head, battling the pounding in his temple probably. And then he flushes the toilet. Only when he shifts his body—sitting back against the basin— do I ease off on calling 9-1-1.

Color has returned to his cheeks. I press my knees on either side of his legs, and I sink low over his lap while I scrounge in my backpack. I'm not the most prepared person in my family, but I always have a water bottle. And lately I've been carrying travel tissues.

I rip open a pack of tissues and dab Banks' lips.

His eyes roam around my features, and before I can tilt my water bottle to his mouth, he takes the bottle from me.

"Prideful," I note.

He almost smiles. "I'm not in a coma. I have hands that I like using."

"Yeah?"

"Yeah, especially on this one girl with the greenest eyes I've ever seen. I could almost drown in them." He swigs water while I start to smile. And he adds, "It's a good thing she's an Olympic swimmer."

"Retired Olympic swimmer."

"Once an Olympian, always an Olympian."

"It used to feel like that." I shrug tensely. "Now I just think…I miss it. I don't want to miss it because even if I experience it again, what's afterwards?"

He swallows water. "Does it matter? Your life doesn't need to be planned out."

"That's the problem—without a direct path and fucking purpose beyond the Olympics and winning medals, people aren't going to think I'm being responsible with my life. And then what?" I hear myself and I cringe.

Responsible with my life.

That's not what I wanted to be. And who am I even trying to please anymore?

"I think you know the answer," Banks murmurs, reading my features well.

I glance at the phone in my hand. "Should I call Akara?" He still hasn't texted us after we gambled thousands of dollars into a gutter. I really had hope that he'd show up.

Banks shakes his head stiffly. "He's not coming to 'Lantic Sidy. He made it abundantly clear he doesn't want shit to do with us today." He reaches out a hand. "Give me Mini-Akara."

I pass him the Akara popsicle stick.

For a second, I think Banks is about to flush him down the toilet. My pulse shoots to my throat. "Banks—" I'm about to stop him.

He jabs the popsicle stick in the role of toilet paper. "Now he's with us."

I let out a breath and a softer smile. "You feel better?"

Banks nods.

Knock knock.

Fuuuck, my heart is on a roller-fucking-coaster, riding up and down. The mole has still been active in January. Banks shoves a hand in his pocket and pulls out his cellphone.

I lean forward and read upside-down.

THE ROYAL LEAKS

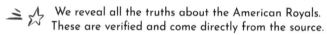 We reveal all the truths about the American Royals. These are verified and come directly from the source.

ROYAL LEAK #1: Sullivan Meadows lost her virginity in a threesome.

ROYAL LEAK #2: Farrow Hale hates his dad, Edward Keene.

#TodaysLeaks #VCard #WhoEnteredFirst? #daddyissues

I pale. "*Fuck.*"

Banks has gone from looking sickly to looking ready to throw himself in a fucking cage match. "I swear to Christ you're being targeted."

"What do you mean?"

"The leaks—you've been named more than anyone else. Why is that?" He fumes, then shuts his eyes in slight pain.

"Alright, okay—fuck the mole. We hate them…just stay calm. Is there a trigger or something that brings on the migraines? Is it the light?"

He shakes his head a few times. "I don't know…I'll be fine. It's passing."

"*Please* let me take you to the fucking hospital after this."

"I'll call a doctor and make an appointment before we leave the bathroom."

After I agree to that, Banks rereads the leaks. "Looks like my dad issues aren't the only ones being put on blast."

Sucks for Farrow, for fucking sure. Or maybe he won't care. He's the most unbothered human being I've ever met.

I'm not as ripped apart at the virginity leak as I thought I'd be. Either because the world already speculates the status of my V-card and this'll just be more of the same…or because I like that they subtly mentioned both guys were there.

I frown more. "Hey, we haven't talked about the virginity thing in forever, Banks. Like from before we even realized our penthouse was bugged. We've been so careful not to say anything about that night out loud."

"They're definitely hoarding information." He nods. "Which means it doesn't even matter if you leave the penthouse. They still have dirt on all of you."

Yeah.

We figured that.

"You think the mole dropped this leak in response to our Instagram post today? Maybe it's their way of trying to tell the world the triad still exists."

Banks lifts his shoulders. "That's a good possibility. I don't know if this'll confuse the public or not."

As I kneel here, I realize a big part of me is hoping they believe in the three of us. Even if that means meeting more paparazzi, even if the cameras never fucking back off. It's easy to feel that strength when I'm alone with Banks in a secure bathroom. Put me in the same hysteria on New Year's Eve…and I don't know…I don't know…

My phone vibrates, and my lungs expand. Akara must finally be calling, maybe to see how I'm doing after the leak. Quickly, I check Caller ID and my hopes burst like a popped balloon.

Banks swigs more water, shutting one eye. "Who is it?" He's breathing through his nose. *He's in pain still.*

"Luna." Before I answer her, I tell him, "I'm not leaving you. I'm *never* leaving you, and wherever you're going in this world or after, I'll find you."

His love for me cascades through his eyes and breathes life into my body. He touches two fingers to his lips and presses them to my cheek. "Because I've been upchucking—or else Lord knows I'd kiss you on the mouth right now."

I almost laugh, but I fucking hurry before my phone rings out. "Luna?"

"Sulli?" She sounds dejected. "You have a minute?"

My eyes grow to the size of Everest. "Yeah, what's up?"

"Is Banks with you?"

"Yeah."

She's quiet for a second. "Can you put it on speaker?"

My lips part, not expecting her to want Banks to be a part of the conversation. I press the button. *What's going on?* "You're on speaker, Luna. Banks is here."

Banks forces both eyes open, curiosity pinging as he glances at the phone. "Luna?"

"Hi. Howdy," she says a shortened, sadder version of her usual upbeat greeting. "Have you all talked to Donnelly recently?"

"No…?" I pry my gaze off the phone. "Banks, have you?"

He hangs his head, thinking. "I haven't talked to him much off comms since…" He winces. "Since the break-up."

Makes sense, I guess. Banks has mostly stayed in the penthouse and only gone back to his apartment to grab his things.

I ask Luna, "Is something going on with Donnelly?"

"Sulli, can we talk in private for a sec?"

Shit.

"Uh, yeah." *I'm not leaving Banks. I'm not being a bad friend to Luna.* I just take the phone off speaker while Banks tries his best not to listen. And I press the phone to my ear. "What's up?"

"I asked Donnelly if he wanted to go to Wawa with me, and he kinda blew me off."

He blew her off? That fucking dick. I try to drop my voice to a whisper. "What'd he say?"

"It was over text. He left me on *read*, and then today, he messaged: *Sorry. Couldn't go.*" She pauses. "It was kinda the first time I asked him anywhere outside of tattooing me. I just thought we were friends…"

"I'm sorry, Luna," I whisper. "That was an asshole move."

Banks makes a weird face at me, and I realize he's been able to hear everything Luna is saying. He's mouthing something to me.

I lower the phone and cup my hand over the speaker. "What?"

"He must've thought she was askin' him out on a date," Banks whispers.

"To Wawa?" Now I make a face.

Banks nods, pretty assured.

I put the phone back to my ear. "Luna, you think Donnelly thought you were asking him out like…on a date?"

"I wouldn't do that to him—my dad would *kill* him if we ever got together. That's not…" She intakes a sharp breath. "Rats. Maybe he did think it was a date…I gotta go fix this. Thanks, Sulli."

"I didn't do much."

"You did a lot, a lot." After a see ya later, we hang up.

I immediately ask Banks, "How'd you know Donnelly thought it was a date?"

"'Cause I've heard him talk about taking girls to Wawa being his ideal date, and if he said no to Luna, then he probably doesn't want to be with her."

I recoil. "He doesn't want to be with her?" My voice is a little hostile. They hooked up, alright. I kind of just want to smush them together like marshmallow and graham cracker.

Banks stares through me. "You do know something about the two of them, don't you?"

I bite my bottom lip to keep from spilling the fucking beans.

"Did they fuck?"

I make a you-smell-that-fart? face, more at myself.

Banks laughs a little. "Alright, maybe it's better if I know nothing."

"Yep."

He nods to himself. "Head in sand."

"You feel any bet—" I'm cut off by another ringing.

Fuck.

I answer the next call on speaker. "Beckett?"

"Sulli," he says. "Are you sitting down?"

Still on the public bathroom floor, I'm knelt on either side of Banks, and my ass has dropped to his lap. "Sort of."

Beckett would be drowning himself in hand sanitizer if he switched places with me and my boyfriend.

"My dad just called me. Apparently, the SEC are investigating our families."

My face falls. "For what?"

"They think we might be behind the leaks in order to manipulate the stock market. It's bad, Sulli."

I stare in a daze at my phone. Un-fucking-believable. Why would we be tanking Fizzle's stocks and Hale Co. and Cobalt Inc.? What good does that do us?

Banks shakes his head at me like he can't believe it either.

"I have to go," Beckett says in a rush. "I just wanted to let you know in case you hadn't heard yet."

"Thanks, Beckett."

We hang up.

Silence stretches between me and Banks, a single thought in the air.

"You first," I tell him.

He takes a breath. "Akara didn't call us."

My chest hurts. "I was thinking the same thing."

Akara would definitely have known about the SEC investigating our families before even Beckett. I'm sure Uncle Connor speed-dialed Akara right after he learned the news. We're not even on Akara's *need-to-know list* anymore. He's just wiped us out like our triad never even existed in the first place.

Some of the public think it was all a lie.

Maybe Akara's starting to believe it too.

52

Banks Moretti

COLD FEET. I FELT THAT towards my dad. Now I'm feeling that feeling again. I'm usually not the one running away, but I'm dreading tomorrow. I shouldn't be wishing for a natural disaster to yank me away from a doctor's visit. But that's where I'm at.

Hoping for a fuckin' tornado.

Hurricane.

Maybe a little tsunami.

While Sulli is showering, I go into the living room and find Farrow lounging on the rug with an apple in hand. He watches Baby Ripley, who waddles into an uneasy stance and giggles before walking like a torpedo.

Farrow is quick on his feet and snatches up his son, stopping him from colliding into the corner of the coffee table. "Where are you headed so fast, little man?"

Ripley giggles as Farrow swings him in a circle.

"You trying to run after wolf scout?"

He kicks his legs out and giggles more.

"He makes me laugh too, but we're not going to tell him that, are we? No, we are not…" He trails off, seeing me come further into the room and lingering.

Farrow gently places Baby Ripley on the rug beside a few of his toys. Ripley plops down and grabs an interactive, educational book. He had his first birthday a few days ago. Only recently has he started walking and racing through the penthouse like an obstacle course.

I even helped baby-proof the penthouse better with Sulli and her roommates.

Babies are fucking cute.

I'm still hoping my brother has one. Or three or four.

Thinking about him reminds me of my family. My mom is over-the-moon elated that my relationship with Sulli is now confirmed to the public. Seeing as how she thought I'd never really settle down. Can't really celebrate with her when it feels like we're two-thirds of a whole and still missing a piece.

"Hey," Farrow nods. "You okay?" He lowers next to his son and helps him flip a page that's stuck together.

I upnod and try to vocalize my feelings. Not always that easy. "You talk to my brother recently?"

After Farrow bites into the apple, he leans back on one hand and swallows. "I talk to him basically every day. Hazard of our spouses being best friends."

Farrow and Thatcher talking every day. I've seen stranger things, but clearly my brother has a new best friend that's not Akara. I never would've thought it'd be Farrow.

Ripley giggles at an animal noise from the book.

Farrow smiles. "That one's an elephant."

His son babbles back.

Just so I go through with this conversation, I force myself to sit on the mod couch.

Farrow sees.

I speak before he can. "Thatcher never told me he planned to do the cheating leak with Jane. Probably because he knew I'd give him hell for even thinking about it. Let alone putting that shit into the universe."

"He didn't tell me either, and Jane didn't even tell Maximoff. I don't think they told anyone but each other."

I nod, knowing that my brother and his wife only conspired together. Thatcher and I talked about the whole thing after the fact.

I crack a crooked smile at a thought. "My brother went rogue. You must be rubbing off on him."

Farrow sucks in breath. "Not really. He pulled some Cobalt plot-twist shit, and man, that's not me." He tilts his head. "But clearly it's in him."

I bob my head again. "Thatcher loves implementing strategies and taking bullets. Always has. And Janie is his other half." They're teammates in this fucked up world.

Farrow assesses me in a quick sweep. "Okay, you didn't come here just to talk about your brother, did you?"

Just say it. "I have a doctor's appointment tomorrow."

His brows shoot up. "Everything okay?"

I nod, automatic, but then I shake my head. "I don't know." I scrape a hand down my tensed jaw. "No offense, Farrow, I fuckin' hate going to the doctor."

His lip quirks. "That's a more common sentiment than you might realize, Banks. It's okay."

I grip my knee, not able to tell him how I grew up rarely going to annual check-ups. Not really wanting to sit here and describe how I don't trust doctors because in my head, they never have anything *good* to say. Why go to a place just to receive bad news?

I'm going to live my life and one day, I'm gonna die.

So it goes.

Now, though, it's different. I want to know that I'll be able to wake up tomorrow and see her. I want to hold her in my arms a year from now. Two years. Longer.

As long as she'll have me.

Farrow frowns harder. "The med team is open to Kitsuwon Securities, so you can talk to me about what's going on."

I nod several times. God, I hate talking about my pain. I'm not broken, and I want to be treated like I can do anything on security. Like I can keep up with SFO, because I know I can.

"Is it your back?" Farrow guesses.

"No." I straighten up. "Maybe you can diagnose me here, so I don't have to go in tomorrow."

A bird squawks from the book, and Ripley giggles loudly. Farrow smiles before looking back to me. "I don't even know one of your symptoms, Banks, so I can't promise you a diagnosis. But I can give you my advice."

Better than nothing.

I swallow hard before telling him, "I keep getting these migraines. After I came back from deployment when I was twenty-two, they started and haven't let up that much since."

Farrow doesn't show anything past his expert-level poker face. "How often do they occur?"

I shrug. "It varies. Sometimes a few times a week. Sometimes once a month. But sometimes they've stopped for months at a time."

"Do you notice any symptoms *before* the migraines start?"

"Like what?"

"Fatigue, nausea, depression, irritability. Anything like that?"

I yank at the collar of my shirt, feeling the cold metal of my dog tags. "Hell, I don't know. Maybe irritability?"

He flips another page for Ripley. "What about at the start of the migraine?" He looks to me. "Do you experience any sensory changes? Flashes of light in your eyes, spots in your vision, strange smells, hearing music when there is none, numbness or difficulty speaking?"

I shake my head. "No. None of that. My eyes just get ungodly sensitive to light."

"The migraines are painful?"

I nod slowly. "Yeah."

He pops something up on his phone and then hands it to me. "On a scale from 1 to 10, where's your pain?"

I'm staring at a pain scale for migraines. Next to each number is a paragraph detailing pain symptoms. "I don't think I'm anywhere near a 7, unmanageable pain. I can still perform daily functions."

If I couldn't, Akara would've sidelined my ass since he found out, not kept me on-duty. I'd be risking his company and Sulli. Hell, *I'd* sideline my ass at that point.

The casino was the first time I needed a bathroom puke break on-duty.

"I'm probably usually a 4 and verging on a 5," I tell Farrow, passing him the phone back.

Farrow takes this in for a long second. "Does your brother know?"

"He knows I get migraines. But he thinks they've died down. He probably would've drop kicked my ass to the ER if he knew they're back and getting worse."

Farrow tilts his head to the side. "He wouldn't be wrong. It's not something that should be left unchecked for too long."

I shrug. "I've survived."

He pockets his phone. "How have you been treating it?"

"Advil, water, sunglasses, some Hail Mary's, and prayers to Saint Gemma Galgani."

His lips rise. "The first few most likely helped."

"Don't knock Saint Gemma. She's come through for me a few times."

He smiles a warm genuine smile. "I'll take your word for it."

"So what's the diagnosis?"

"Are you seeing a specialist tomorrow?"

"Neurologist." I don't mention how she was fully booked and squeezed me into her schedule when she realized who I was. Her daughter is on the middle school swim team and idolizes Sullivan Meadows. Perks of having a talented girlfriend. Plus, Sulli was happy the appointment is only nine days after my Atlantic City migraine.

"Can I skip it?" I ask Farrow.

"No, you don't want to skip. The neurologist might order you either an MRI or CT scan to rule out other causes of your pain. Once those are clear, she'll go through medications that might help lessen the frequency and intensity of your migraines."

I swallow hard. "What if they aren't clear?"

"You don't need to worry about that," Farrow says easily like it's inconsequential. "Stay in the moment. No bad shit is happening until it happens, and it might never happen."

I breathe in that philosophy. These days, I just feel like I have more to lose. More people will miss me if I'm gone.

More people need me than before.

My dumbass shouldn't have gotten attached to more than just Thatcher before checking on my own health.

Farrow must see my stress. "The neurologist might not mention it, but there is something I can do."

"What?" I ask. *I'll take anything.*

"A Daith piercing." He touches the inner cartilage of his ear. "There's some evidence that this piercing helps with chronic migraines."

"Sign me up."

He smiles. "Okay, but come back to me after your appointment tomorrow. I'll pierce you then."

A lion roars from Ripley's book and he lets out a sudden cry.

I almost laugh. "Someone definitely isn't a Cobalt."

Farrow nods. "I'm not sad about it." His eyes meet mine once more. "Don't worry about tomorrow, Banks. You're doing the right thing."

I'm doing the right thing.

It only took me seven years. It feels wrong to say I was scared, but what other excuse do I have? Tomorrow, I finally face a fear.

53

Akara Kitsuwon

SNOW FALLS AND COVERS the city streets of Philadelphia.

Bells rings from the temple, and I stand outside the opened doors. Family and friends dress in white and black as they gather around a casket draped with black cloth.

Even from back here, the smell of jasmine overpowers *everything*.

I look up. Yellow petals fall inexplicably from the sky off unseen trees, the *Cassia Fistula* flower native to Southeast Asia, and they flutter in gentle descent and pool at my bare feet. I stare ahead, through the opened doors. White flowers, my dad's favorites, pile atop the casket.

Someone touches my shoulder.

I don't see who.

They place a small flower in my hand. Petals made of birchwood shavings. I recognize the wooden flower immediately. I placed it under the casket before my dad's cremation.

Laughter and smiles emit from the temple as everyone gathers to celebrate his life. For most people here, this isn't the end of my dad's life, but it still feels like it for me.

Monks chant, and I try to take a step towards the temple.

My feet can't move.

I glance down. The yellow flowers are gone.

Snow compacts over my feet like cement. *No.*

My pulse spikes, and I watch as the temple doors begin to slowly close. *NO!* I try to scream, but my voice is soundless.

I can't miss the ceremony.

I can't miss it! I can't!

You didn't, Nine.

Then why am I living this nightmare?!

Tears prick my eyes, cold whipping around me.

I blink.

I'm inside.

But it's not the temple.

I'm sitting on a metal chair on the outskirts of a boxing ring. Cellos play softly in the background—Bach. My mom stands in the middle, wearing a Mongkhon around her head. A symbol of respect and worthiness, gifted from her Muay Thai trainer. Handmade from rope and cloth. My mom always said her Mongkhon had special powers of protection that'd keep her safe. Before the fight, her trainer would take off the Mongkhon and place it on the top of her corner for good fortune. As a little kid, I believed in all of its symbolism.

Snow falls from the ceilings.

Damn *snow.* Flurries wet my cheeks like tears.

Seats fill around me and cheering crowds overtake and drown the classical music. My mom stands still like a statue, but she's looking right at me. Blinking.

My chest rises and falls heavily. *No.*

Her opponent climbs underneath the ropes and enters the ring. Creeping up behind my mom with stealth.

"Mom, move!" I yell, this time sounds returns to my voice. "MOM!"

But my mom doesn't listen.

She remains right there. Standing. Staring.

"MOM!"

The other fighter approaches quickly. In range for attack.

"MOVE!" I scream, spit flying. Lungs crushing with terror. It's too late.

She lands a single deathblow to my mom's face.

Lights out. My mom just collapses in a heap. Cheers around me are excruciating. People shake my shoulders in excitement like someone scored a touchdown.

I blink.

The room is pitch-black.

Sweat coats my skin.

My breath comes out in heavy waves, and I sit up only to careen into my knees. I cry. Choked sobs rumble through me.

Growing up, my dad and I would discuss my dreams. We'd talk through them, and each time, he'd tell me how intuitive I was. How, deep down, I know myself better than most. "Your conscience speaks to you, Nine," he'd say. "Always listen to it."

I didn't listen to the cliff nightmares.

I shook those off.

Now I'm here. My guilt for disregarding my dad's advice is apparent. I know that's what this is.

Roughly, I wipe at my eyes.

These are harder to experience every night. Harder to wake up from. I understand I'm fighting against my own happiness and it's tearing me apart from the inside out.

Reaching over to the nightstand, I switch a knob to a lamp. Sweat coats my bare chest, and the warm light illuminates the ink along my upper bicep, shoulder, and upper chest: a tattoo of a snake twisted around red roses and yellow flowers, the latter being the national flower of Thailand called golden shower, or *Cassia Fistula*.

I go to grab my phone but accidentally touch my wallet. Leaning out of bed, I curl my fingers around the brown leather and study the wallet under the lamp. My thumb runs over the burned number in the left corner.

9.

Banks gifted me the wallet for my recent birthday. I breathe in a strained breath. Grief rolling through my body, I don't go back to sleep.

I climb out of bed.

Going through the motions, I leave my room, shower, put on my radio, and make a protein shake. By the time light hits the sky, I'm just waiting for Luna to text me when she's leaving the penthouse.

Her *Introduction to Economics for Business* course meets on Tuesday and

Thursdays, and I sit behind her assigned seat. I tried to talk my way out of paying a fee to sit-in on the lecture—I'm not really there for school, anyway—but it was a no-go. The price of auditing that class is now added into Kitsuwon Securities' P&L sheet.

At the kitchen bar, I search through social media for any threats towards Luna.

Comms crackle in my ear. "Banks to Thatcher, I'm heading out to Jersey with Sulli."

"Copy," Thatcher says quickly over the radio.

I frown. New Jersey.

What's Sulli doing in New Jersey? Are they going back to Atlantic City to gamble again?

I shouldn't ask.

You can ask, Nine.

I take a tight breath and text Banks. What's going on in New Jersey?

Casual. Very casual. I'm just a boss checking in on one of my guys and his client. That's all this is.

Seconds later, I get a reply.

Neurologist. – Banks

Shit.

Shoot.

He's finally doing it.

Instinct overpowers logic, and I quickly jump up and grab my jacket. With one hand, I text back: Where?

54

Akara Kitsuwon

NERVES ARE IN *OVERDRIVE* when I show up to the doctor's office. Especially when I see her.

Sulli pops up from her seat in the waiting room. Her green eyes tunnel through me with surprise and confusion and weeks I've missed.

I spent over five years protecting her. *Years* with Sullivan Meadows. *Years* at her side. *Years* hearing her laugh. *Years* feeling her knuckles press into my arm. *Years* seeing her climb to the top again and again.

Years with her love. *Years* with our love.

Whenever I screwed up and we fought, she was still there.

This time, leaving her detail has wrenched me away from those years. Left me looking to my left and right and there's no Sullivan. No laughter, no playfulness, no competitiveness, no love. Just empty.

A void that *I* created.

A void that's killing me slowly with every passing day. Each hour without Sulli is a brutal millennium.

The waiting room is mostly empty. Hovering near Sulli is a temp bodyguard that I employ. Seeing me, he arches his shoulders, lifts his chin. On his best behavior. He gives her enough space.

And he gives me space to approach.

I stop a few feet away. Resisting with all that's in me not to step closer. Not to open my arms for her. Not to pick her feet off the floor and spin her around like we're reuniting after forever.

She halts suddenly, mimicking me. "Hey," she breathes softly.

I haven't really heard her voice in a while.

I miss you, Sul.

Pressure bears down on my chest. Air is too thick to inhale. "Hi," I manage.

Her green eyes carry longing and sadness, and *I* caused that. It cuts me up. Bleeds me out. I push my hair back and then put on a black beanie.

"I didn't think you'd come." She gathers her hair into a messy bun. "I mean, I fucking knew you asked where the doctor's office was, but I thought maybe you'd just Google Maps it and stay home."

"It's a big deal. I want to be here."

"Even though you're not dating us anymore?" She snaps the hair-tie and crosses her arms.

I glance over my shoulder. Behind a desk, a receptionist is on the phone, back turned to us.

Sulli catches me looking. "You're afraid she might hear?" She intakes a hot breath. "Kits, I'd scream it from the rooftops, if I could. It's the fucking *truth*. We were together. I know you want to erase it from your memory like it never happened—"

"That's the very *last* thing I want to do." I cringe into a pained wince. "I don't want to erase *anything* we had from my memory, Sul. I never want to forget you—even if it kills me."

She threads her hands onto her head, like she's coming off a marathon.

"I just don't want anyone to know," I say strongly. "That's it. I'm trying to protect you."

"By hurting yourself," she snaps back. "By hurting me *and* Banks."

"It's temporary," I try to convince myself.

"What is?"

"The pain."

She shakes her head and wipes at her face. "And here I fucking thought maybe you'd changed your mind."

I haven't.

I won't.

She deserves to live her life without being a public spectacle. To wake up and be able to breathe and not be suffocated by the world. I can give her that.

I swallow hard and nod towards the door. "Is he back there?"

She follows my gaze. "No, they took him downstairs to imaging. He's getting an MRI."

Without hesitation, I walk forward and take a seat in the waiting room. Right next to the chair she'd been sitting on.

Sulli frowns down at me. "Why are you staying?"

I rub my hands. "He's one of my men. I need to make sure he's alright." Off her snort of disbelief, I try not to smile hearing the sound, and I just add, "It's a security thing."

"Sure." Sulli lowers into her chair. "Whatever you say, Kits."

Tension piles between us in the unbearable silence. I lean back and glance over at Sulli more than once. Arms crossed over her chest, she glares at the ground.

I'm the one building walls, and *shit,* everything in me is screaming to tear them down.

"How have you been?" I ask.

Her eyes flit to me, softening instantly. "Miserable. Just like Banks." She studies my face. "You?"

I think about lying.

I can be cruel. But not that cruel.

Sliding my thumb across my fingers, I say, "I'm having nightmares again."

She rotates more to me. Our knees knock. "Sorry," she apologizes.

Neither of us move away. I want to say everything but nothing leaves through my lips. As her eyes well, I'm certain she can see how much pain I'm in.

I choke out, "You don't have to be sorry."

"I'm not sorry for falling in love with you, how's that?" Sulli says with a shaky voice.

That gives me too much hope to come back. I pinch my eyes. We're quiet for another tensed beat.

"Your nightmares…?"

I drop my hand. "It's fine."

"They've never been *fine*." She tries to place a comforting hand atop my knee, but I pull away.

Sulli careens back, wincing.

"Sorry," I say fast and hold out my hand. "I don't want you to think there's a door open for *us*."

Please shut the door.

"It is open," Sulli refutes. "On my side. On Banks'. It's been fucking open, and it'll be wide fucking open—"

"Stop," I cut her off. Pain starts piercing all over me, and I take off my beanie and crumple it in my hand. "I need you to be angry at me."

"I *can't*."

My insides are being shredded. "I broke your heart, Sul."

"You broke your own heart *first*," she growls. "You're trying to protect mine. I know what you're doing—I fucking get it, even if I don't like it. You can warn me how you're the bad boy again, Kits, but you're not fooling me this time. You're *my* hero who's risking everything to save me, and I'm fucking telling you that I'd rather leave the safety of the castle with you than be locked in there without you."

I let her words wash over me, but I keep seeing flashes of that night. The mania, the mobs, Sulli being grabbed—*stop*.

I stare at the carpet, then glance over at the receptionist. *Did she hear us?*

The desk is empty, so she must've retreated to the back.

Sulli hugs her arms around herself. When I look over again, she gives me a sad smile. "Loving you is easier than hating you, Kits. It always has been."

Raw emotion threatens to pummel me, and I fight everything.

Minutes later, the office door swings open and Banks and the doctor slip out together.

Sulli and I shoot to our feet.

"We'll be in touch soon," the neurologist says with a handshake before disappearing through the same doors.

Banks turns and freezes. "I'll be damned...you came." Surprise touches his eyes, then confusion when he sees a morose Sulli. "What'd I miss?"

Sulli waves a hand at me. "Akara's just here for *security*, apparently."

Banks frowns, coming closer to us. "Security?"

I stand stiffer. "You're SFO. I just want to make sure everything is going well with you, health-wise."

Banks lets out a short laugh that picks up vigor. "Yeah, right. You're just here to check up on one of your bodyguards." He threads his arms. "You're not fooling anyone, Akara."

"That's what I told him," Sulli says too like they see through me. "Maybe he's fooling himself though."

"He's doin' a bang-up job of that."

I feel myself start to smile. "Fuck, Banks—"

Right as I swear, they both slug me at the same time, left arm, right arm. *The bet I lost.* They haven't forgotten. *They haven't forgotten me.* I smile and grimace, and I can't even wish they would forget—because I wouldn't wish forgetting them on myself.

Banks smiles more. "I do love this gold-star hospitality from my boss. Let's me know you care."

I rub my arm where Sulli slugged. "I do care just as your boss." Before I can ask, Sulli chimes in first.

"How'd it go?" she asks, concern drawing her towards him.

"Is everything good?" I wonder too. He's not torn up or quiet, so maybe the news is good.

He lifts his shoulders. "Don't know. They said they'd call me in a couple hours with the results."

Sulli lets out a long breath. "Two hours. We can wait that out."

"It'll be nothing," Banks agrees and then careens his head back to me. "You want to wait with us?"

What?

I don't move.

I can't.

Banks smacks my chest with the back of his hand. "I could be about to hear some potentially career-ending news."

"You're going to be fine, Banks," I say, letting that statement out into existence. *He'll be fine.* And it's not his career I care about. It's his health.

It's him.

He shrugs. "Still, you can join us."

I shouldn't.

I really, *really* shouldn't.

Feel the moment, Nine.

With a deeper breath and before I can stop myself, I exhale the words, "As your boss, I can do that."

"As my boss," Banks repeats with a shadowy smile. Like I'm full of crap.

I shake my head at him, trying not to smile back. "You think the MRI is going to tell us if you have a screw loose?"

"If so, we should order one for you."

Sulli laughs, and I hear my laugh that feels ancient. Dusty. Newly uncovered.

I missed them.

Feeling it is different than thinking it. And like an idiot, I'm doing both.

Laughter leaves fast as I remember what I should be doing. *You're just his boss. She's just a client.* "Let's head out."

Banks clasps Sulli's hand, and with the shortest glance backwards, I see them share a smile. I'm giving them too much hope.

This is wrong.

Then why do I keep moving?

While I lead out front, the three of us and the temp bodyguard exit the revolving glass doors. I go outside first.

Scanning the snowy Philly sidewalk, a crowd of ten or twelve has amassed, but nothing major. Nothing like New Year's Eve. Seeing the calm just reinforces why I broke up with them.

So she could have *this*.

Banks leads Sulli forward and I hawk-eye the paparazzi who push closer. "Stay back!" I shout, arm outstretched.

"We parked in the deck," Sulli says. "To the lef—" She's cut off.

In a single instant, someone pelts a projectile too fast to catch. Banks only has time to raise his arm to block the assault. *Something* smashes into him and explodes—white powder mushrooms around the three of us and the temp. We're covered. Sulli coughs as I wrap an arm over her shoulders with Banks, about to pull her to the ground in case another projectile is launched.

"CHEATER!" someone screams angrily.

Whoever just assaulted Banks—they thought he was *Thatcher*. The projectile wasn't meant for Sulli. Alarm has snapped me into total focus. I can't see the person through the white, dusty cloud.

"Bernard!" I shout at the temp, and I order him to go detain the heckler.

Banks wafts the air around our faces.

"What…what the fuck is this?" Sulli wipes the white powder out of her eyes. I check on her with a fast sweep. *She's okay.*

I taste it on my lips.

Flour.

With our hair and face and shoulders dusted with baking flour, Banks and I share a brief, readied look.

"Get her out of here," I tell him. "I'll meet you at the penthouse."

SULLI'S BATHROOM.

That humongous *fudging* tub. The water. Him and her.

Still caked in flour, I lean against the sink and grip the counter behind me, trying to peel my gaze off a memory. In a flash of a moment, a second, I can almost feel us in the water. Taking Sulli's virginity against the stone of her tub, the trust and affection and emotion…

It's right there, Nine.

"I can't fucking believe they mixed you up with your brother," Sulli fumes, running a damp towel over her face.

Banks soaks another washcloth in the sink. "It happens." He's unaffected by the blunder. "This is one of those times I'm glad I'm employed by you." He meets my eyes, speaking to me, and a levity inflates my lungs. "Can you imagine the fuckin' old guard after a flour-bomb?"

I start to smile and mimic Alpha bodyguards. "*Back then, we had to deal with repeated flour-bombers in public locations. Like a damn ski slope!*"

Banks laughs.

Sulli smiles over at me. "Was this when Jane and Moffy were babies?"

I nod. "Yeah, way before our time on security. And you weren't even born yet."

"You know the worst one?" Banks says to me, rubbing streaks of flour off his face. "*Disneyland.*"

I groan into a bigger smile. "Don't even start."

"What?" Sulli is confused and excited to hear security's secrets.

Banks explains, "The old guard who went on the Disneyland trip when you were a kid."

"They never shut up about it," I add. "At least the ones who haven't retired." There are only a handful left from that generation.

Sulli tries to shake out flour from her hair. "A lot of the time I forget you two are bodyguards and not just my boyfriends."

Boyfriends. I stiffen.

She realizes her slip with flushed cheeks. "I mean, *boyfriend* for Banks but *friend* for Akara or…whatever the fuck we are…" She reddens more. "Cumbuckets."

Cumbuckets. I missed that.

"It's okay, Sul," I tell her softly.

Banks looks cautiously between us.

Maybe I shouldn't be here, but Banks is still waiting on the phone call…and no part of me wants to walk away.

Sulli tries to rewind the conversation. "I hate that people who *love* Jane are now trying to assault her husband. It's fucked up."

I jump up on the counter, sitting. "Yeah, that's an issue."

Thatcher Moretti.

I still care about my friend; I'll always care—even if he's been pushing me away and we haven't sewed what ripped. For the longest time, it's been me and Thatcher trying to make tough calls. Trying to figure crap out behind-the-scenes and clinking beers after a hard night, leaning on each other when no one else understands the core of the job—and now he's a target for hate.

"Thatcher will be alright," Banks says. "He can take flour to the face as well as I can. It's nothing."

I give him a hard look. "I love you, Banks, but you two need to stop flexing. Just because you can take a hit doesn't mean you should."

His mouth curves up. "You love me, Akara?"

Son of a mother trucker.

I lick my dried lips. *You know I do.*

He slips a toothpick between his teeth with a shadow of a smile. He sees right through my silence.

Sulli begins to smile.

Shoot.

I grip the edge of the counter, not jumping down yet. But I remind them, "I'm leaving once the doctor calls."

That sobers the room.

Smiles vanish.

We go back to dealing with the flour. Banks squeezes dirty water out of the washcloth into the sink. I run a hand through my hair, flour kicking up. I'm *covered.* It'll take more than a sponge-bath to get clean.

Sulli struggles with her hair. "Fuck, it's everywhere."

Help her, Nine.

Before Banks or I can even think of moving, Sulli dashes to the large glass shower, surrounded by two oversized elephant ear plants. Vibrant. Green. Tropical rain forest vibes are sky-high and totally Sulli.

After she turns on the faucet, water hits the black slate and spills into the drain.

She hasn't stepped in yet.

Sulli faces us and pulls off her long-sleeve shirt.

Dang. *She's braless.*

Shoot.

Fuck.

I divert my gaze to the ground. Too late. Her nipples are perked. Yeah, I saw her tits. My muscles flex more.

"I'm getting in," she says. "If you guys want to join, you can."

Guys.

Plural.

Me and him.

I drill my gaze fiercer at the floor. Hearing the unzip of her pants. Seeing her panties fall on top of her shirt.

Hearing the water splash. Sulli must step inside the shower.

"Akara," Banks whispers.

I look up.

He's right in front of me. Brown eyes on mine. Concern pumping from him to me. "You gonna keep beating yourself up and down?" he asks. "Or are you gonna get in?"

I career my head back, conflicted. *I have to protect her.* But Sulli has already contested the defense I want to say out loud.

She's telling me not to guard the castle. To just leave the fortress and follow her and him out.

Banks steps closer, to shut off the sink faucet he left on. Our knees knock together for a second.

I've thought about attraction. Whether I'm attracted to Banks like I am to Sulli. I guess I just keep coming back to one question: Is it possible to be *in* love with someone and not be sexually attracted to them?

Our legs brush again as he shifts away, and we both glance back at the shower at the same time. Sullivan Meadows is already naked beneath the cascading water. As she wipes steam off the shower door, she watches our interaction.

And then she blows a raspberry on the glass.

I burst into laughter with Banks.

Adorable doesn't even cut it.

Banks and I are smiling, and he's quick to shed his shirt, pants, boxer-briefs. One last glance to me, he says, "Stay or leave, it's up to you." Then he runs after Sulli and climbs into the shower. They rinse off under the hot water together. Fog starts to coat the glass.

Everything inside me is calling and beckoning me to just *go*. To her. *With* her.

With them.

What am I doing?

What am I doing?

Like it's the most natural thing in the world, I just move towards them. Jumping off the sink counter, I strip to nothing, and I take confident strides towards the shower. With each step, pain lessens. Weight lifts off me. Until the glass door swings open without me even touching it.

Until I'm inside the rainfall with them.

Until I'm home.

Hands roam. Mine along Sulli, hers along me and him, and we're huddled together. Close underneath the warmth of the water.

I knead my fingers through Sulli's hair. Shampoo foaming as I scrub. She faces Banks while he lathers her toned body with soap, but she tilts her head back a little. Just to smile up at me. "You better be fucking careful, Kits—a girl could get used to this."

"A guy already is," I whisper. Whatever tomorrow brings, I'll handle later—right now, I have to be here. I want to be here.

I can't just walk away again.

I can't.

"Two guys already are," Banks rephrases.

We all share a smile, and I wash Sulli's hair while she nearly melts against my shoulder, eyes shut in ecstasy.

She reaches back, holding onto my neck. Banks pries off a hand wand and rinses off the soap suds along her arms and chest. He teases the water against her pussy, and she squirms against me, arching her hips.

My muscles contract. Heat brewing.

Her eyes snap open, longing pooled in them. After I rinse out her shampoo, she runs a washcloth along my abs, along *his* abs. Like she's wiping a window clean.

Our breaths go shallow. Banks and I wash our own hair, and she watches as our fingers brush back and forth along our heads. She zones in on my biceps that flex a little.

I smile more. "You like what you see, string bean?"

She collects her hair on her bare shoulder. "Is that even a fucking question? You both could sizzle the ground you walk on."

"The earth isn't burning beneath my feet," Banks says, wiping water out of his eyes.

I playfully check beneath my soles. "Shit, mine are on fire. I must be hotter than Banks."

He chucks a washcloth at me. I duck, and Sulli slugs my arm. I was waiting for the curse word penalty. Honestly, I just wanted to feel her skin against my skin.

I'm smiling as I steal the hand wand and squirt Sulli's face.

"Kits!" she laughs before collecting water in her mouth. She spits out a fountain-like stream at me.

We're all laughing.

Soap and washed-off flour swirl down into the drain. Clean. *We're clean.* This can't be the end, but Sulli is reaching for the faucet. Shower shuts off.

I push back my wet hair, droplets streaming down my jaw and abs. Banks rakes a hand through his wet strands, and while Sulli stands naked between our bare bodies—an aching, *sweltering* tension stretches. Pulses inside my veins, inside my core.

Sulli glances from him, to me. From him to me. I watch beads of water rolling along her tits, down her abs, down the long length of her legs and unshaven pussy. My brain is yelling at me to pick her up. To run my hands along the curve of her body—to fill her entirely, until tears squeeze out of her eyes and she cries into the highest damn peak.

Yeah.

I want Sulli.

I need Sulli.

Her body shifts under the heat of my gaze.

"You like what you see, Kits?" Her raspy voice squeezes my cock.

I smile, pushing my hair back again. "Yeah, *Lady* Meadows, you're a total babe who's lit more than just the ground on fire." I'm burning up.

Her lips lift, and once she glances back at Banks, he flexes in arousal.

Sulli chews the corner of her lip and stares at my dick. His dick. Her eyes, though—her eyes are a hand wrapped around my length. Desire pummels. My jaw clenches. *Shit.* I harden even more.

She sees.

I'm not the only one who wants inside her.

Banks grows too.

And then she drops to her knees.

"Sulli," I breathe out.

Steam and heat billow around us.

"I want to, Kits." Confidence encases every syllable. She's taken me in her mouth before. But not Banks.

We move in closer to Sulli and look down at the athletic, competitive American princess.

I don't fight this. If I could spend eternity inside these moments with Sulli and Banks, I would. Not just for sex. It's *everything*. The calm, the laughter, the peace, the levity, the attraction and heat.

The love.

Unrivaled love that I can't find anywhere else—so am I even surprised that I'm magnetized to these emotions, to them?

Maybe I should be stronger and pull away. But I can't.

I just know today.

Right now.

Here.

Where I'm happiest.

I nod Sulli on.

Desire and a smile in her eyes, she wraps her hands around his cock, then my cock.

Banks lets out a low groan, and I suck in a tight breath. I rest a hand on my head, then my other palm on her wet hair.

She strokes us in unison.

My abs tense. Banks' eyes flit from her to me. *Yeah, this is happening.*

He braces a fist against the foggy glass wall, and as my hand shifts from her head to her squared jaw, Banks gathers Sulli's hair, holding the strands back as I guide her mouth around my cock.

I watch her in this intimate position and emotions surge.

She's Sulli.

The girl I've kept safe.

The one I'm still trying to keep safe.

The girl I want to be happy, too.

Her lips are around me, and the sight nearly bowls me over. Pleasure punctures every nerve. A groan catches in my throat.

I nail an aroused glare onto the foggy glass. Sulli loves this setting, and I drink up *her* pleasure. Her eyes rake over my sculpted body that towers over her. His muscular build on her other side.

Sulli sucks tentatively, like she's unsure of the next move. Blowjob expert, she is not, but her inexperience is far from a turn-off. I just want to be careful with her. To protect her. Make her feel the best she's ever felt.

That's all I've ever wanted.

I tighten my grip on her jaw, and I arch my waist. Going farther in her mouth, I create back-and-forth friction with ease. She makes a noise around me. Her breath staggers. Blood rushes down.

I clench my own hair. Trying not to come.

She's stroking Banks with one hand.

I do my best to not thrust far into the back of her throat.

Even as she tries to take more of me. Her eyes scream, *faster, Kits.*

"Sulli," I groan out, so close to fucking her face.

With Banks' hand on her head, he's feeling her move forward and back. She widens her knees on the ground—like she's ready to be filled.

Feeling her need for a break, I pull back. My hardness popping out of her mouth, Sulli turns to Banks' massive cock.

He's not a fan of blow jobs.

"Easy on him," I warn Sulli.

"I won't take you in my mouth or anything, is that okay?" she asks Banks.

He nods. "I'll let you know if I don't like something."

Sulli smiles before licking a trail down his length.

Banks shudders, abs tensing. "Fuck."

Arousal pools in her green eyes. Lighting me up, and as her tongue circles his tip, she reaches over and strokes me.

My muscles tighten. Burn. I want more. Between her legs. Filling her. Watching her squirm and writhe and come.

Our bodies bow towards Sulli. My fist presses on the foggy wall like Banks' fist, our knuckles close to brushing, and as we stare down at Sulli, our foreheads nearly touch.

She fists me harder.

"Sulli," I grunt in pleasure.

Her lips part in shortened breath. She has complete control of us. "Kits...Banks."

He groans.

I wait for it.

Her lips edge away from his dick.

I crouch down and hook my arms underneath her thighs. Swiftly, I bring her up to my waist as I stand. She gasps, her arms curling around my shoulders. Holding a naked Sullivan Meadows in a front-piggyback is dangerous *fudging* territory.

My cock edges against her heat.

She dips her head back and devours Banks with a *wanting* gaze. He kisses her, then she kisses me.

"Let's stay here, Kits," she breathes against my lips. "I like it here."

In the rainforest of her shower.

Banks moves around us, slipping me a readable look.

She frowns at him. "Banks?" Her voice pitches in worry.

"He's getting condoms."

She relaxes in my arms. Waiting for Banks, I slowly drop Sulli to the wet, black slate. Her legs and hips and breasts slip down the length of my body before her feet touch the ground. We breathe in a synchronized, ragged tempo. Her hands burn a path along my abs, and I curve an arm around her waist, drawing her closer.

Closer.

She fits perfectly against my body and wraps her arms around me tightly. An emotion pulling between us.

I'm not going anywhere.

That thought barrels through me.

I'm not going anywhere.

It's okay.

You're home, Nine.

"Sul," I whisper.

"I missed you," she breathes, voice tighter. "I really fucking missed you."

My chest rises and falls heavily. "I missed you like crazy." I hug her closer. She holds on. Not letting go.

Can't live without her.

I've known that, but I felt the truth of it.

Banks returns to the shower with the condoms, and his lips subtly lift at me. I can't help but smile back at him. What would I do without Banks? The age-old question.

The answer: *struggle.*

Be in pain.

Be miserable.

I want none of those things.

Can't live without him.

"I missed you too," I tell him.

He smiles wider, something unsaid passing between us before he breathes, "I love you too, Akara."

Emotion ripples through the shower. Water slick on the slate, but the faucet is still off. Sulli glances between us, heat coursing. "Who's going to take me first?"

I turn to Banks. "You want me to fuck her in your arms?"

Sulli's breath hitches.

Banks starts to smile. "I can fuck her in yours."

"Holy...*fuck*." Her eyes widen. "Is this, really—?"

"It's happening." I quickly and easily lift Sulli in a front-piggyback again.

Her smile explodes.

She totally flexes her strength and makes a show of supporting herself on me. Arms wrapped around my shoulders, legs tight around my waist.

She says, "How's that for a fucking *string bean*?"

"Not bad, string bean."

She laughs with emotion in her eyes. "Say it again."

"Super strong, string bean."

"Again."

I nuzzle closer. "I love you, string bean."

We kiss. But not for long. With one hand on her ass for support she doesn't really need, I reach my hand out as Banks passes me a condom.

Ripping it open, I sheathe myself.

Banks is behind Sulli, and she leans her weight against him. Shoulders to his chest, Sulli slightly turns her head. They kiss and kiss, and when they pry their lips off, he sucks on the nape of her neck.

She lets out a whimper, her eyes on me.

Getting her off is peak fun for me—and I slip a couple fingers inside Sulli. She's already soaked.

While Banks and I are standing, I hold underneath her thighs, and I carefully ease inside Sulli, heat inviting me in with warmth. She gasps at the fullness. Her thighs tremble.

I let out a groan. My eyes want to roll back. She's so tight around me.

She clutches my shoulder and Banks' bicep, and I'm on fire. Dying to push in and out in a hypnotic, mind-altering rhythm.

I sweep her features, ensuring she's okay, and I thrust in that deep, pleasured pace.

"I can't…" Sulli looks between us, melting. *Melting.* She cries out as I keep moving. "Kits. *Kits. Banks.*" He circles her nipples with his thumb.

"You can't take me?" I ask against her lips. "You can't take this?" I don't stop moving inside Sulli.

She breathes back, "It feels so…fucking…" She whimpers as she watches my cock disappear between her legs.

I swallow a groan. "That's inside you, Sul," I whisper. "You want Banks inside you next?"

"Fuck, *yes.*" Her fingers tighten on me. Probably Banks too. Gripping like she's going to plummet a thousand feet.

Still standing up, I shift my hands to her hips. I pump Sulli up and down on me. She leans more against Banks, relaxing into the movement.

He dips his head and takes her mouth in his. They kiss as I make love to her pussy.

Quickening my pace, she breaks from his lips to let out another high-pitched cry. The sound is one I treasure. It stirs me to move faster, harder.

Her mouth is agape, breath jettisoning from her body in overcome waves. Her eyes are lost in us, and my muscles burn. *I love you, Sulli.*

I love you.

I will always love you.

She holds onto Banks for support. I feel her pulsate around my cock. Her eyes roll, and the image sends me over.

I don't stop thrusting until my climax hits me in a solid force. Her orgasm throbs me more, and I quickly slip out so that he can have her.

Keeping her in my arms, I hike her higher on my waist and I spread her wider. "He's going in from behind," I tell Sulli as she tries to see him.

He has the perfect angle.

"In my ass?" she asks with raised brows, like she's game for anal sex right now.

"No way in hell," Banks says.

She frowns. "Why not?"

I try not to smile. "For one, we don't have lube. For another, you're still pretty new to sex. We're not throwing you into the major leagues."

"A league I've never entered," Banks tells her.

"I have," I note.

Sulli is very interested. Her eyes light up with questions, but we'll have time to discuss more.

This isn't the end.

For better or for worse, I made a choice the moment I stepped into the shower. Maybe even the moment I went to the doctor's office.

And I'm not turning back around.

Lifting Sulli a little higher again, Banks holds her ass. She looks over her shoulder. Watching him slip up into her heat.

Her breathing quickens from the new position.

"You okay?" Banks and I ask at the same time.

"Yeah, *yeah*. Fuck. Keep going." Her lips part.

I have the best view of his cock sinking into her so very slowly.

"Oh my fucking *God*," she moans into a cry, her legs quaking in my grip.

I'm getting hard again.

"Banks," she cries. "Banks." Her thighs twitch and shake.

"You're alright," Banks says against her ear.

"Breathe," I tell Sulli.

I watch her take a deep inhale. And then he rocks in, out, in, out. Her lips part in a perfect *O*. Her eyes fixed to me; he pumps inside her heat with deep grunts.

She cries out our names.

Another orgasm ripples through her, her abs tightening. Her toes curl and she lets out the sweetest sounds.

Then Banks curses, "*Fuck*."

Not a good fuck. He keeps cursing. Alarm shoots through me. What the hell happened? She's okay. He's not okay.

He pulls out but keeps Sulli in his arms.

"What's wrong?" I ask, and rub Sulli's thigh softly, keeping her calm.

He shakes his head at me like he can't say. *The leaks*. Right.

"Did I do something...?" Sulli asks.

"No," Banks says quickly. "It was me."

Pulling a hand away from Sulli, he shows us the condom between his fingers.

It's ripped.

55

Sullivan Meadows

THIS CAN'T BE HAPPENING. Like I know condoms aren't made out of impenetrable material, but *fuck*, they should be! Banks 100% came inside of me.

Which would be sexier if I were on birth control.

Cum. Literal *cum fuck.*

I could roll the dice. Not take Plan B.

But the anxiety that rushes up is enough to push me towards a drugstore. Banks *and* Akara offered to go for me. Just so I can avoid the paparazzi.

Fucking tempting. Especially after the flour-bomb. But I thought about Wise Words from Maximoff & Jane, and they'd tell me not to hermit away from the world. When the HaleCocest rumor circulated, my cousins actively went *into* the world with the FanCon Tour. And I want to be *with* Banks and Akara as they adventure off to the drugstore.

I don't want to miss out.

Twenty minutes into the car ride to the drugstore, paparazzi chase after Booger. I sink further in the backseat. Luckily, they're easier to shake off than after the New Year's Eve party. Evening Philly traffic is worse than the media right now.

Banks loses the tail and parks beside a curb, right outside the drugstore.

Over a week has passed since Banks and I confirmed our relationship, and it's obvious that's the reason paparazzi are less aggressive and less active around me. It's not as juicy as the triad rumor.

Even the swimmers at Warwick cranked down their whispering around me. Coach Reed boasted about keeping Banks and my relationship a secret. I'll give him *some* credit. He never fucking blabbed about the half-truth Akara told him at the pizzeria.

The big kicker: Fans online speculate the leak's validity, and I think most truly believe that the idea of a poly relationship is too unusual and outlandish to be real.

It is real.

I hop out of Booger. The black-furred Newfie leaps out behind me. Holding Orion's stars-and-planets leash tight, I make sure this burst of puppy energy doesn't race off. With Luna in class today and visiting Eliot and Tom tonight, I offered to dog-sit.

Orion races for the nearest tree by the parking meter. "Good boy," I tell him, then check left and right. Akara and Banks are already scanning our surroundings.

No paparazzi. No fans in sight. Mayhem gone. What a fucking reprieve. Guilt tugs at me for even letting out a breath of relief. Being *relieved* is like sticking a gold star next to Akara's break-up plan, and I want to X it out of existence.

When their tense features seem to unwind in an *all-clear*, Akara says to Banks, "I just don't see how it happened. You were being careful."

We haven't spoken about the condom break until the last few minutes of the car ride when paparazzi stopped eating our ass.

Banks grimaces, torn up. "It might've been the position."

I elbow his side. "It's not your fault." Orion starts peeing, and I turn my back so he can take a leak in semi-private.

Banks narrows his gaze down the street. "Whose fault could it be then, the fuckin' Boogeyman?"

"The Boogeyman is totally to fucking blame. And the condom manufacturer and the person who created condoms and—"

"The size of my cock," he says pointedly.

"No," I shoot back.

"She's right," Akara says, surveying the street too, then eyeing him. "This isn't on you."

Banks eases a little. "Alright, I'm cool like the wind."

"Are you?" I question.

"No," he admits, "but I'm trying to be. Putting you in this position is never gonna sit right with me. That's all." He lifts his shoulders. Banks cares more about me.

Have I been freaking out about a pregnancy?

Is the sky fucking blue?

I had a "panic" face apparently in the car. To which I told them it was a two-thirds "pregnant panic" and one-third "paparazzi panic". Their concern blanketed me all the way here.

I keep imagining Banks' sperm swimming up inside me. *Please do not create a literal Mini Meadows.* I want to be a mom on my own timeline. No accidents.

Banks stares deeper into me.

I breathe in, and I step closer. "You know—if I had to go through this with anyone, I'm just glad it's you and Akara and not someone like Will Rochester." My ex-boyfriend was nice, but I already know I would've been calling up Kits and Banks to help me get Plan B. In every scenario, they're the ones I trust the most.

They each have my whole fucking heart.

Banks wears that almost-smile. He curves an arm around my shoulders. Hugging me. He whispers in my ear, "I'm here for you, Sulli. Whatever you need."

I hug back just as strong.

Booger shields us a little bit from the few cars that pass along this street. Akara and Banks know Philly like the back of their hands, and they said this area doesn't get much foot traffic.

They're right. We're practically alone.

Sun descending in an evening glow, it's nice being outside without the chaos and onlookers. The handful of pedestrians who pass don't pay us any notice.

As I break away from Banks, I say, "Maybe I should go back on birth control."

"You hated it," Akara reminds me.

Banks adds, "Don't go back on it for us."

For us.

I start to smile, then falter. Akara hasn't officially said he wants to be in a relationship with me and Banks again. Until he says the words, I'm going to keep my expectations low. Like under the ground. Just so disappointment can't touch me.

But I can't deny how *good* it felt having Akara back. Like coming up for air after a long swim. I hang on to those feelings. And I hope.

Just as I go to speak, Banks' phone rings.

The doctor. We're all caging breath. Orion sniffs Booger's tire, and I pull him towards us a little more.

Banks stares at his cell, gaze darkening on the caller ID.

"Answer it," Akara urges.

He does, raising the phone to his ear. "This is Banks Moretti." He puts a hand to his lips. "June 9ᵗʰ." *His birthday.* He must be verifying his identification. He stares at the ground. Nodding. Over and over.

I can't breathe.

Please be okay.

Please.

I can't lose you either.

He nods once more. Face serious and readied. He often looks primed for everything, and Banks will say he's equipped better for hell than for heaven, but he'll run towards both. He'll run towards anything, as long as he's not stuck in place.

"Thanks. You too." He hangs up, then slips the phone in his jacket, and I reach out and clasp his hand. Banks smiles down at me.

"You're smiling—that's a good sign, right?" I ask in one breath.

"Yeah, I guess it is." He inhales strongly. "As far as they can tell, the tests look good."

"You're serious?" Akara questions like Banks might not be telling the whole truth.

I interject, "Don't lie to us. Don't fucking downplay anything—we want to know what's going on."

Banks squeezes my hand. "I'm not lying, mermaid. I promise you two, that's what they said. He told me they couldn't see anything of immediate concern. And it's likely I'm suffering from chronic migraines. I'm gonna have to watch out for things that trigger them."

Akara asks, "Are they going to give you anything for the pain?"

He nods, scrutinizing a guy who disappears in a pawn shop further down the sidewalk. "They're prescribing me some medicine. It should help." He slips a toothpick between his lips. "Farrow's going to pierce my ear too." He explains the Daith piercing, and he finally begins to smile. "Looks like I'm surviving another year or two, maybe thirty if the Lord doesn't take me."

Relief and joy and love burst inside of me. "Thank fuck." I fling my arms around Banks, standing on the tips of my toes. He smiles against my neck, and I'm fucking crying tears of relief.

He reaches out a hand like I do, and we both pull Akara in our hug. He shares the biggest grin with Banks, and we don't part right away.

Triad huddle. A safe, happy, and loving embrace that I want to last forever. We keep our arms around each other, forming a literal circle huddle on the sidewalk. Orion hops excitedly down at our heels.

"Hey, I have your Lord on speed-dial, remember?" Akara tells Banks. "If He tries to take you before you're an old man, we're going to have words."

Banks smiles. "You'll have to phone Hell too. The devil has always wanted me more."

"I'll make sure Sulli is with me. She's a pro at launching meat and sour cream."

"Food fight with the devil," I say into a smile. "I'm in."

Knowing Banks is okay should cement total happiness, but the mole is still at large and the condom recently broke. Good news sprinkled with some bad.

Akara reroutes our banter into a plan. "I'll go grab the Plan B. You two stay out here with Orion."

"Break," I say like a football player as we split up from the huddle.

Banks and Akara are smiling, until they face the drugstore. My stomach flip-flops like a fucking pancake.

Kits leaves, and I watch him go.

My heart thumps a little harder. "You think he'll stay with us?" I wonder while Banks stares inside the store, then down the streets.

He frowns at me. "You don't think he will?"

"He never said that he is. I'm not getting my hopes too high." It'll fucking hurt worse. Like losing him a second time. Before he can respond, my phone buzzes.

Caller ID: *Nona-Frog.*

After the break-up with Akara, my sister has been Team Sulli. She made me a care basket of sweet treats with Audrey, Kinney, and Vada. Iced cookies, cupcakes, and brownies with self-love sayings like *you're awesome, you're a badass, you're beautiful.*

Since this break-up isn't a typical one, no one in SFO or my family has been angry at Akara. Some sort of expected it. He's just trying to protect me. And maybe they can see that our love hasn't disappeared.

I click into the call. "Hey, Nona—"

"I need you to come to the Cobalt Estate like…right now. Where are you?" Her panicked voice pricks my skin.

"I'm close-ish." Fuck, fuck, fuck. Hurrying, I motion for Banks to unlock the door. I climb into the backseat with Orion and shut it. "What's going on?"

"The girl squad is in a pickle. You're on speaker."

"A pickle how?" I frown as Banks hops into the driver's seat. "You're on speaker too, by the way. Banks is here."

"He's a nark," Kinney says from the background.

"Banks isn't a nark," I say, wide-eyed as I picture the kind of trouble these four girls got themselves into.

"Farrow said he is."

Banks shrugs at me in admittance.

I gape at him.

He's narked before? On who?!

Xander, I realize the answer to my own question. Of course he would—Xander is a *minor*. If they found themselves in a truly fucking terrible situation, I think…I'd nark too.

To Moffy and Jane, at least.

Winona cuts in, "*Please* don't tell any of our bodyguards. This is just between you and Banks."

"And Akara," I add, waiting for him to return. *Hurry, Kits.*

Winona gasps. "Wait, wait, does this mean you're all back together? *Sulli.*" She emphasizes my name with happiness. She really is Team Sulli, knowing what I want.

I could say the truth, *I don't know if we're back together yet.* But feeling her happiness is euphoric, and I decide not to puncture it.

"Get that D!" Vada shouts.

"Double D," Winona says, probably with a brow-wag.

"Took him long enough," Kinney says, all blasé-like.

I wait for Audrey to swoon over the line about "love prevailing" or flourishing.

She never speaks.

Panic jolts me, and Banks is the first to ask, "Where's Audrey?"

"That's why I'm calling," Winona says fast. "We just want someone else to check on her. She's not passed out, but she's been puking up the party punch."

"*Party* punch?" My brows rise. "Fuck, Nona did you guys throw a party?"

"It's her pre-birthday," Kinney declares, "without her annoying brothers."

"Except Ben," Nona notes. "Ben is here, and he's not annoying."

"Ben's okay," Kinney mutters.

God, I really hope Akara is at the check-out.

"Are Moffy and Jane on their way?" I ask.

Winona speaks. "No. It's just you. I was going to call Moffy, but we all wanted to see if you could come first."

Maybe because I won't be disapproving of the party or too worried.

And they must not be too scared about Audrey's health or they'd for sure phone Moffy, who'd bring his doctor-husband along.

She called me.

I'm the first call to speed-dial in a mini-crisis.

Wow.

Do I seem like I have my shit together to deal with explosions and fallouts? I mean, I am clearly a hot fucking mess sitting outside a drugstore where one of my boyfriends (if he's still my boyfriend) is buying me Plan B because my *other* boyfriend's condom broke. Yes, this is my fucking life.

But my sister believes I'm responsible and reliable.

What's changed in the past few months?

I've been battling the media and headlines and leaks, and maybe I have proven to people that I'm stronger in the face of those things. More than I even thought.

Akara exits the store, just as I tell my sister, "We're on our way, squirt."

"Thank you! We love you!"

Once we hang up, Akara climbs into the passenger seat with a plastic bag.

Banks tells him, "Crisis at the Cobalt Estate."

Unfaltering, Akara is all confidence and experience. "Let's go."

56

Banks Moretti

SUN HAS SET, AND WE DRIVE up on a *royal* clusterfuck.

"What the fuck," Sulli gapes out the window, and I brake to a sudden stop halfway up the Cobalt's driveway.

Range Rovers, Bugattis, Mercedes, the most drop-dead gorgeous *Ferrari* is blocking our pursuit to the mansion. Christ, I'd love to stick my hands in them. Can't even ogle or salivate over the cars of my fucking dreams when teenagers slam their doors and carry top-shelf booze up to the Cobalt Estate.

I mutter, "Bet they raided their parents' liquor cabinet."

"There is no fucking way Uncle Connor and Aunt Rose know about this," Sulli realizes.

Akara and I are kicked into gear. Alert. Readied.

"Security cameras should be on," I tell him.

"Unless she disabled them." Akara fixes his earpiece cord quickly.

"You calling Epsilon?" I ask. SFE will want to know their clients are around unvetted strangers without their parents' knowledge. Especially after the wrath-inducing incident in the Meadows' backyard with the T-Bags.

"Not yet. You said the girl squad don't want us to nark, and Epsilon will call Connor and Rose."

"Fucking rewind." Sulli peers through the middle seat. "You think *Winona* disabled security cameras? My sister who *values* her privacy?"

I motion to the gaggles of teenagers. "Your sister threw a rager with Bugatti-driving, hundred-year-old-scotch-drinking, gold-shitting teenyboppers."

Sulli tries to maintain seriousness, but she snorts into a laugh. "No, Banks—Winona wouldn't let this many strangers into one of our houses. She's not Eliot or Tom. And not all her friends look this douchey!" She pauses. "But they do shit gold bricks."

Akara smiles but fixes his earpiece cord quickly. "We also didn't think Nona would skinny-dip in Italy after a dare."

"That was different," Sulli defends.

"She's a teenager," I mention. "She's gonna fuck up."

"Not like this." We all unbuckle.

Out of the car, Sulli winds Orion's leash around her hand, better grip so she's not losing the Newfie. Skeletal tulip trees line the driveway, and the three of us, plus a puppy, take lengthy, urgent strides up the pavement.

Our breath smokes the air. We look like a power trio, and teenagers step to the side as we bulldoze forward. I recognize some faces, kids who definitely live in the gated neighborhood. Others aren't that familiar.

In the nut-freezing cold, Akara asks one teen, "You here for a party?"

"Who's asking?" He hides his bottle of scotch in his jacket.

I whisper to Akara, "You're the old fart."

"Says the oldest one here," Akara smiles.

Twenty-nine and still kicking. *Ooh-rah.*

The good news about my migraines has sent me on cloud nine—I have another year with Sulli and Akara, longer, hopefully forever—but I fall back to earth the second we reach the mansion. Frozen fountain in the middle of the circular, crammed driveway, no one is nearing the front door.

It's closed.

Probably locked.

All these kids are hiking their ass over a six-foot hedge. Their friends boost them up, and more help them down on the other side. Sneaking into the backyard.

These aren't guests.

They're party-crashers.

Sulli lets out a worried breath. "Winona."

And we run.

Blood ringing in my ears, legs pumping beneath me.

"Get outta here!" I yell. "GO HOME!"

"COPS ARE COMING!" Akara shouts at the top of his lungs, and the teens loitering around the fountain suddenly shriek and scatter.

Sulli outruns us, but I catapult myself over the hedge first. With one sweep, we've entered wealthy teenage debauchery.

Jesus, Mary, fuck.

Top charting songs blast through outdoor speakers. Crushed beer cans scatter the patio. Sloppy teens splash in the heated pool and cackle (not looking to see if they're clothed). Liquor bottles and white powder line an outdoor bar, and more drunken teens surround an outdoor fire pit and spritz lighter fluid.

Winona.

Kinney.

Audrey.

Vada.

Ben.

Is Xander here?

Pulse pounding, I try to take inventory of the youngest kids in the famous families. I don't see a single one right now.

I help Sulli over the hedge, and Akara lands beside me. He reaches for Sulli's other hand. With the puppy safely under her arm, she drops to the ground. Not letting Orion loose.

"Winona!" Sulli shouts.

"Winona's not here right now," a beanie-wearing guy mocks, "call back later."

Sulli looks sick.

I rage forward and fist his shirt. He drops his beer. I growl, "Where is she—so help me God."

He cranes his neck, wide-eyed up at my six-seven height and skull-crushing gaze. "…get off me." His voice breaks. He pisses himself. Literally, and I let go, feeling marginally bad. *They're trespassing.* Still, these are a bunch of kids to me.

My brother…

Skylar.

He was like these kids. Drinking in excess. Just trying to burn off some kind of steam that'd been building, thanks to our strict dad.

Seeing fifteen-year-olds reminds me how young my brother was— how much life he never got to live.

I'm not here to take anyone's life away. But I am here to protect five, possibly six, young souls. Plus, my girlfriend who's my client.

Nothing can happen to Sulli.

"Party's over!" Sulli calls. "Everyone leave!"

No one moves.

Akara draws my attention to him. "You focus on finding Winona with Sulli. I'll secure the backyard."

That, I can do. I nod.

Akara asks Sulli, "You have a key to the house?"

"Yeah." She whips her macrame backpack around, then lets Orion on the ground.

Akara eagle-eyes the stereo speakers. "Before I call SFE or Connor and Rose, I have an idea. I'll be gone five minutes tops."

I nod to him, "Stay frosty."

"Keep her safe," he says before jogging past the pool.

"Oh my God, that's Luna Hale's dog!" a girl squeals. She squats beside the energetic Newfie and snaps a selfie.

"Hey, stop," Sulli snaps.

"Oh…sorry. I just love Luna." She pats the Newfie.

Sulli picks up Orion protectively. "Don't touch him."

"Jesus, you're acting like I kicked him—Luna wouldn't care. She's cool." The girl makes a snotty-nosed face at Sulli, like she's the "uncool" one.

"You don't even know Luna," Sulli refutes with heat. "Just leave her dog alone and fuck off."

Go, Sulli. I almost smile.

The girl spits out, "Slut," and trots away fast.

I glare at her cowardly ass, then touch the back of Sulli's head in comfort.

She's a little ruffled, still searching for the key to the Cobalt's. "And suddenly I'm really fucking glad I was homeschooled."

"Amen—"

"LEAVE!" Vada Abbey shouts though a kitchen window. Gap-toothed, a BMX rider, and daughter of Garrison & Willow Abbey, she's the least famous of the girl squad.

"WE DIDN'T INVITE YOU!" Kinney Hale yells next, safe beside her friend indoors.

"Come out and say it to our faces!" someone taunts.

"YEAH, COME OUT HERE!"

"WHY ARE YOU HIDING?!"

The cackling is fucking shrill.

Sulli tenses.

I zero in on the sliding glass door. "Your sister."

Winona is inside. Safe. Except wrath is in her eyes. And she starts unlatching the lock from inside.

"No, Nona!" Sulli shouts.

We race toward the door with the puppy. I yell, "STAY INSIDE!"

These kids are hyenas. Waiting to bum-rush Winona and take the party inside the place they're forbidden to go.

Right as we reach Winona, she slips outside. "Akara!" I shout. He's right next to the stereo speakers some meters away. Unable to hear, so I yell in my mic. "AKARA!"

Quickly, he abandons whatever he was doing and jogs towards us.

"GET OUT!" Winona screams at the top of her lungs, launching herself towards the gathering crowds.

I grab onto Winona's shirt while I use my other arm and body to block about ten guys from rushing into the house.

Sulli tries to restrain her sister. "Winona, *Winona.*"

Some shitbag goes for my fucking *gun*. I let go of Winona and twist his arm, putting him in a lock instantly.

He winces, "Fuck, dude."

Shoving him hard, he stumbles away and into the pack of guys. And then I turn to the sliding glass door. Xander is on the other side.

Our eyes meet, and so much flashes through me. This kid I love and protected for years is at a high school party. This kid is safe inside. This kid is *seventeen*.

My gaze screams, *lock the door*, and before I can even say the words, Xander locks the latch.

I nod to him, grateful.

Ben appears in the living room behind Xander. He's wearing a Dalton Hockey sweatshirt. "Is that Nona outside?"

"Stay inside, Ben!" I yell, shoving more kids away. They try to bang at the glass. It's not safe for Sulli or Winona to stand around here.

Akara swoops in and protects the Meadows girls, moving them towards the stereo. "Banks, don't let anyone out or in."

"Copy that—*back off!*" I yell at two guys who try to deck me. I let them hit my arm and stifle a grimace. They're too short to reach my face. With one free hand, I click my mic. "Watch your gun, Akara."

"What's going on?" Thatcher is in my ear.

"You need backup?" Donnelly.

"I'm in town." Oscar.

I tune out SFO comms as Ben yells, "We can't leave Winona outside with Tate!"

One of the T-Bags is here. Somewhere. I scan the drunken party. Security was given their photos. Tate is the tallest one.

Xander is about to fling the curtains closed over the glass door.

"Xander, *no*—" Ben stops him. "We have to go help Nona."

Xander gapes. "Are you nuts? We can't open that door!"

Ben tries to wrestle forward. He unlatches the door, and I pry it closed, letting this one fuckbag pound at my back with a fist.

"Move, man!"

Do not kick a kid.

Pain is background noise to what happens inside the house. Xander shoves Ben back. "STOP!" he screams at him. "Kinney is in here! Your sister is in here! Vada is in here! We're not letting strangers into your house!"

"Winona is outside!" Ben screams back. "If your sister was out there, I'd be out there! You know what Tate told me he'd do to Nona—"

"No," Xander pushes him back again. "No, I can't let you out, man. *Please.* Stop."

I shout to Ben, "Winona's with Akara! She's safe!"

"See," Xander says. "Banks and Akara have everything under—"

"That's him; that's him!" Ben shouts in panic. He rushes forward to leave, but I physically force the door shut and try to spot Tate.

"Where is he?" I ask in a wince over the punches. Alright, I kick at the one fuckbag who thinks *I'm* a punching bag.

"Wrestle Bigfoot!" his friends goad.

Hell to the fucking no.

I drill the harshest glare. "You try, you're getting kneed."

He tries.

I knee him *hard.*

He topples backwards. Everyone laughs, and I shake my head, hating everything about this.

"He's near the pool!" Ben shouts to me. "Let me out, Banks. I have to get out."

"Stop!" Xander tears Ben away, and they wrestle each other and fall onto the Cobalt's coffee table. Shattering the glass beneath their weight.

Fucking *Christ!*

"FIGHT! FIGHT!" People chant and bump closer, hoisting their phones to record the Xander Hale and Ben Cobalt fight.

Goddammit.

Tate—I catch sight of him and his Dalton Swim beanie near the edge of the pool, heat rising over the water in a steaming layer. A few other guys in lacrosse letterman jackets flank him. He's not far from Winona.

I speak into my mic. "T-Bag at the pool."

No response.

"T-Bag at the pool!"

No response.

My mic is fucked, I realize. The cord is ripped. "AKARA!" I yell as loud as I can while he's working on the stereo. "POOL!"

Sulli is holding her sister backwards, and Akara quickly guards Winona.

"Winona! All talk!" Tate shouts. "Let's see how big of a girl you are. You want to take me down! Come at me, bitch!"

I grind my teeth, breathing hot through my nose. What a fucking vile garbage human.

Winona is strangely frozen. Like his voice has scarred some fucking part of her. It shoots *ire* into my bloodstream. She shrinks back into Sulli, and it takes everything in me not to rage forward again.

I'm the only one keeping this door shut.

"Hey!" Akara glares, unable to confront Tate without putting the Meadows girls at risk. "The police are seconds away!"

"Yeah, right. I'm not falling for that again." Tate laughs, then shouts at Winona, "Go hide behind your bodyguard and your slutty sister! What a big fucking pussy you are!"

"What'd you say?" That's not coming from me.

Or Akara.

Or even Sulli.

A new player has entered the ring.

A shaggy-haired seventeen-year-old pumps up his chest against Tate's chest. "Why are you taunting her, dude? This is her uncle's house that *you're* trespassing on. Stop bullying her."

"Who the fuck are you?" Tate sneers.

"Jesse Highland." He gets in his face. "Come at me, *dick*."

Tate swings, and Jesse shoves Tate into the pool. The T-Bag slips over the edge and splashes into the water.

Some people actually applaud.

And then the music cuts out to silence. Followed next by loud police sirens.

"Oh no!"

"Shit. Go, go!"

Teenagers scatter in every direction. Trying to quickly jump over the garden hedge. Trampling over cans and broken glass.

Tate struggles out of the pool. Urgency to leave draining color out of his face.

Thing is, we know where he lives. Rose and Connor even know his parents.

"Busted!" Kinney shouts through the window.

What a fucking shitshow.

I'm still on guard. Not everyone has vacated, and Akara lowers the volume on the sirens. He played the prerecorded sound over the stereo system.

Sulli tells him, "Boss move."

Yeah, at this point, Akara's resumé is stacked to heaven with boss moves. Makes it easy to follow him.

I almost smile, but I shout at the lingering teens, "You all need to go. Except Jesse."

Jesse is with us.

A girl in a pink sweater says, "We were, um…" She pushes up her glasses. "…invited to the sip-in-snow for Audrey's pre-birthday party."

"They're with us!" Vada shouts, right outside the glass sliding door. So is Kinney.

"You sure?" I ask, counting about six teenagers left.

"Yeah!" Kinney chimes in.

So I let go of the door.

Ben and Vada rush outside to Winona, and Xander is trying to sweep up the shards from the glass coffee table. He gives up midway through. Kinney stays with him.

I want to help the Hales, but too much involving security isn't resolved or secure. Stereo is turned off. Sulli, Akara, and I meet up at the firepit to extinguish this blaze. Orion happily circles Sulli's feet.

"Careful," she tells him. Empty wine glasses and bottles litter the area. A couple forgotten scarves hang over chairs.

And suddenly, a tense noise cuts into the cold air.

Knock knock.

Knock knock.

Akara and I share an uneasy look.

We take out our phones.

"Was that a notification for the Royal Leaks?" Vada asks too loudly.

Those six strangers start checking their phones like us.

Akara frowns. "This doesn't make any sense."

Sulli peers closer at his screen.

For fuck's sake. How...?

THE ROYAL LEAKS

 We reveal all the truths about the American Royals. These are verified and come directly from the source.

ROYAL LEAK #1: Sullivan Meadows bought Plan B.

#TodaysLeaks #TheCondomBroke #OopsieBaby #poundtown

Winona, Vada, Ben, and Jesse look up at the three of us in wide-eyed shock. Inside, Kinney and Xander are staring out. And the six strangers gawk in Sulli's direction.

Like our drama has eclipsed and outclassed their drama. Gotta say, this is a first for me.

"I'm not here. This isn't fucking happening," she mutters, a hand to her forehead.

I wrap an arm around Sulli.

"Show's over!" Akara yells, and they try to pry their beady-eyes off us.

The leak confuses the holy hell out of me. The three of us turn more towards the fire, and I ask Akara, "How'd they know the condom broke? We didn't say a fucking thing *in* the penthouse."

"I know," Akara breathes, running a tensed hand through his hair.

"The car can't be bugged," Sulli says. "None of the other leaks came from Booger. They've all originated *from* the penthouse."

Orion lets out a bark.

The three of us lower our gazes.

Cold nips at my skin, and I ask, "Has anyone checked the dogs?"

57

Banks Moretti

WE LEAVE ORION INSIDE the mansion, secured in a bathroom. With a very peculiar-looking device on the inside of his collar. Translucent, three little wires protruding.

I'm no genius, but I'd bet my firstborn that the dog is bugged.

Firstborn.

God, my thoughts. Of course, I'm thinking about *babies* since the condom broke. Being a dad hasn't been on my radar. I've been thinking about being an uncle. But I've always figured if I did have a kid, my dumbass would probably have an accident.

While Sulli is checking on a drunk Audrey Cobalt, I'm securing the perimeter of the Cobalt Estate with Akara. We walk down the driveway, ensuring no one is in the bushes or behind tulip trees. All the cars are gone. Akara already called Rose and Connor, and they're headed home from a Cobalt Inc. engagement in Center City.

They thanked us for keeping the party crashers out of the mansion and clearing the backyard. Epsilon has been called in to inspect the perimeter with us, but we all know this is a win for Akara's security firm.

After Akara updated SFO about the high school party, Oscar spoke on comms, "Kitsuwon Securities 2 – Triple Shield 3."

"Moving on up, boys," Farrow chimed in.

Except Akara hasn't unleashed what we found on Orion's collar yet. It's hard to believe the Royal Leaks could be over *tonight*.

Feels good to be headed there.

Feels like hell knowing it took us this long. "How'd we miss this?" I ask him quietly while we check behind a rose bush. Just a handle of vodka here and a shoe. Someone took off without their Nike.

Akara shakes his head. "It had to have been a cat sitter. That's the only person who would've had access to the animals."

"Grandmother Calloway?" I theorize.

"She avoids the pets like the *fudging* plague."

I furrow my brows. "What motive would a cat sitter have?" Seems unlikely they'd really want to harm the families' stocks and businesses.

"We still have to figure that out," Akara says, texting quickly on his phone. He's either contacting Connor Cobalt or Price. Probably both.

What might've saved us is Sulli dog-sitting during a Plan B run. If that hadn't happened, if she hadn't gone outside even with the potential threat of paparazzi—there'd be no leak and we never would've found the device on Orion's collar.

"She saved us," I tell Akara what I'm thinking.

He slips me a brief glance. "Your big dick saved us."

I let out a laugh.

"And she did too," Akara adds with a smile, but we've fallen quiet fast as his phone buzzes. He checks the text. "Jack is asking about his little brother." *Jesse.*

"What was Jesse Highland even doing here? I thought he'd be in California."

"From what I gathered, Ben heard Jesse was in town and invited him to the party. Ben is friendly with everyone." Akara scopes out another bush. "Jack said that Jesse skipped school and flew out to Philly to come help him with post-production for *Suddenly Famous*."

The docuseries about Oscar and Jack must've stopped filming. I don't pay too much attention to production's schedules unless they get in my way.

I nod a few times. "Skipping school, huh?"

Akara smiles. "*Evidently*, Jesse's mom gave him an earful about it."

I surprise myself as I say, "The only person I probably would've skipped school for is my big brother too." *Skylar.*

Even in the dark, I see Akara's gaze softening on me. "You love him."

"I love him. I hate him. I don't know if that'll ever change, Akara."

He squeezes my shoulder as we move forward together. We quiet as SFE shines their flashlights close to our area of operations, and Akara shouts, "It's all clear here!"

They nod, but Winona's bodyguard—Greer Bell—sends us a death-glare. The Meadows bodyguards aren't that happy we're banging Sulli. And they just found out she needed Plan B.

I wave at him to keep the peace. What I think Akara will want.

Greer flips me off.

Akara flips him off with two middle fingers.

I end up smiling.

He whispers to me, "Meadows family trips with Greer and Wiley are going to be such a *blast.*"

Meadows family trips. To think I could be going on those someday as Sulli's bodyguard and boyfriend—I must've really hit my head. Maybe a migraine fucked me over and I'm actually dead. Seems more fucking believable.

I smile more. Guys like me end up in early graves. Living for the long-run is the most exciting adventure I could ever take.

Akara's statement reminds me of something. "You're back together with Sulli?" If he's going on a Meadows trip, it'd be as her boyfriend. He's still Luna's bodyguard.

"Yeah. We're a triad." He frowns. "Isn't that obvious?" He drops his voice. "We all had sex."

I smack his chest. "I know that. She doesn't."

"What?" His face screws up. "She knows. Sulli *knows.* We said we missed each other...we hugged...it was obvious." He contemplates longer.

"Did you actually say the words? 'Cause she needs it spelled out, Akara."

His face slowly falls. "*Shit.*"

I punch his arm lightly.

He curves inward, already expecting the hit for the curse. "I have to tell her." He glances back up the driveway. We still need to secure the area.

So we move faster, and I laugh.

"What?"

"For someone that's so damn good at communicating with your men, you kind of suck at it when it comes to your girl."

He shoots me a glare and corrects haughtily, "*Our girl.*"

"Excuse me—*our* girl." I wear a crooked smile that disappears. Logistics are hanging unkindly over me. Not a fan of them, but I have to ask, "What about publicly? Are we confirming we're all together then?" It's the biggest jump we've all been avoiding.

Akara comes to a halt at a naked tulip tree. His heavy breath visible in the night. "The threat hasn't changed, Banks. We confirm the poly relationship; she's in danger. Those are the *facts.*"

"I know," I breathe, scraping a hand along my jaw. "But it's not fair if her and I can kiss in public and you two can't do a damned thing. And how long will that really last? You two are never careful out there—"

He rolls his eyes, and I add fast, "SFO *literally* thought you two were together for years."

"We weren't," he combats but then sighs out, knowing now how they *flirt.* Even as "just friends" they flirted like they were screwing behind closed doors.

"Look, your dynamic won't change—and I wouldn't want it to. Neither would Sulli."

"What are you saying, Banks?"

I raise my shoulders. "Maybe the least messy, complicated solution is to tell the full truth. We'll handle the fallout. It's what we do."

"You say our dynamic won't change, but you know *everything* will change," Akara whispers strongly. "Just leaving the house will be a warzone. Every *single* day, Banks. She's not a Marine like you. She could be scarred for life—you saw Winona tonight just dealing with a neighborhood bully. That's going to stay with her for *years*. Intensify that by a thousand for Sulli—that's what we'd do to her."

My eyes burn. "You don't need to convince me it's a dangerous path. I just see things differently. Her safety vs. her happiness—I'm throwing myself towards her happiness."

"That's the thing, Banks. She's not happy when she's not safe."

"She's not happy living a lie—"

"A half-truth."

"Six of one, half a dozen of the other—it's the same shit." I can see guilt eating at her for giving me more and giving Akara less. I can see frustration eating at all of us.

Akara stares up at the crescent moon. "She might not even want to publicly confirm all three of us, and then the point is moot."

I bob my head. "That's true." If she'd rather be more cautious, I'd go down that road with Sulli and Akara.

He speaks even quieter. "Leaving things how they are publicly might be the best route, *especially* if she's pregnant."

I go still, no muscle even twitching. "She's taking Plan B."

"She hasn't yet, Banks," Akara whispers. "She can change her mind."

On the car ride here, Sulli talked about her mom's fertility issues, how difficult it'd been for Sulli to come into the world. If she has a last second change of heart, I'll ride that change with her. But she still seemed set on taking Plan B.

"I think she'll take it," I tell him.

Akara thinks this over. "Even then, Plan B is only 87% effective. We can't be *shocked* if weeks later she's pregnant."

We hold tighter, grimmer gazes. We haven't talked about babies. What that'd even mean for our relationship, but we understand what it'd mean for Sulli's safety.

Pregnancies provoke media attention. It's set in history.

"Highest threat level," Akara says with severity.

"We'll protect her in public, no matter what. We always will," I remind him, and our heads turn as SFE shines their flashlights towards us again.

"Let's finish this," Akara declares. We go back to work, and after the perimeter is secured, he calls Sulli, "Can you meet us at the end of the driveway? We need to talk." He listens. "Okay, great. See you."

We need to talk. His choice of words is something.

I'd bet my second-born that Sulli is freaking out right now.

58

Sullivan Meadows

I SPRINT WITH ALL MY fucking might down the winding driveway. Hair whipping behind me, cold numbing my cheeks—I just run towards Kits.

He's going to say goodbye. He's leaving.

I run like I'm losing time with him. Like there's no time even left. Why can't I have eternity? Why is the world standing in our way?

Let us be.

Heart slamming, legs pumping fiercely, I weave down the path, and the mailbox comes into view. Banks and Akara rotate to face me at the same handsome fucking time—like I'm Kate Winslet on the Titanic, dreaming as two Leonardo DiCaprios spin and extend a hand.

Only in my reality, I barrel past them, unable to break my forceful stride in enough time. And I have to double-back in an arc and sharp breath, "Kits—"

"Sul—"

"I love you," I cut him off strongly. "I fucking *love* you, and I'd rather have you and live in madness than not have you at all. So don't go—"

"I'm *not* going anywhere," Akara emphasizes, concern and distress all over his face. "I would've *never* had sex with you and then broke things off—I'm not trying to emotionally toy with you or confuse you. I'm trying to be better than I was, than I did."

He is.

"You are," I tell him.

Akara inhales, "I was never planning on leaving tonight or tomorrow. I should've been clearer earlier—I thought I was, but I didn't say everything I should've."

I breathe easier, calmer, especially seeing Banks' soft, almost-there smile that rises and rises. "What should you've said, Kits?"

He edges forward. "That I'm *staying*. That I never stopped wanting to be with you and Banks. That it's too painful to be without you. That I can't live without you, Sullivan Minnie Meadows, and I've felt the truth in that. That for as much as I will always protect you, I can never stop loving you, and whatever happens tomorrow, I'm not leaving. I'm never leaving you."

"Not for anything?" I ask, hope surging. We've drawn closer.

"Not for anything," he promises, his hand skimming the edge of my cheek and jaw.

"Even if it's the stupid thing to do?"

"Even if it's the stupidest *fudging* thing in the world—I'm stupidly in love with you." He presses his forehead to mine. "You are my heart when I forget I have one and my happiness in every day. I hope I can be the Kits you've hoped for, the Kits who keeps you whole—"

"You're the Kits I love the fucking most," I interject. "You don't need to keep me whole. Just be happy with me. With us."

Tears slip down his cheeks as he brings me closer and kisses me tenderly. I clutch the back of his neck, feeling our lives flash through our history. Friendship. Flirting. New fights. New roads. Kissing. Love. And still, this is my favorite time with him.

Now.

On a new adventure.

A bigger one.

We pull apart, and Banks is practically grinning. "I feel like a proud Mother Goose."

I laugh, wiping my wet eyes, and Akara shakes his head with a growing smile.

"Just so we're crystal," I say, "we're all together again?"

"Yes," Akara says.

Banks nods, then looks me over. "Where's your head at about the public?"

"I—"

Akara's phone rings, and with the sip-in-snow party from hell, plus the revelation about Orion's dog collar, the interruption isn't surprising but actually welcome. We all want answers and resolutions.

"It's Connor Cobalt." He waits to answer. "I'm going to call a security meeting soon about the leaks. We'll table this? Later but soon."

Later but soon. I nod heartily. "Sounds like a plan."

LATE-LATE NIGHT BACK AT THE PENTHOUSE, ALL of SFO are still absent at a mega-security meeting involving Triple Shield and Kitsuwon Securities. Leaving me alone with my three cousins.

Underneath galaxy lights in Luna's bedroom, Moffy, Jane, Luna, and I camp out on a fuzzy midnight rug in a circle, a bowl of M&Ms and Chex Mix between us.

Usually when we hang out all together like this, I feel our youth. But tonight, I feel our twenties pass between us. What we've dealt with isn't *kid* stuff.

Moffy had his sex life blasted.

Jane had a cheating rumor blow-up.

Luna had her private fanfics condemned.

And I had my health, love life, and sex life totally fucking exposed.

"I think we've come out completely and entirely unscathed this time," Jane says into a sip of coffee, hands wrapped around a pastel pink mug. Wavy hair tied in a cat-printed ribbon. "Don't you feel it, old chap?"

Maximoff smiles. "I'm feeling *partially* charred."

"A teeny bit scratched," Jane agrees.

"Semi-crispy," Luna sing-songs.

"Fucking burnt," I finish.

We all share soft smiles that fade into seriousness with incoming texts.

I pop M&Ms in my mouth and read mine. "Akara says the perp was...Tatiana Grace? Who's that?"

Jane goes eerily still. "Merde."

Maximoff glances from his phone to Jane. "A cat sitter?" He reads his texts. "Farrow said it's bigger than that."

Luna munches on Chex Mix. "I'm lost."

Our boyfriends are texting us updates as the security meeting unfolds, and Luna is the only one without a bodyguard boyfriend.

"I interviewed Tatiana," Jane explains, her face pinched in hurt. "Thatcher said *she's* the one who physically attached listening devices to Orion *and* Arkham's collars. She confessed after they showed the cat sitters the devices tonight."

During every sweep of the penthouse, we always took the puppies out with us, so surveillance teams never found the bugs. Uncle Stokes even brought Orion and Arkham to his house during the holidays.

Jane breathes, "I must've...I must've been distracted by my cats during the interview. I didn't see her touch the dogs, and Thatcher wasn't with me." She buries her face in her palms.

Moffy wraps an arm around her. "It's okay, Janie."

"She seemed *sweet*. She's a single mom living around where Thatcher grew up."

A pit is in my stomach seeing Jane take the fall. "I'm sure she was, Jane. Hey, it's not your fucking fault."

"It could've been any of us," Luna whispers, so softly that I strain my ears to pick up the words.

No wonder her life leaked the least. She's a whispering badass. "I need whispering tips, Luna."

"You just talk like this." Her voice grows so quiet and calming, she could sell ASMR videos.

"Like this," I try to mimic very fucking poorly, and Jane starts laughing. We smile over at her, happy to quell her sadness.

Moffy licks his lips, then gestures his phone around the circle. "So the cat sitter planted the bugs—but why? Makes no damn sense, in any universe."

"In my universe, it makes a lot of sense," Luna says. "The cat sitter is obviously a smuggler of space dust."

Maximoff smiles. "Makes total sense now. Space dust is high currency, and I'm guessing Luna is hoarding a massive amount."

"Tons," Luna grins.

A weird sense of calm passes between us now.

For *two months* we've endured the leaks. Strange to think in a couple hours, maybe even less, this could be the end of the constant unease of what bomb is dropping next.

Our phones go off again.

We all try our best to read out loud for Luna and to piece together information we're given. "Banks just told me Tatiana was a pawn. She was being..."

"Blackmailed," Maximoff says rigidly. "By wealthier 'individuals'."

"More than one person?" Jane muses quietly.

I say aloud, "So Tatiana isn't the mole."

"Oui," Jane nods. "They just used her to plant the bugs."

We text back for more info, but the messages go silent for a little bit. And I take the opportunity to tell them, "Akara and I are back together. Banks is still with me too."

Luna bursts in a smile. "The trio's back in town." She wags her fingers with my fingers, and light illuminates in me but flickers knowing I need to face Moffy and Jane.

Maximoff is harder to read. My big brother in spirit. He straightens up, swimmer's shoulders pulled taut with a sort of protectiveness I've always known and seen. A genuine smile touches his green eyes. "He better not leave again."

Sudden emotion nearly spurns tears. "Is that you saying...you actually *want* us to stay together?"

"Yeah. Totally. Completely. Colossally. *Together.*"

Holy fuck.

I'm stunned speechless.

"It's not really for me to decide what you do." He licks his lips again, empathy so clear now. "You know I have this husband who lives his life so damn *authentically*. He makes me a better person…and all I want is for you to be happy, Sulli, and to be able to live your life so damn proudly too. So whatever you might face out in public or in the media, I'm here if you need me. Just one Bat Signal away."

I immediately reach forward and hug Moffy.

He hugs back.

"That means…everything to me, Mof." To have my family more firmly and supportive on my side—it's the best feeling in the fucking world.

It dawns on me that I've rarely extended the same offer to Moffy. Maybe because he so rarely turns to others for help. The FanCon Tour was one of the biggest times I could be there for him. "If you ever need me, too, Moffy, I'm just one Mermaid Signal away." I'm not sure if he'll ever take me up on the offer, but he's not flinging it aside.

He smiles. "Thanks, Sulli."

We break apart, and Jane mimes the tip of a top hat to me. "I'm here as well. I can't promise I won't always love Banks a little differently since he's my brother-in-law, but I sincerely believe you three are better together as one." She smiles brightly. "Toujours."

I know very few French words, but that one I'm fucking certain means *always*.

I breathe in the word and mime the tip of a top hat back. We share a burgeoning grin, and then our phones go off again.

We fumble for them, and my jaw unhinges at the new texts. No fucking way. I go cold. Stomach roiling. "Did you guys…?" I whip my head up to Maximoff and Jane. She has her fingers to her lips, blue eyes like saucers.

Maximoff's gaze flashes hot. "You've got to be shitting me."

"What? Who?" Luna asks, crunching on Chex Mix.

"Oh shit. Sorry, Luna." My voice is tight, ribs shrinking over my lungs. Anger tries to boil, but shock is overriding any rage. "They know who the mole is. Tatiana ratted them out."

I can't say the name.

The name we all know.

The name I *intimately* know.

I stare haunted at the phone. Like it's a fucking typo.

Maximoff tells his sister, "The Rochester family—they created The Royal Leaks."

Luna immediately turns to me. "Are you okay?"

"Sulli?" Moffy asks.

I swallow harder. "My ex-boyfriend wouldn't...Will is *nice.*" I'm in denial for a hot second, then I pinch the bridge of my nose. "Fuckfuck*fuck*, what if this is break-up revenge?"

And he came after my roommates.

This isn't Jane's fault. It's *mine.*

I feel sick.

"He's dead." Moffy is on his feet.

Jane pulls him down.

He's trying to cool off, and Luna side-hugs me.

"They just said the Rochester *family,*" Jane reminds us. "Will Rochester isn't the only sibling. Wesley, Wyatt, and Winnifred—not to mention, *their parents.* The probability that their parents were going after our parents is high. An old money family trying to manipulate the stocks of their competitors."

The motive is there.

"Will they be arrested?" I ask Moffy and Jane.

Moffy is staring at his phone. "They have as much money as our families. I doubt they left any evidence. They have fall guys."

"Tatiana," I realize. *Fuck.*

"What about her confession?" Luna asks.

"It's just her word," Jane replies sadly. "If there's no evidence, we'll only be able to go after Tatiana for planting the bugs."

We're not cutting the head off the snake. But Akara texts me that the Hale, Cobalt, and Meadows' lawyers are aimed at the Rochesters, and how litigation can be the best form of pressure.

It's time they're under some.

"They're taking down the website now," Jane says. "Look."

I pop up *The Royal Leaks*.

The most recent leak about Plan B is there. I refresh the gossip site, and the web browser says magic words that breathe power and life into us.

Sorry, the page you were looking for does not exist or is not available.

"Fucking finally."

The air untenses for a while, but I have another announcement that jostles my nerves. An announcement that I discussed briefly with Akara and Banks on the drive here. I wait to tell my cousins until we're with security.

Once SFO arrive, we all pick ourselves off the floor and meet them in the living room. The door opens, and we all stand, waiting for our bodyguards.

I expect them to be spent, sort of dragging their heels. Groaning at the long, long fucking day. But they're not exhausted or drained.

SFO come inside with mighty, unrelenting confidence. Like pillars and rocks of our lives. Like they're ready for more.

Donnelly lets Orion and Arkham loose, and Moffy and Luna embrace their puppies. Quinn, on crutches, is invited inside, even though he's no longer SFO. We all signed his cast. And Gabe is a new bodyguard on the small fleet.

They all face us, and we face them.

I breathe in the care, the safety, the protection—not manufactured or some fucking illusion meant to trick and deceive into a false sense of security. They're the reason I came out of New Year's Eve without a scratch. They're the reason the chaos of our lives is livable.

Now it's up to us to live out our lives.

"It's over," Akara declares.

"Thank fucking God," I exhale, approaching Banks and Akara. They hug me, and I let them know I told my cousins about our reunited triad. But I notice a black jewelry box in Akara's hand. "What's that?"

Is he proposing?

No.

No fucking way.

"A gift from Connor," he tells me.

I exhale a breath. Okay. Right. *Makes way more sense.* Banks can see through me. He's watching my expression, and I try to hide my reddened face by urging Akara to open the box.

He shows me the platinum cufflinks.

My lips rise. "That was nice of my uncle."

Very quietly, Akara tells me, "He's not the dad I wanted to impress. But I'll take this win."

I haven't had time to talk to my dad about our newly reunited triad, but I *know* after everything we went through, he'll be in my corner. He promised to protect my love, and that means not being on opposite sides of Akara and Banks.

Before I can respond, Oscar shouts over everyone, "Looks like it's now Kitsuwon Securities 3 – Triple Shield 3." All of SFO start clapping for Akara.

I join in with my cousins.

He points over at me and Banks. Like we solved the fucking mystery. I shove his arm. "Come on, it was the two of you, Hardy Boys."

Akara messes my messy hair. "You were there too, Nancy Drew." He smiles at me. "Claim this win with us."

I'm about to mention how I thought *Jane* was the Nancy Drew. But…then I realize I can be one, too.

"When you put it like that, Kits, you know I'm not going to say no." All feels right. All feels happy, except I'm about to launch more news. No time is better than now. "Everyone, I have something to say." Facing SFO and my cousins isn't as hard as before, but where I'm headed is a whole new adventure. One I've been on before.

And I begin to smile before I say the words.

59

Akara Kitsuwon

EARLY MORNING AFTER the never-ending night and Sulli's big announcement, which she's going to announce to the world today— Sulli wakes at dawn, and I whisper, "It's later and soon." Meaning, we have more time to talk about our public-facing relationship.

"Let's go to the treehouse first," Sulli says to us. "I left something there."

Now the three of us are in winter jackets and crunching snow, hiking through the backyard of the Meadows cottage, and my life is resting in the tips of my fingers. What I want and love, I'm holding.

Sulli.

Banks.

SFO.

Studio 9 is still standing, for now. Kitsuwon Securities is back on track after a few missteps. I even plan to stay as Luna's bodyguard for a little longer, the twenty-year-old fanfic writer who's in pursuit of a business degree. She could use an experienced bodyguard until Quinn recovers, and I want to keep Gabe as the floater.

It feels apropos guarding a future businesswoman.

And I'll be in college. Sitting in lecture halls that I would've taken at eighteen if my dad had lived. Like all things, time circles back around, and I feel like I should be here. Even Sulli agreed I need to maintain course for a little while.

What I want and love, I won't drop.

Yet, I'm scared.

In the last minute.

In the final act where we've finally hung on and begun to breathe.

Could everything just blow up again?

Overcast, the winter sky is gloomy, but our spirits remain high off the wins and our reunion together. The Meadows' cozy but mammoth treehouse comes into view, nestled among thick branches in nostalgic glory. Windowpanes, wraparound porch, a fake smokestack—this is a clubhouse of a kid's wildest dreams.

Sulli reaches the ladder at the tree trunk, and Banks and I stop a couple feet away as our girlfriend plucks a berry and floral wreath off the ladder's rung. Brushing snow off the woven blue flowers and pieces of fern, she comes closer to us.

"My mom made this for me."

I realize, "It's a flower crown."

Banks inspects the berries.

I give him a look. "You know what it's made out of?" Banks understanding *plants* is news to me.

"Not a clue. My thumbs are covered in oil, not dirt."

Sulli kicks my shin, then his shin in soft Sullivan affection. We're hooked on her as she says, "These are winterberries, Forget-Me-Nots, and ferns." She studies the crown with a faraway look. "Banks asked me where my head is at in terms of the public, and I want to be utterly fucking honest with both of you." Sulli lifts her green eyes with tenacity and resolve. Gold-medal confidence that I've seen propel her through finish lines and onto podiums. "I wasn't ready for the mayhem at New Year's Eve. I might never be ready for that kind of attention and aggression every single day of my life, but I can't spend another month, another year—fucking eternity—fearing another leak."

I shift my weight. Seeing where she's going. "We can be careful, Sul."

"Can we, Kits?" She shrugs. "We never have been."

"We can try."

"I don't want to be scared to kiss you. I don't want to feel guilty for kissing Banks. Our love shouldn't be weaponized against us, and it could be at any fucking point in time."

Banks is quiet because he's ready to roll with Sulli into pandemonium. Deep down, I want to be there, too. "I can't get over your threat level, Sul. It's *astronomical* if we confirm our triad, and that's not even considering you might be pregnant."

She shifts a hand in her jacket and reveals the Plan B box. "I'm taking this today—and I know, it's not totally effective. So if you need to consider the threat level of me being pregnant, do that. If even one of you isn't okay with this, we don't have to confirm anything. But I just need you to know what I really want."

The ball is in my court.

Life at my fingertips.

Not just mine.

Hers and his, and what are even the odds? What's the best odds of success? Best odds of happiness? Everything is muddled, jumbled, *scrambled* together with a big *fudging* question mark. Her safety. Our love. Her happiness. Our happiness. Her danger.

Messy.

So very, very messy.

But the messiest things have been the best roads I've ever taken. Trying to keep things neat and preserve my friendship with Sulli— fearing making a move and ruining what we had—would've been the biggest mistake of my entire life. I would've left these life-changing stones unturned. I would've missed out on the three of *us*. Romance. Love for the ages.

I've been trying to *preserve* Sulli.

Maybe I just need to live with the girl and guy I love.

I push back my black hair, breath easing. With my arm movement, a bracelet glides against my wrist. I tug at my sleeve to see braided red thread and beads that spell out *I love Sulli*.

My lips almost rise.

Don't be afraid, Nine. "You really want this, Sul?" I make sure. "Even if the world hurts you and changes you?"

Sulli glances at the crown, then looks from me to Banks, back to me. "I can't promise either of you that I won't change. Maybe I'll get stronger. Maybe I'll get weaker. Maybe I'll cry myself to sleep some nights. Maybe I'll regret it some days. Maybe I'll be happy most weeks. Maybe, just fucking maybe, you'll change with me. You'll stand with me through the sad and happy, the peaceful and the loud, through the whole fucking adventure. Just maybe…you'll want that too."

Banks and I exchange a look of certainty.

With a shadow of a smile, he says, "Come what may."

I smile more. "Feel the moment."

Sulli eyes me, then him. "That's a yes?"

"That's a definite yes," I nod. "Kneel, Lady Meadows."

She drops to the snow. Exhilaration and euphoric bliss teeming between us.

Banks asks her, "Can I borrow this?" He reaches for the flower crown.

"You fucking may." She bursts in a bigger, overcome smile as we stand side-by-side, towering over her athletic frame.

I look to Banks. We've fallen in love with the same lively, endearing, courageous girl, and the irreplaceable feelings I share with him—the true depth of feelings we all share—I can't leave behind. Like pieces of soul and breath. Greater than love. A reason for living. A reason for being.

He looks to me. It's the three of us.

It's always going to be the three of us.

"Let's crown our queen," I tell him, and together, we rest the winter crown on Sulli's wild, dark brown hair.

When she rises at six-feet tall, she clasps our hands, "To the treehouse. Let's do the huge thing."

Two announcements to make now.

Everything will undoubtedly change, but what I fear more is an unlived life. Without reservation, I walk forward with them, and I climb the ladder, leading the way.

60

Banks Moretti

PAPER FLOWERS AND PAPER birds dangle from inside the treehouse. Almost slammed my head into the ceiling, but I duck while Sulli switches on a portable heater and we shrug off jackets.

"We're all set on posting a video to my Instagram, right?" Sulli asks, taking a seat on a mound of colorful pillows. Flower crown in her hair, she's still a fucking smokeshow, but *God*, am I proud to be next to her, of being witness to the woman she is and of who she might become.

And I'm proud of him. Our friendship has grown into something unexplainable. A feeling, a heartbeat, an inseverable tether. Whatever future holds, Akara has to be there. I didn't think I could love him more, but somehow, some way, I do.

"Akara?" I ask since he'll have stronger opinions on the announcement strategy.

"A video works great." He takes a seat on her left.

I sit on her right.

With Sulli between us, she first tears open the box of Plan B. I hand her the water bottle after she swallows the pill. She's an untiring current, and right now, nothing is slowing her powerful stride.

I slip a toothpick between my rising lips.

"Just do what you'd always do with me," she tells us, throwing the box in the corner.

I bite down on the toothpick. "Alright, alright, alright." I curve a strong arm over her shoulders. She leans her weight into me.

Akara tosses a strand of hair at her face. She elbows him with a smile, "While we're recording, Kits."

"You left that part out, Sul," he teases.

She wags her brows and pops open her camera app, then switches to *video* function. To align all three of us in frame, I angle myself and cock my head. Akara fits on a beanie, looking like a pro-skateboarder. I watch Sulli's smile mushroom until she bites her lip.

"Fuck, you two are way too hot for this—like, Banks, your eyes are seriously fucking smoldering."

I'm just staring at Sulli.

"Kits, you look sexy cool, and I look…" Emotion touches her gaze, seeing herself in the camera. Sitting tall, steadfast, confident—a girl who knows exactly what she wants. Who's unafraid to chase after love and life.

Akara and I are grinning down at Sulli.

"Wow," she breathes.

Her finger hovers over the red *record* button. Waiting just a beat.

Akara reminds her, "We can take multiple videos and pick the best one."

"Yeah, I know."

I touch the back of her head reassuringly before my hand falls to her shoulder again. "You've got this, mermaid."

She exhales one last time. "One-hundred-fifty miles per hour. No brakes." And then she presses *record*. Without a pause, she begins, "Hey, if you don't know me, my name is Sullivan Minnie Meadows. I'm twenty-one—I'll be turning twenty-two in February. And some of you might know me as the daughter of Ryke and Daisy Meadows. Others might know me as an Olympic swimmer. If you're closer to me, you probably know me as the girl who eats too many sweets and curses too fucking loudly."

My mouth curves up, and maybe I should be watching the video screen. But I can't take my eyes off the 3D-real-life Sulli.

"Lately, there's been a lot of speculation about my love life—but before I talk about that, I want to make an official, *formal* announcement."

She's doing the thing.

After a short pause, Sulli says, "I'm going to compete in the Olympic Team Trials in June. I'm out of retirement. And I'm shooting for the summer Olympics."

I can't wait to see her race for gold.

She's already emailed Warwick University about ending her coaching position. Whether or not she's pregnant will put a screwball in her Olympic plans, but that's not in the forefront.

Next, Sulli says, "Now about my love life, which I know is juicier."

Akara flings her hair at her face again.

She snorts, "Kits."

I shift my toothpick, and Sulli devours me in the camera. My chest rises, and back to the recording, we all look straight ahead.

Nothing can bring me down. I've got the girl. I've got the guy. Screw the world to hell if they think they'll take them away from me again.

Death might not be as close. But hell, I'm excited for the life I'm living.

Her green eyes flame with a determined fury. "I'm in a relationship with Banks Moretti and Akara Kitsuwon. A *poly* relationship. And I love them equally. That's the fucking gist of it. But if you have issues, please kindly refer to the fucking caption of this video."

With this, she hits the *stop* button.

Something washes over all of us.

I say first, "That was the one."

"Definitely," Sulli agrees. "That felt *right*."

"It felt *fudging* right," Akara says, smiling at us.

Sulli begins to insert the video onto Instagram. She captions the post, and my lips rise reading the words. That's our Sulli.

She nods strongly and reads them out loud, cementing what we all believe.

"To whom this may concern," she recites, "*fuck you*."

She posts the video.

I smile. "Get some."

ACKNOWLEDGEMENTS

The love Akara, Banks, & Sulli share has been a whirlwind, and it's given us such life & happiness. We hope *Fearless Like Us* has brought some happiness & hope to you. As Banks' grandma (and our grandma) would say, *be happy*. We hope you're all happy today, and if you're feeling a little blue, we hope these characters can be a source of love for you. They'll always be here. And this triad's love story is not over yet.

Akara, Banks, & Sulli officially have the longest book in the Like Us Series (so far!), and that means this book took some extra love and care to get exactly right. Big thanks to our mom for her support and editing skills. You're the calm during our deadline-mode panics and the queen of catching our worst typos. Without you, these books would never sparkle. We love you a waffle-lot.

Thank you to the admins of the Fizzle Force—Lanie, Jenn, and Shea—for your continued support, for everything you do behind the scenes, and for always throwing the best pre-release parties.

Thank you to our agent, Kimberly, for finding this book a home in audio. We truly love when these characters get to come to audio life.

Thank you to the patrons of our Patreon for being a huge source of light and love in our lives. We know we always say this, but we truly would not be full-time writers without the support from Patreon. You all fuel our creative wells and keep us inspired daily. Thankyouthankyouthankyou!

Thank you to the bloggers, bookstagrammers, booktokers, reviewers, and readers who shout about the Like Us series from the rooftops. With so many stories out there to consume and recommend, we're forever honored that you've chosen to spread the word about these books.

Thank you to *you*, the reader, for picking up Book 9 in the Like Us series and continuing this journey with us and these characters. Without you, these stories wouldn't breathe and live on past creation. We're so very grateful you picked this one up. And we hope you'll continue this awfully big adventure with us.

All the love in every universe,
Krista & Becca

PRONUNCIATION GLOSSARY

The Italian used in this book is an Italian-American language developed by Italian immigrants. It is an incomplete language and uses Italian, English, or both. Different Italians speak different dialects in certain areas, and what is used in the Like Us series is prominent on the East Coast. Words may vary in pronunciation and spelling in different communities.

gabbadost': pronounced gaa-baa-dahst (Origin: capa dura/capa tosta)

mapeen: pronounced maa-PEEN (Origin: moppina)

musciad: pronounced moo-SHYAAD (Origin: musciata)

scustamad': pronounced skoo-stoo-MAAD (Origin: scostumato)

stunad: pronounced stoo-NAAD (Origin: stonato)

vaffangul': pronounced VAA-faan-GOOL (Origin: vai a fare in culo)

Ingram Content Group UK Ltd.
Milton Keynes UK
UKHW021310030523
421166UK00001B/101